Praise for Brenda Novak

"Novak's story is richly dramatic,
with a stark setting that distinguishes it nicely
from the lusher world of other romances."
—*Publishers Weekly* on *Taking the Heat*

"Readers will be quickly drawn in to this well-written,
multi-faceted story that is an engrossing, compelling read."
—*Library Journal* on *Taking the Heat*

"*Cold Feet* left me breathless.
Any book by Brenda Novak is a must-buy for me."
—*Reader to Reader Reviews*

"Novak's *Cold Feet* is a nail-biter....
The plot is riveting, the ending delightfully unpredictable
and the characters compelling."
—*Romantic Times*

"This story should appeal to readers who like their
romances with a sophisticated touch."
—*Library Journal* on *Snow Baby*

"A one-sitting read! Kudos to Brenda Novak
for an insightful and emotional story
that tore at my heartstrings."
—*The Best Reviews* on *A Baby of Her Own*

"Novak is an expert at creating emotionally driven
romances full of heat, sensual tension and conflict that not
only satisfy her characters but her readers as well."
—*Writers Unlimited* on *A Husband of Her Own*

"Once again, Brenda Novak delivers a stunningly
magical performance.... Novak's fans will easily
recognize her unforgettable style and characterization
from the first chapter."
—*Wordweaving* on

"[*A Home of Her Own*] ke
Kleenex in hand, totally en
a forget-about-dinner, ju
—*Rom*

Books by Brenda Novak

HQN Books
EVERY WAKING MOMENT

HARLEQUIN SINGLE TITLES
TAKING THE HEAT
COLD FEET

HARLEQUIN SUPERROMANCE
899—EXPECTATIONS
939—SNOW BABY
955—BABY BUSINESS
987—DEAR MAGGIE
1021—WE SAW MOMMY KISSING SANTA CLAUS
1058—SHOOTING THE MOON
1083—A BABY OF HER OWN*
1130—A HUSBAND OF HER OWN*
1158—SANCTUARY
1195—A FAMILY OF HER OWN*
1242—A HOME OF HER OWN*
1278—STRANGER IN TOWN*

*Stories set in Dundee, Idaho

HARLEQUIN ANTHOLOGIES
MOTHER, PLEASE!
"What a Girl Wants"
MORE THAN WORDS (Volume 1)
"Small Packages"

BRENDA NOVAK

EVERY WAKING MOMENT

HQN™

ISBN 0-373-77045-6

EVERY WAKING MOMENT

www.HQNBooks.com

Printed in U.S.A.

To my husband, Ted,
who's stood behind me for twenty years.
Even in the beginning, through the lean times,
he supported me financially when I started flying off
to every writers' conference I could feasibly attend.
He's constantly searching for the next computer,
software, keyboard, chair and anything else that might
make my job easier. He listens to every story I write
and tells me, even when I'm sure he's wrong, that
what I've written is good. And he props me up when
I get too tired or overwhelmed. What more can a wife
ask? I've always been able to depend on his love.
For that, I'm eternally grateful.

Dear Reader,

When I'm not writing romantic-suspense novels, I'm writing relationship stories for Harlequin's Superromance line (the longest and most mainstream of the various series). I've found it to be a great mix. If I'm craving danger and intrigue, I dig into one of my "bigger" books, like this one. If I miss the cozy comfort of a good relationship novel, where there's rarely any threat of physical danger, I write another story set in the fictional town of Dundee, Idaho. They're different styles of books—and yet they're similar in many respects. I like creating characters who have an interesting past, a conflicted present and the hope of a fabulous future.

But back to this story.... I've long found it fascinating how some people feel compelled to control others. I've never really understood that compulsion, which is part of the reason for my fascination. It can become such a driving need, one that causes all kinds of trouble, sometimes resulting in murder. In *Every Waking Moment* we have two villains who can think only of fulfilling their own desires. They set off a chain of events that change the hero and heroine forever. But some characters really deserve a "happily ever after" and, after you read this story, I think you'll agree with me that Preston and Emma fall into that category. I enjoyed seeing how they'd react when faced with certain daunting challenges, but I especially enjoyed seeing them triumph in the end.

I love to hear from readers. Please feel free to contact me through my Web site, www.brendanovak.com, where you can enter to win a $500 shopping spree at the store of your choice, check out excerpts and reviews for this and other books, see what's coming in the future, or help me reach my juvenile diabetes fund-raising goal. If you don't have an Internet service, write to P.O. Box 3781, Citrus Heights, CA 95611.

Stay safe!

Brenda Novak

CHAPTER ONE

VANESSA BEACON'S HANDS SHOOK as she stared down at the California driver's license she'd had her gardener purchase for her several months ago. The photo was hers, along with the physical characteristics. Hair: Bld; Eyes: Bl; HT: 5-06; WT: 120. The name, birth date and address, however, were not. The name read *Emma Wright*. Vanessa had chosen "Emma" because it was her mother's middle name. "Wright" she'd selected as a reminder. She was doing the *right* thing. She had to believe that wholeheartedly or she would never have the courage to take such a risk.

The clock ticked loudly on the wall of her expansive chrome-and-marble kitchen. It seemed even louder than Manuel's new plasma television, which she'd turned on in the living room to occupy their son, Dominick. She'd gone through her and Dominick's suitcases, checked for his new birth certificate, her driver's license and the two prepaid credit cards she'd purchased as additional identification, plus the teaching credential in her new name. She also counted her cash and packed her maps. But she couldn't help worrying that she'd forgotten *something*.

God, she couldn't make a mistake. Dominick's life might depend on what she'd forgotten.

Mumbling a silent prayer that she could think straight despite her racing heart, she once again sorted through the backpack she'd hidden in the attic for the past three weeks. A small, handheld cooler contained three types of insulin—NPH, Regular and the fast-acting Humalog. Outside the cooler and loose in the backpack, she'd packed two hundred Ultra-Fine needles for Dominick's three or more daily injections, two blood-glucose monitors, arm and finger pokers with plenty of test strips and two boxes of extra lancets. There was also a biohazard sharps collector, which was so large and bulky she'd almost taken it out a number of times but didn't in the end because she had to have somewhere safe to toss the needles. She'd included KetoStrips to test for protein in Dominick's urine, an emergency glucagon kit—in case he ever passed out, God forbid—and a tube of oral glucose gel for use in smaller emergencies. Besides all that, she'd packed his logbook to record his blood-sugar readings, and plenty of carbohydrates disguised as granola bars, trail mix, fruit and individually packaged chips for her son's mid-morning and mid-afternoon snacks. She'd nearly required a small suitcase just to transport his diabetes supplies. But every item was absolutely essential. One missed insulin injection could quickly result in ketoacidosis, a life-threatening condition.

I have everything. There's nothing to worry about.... Vanessa closed the bag. A glance at the clock made her feel weak in the knees. It was after ten. Juanita should've been here fifteen minutes ago. Would she come at all? Or had Manuel gotten to her?

Vanessa cautioned herself against the paranoia that threatened. Manuel always watched her closely, but she was sure he had no idea she was about to disappear. She could trust the gardener. Carlos had proved himself with his secrecy on the false ID and the car he'd bought for her. Juanita would come through, too—*if* her loyalties were what Vanessa believed they were, and *if* she clearly understood what Vanessa wanted her to do. Vanessa thought she did. Manuel had insisted on hiring a nanny who could speak only Spanish, so his son would learn his native tongue, he said. But there were plenty of bilingual nannies, especially in San Diego where they lived. No, it wasn't solely for Dominick that Manuel had selected Juanita. Manuel liked the idea that Vanessa wouldn't be able to communicate with her. Isolating Vanessa gave him that much more power and control.

Fortunately, it wasn't quite that simple. He didn't know it, but during the four years they'd been living together, she'd taught herself enough Spanish to speak and understand most of what she heard. At first, she'd done it to help while away the empty hours of her day, since Manuel wouldn't let her return to school or get a job. Later, she'd wanted to understand the strange phone calls he received at night and to decipher what the Rodriguez family discussed during the frequent meetings they held in the conference room off Manuel's home office.

But she didn't want to know about Manuel's business dealings anymore. Or his family's. His family was the main reason Manuel had never married her, even after she'd had Dominick. His mother refused to accept her, ostensibly because of her nationality, but Vanessa knew it went a little deeper than that. Mama Rodriguez couldn't tolerate the thought of another woman in her favorite son's life. Period. It was a fact Vanessa had once lamented, but no more. She'd learned enough about Manuel's mother, his whole family, to be thankful for their rejection.

Dominick came in from the living room, his round face a picture of impatience. He'd just turned five two months ago and would've been starting kindergarten in a few weeks. She hoped she'd be able to get them situated soon so he could go to school this year. "Mo-om, I thought you said we were going to leave!" he said.

Vanessa attempted a reassuring smile, even though she was sweating profusely and feeling as though she might faint. Juanita *had* to come. She had the car Carlos had bought. And if she didn't appear soon, it meant Manuel had figured out what was happening. He'd take Dominick to Mexico and Vanessa would probably never see her son again. Manuel had certainly threatened that often enough—whenever she tried to establish some independence. He'd made his point when she'd tried to leave the first time. Her father had passed away several years before she met Manuel, and her brother had been killed in a motorcycle accident not long after, but her mother and married sister lived in Phoenix. She'd gone to them, and wished she could do so again.

But she wouldn't make the same mistake twice. Manuel had tracked her down and dragged her back—then let her know, in no uncertain terms, that he wouldn't tolerate her leaving in the future.

Don't think of that. Don't remember....

"We're waiting for Juanita," she said, aching to pull her child into her arms. She didn't know what she'd do if she could never hear Dominick laugh again or tell her how much he loved her. But she knew a clingy, desperate hug wasn't what he needed at the moment. She didn't want to communicate her anxiety to him any more than she already had.

"You said she was coming a long time ago," he complained. "Where *is* she?"

Vanessa had no idea. Juanita had worked for them for nearly a year and was never late. Where could she be today?

Without her support—and the car—Vanessa and Dominick would never get away.

"Maybe she had a flat tire." *Please let it be that.* "I'm sure she's coming."

The phone rang. Vanessa quickly gave Dominick some markers so he could write on the dry-erase board attached to the fridge, and approached the desk in the corner.

Anxiety stabbed through her when she recognized Manuel's cell-phone number on the caller ID. He was supposed to be on a plane to Mexico. He left the country often and stayed sometimes for several days, sometimes for a couple of weeks. He claimed to import marble from Culiacán, but Vanessa had long suspected that he imported more than marble.

The steady bursts of noise jangled her already frayed nerves. Should she answer it?

She wasn't sure she could keep her voice level. Hoping that his plane had simply been delayed, that he'd be gone soon, she decided to let the answering machine take it. But she should've known she couldn't avoid him so easily. Her cell phone, which was sitting on the counter, started ringing only a few seconds later. Manuel hated it when he couldn't reach her. She knew he'd keep trying, again and again and again, until she finally picked up, even if it meant missing his flight.

She couldn't let him miss his flight.

When she continued to hesitate, Dominick glanced up from his drawing. "Mommy?"

Spurred by the curiosity in her son's voice, Vanessa arranged her expression in a blank mask to hide the fear and loathing Manuel elicited, and retrieved her cell. "Hello?"

"What's going on?" Manuel demanded without a greeting.

"Nothing. Why?"

"You didn't answer the house phone."

"I told you last night that I might run a few errands this morning."

"You haven't left the house."

A prickly unease crept up Vanessa's spine. He'd spoken with such certainty. "How do you know?"

"A good guess."

She didn't believe it was a guess at all, and judging by his flippant tone, he didn't care whether he'd convinced her. Somehow he always knew where she was. She'd scoured every inch of the house and been unable to find any type of listening device or video camera, so he must have hired someone to watch her. Which made Juanita absolutely integral to her plan.

Dominick went back to drawing, and Vanessa moved to the sink to stare out the kitchen window at the perfect summer day, wondering for the millionth time who was out there.

"Why didn't you pick up?" Manuel pressed, unwilling to let the subject go.

"I was—" she swallowed to ease the dryness in her throat "—in the bathroom."

"I had a phone installed there, remember? For your convenience."

Not for her convenience. So she wouldn't have even the bathroom as an escape from him. "I refuse to answer the phone while I'm in the bathroom," she said. "I haven't used that extension since you put it in. You know that."

He chuckled softly. "*Querida,* you can be so stubborn."

Manuel had no idea. But he was about to find out—if only Juanita would arrive as promised.

"What do you need?" she asked.

"I'm calling to check on you."

Check on her? Not in a loving way. Vanessa could hardly tolerate the sound of Manuel's voice or the pretense of his caring. When she'd first met him, at twenty-two, she'd just graduated with a teaching degree. He'd been older, twenty-five, and had seemed energetic and ambitious—but loving and kind, too. He'd changed so fast….

Maybe she'd never really known him. Maybe the man he used to be was simply a persona he adopted when it suited him. In any case, she barely recognized him anymore. His dark eyes, once the color of melted chocolate to her, watched her too carefully, frightening in their obsessive intensity. And the thick black hair she used to love, especially when it fell across his brow, he now slicked back in a dramatic style that added to the impression he gave of being as hyperaware as he was hypercritical.

She brought a hand to her chest, preparing herself for the answer to her next question. "Aren't you going to Mexico today?"

"The trip's been postponed."

Her muscles tightened. *No! Not when I'm so close.* "Until when?" The knocking of her heart against her ribs made it difficult to speak.

"Come on, *mi amor.* You know better than to bother your pretty head with business."

A dodge. Typical of him. As was the condescension in his voice. He didn't like her knowing his schedule. Except for the odd occasion, he typically sprang news of an impending trip only the night before.

But Juanita still wasn't here, and Manuel hadn't said why his trip had been postponed. Did he realize she was planning to leave him?

"Will you be home for dinner, then?" she asked.

"Of course. I always spend my evenings with you, if I'm available."

Bile rose in Vanessa's throat at the thought of postponing her escape until Manuel's next trip to Mexico. Holding out until he was far from home would be the wisest course. She and Dominick needed the lead time. But everything was already arranged. And staying meant she'd have to suffer through more nights in Manuel's company, nights that always ended, at some point, with her lying beneath him. Manuel had an insatiable sexual appetite and demanded she perform some kind of sex act for him daily, often two or more.

"Maybe you could mention to Juanita that I'm in the mood for *meñudo*," he said.

Even the prospect of sharing another interminable dinner with Manuel made Vanessa ill.

She frowned at the cigarette burn her husband had inflicted on the inside of her wrist four days ago. Manuel loved to deal out little reprisals for anything that displeased him—

Dominick rounded the kitchen island. Quickly hiding the injury, she rubbed her son's back as he came over to hug her leg.

"What's wrong, Mommy?" Worry clouded his innocent eyes.

She held a finger to her lips to indicate silence. She didn't want Manuel to overhear.

"I'll tell her to make it for dinner," she said into the phone.

"And I'm going to need those suits I had you take to the cleaners," he added. "Can you pick them up for me while you're out?"

Her life was closing in on her again. "Of course."

"Thank you. You're such a wonderful wife."

"I'm not your wife," she said.

"As far as I'm concerned, you are. Every man should be so lucky."

Vanessa's nails curled into her palm at his assumption and false praise. He threw her a few compliments from time to time—figuring that would keep her happy. But he'd never trusted her or loved her enough to let her be truly happy. Or to stand against his family and marry her, as she'd once wanted. Or to treat her as an equal instead of chattel.

"How do you want me to pay for it?" she asked because she knew he'd expect this question. Their gated, ten-thousand-square-foot mansion provided proof of his wealth. But he kept such a tight rein on their money that it had taken her nearly two years to save the funds she'd given Carlos for the car. She'd only managed to accumulate that much by returning small items she hoped Manuel wouldn't miss—even groceries—and hiding the money between the insulation and the wall in the attic.

"I'll call the bank and add an extra hundred to your account," he said.

"Fine." She grimaced at his stinginess. He allowed her no standing balance. He waited until she had a specific need, one he could easily verify. Then he called and transferred enough to cover the expense. One hundred bucks would barely pay his dry-cleaning bill; Manuel clothed his lean, sinewy body almost exclusively in the finest hand-tailored suits.

"Thank you, *querida*," he said. "What else do you have planned for the day? What is my *hijito* doing?"

She glanced at their son. Dominick was so unlike his father, so much more similar to her side of the family—especially the younger brother she'd lost the year she and Dominick had moved in with Manuel. Large for his age, Dominick had sandy-blond hair, eyes that were an unusual shade of green, and golden skin that still retained the softness of a baby's. "He's standing here, waiting to go to the store."

"He should be reading, Vanessa. You know I want him to read."

"We'll read when we get back."

"Let me transfer the money to the credit card I've given Juanita. She can do your shopping and pick up my dry cleaning. I don't know why you like doing such menial tasks."

Maybe it was because she had nothing else to do. Manuel insisted that Dominick needed one hundred percent of her attention, but she believed there should be more to life than following her son around, watching over his every move, correcting all his mistakes, stealing the same privacy and independence from him that Manuel had already taken from her.

"I like to get out once in a while," she said. *If you only knew how badly I'm dying to get out right now.* "It's good for me."

"So you're always telling me."

She *had* to leave. Right away. She couldn't survive the helplessness any longer.

"But today…today you might be right," she said. "I've got a headache. Why don't you go ahead and put the money on Juanita's card. I'll have her take Dominick out to run errands while I lie down."

"Fine."

"I'll see you tonight," she said, eager to get off the phone. Tears burned at the backs of her eyes, tears of disappointment and bitterness toward the man who had systematically cut her off from friends and family.

At least he didn't know what she had in store for today. If he did, he would've said something about the way she'd set him up—wouldn't he?

"Te amo," he said.

She couldn't say it back. She hadn't been able to for years.

"Goodbye." She hung up then slumped over the kitchen sink, afraid she was going to be sick.

The sound of keys jingling and the front door opening brought her head up. Dominick dashed off and, a moment later, marched into the kitchen ahead of Juanita, who met Vanessa's eyes with a fearful expression.

"Are you ready, my friend?" she asked in Spanish.

"Where have you been?" Vanessa replied in the same language.

"I had a neighbor check the engine of the car. I couldn't let you go without knowing you and Dominick would have a reliable vehicle."

Vanessa feared the car might be stolen property. It should've cost a lot more than it did. But Carlos hadn't admitted anything, and she hadn't asked. What was the point? She had to take what she could get; she didn't have a choice. "Why didn't you tell me? Or call?" she asked in English.

Juanita scowled and moved closer, gazing around the kitchen as if looking for the camera Vanessa had searched for repeatedly. "I thought of it too late yesterday, and we agreed never to discuss this over the phone." She lowered her voice so Dominick, who'd started using the dry-erase board again, couldn't hear. "He called me last night, you know. He asked how Dominick was doing in his studies, but he also asked many questions about you."

"Like what?" Vanessa whispered.

"What you do while he's gone, where you go, whether you try to communicate with me."

"What did you tell him?"

"Nothing." She removed the long heavy coat, sunglasses and head scarf Vanessa had asked her to wear. "Put these on and go. Right away. It isn't odd for a little old lady like me to dress so warmly, even in the summer. And the engine of the car is good, strong. You should be fine."

Vanessa hesitated as she accepted the clothing. "But he didn't go to Mexico, Juanita. He's still here, in town. He wants you to make *meñudo* for dinner!"

"So…are you going to wait?" Juanita leaned around the island to check on Dominick.

Vanessa could see that he was still happily occupied. But she put Juanita's belongings on the center island and pulled Juanita into the formal dining room. "I don't know what to do."

"You have to go," Juanita said. "He senses something. I know he does."

"But now that he's coming home tonight, you won't be able to tell him I was here when you left at dinner but gone when you returned in the morning. What will you say to him?"

"Don't worry. I'll say I was running late and you were already gone when I arrived."

Vanessa checked Dominick again. He'd given up on the dry-erase board but was busy arranging magnetic letters into the small words she'd taught him to spell. "He'll want to know why you didn't call when I didn't return."

Juanita pulled thoughtfully at her lip with her teeth. "I'll have Carlos take me home early," she decided, "before I would expect you back, then I'll tell Manuel I felt ill and didn't want to infect Dominick."

"And if someone's watching the house? What if they see me like this and tell Manuel you left with Dominick—and never came back? With Manuel coming home, it's all so much more *immediate*."

"Calm down, my friend. We've talked about this before.

I'm just the housekeeper. No one pays attention to when I come and go. If someone says I left with Dominick and never came back, I'll say they are *loco*. My son dropped me off in the morning. Carlos took me home when I felt ill. In between, I never went anywhere or saw anything out of the ordinary. How can Manuel argue with that? It is simple, eh? Besides, he doesn't even think we speak the same language, remember?"

"Sí." Vanessa struggled to regulate her rapid breathing. He'd never suspect Juanita. He trusted her. Everyone trusted Juanita.

Nodding decisively, she ducked back into the kitchen, covered her head with the scarf and put on the coat. It was now or never. She was leaving; she couldn't look back. Somehow she'd provide a life for herself and Dominick, a life that had nothing to do with the man who tried to own her.

Their return distracted Dominick from his magnets. "Why are you dressing up like Juanita?" he asked with a scowl.

"This is the special game we've been practicing for," she told him, adding Juanita's sunglasses and dark lipstick to her disguise. She'd been terrified that Dominick might mention the "game" to Manuel. But it was a risk she'd had to take. Fortunately, they played games of pretense quite a lot, and it had never become an issue. "We're going to see if anyone can tell who I really am."

"Am I going to dress up, too?"

"No, you're going to act like I'm Juanita, remember? When we step outside, you'll hold my hand and walk to the car the same as you do whenever Juanita takes you shopping or to the library."

"That's not how it goes. I'm Max, from *Where the Wild Things Are,* and you're a lady named Emma."

Vanessa had chosen the name Max because it came from Dominick's favorite book. He responded well to it. And, equally important, it was a name Manuel would never connect with him. "We'll do that, too. Just as soon as we drive away."

"Oh, I get it! You're going to be Juanita first, *then* Emma." He seemed excited—until he followed them into her bedroom and noticed, for the first time, the two suitcases she'd packed. He watched Juanita cover one with a big black garbage bag and take it out to the back porch.

"Why are we throwing away our suitcases?"

"We're not," Vanessa said, doing the same with the other one. "Carlos is going to get them for us."

"Is he playing, too?" Dominick asked as they walked into the kitchen.

Vanessa slipped the backpack into a garbage bag and carried it to the back. "Sort of. We'll meet him down the street."

"But why do we need suitcases? Are we going somewhere far away?"

"Yes," Vanessa said, feeling such relief in the word that she reached out to squeeze Juanita's hand.

"Where?" Dominick asked.

Across the country, as far as I can take us. "You'll see. It's a surprise." She stood in the living room to make sure Carlos saw their luggage. Had he noticed Juanita pull up outside?

The gardener came almost immediately. Good. Glancing inside the house from the patio, he nodded as he picked up the first bag and carried it around to the front, as if he was loading more clippings into the bed of his truck.

Fear turned Vanessa's legs rubbery as she hurried to the front door and gave her nanny a tight hug. "You'll be okay?" she asked in Spanish.

"Of course. We have it all planned out."

"I could never thank you enough."

Juanita took a piece of paper from her pocket and slipped it into Vanessa's hand.

"What's this?"

"My sister Rosa's number. We can communicate through her. Call me if you need anything."

Vanessa stared down at the crumpled paper in her hand. "You never even told me you had a sister—"

"Exactly. Manuel doesn't know about her, either. I keep my business to myself, eh?"

"Where does she live?" Vanessa asked.

"About an hour from here."

In a moment of pure panic, Vanessa squeezed her friend's arm. "Go to her, Juanita. Go to her and never come back here." She leaned close so she could whisper the rest into Juanita's ear. "Manuel, he…he isn't right."

"You're the only one he hurts," Juanita whispered back. "Just be safe, my beautiful friend. And be happy."

Vanessa waited while Juanita said goodbye to Dominick. Then she took her son's hand. Keeping her face down and stooping a bit like the older woman, she led him out the front door into the mellow sunshine of a clear August day.

The nondescript white sedan she'd asked Carlos to purchase sat in the circular driveway, representing the freedom she'd craved for so long. She wanted to race toward it, buckle Dominick safely inside and put the metal to the floor as she tore away. But she forced herself to walk very slowly, like Juanita. She'd be gone soon. Then she wouldn't be Vanessa Beacon anymore. She'd start over as Emma Wright, and Dominick would be Max.

CHAPTER TWO

"EMMA, EMMA, EMMA," Emma chanted, trying to get used to her new name. She gripped the steering wheel of the white Ford Taurus so tightly her shoulders ached. She'd been heading north on Interstate 5 for nearly six hours, but the miles didn't seem to be passing quickly enough. Probably because she kept imagining that Manuel had figured out she was gone and was already coming after her.

She checked her rearview mirror, something she did every few seconds, and increased her speed to eighty. A red Toyota 4Runner was following her and had been since she'd come out of the Tehachapie Mountains, the section of interstate called The Grapevine that separated the Los Angeles Basin from the San Joaquin Valley.

Interstate 5 wasn't like Highway 99, which ran parallel to Highway 5 through the central part of California. Interstate 5 bypassed most of the small farming communities between Los Angeles and Sacramento. The people on this newer road were typically traveling across the state, so the fact that someone had followed her for so long wasn't *that* unusual. Except she didn't recognize any of the other cars around her. People passed her all the time, or she passed them, but they soon drew apart.

"Mommy, I want to go home," Dominic—Max—said from

the back seat. He was bored with the action figures she'd brought for him to play with and had been asking to get out of the car for the past few hours. She'd stopped once in Los Angeles to feed him, test his blood and give him insulin. But Emma couldn't afford to let him have another break yet. She felt the tick of every second. As close as freedom suddenly seemed, she was still only a heartbeat away from failure and terrible reprisal. "I'm sorry, babe. Mommy can't stop now."

"Why not?" he asked, jingling the chain around his neck that held the dog tag she'd had Carlos purchase. It was engraved with Dominick's new name and medical information.

She checked the red Toyota again. Two occupants. She didn't think she'd ever seen either man before. But they could be a threat all the same. Maybe they were the ones who'd been keeping an eye on the house. Maybe her disguise hadn't fooled them, or they'd seen Juanita pass by the kitchen window a few minutes after she'd left....

"Mom?" Max persisted when she didn't answer. "When are we going home?"

She watched the needle on her speedometer edge up to eighty-five. "We're not." Glancing in the rearview mirror, Emma saw her son tucking the metal tag inside his T-shirt.

"Ever?"

Emma didn't want Max to have to face the reality of forever. She knew he might not find the same relief in it she did. So she kept her answer vague. Especially because she didn't know *what* might happen. "Not for a while."

"What about Daddy?"

"What about him?" She was too preoccupied with the Toyota to focus fully on Dominick's questions. Max, she reminded herself. She had to become accustomed to it. But she couldn't concentrate. Had the men in the other car been following her longer than she thought? Could she have missed seeing them somehow?

"Isn't he coming with us?"

"No, he's in Mexico," she said to make the situation easier for *Max* to accept. If her son reacted to this news the way he normally did, he wouldn't ask about Manuel again for days, maybe even weeks. Soon, one month would blend into the next, and Max would adjust to his new life and eventually forget the old. The transition wouldn't be easy, but time would help.

"Won't Daddy be mad that we're going on vacation without him? He doesn't like it when we leave."

"I know." She sped up yet again, so the Toyota couldn't draw even with her.

"I think Daddy's gonna be mad," he said.

Max was right, of course—Manuel was going to be furious. But she felt no guilt for separating him from his son. She had to think about what was best for Dominick—*Max*—had to guide and protect him so he wouldn't grow up to be like his father or get involved in the family "business."

"Daddy's busy. He doesn't even know." She adjusted her mirror again, relieved to see that the Toyota had finally dropped back a little. A moment later, however, she realized why. A highway patrol car was coming up fast, in the other lane.

Vanessa—Emma...she was Emma—immediately eased off the gas, but it was too late. The red SUV passed by with scarcely a glance in her direction, while the patrolman came up behind her and flipped on his lights.

Damn it! What was she going to do now? Her first panicked impulse was to run. But she had Max in the car.

Turning on her blinker, she slowed and pulled off the Interstate onto the shoulder, and the patrolman did the same.

"Why are we stopping?" Max asked.

"Because we have to. There's a policeman behind us."

When the car was no longer moving, her son unlatched his seat belt and climbed up on his knees to stare through the back window. "What does he want?"

"I don't know yet. Just don't say anything while he's here, okay?"

"Why not?"

"It's all part of the game we're playing. No matter what I say, you don't talk."

"How come?"

"I don't have time to explain. Just be quiet back there." Emma hated to use bribery with Max. It set a bad precedent, but she wasn't sure what she might have to say to the patrolman and didn't want her son to contradict her. "If you keep quiet, if you don't say even one word, Mommy will buy you a toy at the next town, okay?"

"Okay!" His enthusiasm gave her hope that he would actually remember and comply, but Max's natural frankness was only part of the problem. She had no idea what would happen if she gave the patrolman a fake ID and he ran it through his computer. How much scrutiny could her new driver's license withstand? And what was she going to do when the officer asked for registration and proof of insurance? The car could be stolen property.

Real or fake ID? Either way, she could be in trouble.

Breaking into a cold sweat, she felt in her purse for her wallet.

The patrolman's boots crunched on the gravel shoulder as he approached. In her rearview mirror, she could see the pant legs of his taupe uniform, his black utility belt and holstered gun, and his badge, which glinted in the bright light of early afternoon. As he drew closer, in her side mirror, she made out a fiftyish face with salt-and-pepper hair showing beneath his trooper's hat.

She'd let the red Toyota spook her into making a dreadful mistake. How could she have been so stupid?

Wiping away the perspiration on her upper lip, Emma pushed Juanita's sunglasses closer to the bridge of her nose and pulled the scarf forward. Then she lowered the window.

"Good afternoon," he said, his manner professional.

"Hello." She took note of his name—Daniels—and tried to smile confidently. A lot depended on her performance in the next few minutes.

He bent his head to glance at Dominick, who was dangling over the seat in an effort to see him. "Where you headin' today?"

"Sacramento." Emma wanted to embellish the lie by saying she had family there, but she was afraid such a comment would draw Max into the conversation despite her bribe. They'd visited her family in Arizona two years ago, when Emma had tried to leave Manuel, and Max had loved it. He constantly begged her to take him on another "Zona vacation."

"May I see your driver's license?"

Offering up a silent prayer, she handed him her real license.

"Is this address correct?"

"Yes. Is something wrong, Officer?"

"You were speeding. Going nearly ninety miles an hour, Ms.—" he studied her driver's license "—Beacon."

"I'm sorry," she said. "My son has diabetes, and I'm in a hurry to reach the next town so I can get him some food." She shifted to make sure the backpack containing Max's diabetes supplies was completely closed—and prayed that Max wouldn't pipe up to remind her of all the snacks they had in there. She hated to lie, especially in front of her son, but if she didn't do *something*, their bid for freedom and safety could easily end in the next ten minutes. Fortunately, Max thought it was all a game.

"What does he need to eat?" Daniels asked.

"Fifteen grams of carbohydrate, but he needs to do it right away or he could have an insulin reaction. He was just recently diagnosed, so I'm still getting used to the whole thing. Had I been thinking, I would've prepared better when we stopped in L.A., but I gave him lunch and forgot all about buying an emergency stash. For the past few minutes, I've been so worried he'll go low and pass out that I haven't been watching my speed."

Emma risked a glance at Max in the rearview mirror, hoping he'd hold his tongue. Her stomach lurched when he didn't.

"I need to eat something?" he said.

"Yes, sweetheart. You didn't finish your lunch." At least that part was true.

Daniels seemed to soften, but he didn't return her driver's license, tell her to be more cautious in the future and let her go as she'd hoped. "We'll get you on your way as soon as possible," he said. "May I see your registration?"

"I'm telling you, I don't have time for this." She let the panic rising inside her enter her voice. "Maybe you could follow me to the next town."

His eyes cut to Max. "I'm sure I've got something to eat in my car. I'll get it before you leave, if he's okay for the moment."

Emma looked at her son. It was hardly possible to claim Max wasn't okay *for the moment* when he appeared as alert, happy and curious as he did.

Shit! She'd gambled and lost. How badly she'd lost remained to be seen.

She rummaged through the glove box, completely unsure of what she might find there, and managed to come up with a Certificate of Registration. Along with the registration, she found a sealed envelope with her new name on it, but she had no idea what it could be and wasn't about to open it right now. Shoving the envelope back in, she gave Officer Daniels the registration.

His eyes flicked over it. "This car is registered to a Maria Gomez?"

Emma had no idea how to respond. She could only hope that if the car was stolen, it hadn't been reported yet. "Yes. Maria's a friend of mine."

"This might take a minute." He walked back to his patrol unit. She could see his head and shoulders in her side mirror as he sat behind the wheel with his door slightly ajar, could hear the faint murmur of his voice as he spoke into a crackling radio. Was he running her license plate through some computer? If so, what would he find?

A semi rumbled past, muting all other sound. Several cars whizzed by, too. Emma's hand hovered over the gearshift. She was tempted to join that stream of traffic, to run while she still had the chance. She couldn't go back to Manuel. This time she'd lose Max for sure.

"Did I do good, Mommy? Do I get a toy?" her son asked.

"You did great, babe. But it's not over yet. Be quiet a little longer, okay?" Resting her hand lightly on the gearshift, just in case, she watched the patrolman walk back to her.

"We're almost done," Daniels said, and handed her the registration certificate but not her driver's license, which he'd attached to the clipboard he carried. From what she could see, he was writing her a traffic citation.

She let go of the gearshift. Daniels must not have found

anything on her or the car, or he would've said something by now. That the car hadn't raised a red flag surprised her, but the fact that she wasn't in the computer didn't. She knew Manuel would involve the police only as a last resort. He had too much to hide to draw that kind of attention. And because he'd found her so easily last time, he'd feel confident he could do it on his own.

"May I see proof of insurance, please?" the officer asked.

Suddenly hopeful that she'd have the chance to recover from her foolish mistake, she rummaged through her purse again and provided her insurance card.

He compared it to her driver's license and passed it back. "Sign here, Ms. Beacon." He held the clipboard out to her. "If you'd like to protest this action, instructions are on the other side. Signing the violation isn't an admission of guilt."

She didn't care if it was. She'd sign anything to be able to get back on the road.

She scribbled her real name at the X and accepted her pink copy. But he stopped her before she could roll up her window.

"Ma'am?"

"Yes?"

He pulled a candy bar out of his pocket and gave it to her. "I had this in my lunch today. Hope it helps your little boy."

"Thank you."

"No problem." He leaned down to look in the back seat. "You're a handsome kid," he said. "What's your name?"

Charmed by the promise of candy, which he preferred to toys since he lived on such a restricted diet, Max didn't hesitate. "Dominick," he said, smiling broadly and completely forgetting his pretend name. "Dominick Escalar Rodriguez."

Emma's grip tightened on the steering wheel until her

knuckles grew white. "Get your seat belt on," she told her son, her voice as normal as possible even though she was dying to escape—before anything else could happen. "You don't want Mommy to get another ticket, do you?"

Grudgingly, Max flopped onto the seat and buckled himself in. "Are we going home now?"

The patrolman stepped away from the car. "You're heading in the wrong direction for that, I'm afraid."

"We're taking a little vacation." Emma rolled up her window and, at the first break, merged into traffic. She was extremely lucky to be driving away. But she had no idea how long her luck would hold.

She needed to get out of California. Fast.

EMMA FELT SAFER once darkness fell. She hadn't initially planned on venturing into Nevada, but after her confrontation with the California Highway Patrol, turning east instead of continuing due north seemed wise. And though she never would've anticipated it, she liked the harsh wilderness that made up this part of the state. She also liked the western feel of the tiny mining towns she passed. Carson City, Dayton, Ramsey Station, Silver Springs, Frenchman… Some weren't even big enough to appear on her map. Others had a small casino that doubled as a motel or an old-style theater with the marquee advertising a movie—usually not a new release by the rest of the country's standards. There was always a church or two, a diner, a gas station, maybe a post office, sometimes a public library or municipal building. In each one she saw older, well-kept homes at the center of town and some cheaper, not-so-well-kept homes at the edges, plus a handful of single-wide trailers scattered here and there, and more than the usual ratio of four-by-fours.

Nevada was truly the last bastion of the Old West, Emma thought as she dodged a tumbleweed blowing across the highway. Folks here didn't have spectacular coastline views and multimillion-dollar homes. They didn't even have many trees—just sagebrush, mostly. But they lived a simple life in wide-open spaces. And they seemed more likely to mind their own business.

She rubbed her burning eyes. Max had fallen asleep in the back seat hours ago, after a short dinner break at Lake Tahoe. If she wasn't so tired, she would've preferred to forge ahead, but hour had marched after hour and it was nearly eleven. She'd been driving all day and the tension in her muscles was making her back ache. She needed to find a place where they could spend the night, and she needed to test Max to be sure the insulin she'd given him with his meal hadn't pulled his blood sugar too low.

Reaching over the seat, she touched her son's head. He wasn't sweating, which was a good sign. He seemed to be sleeping peacefully. She could probably wait another thirty minutes to test him, until she found a motel. But she was never completely certain of such a decision. Battling diabetes was as much a guessing game as anything else. Except, like their game today, there wasn't anything fun about it.

A loud *thump, thump, thump* warned her that she'd just swerved into the center of the road. Momentarily startled, she jerked the car back into her own lane. She was practically alone on the highway, but she had to stop driving—before she crashed into a ditch or a telephone pole.

Fortunately, she saw city lights ahead.

MANUEL STRODE around his desk and slapped down a map in front of his trembling gardener. *"Where?"* he shouted. "Where is she going?"

Sweat trickled from Carlos's temples, and his dark eyes darted furtively toward Richard and Hector, two of the men who worked for Manuel. "I—I do not know."

"That's what you told me the last time I asked," Manuel growled. "Say it one more time, and I'm calling Border Patrol. Your American Dream will disappear like that." He snapped his fingers for emphasis.

Though heavyset, Carlos wasn't very tall. At Manuel's words, he seemed to shrink into himself. "W-what makes you think *I* help her, *amigo?*"

"Carlos, I saw you." Hector unfolded his lanky body from the chair where he'd been sitting several feet away, shoved a hand through his long dishwater-blond hair and moved closer. "I keep an eye on the house, you know? This morning, when I was turning into the neighborhood, I saw you talking to someone in a white Taurus." He scowled. "Only I thought it was Juanita."

"*Sí*, it *was* Juanita," Carlos insisted. "I already tell you that."

Manuel couldn't help himself. He hauled off and hit Carlos so hard he could feel the gardener's nose break beneath his fist. Carlos's head snapped back against the wall, and he nearly fell from his chair. The blow seemed to surprise everyone, but only because it came without warning. Manuel knew his men weren't opposed to violence—they thrived on it.

Carlos's arms flew up to protect himself from further blows, fear gleaming in his eyes.

"Don't make me do that again," Manuel said, shaking the sting out of his fingers. "Tell me what I want to know or I swear I'll have you deported."

Carlos began to sputter, *"Amigo…"*

"I'll have your mother deported, too," Manuel added.

"She's old and sick. She doesn't need to have Border Control knocking at her door, eh?"

Pulling his hands away, Carlos stared down at the blood on his palms. "*Señor,* please…*por favor.* No trouble. I—I have a family."

"Then tell me what you know about *my* family!" Manuel wanted to hit him again. This man had cost him Vanessa and Dominick. He wanted to kick him until he was nothing more than a bloody blob on the floor.

Carlos must have sensed the malevolence inside him because his trembling grew worse.

"Whose car was Vanessa driving?" Manuel pressed. "Where did she get it?"

When he said nothing, Manuel hit him again. Twice. He would've kept hitting him, except Hector finally pulled him away. "Manuel, not here. You're not thinking."

He *wasn't* thinking. He couldn't think. Since he'd come home to find Vanessa and Dominick gone, and had begun to suspect the worst when they didn't return, he could only *want*. He wanted Vanessa and Dominick back, and he wanted to punish this man for helping them leave.

Richard, who was nearly as tall and skinny as Hector, but had red hair, put a calming hand on his shoulder. "Call Border Patrol instead, okay?"

It took Manuel several seconds to regain control. He was still breathing hard when he walked around his desk and called information. "Border Patrol, please."

Tears streamed down Carlos's face as Manuel took the number. When Manuel hung up, then lifted the receiver again, Carlos finally lurched to his feet. Blood streamed from his nose. His lip was cut and beginning to swell. And one eye was half-closed.

"Wait, *por favor.* Listen to me. She was so unhappy. I—I had to help her."

"Where did she get the car, Carlos?" The menace in Manuel's voice was a promise he intended to keep.

Forgetting about his damaged face and the blood, the gardener rocked nervously from foot to foot. "It belonged to my mother. Vanessa, she—she no have much *dinero,* you know? And when she come to me, I—I feel sorry for her. So I tell my mother I will get you another car soon. We will save. We have plenty of opportunity in this country."

"Illegal aliens can't register a car here, Carlos," he said. "Who's listed on the registration as the legal owner?"

Tears mixed with the blood running down his face. *"Mi amiga."*

"What friend?"

"Her name, Maria Gomez."

Manuel had never heard of her, but it didn't matter. Hector might have let Vanessa slip away earlier, when he thought she was Juanita, but he'd written down the make, model and license number of the car she'd been driving. He did that with every car that visited the house.

"What else?" Manuel demanded.

Carlos attempted to wipe the blood from his nose. "That is all," he said. "I give her my mother's car. No more."

Hector pulled the bandanna he wore almost everywhere off his head and mopped his own face with it. "What do we do now?"

Manuel glared at Carlos, wondering whether he needed to have Hector or Richard kill him. He deserved to die, but it was never easy to get rid of a body. And for a man like Carlos, deportation would hurt badly enough. "We call the police."

"What?" Richard cried.

"I thought you didn't want to involve the police," Hector said, obviously just as spooked.

Richard and Hector had spent most of the past decade avoiding the law. But the police could be a powerful tool, if used in the right way.

"I don't," Manuel said. "We won't have anything to do with the call. At least not directly. Carlos and his friend Maria will simply report the Taurus as being stolen." He smiled. "Then the police will start looking for it, too."

ACCORDING TO THE MAP, Fallon served as the agricultural center of Nevada. But it was too dark to make out the surrounding farmland. As she came into town, Emma saw a string of restaurants and stores that were far more modern than any she'd noticed in Nevada since Carson City—a Jack in the Box, a Dairy Queen, even a Wal-Mart. A few budget motels sat right off the highway, but she didn't want to stay in those. She was hoping to find a little hideaway where she wouldn't have to worry that someone driving past might spot her car. She had no way of knowing if Officer Daniels had later realized that she was someone he should've detained.

Doubling back when she reached the end of town, she turned left at a sign that said Yerington to see what might be off the main drag. But Fallon didn't seem to be nearly as deep as it was long. Almost immediately, she left the city behind and started into the country. The inky-black sky looked like crushed velvet overhead, and the smell of livestock and green growing things drifted through her closed vents.

It wasn't a bad turn to have taken, though. About a mile from the highway, she found exactly what she'd been hoping for—a small, low-profile motel. A sign in front read Cozy

Comfort Bungalows and the word *Vacancy* glowed red in the bottom right corner.

Weak with gratitude and eager for a short reprieve, Emma wondered if a motel like this was ever full. Fortunately for her, she didn't think so.

She pulled into the gravel lot outside the long, narrow series of attached rooms, which weren't bungalows at all but your basic budget motel, and parked as close to the office as she could. Then she contemplated whether or not to carry Max in with her while she registered. He was getting so heavy.

After a moment's hesitation, she decided to lock the doors and watch the car instead.

The office was closed tight, but a porch light illuminated the space around the door. A sign above a buzzer on the wall read After Hours Ring Here.

Emma pressed the buzzer several times during the next five minutes and heard it go off, but didn't manage to rouse anyone.

Thank goodness she wasn't trying to hold her sleeping fifty-pound son.

"Is anyone home?" she called, opening the screen door to knock on the wood panel behind it.

A brown minivan pulled into the lot. At first Emma felt relieved that she wouldn't be the only one trying to drag the innkeeper from his bed. But when the van's engine rattled to a stop and the driver got out, she began to wonder if it was wise to be standing in the middle of nowhere alone. Whoever this man was, he didn't look reputable. He didn't look like someone who'd be driving a minivan. Nor did he resemble a Nevada native—there wasn't anything western about him. Dressed in a pair of faded, holey jeans and a sweatshirt turned wrong-side-out, he had at least two days' razor stubble covering a strong jaw and chin, and windblown blond hair. It brushed the collar of his sweatshirt in back and fell unkempt across his forehead.

"No answer?" he asked, shoving his hair out of his eyes.

Sticking her hand in her purse, she searched for a little security—in the form of the small can of mace Carlos had given her when she met him to retrieve her luggage. "Not yet."

He opened the sliding door to his back seat, slung a black bag the size of a laptop computer over one shoulder and grabbed a large duffel. When he came toward her, his movements were well-coordinated, which allowed Emma to relax a little. He didn't seem drunk or otherwise out of control. And when she could see him more clearly, she realized he didn't look *dangerous,* exactly. He was far too handsome for dangerous. He had a straight nose, well-defined cheekbones and lips almost too sensual to belong to a man.

"Maybe we'll have to go somewhere else," she said.

He shook his head. "She's here."

The way his hair moved, Emma could tell it was clean. He seemed oddly refined despite his careless attitude, his thick whiskers and worn-out clothing. His nails were neatly clipped; thanks to the floodlights on the building, she could see that as he gripped his bags. His teeth were perfectly white and straight. And he had a body like Manuel's, lithe and lean with broad shoulders and a tapering waist—an ideal build for an expensive tailored suit.

So what was he doing wearing such tattered jeans? Was he some kind of dot-com guy who'd lost his job and fallen on hard times? Why was he at this hole-in-the-wall motel in the middle of a Wednesday night?

Whoever he was, he had a story. Emma wondered if most

of the people who stayed at the Cozy Comfort Bungalows had a story.

He didn't bother ringing the buzzer. Opening the screen door, he used his fist to bang far more loudly and decisively than she would have dared.

A moment later, an inside light snapped on and an old woman with white hair and arthritic hands came to the door. "Oh, Preston, I thought it might be you," she said, peering out at them. The smell of cats and Mentholatum wafted out of the house behind her. "You're back already, huh?"

Emma released her can of mace and hiked her purse higher on her shoulder. He *frequented* this place? Somehow that seemed as incongruous as such a handsome man dressing like a bum.

"Just for tonight, Maude," he said. "I have to go to Iowa tomorrow."

"Iowa!" she cried. "Surely you're not *driving* there."

"I drive everywhere."

"Well, at least you've got a lady friend with you this time."

His light-colored eyes focused briefly on Emma. "She's not with me. I think she wants a room."

Emma cleared her throat and spoke up. "Yes, please."

"Sure, honey," Maude said. "Let me get Preston his key. He likes the end unit, don't you, Preston?"

Maude didn't seem to expect an answer, because she turned away. When she reappeared, she handed Preston the promised key and a Ziplock bag filled with homemade cookies. "Get some sleep. I'll be making pancakes in the morning, if you're interested."

"Thanks," he said, but he didn't refer to the cookies, as Emma would have done. His voice was so noncommittal she couldn't tell whether he'd be joining Maude for breakfast or not.

Emma watched Preston Whoever-He-Was walk away. Maude's eyes lingered on him, too.

"Poor guy," she said. "From what I can gather, he's really been through the wringer." She adjusted the plastic cap she wore to keep her hair from getting mussed while sleeping. "Anyway, you'd like a room. Let's see what we can do...."

Because of her sleeping son, Emma waited outside while Maude handled the paperwork. Ten minutes later, she unloaded her suitcases from the car and returned for Max. He was difficult for her to carry, and she wasn't sure how she'd get him into the motel without pulling a muscle, but she certainly didn't want to wake him. She needed him to remain asleep so she could get some rest, too.

"Boy, you're getting big," she muttered.

"Are we home yet?" he asked, but she didn't respond. She didn't want to upset him by saying no, which turned out to be a good decision because he was asleep again as soon as his head landed on her shoulder.

Just a few more steps, she told herself. *Almost there...here we are...* But her door was shut; the chair she'd used to prop it open had slid out of the way.

She hoisted Max farther up on her shoulder and tried the handle. Locked. *Damn.*

Bending one knee to help support her son's weight, she leaned against the side of the building so she could get the key out of her pocket.

"You have a son?"

The voice startled her. The man Preston was standing in the shadows holding an ice bucket, but until he spoke, she hadn't noticed him.

"Yes." She thought he might ask Max's age, his name, maybe a few other details—typical small talk when confronted with someone's child—but he didn't. He stared at her and Max through his longish streaky-blond hair, his expression unreadable. Then he came forward, took the key she'd just pulled out of her pocket and opened her door.

"Thanks." She deposited Max on the bed and pivoted to find Preston looking in at them, key still in the lock, his hand on her door so it wouldn't swing shut.

"Good night," she said, a little disconcerted that she and Max had suddenly claimed so much of his attention when he'd been completely uninterested in her before.

He didn't answer. Unless Emma imagined it, which could have been the case, a raw, almost savage expression crossed his face. An expression he quickly masked before tossing her the key and letting the door close with a quiet click.

CHAPTER THREE

ALTHOUGH IT WAS nearly midnight, Emma couldn't sleep. She'd expected to drop off immediately and wake only once during the night—when the alarm rang at three and she had to get up to test Max's blood. But her mind wouldn't release the worries that kept her one-hundred-percent conscious. She kept reminding herself of their new names, frightened at the thought of forgetting. And, as if her preoccupation wasn't enough, she could hear the television going in Preston's room next door. Had he fallen asleep with it on? Probably.

She sighed. It didn't matter; she couldn't relax anyway.

Climbing out of bed, she pulled a sweatshirt over her T-shirt and pajama bottoms, and crossed the room to stare out the window. After putting Max to bed, she'd moved the Taurus to the far end of the lot, where it sat in almost total darkness, well hidden from the road. She probably should've asked Carlos if it was stolen, so she'd know whether or not to fear the police as well as Manuel. But Carlos had been so sweet about helping her, she didn't want to offend him. Besides, she was desperate. She would've taken it regardless.

Maybe in a few weeks she'd be living in a small town somewhere in the midwest, where Manuel would never think to look for her, and she could park the Taurus in her garage and walk to work.

She smiled at the thought of owning a little yellow house with flowers in front, of teaching first grade at the local elementary school. She'd have her son, a new name, a new life.

Another chance....

Suddenly remembering the envelope in her glove box, Emma checked to be sure Max was still sleeping peacefully. Then she grabbed her can of mace, put on a pair of flip-flops so the rocks wouldn't cut her feet, and slipped out of the room. The envelope had to be from Juanita. Or maybe Carlos. She hadn't told anyone else her new name.

The night had cooled quite a bit. A chill wind swayed the trees lining the property, making her shiver. Normally she would have liked the creaking of the branches, the low rustling of the leaves, but tonight those sounds seemed stark and lonely, almost eerie. So did the gurgle of the water flowing through the canal not far away. Maybe that was because, crazy as it seemed, she felt as if Manuel might show up at any moment.

Imagining him lunging out of the dark, laughing at her puny efforts to get away from him, made the hair stand up on the back of her neck. She froze for several seconds, her hands sweating on the mace as she turned in circles, squinting into the shadows near the motel.

Nothing. She couldn't see or hear anything unusual. Except for the sound of her neighbor's TV, which filtered out through his open window, the wind and the canal made the only noise.

The door to the Taurus groaned as she opened it. She couldn't see much, especially inside the car. The dome light was broken, but everything else was in pretty good shape, considering that the vehicle had only cost her twenty-five-hundred dollars.

Searching the glove box, she easily located the envelope and took it back to her room, where she shut herself in the bathroom to read it.

At first glance, it looked like a letter from Manuel. She instantly recognized his jagged scrawl. But closer inspection revealed that it was a photocopy of something he'd written and not a letter at all—a list of names, addresses, phone numbers and a few dates.

Someone, presumably Juanita, had jotted a quick note in Spanish at the bottom of the page:

Si él te encuentra... If he finds you.

Perplexed, Emma examined the names. Where had Juanita found this? In Manuel's office? It was possible. While Manuel typically kept his office locked against Emma and Max, he allowed Juanita to clean in there occasionally.

But Emma had mentioned to Juanita, several times, that she believed Manuel's business wasn't quite what it seemed. Juanita had never let on that she agreed.

So who were the people on this list? Several lived in Mexico. Some lived in San Diego. One had no address.

Did she finally have proof of what she'd long suspected?

Juanita's note was too cryptic to tell. On several occasions, Emma had overheard Manuel's family talking about shipments and carriers and accidents in the desert. But those few snippets of conversation hardly *proved* that Manuel was involved in anything illegal. And although she'd been as vigilant as possible, looking for some kind of leverage, she'd never been able to find anything more damning.

Returning the paper to its envelope, Emma tucked it away in her purse. She needed to decide carefully what to do with it. If this paper was what she believed, it could mean her freedom—or maybe her death.

FINALLY, AT ABOUT ONE o'clock, the exhaustion of the day overcame Emma and she slept. But only for two hours. At three, the alarm clock woke her to test Max's glucose levels.

Almost too tired to move, she hit the button that would stop the ringing, dragged herself out of bed and stumbled to the bathroom. She'd left his testing kit on the counter so she could find it without rummaging through everything. But her eyes were too grainy to open all the way. Especially once she flipped on the light.

Hunching over the sink, she splashed water onto her face. Then she wiped her hands, inserted a test strip into the glucose meter and retrieved the lancet that would draw blood from the end of Max's finger. She hated poking him. For her, that was the worst part of his daily care. The three or more injections weren't half as bad as continually pricking the sensitive pads of his little fingers.

But the ramifications of not testing were even worse. Blood sugar that was too high or too low could kill him, and he could go either way unexpectedly and very quickly. So she did what she had to do.

Moving into the bedroom, she gently pulled her son's small hand from beneath the blankets, pressed the lancet to the end of his index finger and tripped the spring. He winced but didn't wake. A moment later, she was able to squeeze out a drop of bright red blood, which was quickly drawn into the edge of the test strip. Then she stood, sleepily scratching her head as she waited for the reading.

When the meter beeped, she held it up to the light coming from the bathroom. Two hundred and eight-four. He was a hundred and eight-four points too high. She hadn't compensated for his lack of exercise as well as she'd hoped. But he didn't show any visible symptoms when his glucose levels fell in this range, no sweating or blotchiness, so it was difficult to know.

Fresh worry gnawed at her as she headed back into the bathroom to draw up more insulin. She pictured the blood circulating through her son's body as a thick sludge that was damaging his eyes and his kidneys—and possibly his nerve endings and heart. Somehow she had to do better in accounting for all the variables. She was his only defense. But just when she thought she'd figured out how his body processed certain foods, he'd grow and everything would change.

Tears sprang to her eyes, tears she fought so she could read the tiny marks on the syringe. She was responding to the effects of stress and exhaustion as much as the daily concern she felt for her son. She knew that—just as she knew crying wouldn't solve anything.

Max whimpered when she pinched the back of his arm and inserted the needle. But afterward he rolled over and continued to sleep.

She dropped the syringe into her sharps container and sat on the bed, lightly running a hand over his short crew cut. Already interested in copying the older boys he saw in their neighborhood and on TV, he insisted on putting gel in his hair to make it spiky. She smiled as she remembered him coming downstairs wearing a T-shirt he'd cut at the bottom and sleeves to mimic the young man who cleaned their pool.

Max meant everything to her. She wished she could take the finger pricks and injections for him.

Suddenly she realized that the television next door had been turned off. At last. The peace and quiet felt almost profound. Getting up, she crossed the room to check the car again and saw someone outside.

Her heart jumped into her throat. But another look showed her it was only Preston, standing in front of his room.

What was he doing?

She watched him for several minutes. He was smoking and staring into space.

He's like me. He can't sleep. But he appeared to be more than restless. He appeared…desolate, which struck her as odd for someone so young, fit and handsome.

She recalled Maude's words: *He's really been through the wringer.* What had happened to him?

It was really none of Emma's business. She needed to go to bed so she could get up early and leave this place. But empathy and her own need for human interaction warred with her common sense. Maybe she should reach out to him, somehow help him get through the night. It might help her at the same time. One night wasn't much, but Emma knew that when it was late and dark and lonely like this, one night could drag on forever.

Grabbing her protective spray just in case, she propped a shoe in the door so it wouldn't shut and stepped out. "Having trouble sleeping?" she asked, being careful to hide the can behind her back.

He hadn't turned when she opened her door. He didn't glance over at her now. "Always."

She inched a little closer, trying to seem casual and relaxed. "They make sleeping pills for that, you know."

He took another drag on his cigarette, letting the silence stretch as he leaned against one of the posts that supported the overhang. After a few seconds, he turned his head to study her. "Are you interested in a smoke?"

"No."

"Then what? Small talk? Entertainment?"

"I don't expect you to entertain me, and I don't like small talk," she said. Manuel had cut her off from everyone and everything, except the faces she passed in the grocery store or on the street. She was sick of meaningless smiles and nods and comments on the weather. She craved real friendship, deep conversation. She doubted she'd get that from a brief encounter with a stranger, but connecting with someone for even a few moments was better than more isolation.

"Fine, then here's the truth," he said, a shrug in his voice. "I can't trust myself enough to buy sleeping pills."

"Because…"

Smoke curled from his lips. "What do you think?"

He was intimating that he might hurt himself, of course. But something about his words didn't ring true. She was fairly sure he was just trying to shock her. "What am I supposed to say to that?"

"Nothing. You're supposed to realize I'm probably unstable and scurry back to your room."

"What if the fact that you've considered suicide doesn't scare me?"

"It should."

He liked playing the part of an I-don't-care-if-I-live-or-die badass, she thought. "Maybe I understand how you're feeling. Maybe I've been there." She'd once sat staring at a bottle of sleeping pills for three hours. Taking them would have been the easiest way to escape Manuel. He made her feel so insignificant, so angry and helpless. It was the defiance suicide represented that had appealed to her, the dramatic final exit. *Control that, you bastard.*

If not for Max, she might have done it.

The wind blew Preston's hair across his forehead as he flicked his ashes to the ground. "You're telling me you're nuts, too?"

She toyed with the mace behind her back. "Feeling desperate isn't the same as being nuts."

"It can be." He scowled, studying the cigarette pinched between his fingers. "Anyway, you don't know me. And you've got a kid in there."

His eyes held too many secrets. She gazed out across the lot. "Maude seems to think you're okay."

"That doesn't mean anything. You barely met her," he said, bringing the cigarette back to his lips.

"Are you telling me I can't trust either of you?"

The cigarette moved as he talked. "I'm telling you that you can't trust *anyone*."

"You have some serious issues."

"We all have issues." The way he looked her up and down would have made Emma nervous, except it was so...orchestrated. "You're not even dressed," he added.

She arched an eyebrow at him. "I'm well covered."

"Those pajamas aren't the most attractive pair I've ever seen."

"I'm not trying to impress you, so quit trying to intimidate me."

He crushed his cigarette beneath his heel and didn't respond.

"Do you want to talk about it or not?" she asked.

Shoving off from the post, he rounded on her a little too quickly. She hopped back out of reach—and dropped her mace on the ground in the process.

He eyed it for a second. "There you go. *Now* you're using your head." Picking it up, he gave it back to her. Then, with a humorless chuckle, he disappeared inside his room.

So much for starting a Tortured Souls Club, Emma thought as she looked down at the small canister. But it was just as well. She was never going to see Preston Whoever-He-Was again. And she had enough problems of her own to worry about. She needed to get some sleep. The more states she managed to put between herself and California tomorrow, the better.

WAL-MART WAS BUSIER than Emma had anticipated. Evidently it paid to be the only superstore in town, even in a town the size of Fallon.

Max helped her push a shopping cart down the aisles as she looked for the bottled water. She'd planned to be on her way by now—hours ago, actually. But she'd been exhausted. When Max had slept in, she did, too. And by the time they'd showered, dressed and packed, the stores were open. So she'd decided to take advantage of the local Wal-Mart to stock up on bottled water before venturing any farther into the desert.

Unfortunately, it hadn't been the quick stop she'd anticipated. First, Max needed to use the restroom and took so long, complaining of a stomach ache, she was afraid he was getting the flu. Then she had to feed him, so they ate at the McDonald's in the store. At that point, she couldn't put off his insulin injection, which necessitated another trip to the restroom. And on the way back, he'd spotted the toy aisle and insisted he be allowed to choose a toy as his reward for being so good while the police officer talked to Mommy yesterday. Because Emma didn't have the heart to tell him he hadn't been as quiet as she'd requested, she'd given in and let him pick out a magnetized game designed for travel. But now she was getting nervous and more than eager to leave.

"Hey, Mommy, they have gum," Max said once they'd found the water and were finally standing in the checkout line.

Emma thumbed through the latest issue of *People*. "I've got some sugarless gum in the car."

"I don't like that kind."

She glanced at the candid photos of various stars. "It's better than nothing, isn't it?"

"How 'bout a sucker?"

Emma looked over the top of the magazine, wishing the checker—a gray-haired man with wire-rimmed glasses—would hurry. Checkout was never fun for the mother of a diabetic child. Everything Max loved but should avoid was displayed at eye level. "I don't think so, honey."

"Please? It could be my emergency snack."

Except that his emergency snack never lasted until an emergency. "I really want to keep your blood in its zone, okay, baby? You had that candy bar the policeman gave you yesterday, which didn't really fit into your meal plan."

"What if I take an extra shot?"

"I just gave you your insulin."

His shoulders drooped and his bottom lip came out. "What if I eat only half of it?"

Emma picked up the sucker and checked the carbohydrate totals on the back—twenty-one grams. "I guess you could have it for your afternoon snack," she said, although she knew Max would start begging her for it the moment they got in the car.

All too familiar with their typical negotiations, he began to press her even before that. "You mean for lunch?"

"I mean for snack at three o'clock." She'd have to take away a healthier food in order to let him eat the sucker, but she didn't want to make his life miserable.

Forever conscious of the fact that her money had to last, Emma put the magazine back in the rack, paid for the water, candy and Max's game, and hurried from the store. She was so intent on avoiding the other shoppers and traffic moving through the lot that at first she didn't notice the cop car parked at a slant behind her Taurus. It was Max who pointed it out to her.

"Look, Mommy. There's another policeman."

Emma leaned around the large family in front of them to see what he was talking about, and felt her stomach drop. Sure enough, a police officer circled the Taurus, shading his eyes to see inside it.

God, it *was* stolen, just as she'd feared! Why else would they be so interested?

What now? Grabbing Max's hand, she darted back into the store. She'd noticed another exit over by the tire center. She'd slip out there. But then what? She couldn't leave her car.

"What are we doing now, Mommy? Where are we going?" Max asked as she hurried him down one aisle and then the next.

Emma could hardly breathe. Their suitcases were in the trunk of the car. She had no choice but to leave behind almost everything they owned. Thank God she had the backpack with Max's diabetes supplies and her purse.

"Mommy? What's wrong? Are you crying?"

"No." Obviously, her panic showed. "I'll tell you what's happening in a minute," she said, scrambling to decide what to do. She had to get out of Fallon right away. But she no longer had transportation. And, as far as she knew, this town didn't have any bus service.

The vision of a beat-up brown van flashed through her mind, along with a snippet of conversation.

I have to go to Iowa tomorrow.

Iowa! Surely you're not driving there.

I drive everywhere.

Preston was leaving town today. He was going far, far away. And he had a van.

He might be her only chance to escape.

But it was nearly eleven o'clock. What if she'd already missed him?

PRESTON HOLMAN BLINKED at the ceiling overhead. He needed to think of five good reasons to get up. That was the exercise, wasn't it? The therapist he'd seen at his ex-wife's insistence had told him to face each new day by making his list of five.

He glanced at the gun on the dresser. As usual, he could think of only one. Ironically, it was the same thing that had caused his divorce. But it got him out of bed every day.

Rolling off the mattress, he landed on his feet, peeled off his boxer briefs and strode to the bathroom to take a quick shower. He might have suffered a setback yesterday when the pharmacist who knew Vince didn't hear from him as he thought he might. But Gordon, the private investigator he'd hired to help him track Dr. Vince Wendell, had called afterward with better news. And even if this new lead didn't work out, Preston would still find him—somehow, somewhere. Dallas was counting on him, and he wouldn't let his son down again, regardless of the cost.

A knock echoed through the room before he could start the water. He didn't generally receive visitors. He'd quit associating with friends and family over a year ago—about the time he started carrying a gun.

It had to be Maude. She was the only person he knew who refused to notice or care that he didn't want to be bothered. He supposed that in some perverse way he liked her motherly clucking. After all, he'd been searching the state of Nevada for months and always came back here.

Pulling on a pair of jeans, he fastened the buttons and shoved his gun in a drawer.

A shaft of sunlight blinded him as he opened the door, reminding him that he should've been up hours ago. He would've been, if it hadn't taken him until five in the morning to fall asleep.

Raising a hand to shield his eyes, he blinked when he realized two people stood on his stoop—and Maude wasn't one of them.

"Can I help you?" Keeping his gaze firmly affixed to the pretty woman he'd met last night, he refused to acknowledge the stocky, all-American boy at her side.

She dropped four quarters in her son's hand and asked him to run to the office to see if Maude would sell him a diet soda.

The boy trotted off, and she gave Preston a hesitant smile, which faded quickly when he didn't return it. "I'm sorry to bother you, but…"

"What?" he prompted when her words faltered.

Her eyes drifted to his bare chest. Then she lifted her chin. "I heard you say to Maude last night that you're heading to Iowa today. Is that true?"

It was his turn to grow leery. "Do I really want to answer that question?"

"Why not?"

"Because I can't see where you're going with it, which makes me a little uncomfortable."

"I'm not going anywhere with it. Well, of course I am, but…" She wiped her palms on her expensive linen shorts before folding her arms in a jerky, nervous movement. "My car's been stolen."

"From *here?*" He stuck his head out to check the far corner where, for whatever reason, she'd parked her car last night. The white Taurus was gone, all right, but he had a hard time believing it'd been stolen. Fallon had very little crime. He typically left his keys in the van.

"Not here, exactly," she clarified. "At Wal-Mart."

"Are you sure you didn't forget where you parked?"

Her lips thinned. "I didn't forget where I parked. My car is gone and my luggage with it. Max and I had to walk three miles to get back here."

"Do you need to use my phone to call your insurance agent or... something?" he asked, still at a loss. He didn't know this woman. What could she possibly want from him?

"No." Her nails made indentations in her arms, beneath her white, short-sleeved sweater. "My insurance agent won't be able to help me."

"Because..."

"I only carried liability coverage. My boyfriend and I recently split up and...and I couldn't afford anything more comprehensive."

Preston considered her troubled face. She had ice-blue eyes with golden lashes, a small, elegant nose, a generous mouth, and the most beautiful sun-kissed skin and long blond hair he'd ever seen. Was she using her looks and that bad-luck story to see how much she could take him for? She was probably accustomed to getting whatever she wanted.

But he wasn't a good mark. He traveled light. And he carried a gun.

"I'd offer to let you call your family or a friend or someone else," he said. "But something tells me you're not here to use the phone."

"No."

"So...what, then?"

She glanced over at the dirty brown minivan he'd picked up at some two-bit used-car lot along the way. He'd fallen asleep at the wheel and wrecked his truck—the only thing he hadn't given his wife in the divorce.

"Actually, I was hoping maybe we could hitch a ride with you."

The moment of truth. "Hitch a ride where?" he asked.

"Iowa."

"What?"

"You've got room." She appealed to him with those incredible eyes, and for the first time, Preston noticed how pale and drawn she was under that tan. "I have family there—in Iowa, I mean."

"We're complete strangers!"

"I know."

She was also too thin. But he couldn't do anything for her. He couldn't stand the idea of having her boy in the car. And the loaded weapon was something else entirely. "Forget it. Won't work."

"Why not?"

"It takes three days to get there."

She grew more agitated. "What about Salt Lake City? That's closer."

He wasn't taking her anywhere. He started to shake his head, but she grabbed his arm. "Please?"

Damn it! Preston closed his eyes. Since the tragedy that had changed his life, no one dared approach him, let alone ask him for a favor. He was too filled with rage, too hungry for vengeance; all that negative emotion made others uncomfortable. So how had he suddenly found himself in this predicament?

He opened his eyes to stare down at the hand still gripping his arm so beseechingly—and saw a nasty-looking sore. It was only the size of a nickel, but he was willing to bet it hurt like hell, and it didn't seem to be healing.

Taking hold of her wrist so she couldn't immediately recoil, he said, "Where'd you get this?"

Her eyes slid to the injury. "It was an accident."

He made no effort to pretend he believed her. "An accident?"

"I bumped into my boyfriend when he was smoking a cigarette and burned myself."

"This isn't the type of burn you get by accident. It's too deep."

When she didn't answer, he dropped her hand. "Are you going to tell me the truth? Or do we say goodbye right now?"

"Okay." She seemed to deflate a little more. "He's got an anger problem."

"Your boyfriend?"

"Yeah."

"He did it on purpose?"

"You already know that."

"Sounds like quite a guy."

She said nothing.

"You two split up?" he asked.

"Yes."

"Where is he now?"

"Not here, which is all that matters. And I can pay for gas. Surely that's an incentive to let me ride with you for a few hours. You look like you could use the money."

"I look like a lot of things," he said. "A lot of things I'm not." Remembering the sleeping boy she'd held in her arms last night, the same boy who'd just dashed off to get a soda, he let his breath out in a long sigh. "If it was only you, it'd be different, but you have a kid and—"

"You're worried about Max?"

It'd been two years, but the sight of a young boy still made Preston feel as though someone had driven a stake through his heart. "Kids don't do well on long drives. They get bored, they whine, they beg, they have to go to the bathroom every five minutes—"

"Not my kid," she interrupted quickly.

"*Every* kid."

"Max is a good boy. He…he's very low maintenance. You won't even know he's in the car, I promise."

As if on cue, her son came running back, carrying a diet cola, which he'd already opened. "She had one, Mom," he said. "She gave it to me. She wouldn't even take the quarters."

Preston kept his eyes averted from the boy's young face. The voice affected him badly enough.

"How nice of her," Emma said. "I hope you remembered to thank her."

"I did. She gave me a cookie, too. Can I eat it?"

A frown creased the woman's forehead as she regarded her son. "You already had a sucker."

"But we walked a long way."

She glanced fleetingly at Preston. "Not now. We'll talk about it later."

"Pul-leeze, Mom?"

The conversation sounded all too familiar. "See?" Preston said. "It won't work."

"He's only asking me for a cookie!" she said.

"You'd better find someone else to give you a ride." He backed up and started to shut the door, but she put a hand on the panel before he could.

"Wait! You can't turn me away. I…I need your help."

Preston still wanted to refuse. He would have—if not for that damn burn and the desperation in her eyes.

"Please!" she said again and, suddenly, he let go of the door. The opposing pressure sent it crashing into the wall. She flinched; he didn't.

"Fine," he snapped, "but you'd better keep that boy quiet."

The woman grabbed her son's arm and pulled him slightly behind her. "He won't make a peep, right, Max?"

Max looked confused, which made Preston feel even worse. He knew he was being harsh and unreasonable. But he couldn't help it. "If either of you gives me any trouble, I won't feel the least bit guilty kicking you out at the first town," he said.

She stiffened but nodded obediently. "I understand."

CHAPTER FOUR

EMMA KNEW SHE SHOULD test Max's blood. Soon. Because she was trying so hard to keep him quiet, she'd been giving in too easily whenever he asked for something to eat. With no exercise to compensate, he *had* to need extra insulin. But after claiming that her son was "low maintenance," she didn't dare whip out his testing kit and reveal what a monstrous exaggeration that had been. Preston Holman, who'd introduced himself once they hit the road, seemed to have no tolerance for children. She feared he'd use Max's special needs as a reason to dump them long before they reached Utah.

If Max could hold out until they had to stop, she could walk him into the ladies' room and take care of him without a lot of fuss. Only they were in the middle of nowhere, and Preston didn't seem inclined to pull over just for the fun of it. Neither did he talk much. They'd been driving for nearly three hours, and he'd scarcely said a word. She got the impression that he saw her and Max's company as an endurance test, that he was busy counting the minutes until he'd be rid of them.

The slightest irritation could make that happen sooner than she wanted.

"Mommy, I'm hungry," Max complained.

Emma knew he couldn't be hungry. He'd been snacking like crazy, which was what had her so worried. "You're fine."

"I want a cookie."

She glanced quickly at Preston, whose eyes seemed fastened on the road ahead of them. He hadn't looked at her, or her son, more than a couple of times since they'd left. She hoped he was in his own little world, deep in thought, and wasn't paying attention. But the way he gripped the steering wheel with both hands when Max added a whiny "pul-leeze" indicated otherwise.

"You've had enough sweets," she said softly, praying Max would accept her response and go back to playing with the magnetized checkers she'd bought him at Wal-Mart.

But he'd grown bored with that game, along with his action figures and his coloring books. "When will we be there?" he asked.

"Not until dark."

"Will it be bedtime?"

"Yes."

"What's taking so long? I want to eat."

A muscle flexed in Preston's cheek. Loosening her seat belt, Emma turned to face her son and lowered her voice. "I gave you lunch already, honey, you know that."

"Can I have my afternoon snack?"

Emma bit back an irritated exclamation. No matter how tense she was, she had to remain calm. "You've already eaten plenty of sweets."

"But I'm hungry!"

"Then you can have some—" She was about to say protein, but she knew that would sound like an odd response to Preston. Parents of normal children didn't typically talk to them in terms of carbohydrates and proteins. "Some string cheese or lunch meat."

"I don't want any cheese or lunch meat!"

Max was tired of the foods she typically used as substitutions. Just as he was tired of riding in the car. "If you'll take a nap, it'll make the time go faster, honey. Then, when we stop, I'll let you choose something you'd like to eat, okay?"

"I want to go home," he replied, and started crying.

Torn between his distress and her fear that Preston would drop them off at the first opportunity if she couldn't get her son to quiet down, Emma gritted her teeth. "Max, please stop—"

Suddenly Preston reached down and tossed a whole box of cookies into the back seat. "Let him eat," he growled.

With a final sniff, Max stopped crying and recovered the cookies. But Emma couldn't let her son continue to binge. Without enough insulin, his body would be forced to use fat for energy, which would create ketones. Ketones could kill body cells. If they built up, they could lead to coma.

"I have to use the restroom," she announced crisply.

Preston's scowl darkened. "Now?"

"Now."

He waved at the flat desert surrounding them. "There isn't anywhere to stop."

"When will we reach the next town?"

"Not for a couple hours."

There wasn't even a tree for cover. Just sagebrush. But Emma could hear the rattle of the inner bag as Max reached into the box for one cookie after another. "I'll make do," she said. "Please stop."

PRESTON CHECKED under the hood, where he'd stashed his gun. Fortunately, the bungee cord he'd borrowed from Maude had done the trick. The weapon hadn't moved.

Relieved, he leaned against the front bumper and lit a cigarette while waiting for Emma and her boy to take care of business on the opposite side. Barely two years ago, when he'd still been a husband and father and a successful stockbroker in San Francisco, he'd also been a triathlete. He'd conscientiously avoided anything that might impair his physical performance. He'd eaten healthy foods, lifted weights, cross-trained. He'd certainly never dreamed he'd ever find himself standing at the side of a desolate highway in Nevada, leaning against a rattletrap van—the only vehicle he owned— hiding a gun and sucking on a cancer stick.

Life was full of surprises.

With a careless shrug, he embraced the nicotine, halfway hoping it *would* kill him, then let the smoke escape through his lips in a long exhalation. "You done?" he called. Gordon's lead on Vince Wendell's whereabouts was the best one they'd found since the doctor had left Nevada. Preston was anxious to get back on the road. He shouldn't have picked up any passengers, particularly a mother and child. But that burn on Emma's hand still bothered him—what kind of cruel bastard purposely burned a woman? And he had to admit that giving them a lift wasn't *that* big a deal. They'd reach Salt Lake in one day. He could handle one day.

"Um...not yet," Emma answered.

Preston could hear Max talking about a rock he'd found. Emma tried to convince him to leave it behind. When Max refused, she told him to put it in his pocket. A few seconds later, she scolded him for getting into the dirt.

Preston hated to see her mollycoddle the boy. He wanted to tell her that a little dirt never hurt anyone. He would've told her that if Max was his son. But his son was dead. And Preston refused to get involved in Emma and Max's lives. He was just biding his time until they reached Salt Lake.

"Domin—Max, cooperate," he heard her say.

"You almost forgot," he laughed.

"Calm down. You know we have to do this." Her voice dropped to a whisper after that. Preston couldn't decipher what she was saying until she finally called out that they were finished.

"Did you have Max go, too?" he asked. The last thing he wanted was to have to stop again.

"Yes."

"Good. Hop in." He put his cigarette out in the dirt and turned—then froze when he found Max standing at the back bumper, watching him.

"You *smoke?*" the boy said.

Where was Emma? She was supposed to be watching this kid, keeping Max as far away from him as possible.

His heart started to pound at the frank curiosity in the boy's eyes. Glancing through the windows, Preston saw Emma cleaning her hands with something on the other side of the van.

"My mom hates it when people smoke," Max volunteered. "She says it's stinky. And sometimes it eats a hole in your throat."

"She's right." Preston pulled open the driver's-side door, then hesitated. The highway wasn't busy, but he couldn't get in and slam the door as he longed to, in case Max happened to step into the road while no one was watching.

"My dad smokes, too," Max said.

Although he didn't really want to talk to Max, this piqued Preston's curiosity. Was Max's father the same man who'd burned Emma? "Where is your dad?"

"Mexico."

"How long has he been there?"

Max shrugged. "I don't know."

"Max?" Emma called.

The boy darted back around the van. "What?"

"I told you to stay right here."

"He smokes," Max said loudly.

Emma lowered her voice. "That's none of our business."

"I told him you hate it."

"Thanks a lot."

Preston couldn't prevent the rueful smile that curved his lips at the sarcasm in her voice. Children didn't understand polite subtleties. They were honest, fresh, innocent….

Dallas had been the same way.

Memories of his son invited the pain he'd been working so hard to suppress. Preston had let him down. Terribly. He'd let Christy down, too. But especially Dallas.

Emma came around the van, holding Max's hand. "Would you like me to drive for a while? Maybe you could nap."

Reluctantly, Preston raised his head. She looked fragile and worried, like Christy had two years ago. He wondered what other horrors, besides the burn, had created the haunted expression in her eyes. At the same time, he didn't want to know. He couldn't get involved, couldn't care. There wasn't anything left inside him except a ravaging desire to hold his son again, which would never happen, and the determination to punish the man responsible.

"Just get in the van," he said, and hoped she would simply do as she was told.

She didn't. "Are you okay?"

He'd broken into a cold sweat when the emotions had overwhelmed him. He struggled to pull himself together, but he couldn't erase the images emblazoned on his mind: Dallas soaking the sheets with a raging fever. Christy's whispered prayers and constant pleading. Vince's odd behavior. And, at the end, six-year-old Dallas lying innocently in his coffin, stiff and cold and gone forever.

Emma and Max made his loss jagged, new. Every emotional wound he had that was connected to the past two years felt like it had just burst open.

He reached for the side of the van to steady himself.

"Is it the cigarettes?" he heard Max whisper to Emma.

"Why don't you find another rock, okay, buddy?" she said. "But search on the other side of the van, away from the road."

Now that Max had permission to dig in the dirt, he seemed unwilling to leave. "What's wrong with him?"

"He'll be all right. Go ahead."

Max finally did as he was told. Except for the occasional car shooting past them on the highway, the silent stillness of the desert settled around them, almost as stifling as the heat.

"Are you ill?" Emma asked.

Preston breathed deeply, summoning the strength and willpower to avoid the jaws of the dark depression that sometimes gaped after him. He knew it came from the betrayal and the rage and the guilt. In a sense, he'd been as much of a victim as Dallas. But he wouldn't remain a victim. "No."

"Then what's wrong?"

"Nothing." He thought of the gun, and the promise that sustained him. It'd all be over soon....

"Give me the keys," she said. "I'll drive for a few hours."

He looked up to find that she was still staring at him. "No." He was feeling better, back in control.

"Why not take a break while I'm here to help?"

A semi honked as it passed, and the subsequent blast of hot wind blew her long, silky hair across her face. "Because I don't need a break. I'm fine."

He'd used his gruffest voice, but she didn't seem to notice.

She brushed her hair out of her eyes and tucked it behind her ears. "Come on, you can worry about being a tough guy tomorrow. You'll have two more days of driving to manage on your own."

A tough guy? He wished he was tough. He wished he were as tough as Christy and could have resumed his life the way she had. All through Dallas's ordeal, Preston hadn't been able to shed one tear. He still hadn't released the pain buried inside him. Christy, on the other hand, had sobbed from the beginning. And now she was remarried. The invitation to her wedding had included a picture of her smiling brightly at the side of a man who used to be their neighbor.

You have to forget and move on, she'd told him only months after Dallas's death. *For* our *sake. For the sake of our future. Let Dallas go, Preston. Please. Let him go so I can, too….*

But Preston couldn't let go. Not then; not now. So Christy had moved on without him.

He had to admire her survival skills. She certainly wasn't as fragile as he'd once thought.

"Hello?" Emma prompted when he didn't answer right away.

"I can drive." It wasn't easy to accept kindness from someone he was so reluctant to help.

Her eyes appraised him coolly, almost mutinously. "You need a break."

Preston almost got in. But…if she was going to be so stubborn about it, he didn't see how it could hurt to let her drive.

Without another word, he tossed her the keys and stalked around to the other side. Since his divorce, he'd never been a passenger in his own vehicle. He doubted he'd managed to sleep, even if he wasn't driving. Since Dallas's death, it seemed he could never shut down completely. He feared too many things—that Vince would slip through his fingers. That he'd crumble and never be able to put the pieces together again.

But twenty miles down the road, Max nodded off. And the thrumming of the tires, combined with the movement of the car, slowly eased the tension knotting Preston's muscles. Soon, his eyelids felt so heavy he could scarcely lift them.

"Quit fighting it," Emma said softly. "Nothing bad will happen if you close your eyes for a few minutes."

That's what she thinks, he told himself. She didn't know any better.

He tried to shake off the sleepiness so he could take over at the wheel. But a merciful darkness drew near, buffeting him like a gentle current. And then, finally, there was nothing.

MAX AND PRESTON SLEPT through the next hour. With a blues CD playing in the background—something Emma was surprised to find in Preston's odd assortment of music—she relaxed for the first time since leaving San Diego. Manuel would never expect her to be traveling in a brown minivan with a man. It didn't hurt that the color of Max's hair and eyes was so similar to Preston's. The three of them weren't likely to raise any eyebrows—they looked like a little family.

How her son could resemble a stranger more than his own father, Emma didn't understand. Because of Max's unusual coloring, Manuel's mother had often intimated that he couldn't possibly belong to Manuel. But Emma knew she could prove it with a paternity test if she wanted to. She'd never slept with anyone else.

"What are you thinking about?"

Emma blinked and glanced over to find Preston studying her from beneath his thick, gold-tipped eyelashes. "Nothing, why?"

"You were frowning."

Manuel's family had a tendency to bring out the worst in her. But there was no reason to go into all of that. She and Preston were sharing a ride, nothing more. He'd drop her off in Salt Lake City late this evening, and she'd never see him again. Then she'd have to plot her next move—with no luggage, no car and little money—from the valley at the base of the Wasatch Mountains where she and Manuel had once attended the Winter Olympics.

"We're only forty minutes or so outside Eureka," she said, instead of responding to his comment about her expression.

"Have you ever been to Eureka?" he asked.

"I've been to Eureka, California, but not Eureka, Nevada. I've never traveled this road before."

He gazed out at the scenery. "They call this the Loneliest Road in America."

"Really?"

"Interstate 80 has more traffic."

"So why'd you choose Highway 50?"

"I don't like crowds."

"I've noticed." She purposely spoke in a biting tone. "I've never met anyone who hates children as much as you do. You remind me of Ebenezer Scrooge."

She thought she saw him wince, but she could feel little real sympathy for someone who didn't like Max.

"You're getting your stories screwed up," he said. "Scrooge hated Christmas."

"I don't have anything screwed up. He was a miserly old man who hated everyone, especially children."

"I could've left you in Fallon," he pointed out.

Emma had to concede that was true. Maybe he was helping them grudgingly, but at least he was helping them. "You're right," she said. "I'm sorry."

He didn't say anything. He kept his face averted but she could see his reflection in the glass: the marked angle of his cheekbone, the squareness of his stubbly jaw, the slight cleft in his chin.

"Have you been on this road a lot?" she asked.

His focus didn't change from the desert surrounding them. "I've been all over Nevada in the past seven months, although I've mostly stayed in Fallon."

"But you didn't get a job or buy a house there?"

Finally he looked over at her. "No, I usually stayed at Maude's."

From the appearance of his van, he'd been living in motels for quite some time. She wanted to ask what had happened to him, why he didn't seem to have any roots. But she knew he wouldn't take kindly to the question, so she resorted to something less personal. "The towns along this road look sad to me, like they're dying."

"The mines have closed down, but the people out here are tough," he said. "They'll make it."

She considered him against the backdrop of the monotonous landscape. "I didn't think so when I first saw you, but…you seem to fit in here."

"I look like the miner type to you?"

"Not at all."

"So what's the connection?"

When she didn't answer right away, he grimaced. "Never mind."

"What?"

"I'm Scrooge, remember? You think my soul's as barren as the land around us—or something equally flattering."

"No. Actually, I think you and the desert possess a sort of…stark beauty," she said.

His eyebrows lifted. *"Beauty?"*

She chuckled. "Does that offend your masculinity?"

"It surprises me."

"Why?"

"You have to ask? I haven't shaved for a couple days. I can't even remember the last time I had a haircut."

"I'm not talking about your hair." She made a point of eyeing his T-shirt and holey jeans. "Or your fashion sense."

"Then what *are* you talking about?"

"Your face. Your body."

Even Emma heard the frank admiration in her voice. Their eyes met, and she wished she'd been a little less honest. A few seconds earlier she'd somehow hurt him, and had overcorrected. That was all. But the intensity of his gaze reminded her that she didn't know him very well and, except for her sleeping son, they were alone in the middle of nowhere.

"I didn't mean that the way it came out," she said, making a point of counting the yellow dash marks flying toward them. "I—I wasn't coming on to you or anything."

He didn't speak for several minutes. When he looked at her again, the flicker of interest in his eyes was gone. "Is the man who left that burn on your hand Max's father?" he asked.

"Yes."

"You called him your boyfriend."

"We were never married."

"Why not?"

"His family objected."

"And he gave in? In this day and age?"

"He has a close-knit family."

"I still find that hard to believe. How long were you with him?"

"We were together for six years. We lived in the same house for five."

"You moved in together after Max was born?"

"Yes."

"And when did you leave him?"

Emma couldn't believe she was divulging so much. But talking seemed the quickest way to ease the sudden tension that had sprung up between them. "Two days ago."

There was another pause. Thinking the conversation had come to an end, she reached over to turn up the music. But Preston caught her hand. "Are you on the run, Emma?"

It was the first time he'd used her new name. Called her by any name.... Conscious of the smooth baritone of his voice and his strong, warm fingers clasping her wrist, Emma drew a deep breath. "What do you think?"

"I think a woman doesn't plead with a complete stranger to take her and her son across the country unless she has no other choice."

Emma didn't respond. What could she say? He was right.

"Do you suppose he's following you?" he asked.

She knew Manuel would try. But she didn't want to spook Preston any more than she already had. "I hope not."

He turned her arm over and ran his thumb very lightly across the raw, red burn. "A man doesn't give up a woman like you, or a son like Max, unless he has to."

Emma wasn't sure if he was talking to her or to himself, but for her own peace of mind, she wanted to answer. "He has to," she said simply. "I'll do absolutely anything to make sure we never go back."

CHAPTER FIVE

MANUEL STOOD at the window of his Sacramento hotel, gazing down at the busy street below. Where was she? If he didn't catch Vanessa soon, he might *never* find her.

Contemplating life without her made it difficult to breathe. He couldn't believe she'd gotten away from him; he still hadn't completely dealt with the shock of it. But he told himself he wouldn't have to. He'd eventually figure out what she had planned, where she was going. He wouldn't allow her to humiliate him in front of his whole family.

I told you she couldn't be trusted. I told you to quit thinking with your dick, his mother had said. *You should've taken Dominick and moved on years ago.*

His brothers had clucked their tongues and acted smug, knowing full well that their own wives would never have the courage to defy them. *She doesn't know her place,* José had said, the comment an obvious suggestion that Manuel should teach her.

It was high time he did, Manuel thought. Once he found Vanessa, he'd give her a lesson she'd never forget. She wouldn't even be able to brush her teeth without permission. He'd prove to his family that he could handle her, that he could handle *any* woman.

But first he had to find her, and reporting the car stolen had netted him only one lead. He knew Vanessa had been pulled over while traveling north on Highway 5. That piece of information had led him to Sacramento, but he didn't know where to go from here.

Pinching his neck, he turned to the phone. He'd already contacted Vanessa's family and all her old friends. They claimed not to have heard from her and sounded so genuinely surprised by his call that he believed them. He probably shouldn't have wasted the time. After what had happened before, the odds weren't good she'd go back to them again.

Should he call the police and report that Vanessa had kidnapped their son? That she'd been kidnapped herself? He wanted to—but he couldn't. There was always the chance that Vanessa had learned more about his business than he realized. If she aroused suspicion and the police launched an investigation, it would put his whole family in jeopardy. His mother said there was no need to invite trouble, to forget about Vanessa.

But that was easy for his mother to say. She'd never liked Vanessa, wanted to be rid of her. She didn't understand that he'd never met anyone who could arouse him the way Vanessa could.

Maybe he should fly to Arizona, just in case she decided to break her silence long enough to—

The telephone rang.

Crossing the floor in four strides, he snatched up the receiver. "Hello?"

"It's Richard. I've got news."

Manuel's heart began to pound. "You've found her?"

"No. But the police called. They've located the car."

"Where?"

"Fallon, Nevada."

"When?"

"This morning."

"Was it abandoned or something?"

"They found it in the parking lot of a Wal-Mart. They waited for the driver to come out, but no one ever showed."

"Damn it!" he said, and kicked the desk chair across the room.

Richard remained silent.

Manuel rubbed his face, grappling for control. *Don't let the panic win. Calm down. Think. Nevada…*

Quickly, he spread out the map he'd purchased and searched the state to the east of California. Fallon…Fallon…

Finally he pinpointed the town. It was on Highway 50, not far from the California-Nevada border. If Vanessa didn't have a car anymore, she was probably still there. Or somewhere close.

He felt a powerful surge of hope. Now the search was narrowing.

"Manuel, are you there?" Richard asked.

"Call Hector and everyone else. Tell them to get their asses to Fallon."

"Don't you want to go there yourself?"

"I'm on my way. But Fallon's not very big. If she's there, it shouldn't be hard to find her. What we have to do is set up an outside perimeter. How far could she have traveled from Fallon if she left around the time the cops found her car? We'll mark that on a map. Then some of us will stay in Fallon and the rest will fly to the outer line of that perimeter and slowly move in toward the center."

"Sounds smart," Richard said.

It *was* smart. Finding that car was the lucky break he'd been waiting for.

AT EUREKA, Preston took over the driving. The change woke Max, who wasn't too happy about having to get back in the van after their brief stop. But Preston was glad to trade seats with Emma. The nap had revived him, and he felt more comfortable behind the wheel. Soon they'd reach Ely, then Wendover. Beyond Wendover, they'd have a final two-hour stretch across the salt flats, then they'd arrive in Salt Lake City.

"When can we eat?" Max asked.

Preston could see Emma fighting sleep. At the sound of her son's voice, she jerked her drooping eyelids open and looked at Preston. "Do you think we could get some dinner in Ely?"

He nodded, wanting to tell her she could go ahead and relax. A normal person, a person with any compassion, would do that. But Max was wide-awake and talkative, and Preston didn't want to be left alone with him. The memories crowded too close.

"We'll stop soon," she told her son.

"When?" Max asked.

"In about an hour."

"An hour! That's too long."

Preston felt the same way. Glaring down at the odometer, he willed the miles to pass more quickly.

"Hey, Mom. There's a rabbit!"

Max's squeal of excitement startled Emma, who'd been about to nod off again. "What, honey? What did you say?"

"Did you see it? Huh, Mom? Did you see it?"

She covered a yawn. "See what?"

"The *rabbit*," Preston muttered.

The exasperation in his voice acted like a jolt of caffeine. It also resurrected the tense expression she'd worn earlier. "Sorry," she said, but he didn't know if she was talking to him or to Max.

"You're not looking," Max complained.

"I am now," she said.

Preston watched Emma gather whatever reserves of strength and patience she had left and turn toward the window, presumably in search of wildlife. But he couldn't expect her to continue acting as a buffer between him and her son. He couldn't be that much of a jerk. He didn't know her whole history, but he was beginning to understand that her life hadn't gone much better than his. If he was going to drop her off in Salt Lake, the least he could do was let her get some sleep along the way.

Still, he cringed at the thought of dealing directly with Max.

He put off what his conscience dictated, hoping the guilt would recede. But it didn't, so he finally reached out and squeezed her shoulder.

When he touched her, she gaped at him in astonishment.

"Go to sleep," he said briskly.

She shook her head. "I'm getting my second wind."

"Bullshit. You're exhausted."

"Did you say the 's' word?" Max asked.

"Max, it's none of your business," Emma warned.

"He said the 's' word, Mom. I heard him."

"That's okay," she replied. "It's not up to us to tell Mr. Holman how to speak, especially in his own car."

"Can *I* say the 's' word?"

"Absolutely not."

"*He* did."

"I'm bigger than you," Preston chimed in. "When you're my age, you can decide what words to use."

Max seemed satisfied with this answer, but not thirty seconds later Preston heard him murmuring, "Shit…shit, shit, shit."

Evidently, Emma heard him, too, because she twisted in her seat. "Max! What do you think you're doing?"

Preston adjusted the rearview mirror to see Max's eyes widen. "Practicing," he said innocently.

Emma shook her head, and Preston couldn't help laughing. "Rest," he told her. "You can worry about cleaning up his language later."

"You're smiling," she said as though she was amazed that he could.

Preston instantly sobered. "Just get some sleep."

"If my son says *shit* one more time, you're going to have to take us all the way to Iowa."

"Do you really have family there?"

With a yawn, she laid her head back. "No."

EMMA CLOSED HER EYES but refused to relax completely. She had to remain cognizant of what went on in the car. Although she was beginning to doubt that Preston was really as unfeeling as he wanted her to believe, he made no secret about his dislike of children. She'd seen the way he looked at her son, as if he couldn't bear the sight of him, and had no intention of letting Preston say or do anything unkind to Max while she slept.

"Are we almost there?" Max asked.

Knowing this question would probably annoy Preston more than any other, because Max asked it so often, Emma tried to summon the energy to answer. But Preston responded before she could, and with far more patience than she'd expected.

"We've got another thirty minutes or so."

"Thirty minutes? Is that long?"

"It's half an hour."

"Is half an hour long?"

Preston chuckled. "Not really."

"Can I have some ice cream when we get there?"

Emma made an effort to bring words to her lips. She'd given Max an insulin injection when they'd stopped, but his glucose level had reached 450 mg/dL, which was very high. She didn't want him to have any more treats until she could get his blood sugar under control. "Don't let him have another cookie, okay?" she mumbled.

Unless she was mistaken, Preston's voice sounded almost gentle. "You're supposed to be sleeping, remember?"

"He's had enough sweets."

"I won't give him anything. We're about to have dinner."

She thought she said okay, but wasn't sure. Exhaustion made her limbs heavy, her tongue unwieldy.

"My dad's gonna be mad if we don't go home soon," Max announced.

The hot sun, glaring through her window, made Emma feel warm and lazy—as though she were lying at the side of their pool. Despite that, she realized her son was attempting to enforce his will by appealing to the power his father had always held in his life, and felt guilty for dragging him so far from home. They'd had to leave Max's aquarium behind, his comfortable bedroom, his toys. Now they were struggling to deal with his health issues on the road. And they had almost nothing.

Except the chance at a new life, she reminded herself. She conjured up the little yellow house she'd imagined so often, and smiled inside. Soon they'd be safe *and* free.

"Does your dad ever play ball with you?" Preston asked conversationally.

"No."

Emma let herself relax a little more. Maybe Preston wasn't

so bad. He was even trying to entertain her son. But his question almost made Emma laugh. Manuel wanted Max to excel at baseball, yet he couldn't be bothered to stand out in the yard and play catch. He hired a private coach to work with him twice a week. Emma threw to him every other day.

"What's your father like?"

The answers streamed through Emma's mind like ticker tape: *Controlling, obsessive, fanatical...*

"He's tall," Max said.

"Did you live with him?"

Unfortunately...

"I still do."

Not anymore, Max. Never again....

"So does he know you're gone?"

"Um..." Max seemed a little puzzled. "He's at work right now," he answered at last.

"What does he do when he's at work?"

Wouldn't we all like to know....

"He wears a suit."

"A suit, huh? Do you see him very often?"

"When he comes home."

"Do you like it when he's home?"

"Yeah. Sometimes he brings me a fish for my big tank."

The fish Manuel brought home for Max's aquarium seemed to swim through Emma's thoughts. Shimmering. Colorful. Resplendent. And occasionally ferocious enough to eat the other fish in the tank....

"Then he takes my mom into the bedroom," Max added out of nowhere.

Emma imagined Preston's surprise that this comment would come from a five-year-old. She didn't like her son volunteering such intimate information any more than she liked the way Max must feel about those occurrences; they'd obviously made an impact. But she felt strangely disconnected from the conversation. She was drifting in and out, baking in the hot sun. Sometimes she was beside the pool. Sometimes she was cooking in the house. Sometimes she was riding in the Hummer with Manuel at the wheel....

"What do you do while they're in the bedroom?" Preston asked.

"I watch my new fish," Max said.

Emma's sluggish mind slowly presented a picture of her son standing in front of his aquarium while his father dragged her into the bedroom and locked the door. It never concerned Manuel, even when he hadn't seen Max for a couple of weeks, and the boy was starved for his attention. Nor did Manuel care about the fact that Emma felt awkward and self-conscious with their child only a few feet from the door when he insisted on having sex with her. More often than not, Manuel went so far as to fasten her hands to the headboard. He liked bondage, but he rarely tied her feet. He wanted her to struggle. He relished having the power to subdue her while she tried to resist. Of course, if Max was awake in the other room, she had to do it silently, which Manuel enjoyed even more.

The heat became overwhelming. Too hot. Miserable. She wanted to find some relief. But there was no escape. Just as she feared there was no escape from the man she'd already lived with for five years. He'd never give up. He'd find her—

A hand touched her shoulder. She instantly recoiled.

"Emma?"

It was Preston. Breathing hard, she stared at him until the fact that he wasn't Manuel could sink in.

"You seemed...agitated," he said.

"The sun, it's...hot on this side."

He opened her air vent, which had apparently been closed, all the while watching her. "Are you sure you're okay?"

Letting her eyes drift shut again, she nodded while waiting for her galloping pulse to slow. She still longed to slip into a peaceful sleep. But she knew she'd never relax now. Her dreams had made Manuel feel too close. She imagined him speeding down the highway, quickly closing the distance between them.

When Preston spoke a few minutes later, he lowered his voice as though he thought she was asleep, but Emma heard every word.

"Is that where the accidents happen, Max?" he asked. "In the bedroom?"

"What accidents?"

"Were you there when your mother burned her hand?"

"She burned her hand?"

Emma hadn't mentioned the injury to Max. There seemed little point in making up a story to cover something he hadn't noticed.

"You didn't know?" Preston said.

"Maybe I was at the library with Juanita."

Not the library. The park. Emma remembered well, because she'd been so grateful that her son was gone during her last big argument with Manuel.

"Who's Juanita?" Preston asked.

"My nanny."

"You have a nanny?"

"Yeah. She's from Mexico," he said proudly.

"Does she speak English?"

"No. She speaks Spanish like me and my dad." Max had used the same kind of superior tone Manuel often adopted when speaking of his heritage, but if Preston was aware of the change, he didn't react to it.

"I see. What about your mommy? Does she know Spanish, too?"

Max hesitated. Until the morning they'd left San Diego, and Juanita had shown up late, Emma had been careful around him. She wasn't sure her son knew the extent to which she could both speak and understand Manuel's native tongue, but finally Max said, "Sometimes."

When I need to, Emma thought smugly. Manuel had tried to alienate her from his people, but it was his people who had made her escape possible. His people and the enigmatic man beside her, whose rare but gorgeous smile she already knew she'd never forget.

"WE HAVE A PROBLEM," Preston said.

Emma's nerves grew taut as she searched his face. They were only fifteen minutes from Ely and dinner. So close. But her escape had been ill-fated from the start. First Manuel hadn't flown to Mexico as planned. Then she was pulled over by the CHP. Then she found that cop circling her car this morning and had to beg a ride from a complete stranger.

Instinctively, she craned her neck to look through the back window, expecting to see Manuel bearing down on them. He'd told her she couldn't escape him. He'd promised that if she ever tried, he'd come after her, no matter how far he had to go, no matter how long it took. And she believed him. But except for the slower-moving RV Preston had passed only a few moments earlier, they were alone on the road.

"What kind of problem?" she asked, trying to stem her sudden deluge of fear.

"The engine's overheating."

The engine had been running a little hot while she was driving, too, but she'd thought that was more or less normal.

They were traveling through the desert, after all, relying heavily on air-conditioning, which tended to tax the system. She'd assumed the van would be okay, especially since Preston hadn't seemed concerned when she'd mentioned it earlier.

Evidently, that had changed. "How bad is it?" she asked.

He frowned as he applied the brake. "The gauge is showing red. We have to pull over."

The tires crunched as they parked on the gravel shoulder.

"We're getting out?" Max said eagerly.

"For a few minutes," Emma told him, and glanced at her watch. It was after six. Considering the amount of insulin she'd given him at their last stop, he'd be going low if she didn't feed him soon. And they'd already eaten most of their snacks. "You don't happen to be a mechanic, do you?"

"I know stocks and bonds," Preston said. "Not cars."

Stocks and bonds. Somehow that seemed too yuppyish for Preston Holman, but Emma's worry about their situation curtailed her surprise. "What do you think could be causing the problem?"

He bent over to pull the lever that would release the hood. "I'm guessing it's the water pump."

"That's not good. If it's the water pump, the van will only overheat again once we get back on the road."

"Exactly." He looked behind his seat and located a gallon of water. "At this point, I'm just hoping we can make it to Ely."

"Then what?"

He brought the water into the front and opened his door. "I'll have to get it fixed."

Emma frowned. "But if Ely's anything like the towns we've passed, they might not have a garage."

"Ely's got nearly five thousand people. There'll be a garage." He sounded tense, impatient.

"It's after six o'clock," she said. "The repair place, if there is one, will probably be closed."

"Then we'll have to get a motel."

Damn. A motel meant they wouldn't be continuing on tonight, and she didn't feel she'd gone nearly far enough from where she'd almost been picked up for grand larceny. Not to mention California and Manuel....

"You'll take us with you when you go on, won't you?" Emma hated to press her luck. She knew Preston wasn't any happier about the delay than she was. For whatever reason, he was in a big hurry to reach Iowa. But she had to ask.

He stepped out, not answering.

"Preston?"

It was the first time she'd used his given name, and she knew he'd noticed when he replied, "What was that, *Emma?*"

"You heard me," she said, refusing to pander to his dark mood.

His eyebrows gathered as he glanced at Max, who was already clambering out the other side. "I don't know. Maybe I'll take you as far as Wendover and put you on a bus."

Sighing, Emma watched him go around front and open the hood. When he bothered to be nice, it was almost impossible not to like him. But Preston wasn't nice very often.

He's really been through the wringer....

Whatever happened to Preston Holman had definitely left a mark.

WHEN THEY LIMPED into Ely more than an hour later, Preston's nerves were shot. They'd had to stop every few minutes to let the engine cool, which turned what should've been a short drive into something interminable. They were hot, irritable and hungry. Because he'd had to get under the hood so many times and didn't want Emma or Max to see the gun he'd hidden there, he'd tucked it into the waistband of his jeans, where it was digging into him. And Max's pleading to stop, to eat, to unfasten his seat belt or go home had become a litany. Preston couldn't wait to be rid of his passengers. Fair or not—maybe because they were to blame for the other unsettling emotions he'd experienced today—he held them responsible for this recent trouble. He shouldn't have let Emma and Max ride with him. He'd known they'd be a problem.

"There's a garage," Emma said, pointing helpfully as he stopped at one of the few traffic signals in town.

A blue corrugated metal building on the left boasted a red-lettered sign that read Mel's Auto Repair. But the garage doors were down and the office looked empty.

"They're closed." Which wasn't any wonder at nearly seven-thirty at night.

"Looks like it," she said.

Swallowing a sigh, Preston headed back to the motel they'd just passed. He'd get a room, some dinner and some sleep, in that order. Then he'd deliver the van to the shop early in the morning and see about getting the hell out of this place. And Emma and Max...

He didn't know what they'd do. If they were still around when the van was ready, he supposed he'd take them to Wendover as promised or maybe even Salt Lake. But he certainly wouldn't be upset if they decided to find another ride in the meantime.

"I'm staying here," he said as he gestured at the Starlight Motel and mini-casino. "Where do you want me to drop you and Max?"

Catching his not-so-subtle hint that they go elsewhere, she blinked at him as though momentarily lost, then lifted her chin. "Um…there was a smaller motel down the street. Maybe that'll work."

"That's a dive," he said. "Why not let me take you to the Hotel Nevada?"

She bit her bottom lip. "No, I think the other place will be less expensive."

"It'll probably be a difference of, what? Ten bucks?"

"The smaller motel will be fine."

Preston bit back a curse. Was she that worried about *ten* bucks? He thought of the burn on her hand, and her words, *I'll do absolutely anything to make sure we never go back,* and hated himself for dumping them. She was on the run with a kid and no car; she was desperate.

But he wasn't the man to help her. He had only one purpose left in life, to seek and destroy, not play the part of the Good Samaritan. Besides, Emma didn't need him, not really. A woman who looked as fine as she did could probably take her pick of Good Samaritans—good *male* Samaritans, anyway.

Fleetingly, he realized she could hook up with someone more dangerous than the man she was running from, but he refused to acknowledge it.

"Whatever you say." He wheeled the van around, but when they reached the small, dingy front office of the Feel Good Motel, Preston couldn't bear to let Emma get out without giving her some money. At least she and Max would get a good dinner tonight. That was something, wasn't it?

The fifty landed in her lap before she could climb out. She stared down at it, then closed her eyes and shook her head in obvious disgust. "I don't want your money," she said, throwing it back at him. "I was asking for a ride to somewhere you're going anyway. But I can see now that we're too much of an inconvenience. You can't be bothered with a woman. Especially a woman who has a *child*, God forbid."

Preston clenched his jaw as her words hit him where he was most vulnerable. "I didn't say I wouldn't take you to Salt Lake. I just thought—"

"I know what you thought. You've made it crystal clear that you don't want us around," she said, and got out. "Come on, Max. We're done riding in this car."

"Take the damn money and at least get a decent room," Preston said.

"Damn," Max repeated. "Can I say shit *and* damn when I get big?"

"No," she snapped. "And you can't do anything else like Mr. Holman, either. If I have my way, your heart will never be three sizes too small. Say goodbye to Mr. Scrooge."

"Mr. Scrooge?" Max echoed.

Preston didn't hear Emma's response because she'd already slammed the door. He watched her grab her son's hand and stomp into the office. She didn't even have any luggage. She carried only a backpack and a purse, a purse with apparently little money.

Dropping his head into his hands, Preston massaged his temples. She'd alluded to *The Grinch,* not *A Christmas Carol.* She had her Christmas stories screwed up, after all. But it didn't matter. His heart *was* three sizes too small.

He hesitated a moment longer but, ultimately, the gun pressing into his back reminded him that she'd be better off making other plans, plans that didn't include him.

CHAPTER SIX

MAX GIGGLED at a Tom and Jerry cartoon while Emma lay down across from him on one of the beds in their moldy-smelling motel room. They'd already walked to Elmer's Drive-In next door, where she'd bought her son a hamburger and fries and given him what she hoped would be his final injection for the day. Happy to be out of the car, he was momentarily entertained, which came as a much-needed relief to Emma.

But she was getting hungry. In order to save money, she'd nibbled on a few of Max's fries instead of buying herself dinner. Preston had scoffed at a mere ten bucks, but to Emma, every dollar counted. She had only twenty-five hundred to her name. If she and Max didn't want to be out on the street when they reached the midwest, they'd need first and last month's rent and deposit, and enough money to support them until she could find a job.

Twenty-five hundred wasn't much to begin a new life with, especially a life filled with so many unknowns. She'd never used her degree. Would she be able to find work as a teacher? If not, would there be something else? Would they even be able to make it to Iowa? And without a car, how would they get around after they settled down?

She knew Preston had been her best bet for immediate

transportation, but she didn't regret what she'd said to him. She couldn't ride with him anymore. The stress of trying to keep Max quiet for miles on end was making her crazy. And she couldn't tolerate feeling like such a burden. She'd tried to be nice. She'd helped Preston drive and offered him money for gas. He'd refused, but she couldn't spare him any kind feelings for that. Nothing seemed to make a difference. He just didn't want them around. Period.

So what was she going to do?

No brilliant ideas came to mind. Emma knew she and Max could languish in Ely for days, even weeks, if she couldn't find someone else to give them a ride. They couldn't take a bus, even if Ely had service. Manuel—and maybe the authorities, if they bothered to search for car thieves anymore— would be keeping too close an eye on such an obvious alternative.

She'd figure something out, she told herself. Later. First, she'd get some sleep so she wouldn't have to feel the hunger pangs. In the morning, she'd think of an answer.

Please, God, let there be an answer.

"Mommy, can we go swimming?"

Emma realized her eyes had drifted shut and forced them open. What had she been thinking? She couldn't go to sleep right now. After napping so long in the van, Max wouldn't be tired for a while yet. She needed to bathe him and test his blood one last time. Then she had to set the motel's alarm clock to get her up at three and test him again.

She rolled onto her side, dragging one of the pillows with her. "This motel doesn't have a pool, sweetheart."

"But I'm hot."

So was she. The Feel Good Motel didn't have any air-conditioning, either—at least of the effective variety. A window unit rattled and hummed and managed to stir the air, but certainly wasn't pumping out anything cool. "It'll get better after dark. We'll open the windows."

"Can't we find a swimming pool?"

"I don't know where to look."

"Mr. Holman has one at his motel."

Leave it to Max to notice. Emma had been too preoccupied with Preston himself. "Are you sure?"

"Yeah, I saw it. We could go over there."

"No, honey. Mommy's tired."

"Please? Just for a little while?"

Emma thought of their suitcases sitting in the trunk of the Taurus, which had, no doubt, been impounded by the police. "We don't have our swimsuits."

"Yes, we do." Max hopped up and dashed over to the backpack where she stored his diabetes supplies. The moment he touched it, Emma remembered stuffing their swimwear in a side pocket the night before they left. Exercise made a real difference with Max's diabetes, and compared to a bat and ball, swimsuits took up no room at all.

Pulling out her black bikini, along with his red, white and blue swimming trunks, he grinned broadly as he waved them at her. "See?"

"The pool is for patrons," she said.

"What's a patron?"

"Someone who's paid to stay at that particular motel."

"Mr. Holman is paying for a room there. Can't we ask him if he'll let us swim in his pool?"

No! After the way they'd parted, Emma refused to ask Mr. Holman for anything. But how could it hurt to sneak in and take a quick dip? If they got caught, the Starlight Motel wouldn't do anything worse than kick them out. And the exercise would be good for Max. She could probably use some herself.

"Okay," she said. "As soon as I call Juanita's sister, we'll go over there and see if we can get in."

"Can Juanita come, too?"

"She's too far away."

"Why are you calling her sister?"

"Just to check in, see how Juanita's doing." And to get a message to her. Emma wanted to find out where Manuel was right now, so she'd know if she and Max were safe for the moment. She also had to figure out the significance of that document Juanita had placed in the glove box of the Taurus.

Sitting up, she dragged the phone closer, dug Juanita's slip of paper out of her purse and dialed Rosa's number. She'd paid for the room with cash, but the motel manager had insisted she leave a credit card on file for incidentals, which meant telephone calls. In this motel, there wouldn't be a minibar or workout room or any other amenities. Fortunately, she'd been able to use one of the prepaid cards Carlos had bought for her. A phone call to California wouldn't cost much—and Manuel couldn't trace the charge because this card was in her new name.

"*Hola?*" A high, thin voice answered on the first ring.

"Rosa."

"*Sí.* Who is this?" came the hesitant response.

"I— I'm sorry to bother you. Juanita gave me this number and said I could call. My name is Emma."

"Vanessa?"

Apparently Juanita had confided in her sister, or Rosa wouldn't have connected her new name to her old one. "Yes."

The other woman drew a shuddering breath and Emma realized she was sobbing. "She went to bed last night, as usual, but when I called her early this morning, she was gone. She didn't go to work today. No one can tell me where she is. We've called the police, everyone. They say she probably went back to Mexico to visit Nanna. But she wouldn't go without telling me. I've been to her house. She didn't even pack a bag."

Chills slipped down Emma's spine like icy fingers. "Where's Carlos?"

"Is he the gardener Juanita told me about?"

"Yes."

"I don't know. I haven't been able to reach him, either." Rosa released another tortured sob. "Something terrible has happened. I know it."

Panic seemed to be crushing Emma's chest. "Have you heard from Manuel?"

"That *loco* son of a bitch is the first person I called," she said vehemently, forgetting her tears in a rush of anger. "He isn't home. He's already out looking for you."

Emma had expected as much. But she hadn't expected anything to happen to Juanita. Juanita had helped her, and now she was gone? Maybe Carlos, too?

What did it mean? Emma was afraid to even imagine, but she knew deep in her bones that Juanita hadn't left on her own. Could Manuel really be *that* obsessed, *that* dangerous? If so, he was even worse than she'd guessed.

"Have you tried Manuel's cell phone?"

The quaver in her voice drew Max's attention. "What's wrong, Mommy?"

She was too distraught to respond.

"He doesn't answer," Rosa said.

"What about the office?"

"One of his brothers, José, was there. He said maybe Carlos was picked up by Border Patrol."

Emma cringed as she pictured Carlos's kind eyes and sincere smile. He'd been so proud to be working in America, earning money to send to his family. He'd wanted to save up enough to build a house back in Mexico. And now he'd lost his paycheck.

Loathing nearly dripped from Emma's pores. "*Maybe?* If I know Manuel, he called them."

"José said Juanita was probably picked up, too. But she has her green card. They can't take her back."

"What does José have to say about Max and me? Anything?"

"He told me they think you've been abducted."

Of course. Manuel could never admit that she might leave on her own. Saving face, even to his relatives, *especially* to his relatives, was too important to a man like him.

Emma struggled to combat the rage that left her shaking. "Did José seem nervous, upset?"

"No. He said they'd have you back within a day."

Another tremor passed through Emma as she tried to keep the phone pressed to her ear. They knew something, knew where she was or where she was going…something.

Suddenly it felt as though he was like a hawk gliding high overhead. Any move she made would bring him swooping down on her.

"I got the impression he's hired help. A lot of it," Rosa added, sniffling.

The walls of the tiny motel room seemed to be closing in on Emma. She felt so helpless. She wanted to rush out and start hitchhiking, simply disappear. But from what she could tell, Ely didn't have many hitchhikers. Standing thumb out at the side of the road would only make her more conspicuous, especially with a child in tow.

"What do you think I should do about Juanita?" Rosa asked.

"Call the police again," Emma told her. "Right away."

"What good will that do? They won't even file a missing person's report until—"

"Tell them you believe Manuel's responsible for what happened."

"Do you think he killed her?" Rosa asked, her voice hoarse with fear.

Emma couldn't accept the possibility that the man she'd lived with could be capable of something that heinous. She remembered sitting outside on the lawn, talking to him for half the night when they first met. He'd been so charismatic, such a charmer. But he'd changed....

Please, God, protect my sweet friend. Don't let her be hurt.

"No. No, of course not. I'll call you in the morning to see if you've heard anything," she said, and hung up.

WHEN PRESTON HEARD Max's childish voice, he lifted his head from the rim of the Jacuzzi and blinked in surprise. Darkness prevailed in his corner of the pool area, but the floodlight attached to the building confirmed that he wasn't merely hearing an echo of the two people he couldn't seem to forget. The boy rushing toward the water was definitely Max, and the slender woman with him, setting two towels on a chaise, was Emma.

"Mom, watch me dive in," Max hollered. "Watch me, okay? Are you watching?"

"Shh..." she replied. "I'm watching."

"Here I go."

She stood at the edge of the pool while he made a big splash, then glanced around as though she feared someone might notice him. Her gaze touched on the people talking just outside the office, the car turning into the driveway, a man carrying something to his car. She even focused briefly on Preston in the Jacuzzi, but he could tell she didn't recognize him. Two other men relaxed across from him, so he wasn't alone. And he was sitting so low in the water he knew she'd be lucky to see all of his face, especially amid the steam and the shadows.

"Come on, Mom. Get in," Max said.

Emma removed the T-shirt she'd worn over her swimming suit and walked to the far end of the pool, where she stood on the steps.

"Aren't you going to swim with me?"

"Maybe in a minute."

She didn't seem nearly as enthusiastic about this outing as he did. She seemed nervous, distracted. Preston wondered if she could be that worked up about the possibility of being caught in the wrong pool, or if the tension she'd felt all day was simply getting to her.

The guilt that had plagued him earlier for dumping her and Max threatened to reassert itself. But the man across from him drew his attention before he could beat himself up too badly.

"Would you get a load of that?" the man said with a low, soft whistle.

His friend turned to see what "that" was and spotted Emma in her black bikini. "She's got one heck of a body, doesn't she?" he said, and began to elaborate on the attributes he particularly admired, beginning with her "gorgeous tits."

Preston hadn't ogled a woman since he was a randy teenager. The conversation sounded almost foreign to him. Inconsequential. He'd been too busy with more important things, things that had changed or could change his life. Dallas. Vince. The truth. Occasionally, he had dreams about making love to Christy, but his physical appetites always took a back seat to the goal that consumed him from the moment he woke up.

Now that he allowed himself to think about sex, however, Preston realized he missed Christy's warm body in his bed, her welcoming embrace. If he'd been less bitter, he knew he would have missed her more, maybe even a lot. Until Dallas died, their marriage had been a good one, full of comfortable companionship and peace.

But all good things come to an end....

Whoever said that was a freakin' genius, he decided.

Shifting in the hot water, he leaned a little to the left to get a better view of Emma. The men across from him, truckers judging by their conversation, had already moved on to other topics. An encounter with a porn star. Long legs. High heels. A hooker in Memphis. The women they talked about seemed interchangeable. But women weren't interchangeable to Preston. They never had been. Maybe that was why he'd scarcely thought of sex since he'd split with Christy.

He closed his eyes and laid his head back, but Emma in that black bikini made it impossible to relax. Evidently his libido was making a comeback.

Opening his eyes, he studied her legs, the perfect breasts his companions had already noted, her smooth golden skin— and felt his body react almost instantly.

You have a sort of stark beauty.... Your face, your body. He'd felt a definite sexual undercurrent during that exchange, but he'd also known he'd never take advantage of a woman with a kid. So he'd told himself she hadn't meant anything by the compliment and immediately squashed his reaction.

But things were different now. They'd parted ways and,

after tonight, would probably never see each other again. Which meant he was safe to let his imagination wander where it would. Considering his arousal, he couldn't get out of the Jacuzzi right now anyway.

Hooking his arms over the sides, he hauled himself up a few inches so he could see her move deeper into the pool. She gathered Max into her arms, brushed his wet hair off his forehead and kissed him. Then she gave him a ride on her back.

The domesticity of the scene made Preston uncomfortable about the fact that, in his mind, he'd just pulled off her swimsuit. But not uncomfortable enough to stop the fantasy now that it was getting exciting. It seemed like an absolute eternity since he'd felt a woman beneath him.

He imagined Emma inviting him to her room. Conveniently, Max wasn't anywhere around, which was the beauty of dreams. People could appear and disappear at will. And they could react in ways that were exactly opposite to what they'd do in reality.

He pictured her offering him a teasing smile as she slowly untied her swimsuit top and dropped it on the ground. She closed her eyes and let her head fall back when he stepped over to her—touched her. Suddenly Preston felt no guilt at all for leaving Emma and her son at the shabby motel down the street. Considering how badly he wanted her legs around him, she and Max were much better off without him.

THE OUTSIDE AIR and the water in the pool were warm, but Emma still felt chilled inside—too chilled to enjoy swimming. She tried to entertain Max, to act somewhat normal, for his sake. He'd already been through so much in the past two days. But she was too wound up, she could barely move or even speak.

Juanita's gone. Do you think Manuel's killed her?

Emma wished she could say no to that question with *real* confidence instead of the thin veneer she'd put on for Juanita's sister's sake. But the glint of excitement in Manuel's eyes the night of their last argument, when he'd grabbed her hand and purposely burned her, was truly frightening. His expression in that moment, his lack of remorse later, had left an indelible impression. Although he hadn't been physically abusive in the early years, the power his money afforded him seemed to be turning him into some kind of monster, a monster that fed on power and control.

And the more control Manuel achieved, the more he wanted. But was he capable of *murder?* The man she'd once loved? The father of her child?

She remembered the way he used to be when they first met, when he was apart from his family and they were on their own. He'd been sexy, confident, outgoing—a natural leader. Everyone had liked him, especially women. He still had those traits, but they were exaggerated now, stretched so far out of proportion they made him into someone dark and twisted, someone too warped to function normally. He acted as if he were above the law, as if he reigned supreme....

He said they'd have you back within a day.

"Mommy, watch me!"

She nodded absently at Max, still struggling to put her thoughts in order. Even if Manuel knew she was in Nevada, he wouldn't be able to find her.

Or would he? There were only two main highways, and she hadn't moved far enough, fast enough.

"Mo-om, are you looking?"

Emma forced herself to turn and focus, and that was when she noticed the men sitting in the Jacuzzi in the far corner.

She'd made a mental note of them before, of course, when she'd first arrived. She was too afraid that she'd run into someone working for Manuel not to pay attention to the people around her. But something had changed.

The two who'd been talking were still talking. Their voices came to her as a low murmur. Nothing different there. It was the other man. He watched her a little too closely. She could feel his acute interest like the sun scorching her skin on a hot beach.

Throwing back her shoulders, she challenged his gaze—and finally recognized the eyes staring back at her. They belonged to Preston Holman.

Max's hand swept against her as he swam by, and she pulled him to the surface.

"Hey, why'd you stop me? I was going to touch the side of the pool without taking a breath, like Daddy does."

"We're going back to our motel now," she said.

"I don't want to! We just got here."

"It's late, time for bed."

"Already?"

"We have to get up early." She had no idea what might happen tomorrow, but she knew she'd better think of some way to get them out of Ely as soon as possible, even if she had to spend the rest of her money on a car.

She glanced over at Preston once again. Now that she'd caught him staring at her, she expected him to scowl and turn away. But he didn't. He flung the wet hair out of his eyes as his lips curved in a sexy grin.

How many women had felt their hearts pound at the sight of that devastating smile? she wondered. And why was he suddenly flashing it at her? He couldn't be making any overtures of friendship. He'd already let her know, in a million ways, that he wasn't interested in anything to do with her.

Climbing out of the water, she gathered her son and grabbed her towel. Then she threw Preston a look that said "Good riddance," and left.

But just as she and Max were about to cross the street to the Feel Good Motel, Emma spotted a tall man with long straggling hair going into the office. She knew immediately that it wasn't Manuel. But something about him seemed familiar.

CHAPTER SEVEN

WHERE HAD SHE SEEN him before? Emma couldn't remember. He was tall, probably six-four, but thin, almost gaunt. As he spoke to the motel manager, he raised a hand to his waist as if to say "The boy's about so tall." At least her imagination insisted on that interpretation. But he was wearing a bandanna around his head and a leather vest, and he looked dirty, rough, which wasn't Manuel's style at all. Manuel was slick and sophisticated, wily and articulate.

"Why did we stop?" Max asked.

Emma didn't know how to explain the hair standing up on the back of her neck or the strange sense of familiarity that had washed over her.

"Mom?" Finally Max sounded tired.

"We're waiting for traffic to clear," she said. But the street had been wide-open for the past three or four minutes, and she couldn't bring herself to cross it, to move any closer to that man.

Max tugged on her arm. "Come on."

Who was he? Had he been to the house before? Occasionally men stopped by to speak briefly to Manuel in his office. This could definitely be one of them. Or maybe she was imagining the danger, jumping at shadows, like she had with that red Toyota on Highway 5.

That had to be it, she decided and, taking Max's hand, she

stepped off the curb. This guy was only renting a room. Any minute, he'd sign a charge slip and stride out of the office with a key in his hand.

But the manager's wife ushered him outside right away before he could sign anything. So Emma hopped back onto the sidewalk and drew Max into the shadow of the overhang on the gift shop.

The manager's wife led the man across the parking lot. They paused every so often to speak, but it wasn't difficult to see where they were heading. When they stopped in front of Room 21 and knocked, Emma knew her worst fears had come true. Room 21 was *her* room. Manuel, or rather someone connected to him, had found her.

"Mommy, can I have my eight-thirty snack?"

"In a minute." A lot could happen in a minute. In *this* minute. She and Max couldn't keep standing where they were, staring in shock and terror.

It looked as though the manager's wife was taking out a master key.

Emma searched her mind for what they'd see as soon as they opened the door, and barely managed to stifle a whimper. Max's biohazard container was sitting on top of the TV. The moment the tall man saw it, he'd know for sure that he'd found her. How many other women in Ely, who'd just rented a room, had a young diabetic son?

A horrible realization brought Emma's hand up to her mouth. Max's diabetes supplies! The backpack she'd packed so carefully before leaving San Diego was in the room, along with the biohazard dispenser.

"Can I have some ice cream?" Max asked.

Emma shook her head vaguely, distracted. Max needed the things in that backpack to survive. What was she going to do?

She had to get Max's meds.

She couldn't return to the room.

She had to think. *Think, think, think!*

Slowly, her brain started functioning again. Max's tester kit was in her purse. She carried it everywhere. Provided she had enough needles, test strips and insulin in that small black pouch to get him through the night, she could buy more supplies in the morning, when the local pharmacy opened.

After rummaging in her purse, she came up with his kit and confirmed that she had a bottle of test strips, all three types of insulin and a needle. Then she told herself to breathe. She had a plan. With any luck, she could replenish what they'd lost.

But it was a risk she didn't like taking. Buying the other products again would cost more than two hundred dollars. And it wasn't only Max's diabetes supplies they'd lost. They'd walked to the pool with only T-shirts over their swimsuits. They didn't even have pants....

Clarity suddenly cut through her panic. Money didn't matter. Clothes didn't matter. Nothing mattered except Max. And *he* was what she stood to lose if she didn't pull herself together and start moving.

Whirling, she hurried her son back toward the Starlight Motel.

"I thought we were going to bed," Max said, frowning in confusion.

"Maybe later," Emma murmured.

"Are we swimming again?"

"No." Emma pictured the small police station they'd passed when they came into town and wished she could go there for help. She'd almost called the cops a million different times. But she had only one burn mark to prove Manuel could be cruel. The emotional scars didn't show. He looked and acted the part of the consummate businessman, the perfect father, the considerate neighbor. And he was such a convincing liar. He'd blame everything on her, make her appear so emotionally unstable that the police wouldn't do anything.

She could already hear what they'd tell her: *I'm sorry, ma'am. We can't very well arrest him before he does something wrong, can we?* And she could also imagine her own helpless response: *But afterward it'll be too late.*

She couldn't count on the police. She could count only on herself. She had to be strong for Max.

Max was jogging to keep up with her. "Where are we going?"

Emma slowed as they reached the pool area. "Here."

"Why?"

Because she couldn't rent another room, not in such a small town. Once Manuel and the men working for him realized she wasn't coming back to the Feel Good Motel, as they probably expected, he'd keep hunting for her. He'd ask every motel manager in Ely if a woman with a boy about five years old had checked in. Simply renting another room wouldn't buy enough time; she needed somewhere to hide for the night.

"I want to watch TV," Max said.

"Good."

"What are we doing?"

"Looking for Mr. Holman."

"Why?"

"To see if he'd like to have a slumber party."

"With us?" The prospect of a party left Max excited and not tired at all, but the fact that her son might be up for a while longer was the least of Emma's worries.

She located Preston still sitting in the Jacuzzi, his head barely visible above the steam coming off the hot water. *Thank God he hasn't left.* But the sight of him didn't raise her hopes by much. She had to figure out how to convince him to help her. She'd already offered him money, friendship, assistance. He didn't want any of it. To make matters worse, ten minutes earlier she'd given him a look synonymous with flipping him the finger.

She searched frantically for possibilities, none of which would work. Then she remembered the quality of the smile Preston had worn when she'd caught him watching her in the pool, and felt a sinking sensation in the pit of her stomach. She did have one thing to trade. She'd never dreamed she'd ever consider what was going through her mind right now, but as she gazed down at her son, she knew she'd do anything. Squeezing Max's hand, she only prayed it would be enough to provide what they so desperately needed.

"Mommy, a slumber party *with us?*" Max repeated, insisting on an answer.

Pasting a smile on her face, she nodded. Fortunately, her son would be fast asleep when the real party began.

"MR. HOLMAN!" a young voice cried.

Preston turned to see Emma and her son standing at the fence a few feet away.

"C-can I talk to you for a moment?" Emma asked when she caught his eye.

One of the other men in the Jacuzzi murmured to his friend, "You can talk to me, sweet thing," and they chuckled together. But Preston didn't view Max and Emma's return as a good thing. Whether she looked like a pinup model in that bikini or not, he was glad to be rid of her. He didn't want to worry about hiding his gun, didn't want the extra trouble. He'd fought too long and too hard to find Vincent Wendell, made too many promises to Dallas, to allow himself to be distracted, even momentarily.

But he couldn't leave her standing at the fence.

Smothering a curse, he got out of the hot water and stalked over. "Is something wrong?"

"Do you want to have a slumber party with us?" Max asked before Emma could reply.

Preston knew his expression had to reveal his opinion on that subject, but Max didn't seem to notice.

"Say yes," Max said. "I've never been to a slumber party."

Preston looked at Emma. "Is this some kind of joke?"

She motioned him closer. As her cool hand touched his overheated arm, he wasn't sure if she shivered or he did, but he could tell the kiss-my-ass attitude she'd adopted when she left the pool was long gone.

"We—we can't go back to our room," she whispered in his ear.

Preston scowled at Max, who was trying to wiggle between his mother and the fence.

"What did you say, Mommy?"

Emma met Preston's eyes and didn't answer her son.

"Why not?" Preston asked.

"Manuel's there. He's found us."

This could have been a last-ditch effort to hitch a ride, but Emma was trembling too badly for him to believe she was lying. "Max's father?"

She nodded.

He scrubbed a hand over his face. How in the world had he been unlucky enough to bump into these two? They were like bad pennies.

"Go to the police," he said at last. "There's nothing I can do for you."

He started to step away, but she reached through the fence in time to catch his arm. "I—I'm not asking for a favor. I'm offering a trade. I thought maybe…"

Her words faltered.

"What?"

She tugged to get him to move closer, and he reluctantly let her whisper in his ear again. "I saw you…looking at me a few minutes ago."

He could smell the scent of her shampoo. "Doesn't hurt to look," he said.

"You…" She cleared her throat and tried again. "You seemed to like what you saw," she said hopefully.

He tried not to picture her without the T-shirt she was wearing over her suit now. "What if I did?"

"I'd be willing to make you a deal."

"I'm not following this conversation."

He moved with her as she inched away from Max, and her voice dropped so low Preston could scarcely hear her. "I'll give you what you want, if you'll give me what I want."

The trembling he'd noticed earlier had reached her voice, which told him she wasn't merely repeating an offer to help out with gas. "Are you saying you'll have *sex* with me?" he asked in astonishment.

For all his surprise, he'd managed to keep his voice low, but Max hadn't allowed them any space. He pressed between Emma and the fence again, and she put her hands over her son's ears before she responded.

"If you have to spell it out, that's exactly what I'm saying."

Her stiff posture and the stoicism in her face told him she found the idea of sleeping with him about as appealing as facing a firing squad. And that pretty much took care of his fantasies. He couldn't imagine having any fun if she was only tolerating the experience. Besides, he could already tell that Emma wasn't the quick and easy type, and he wasn't about to become embroiled in an emotional mess.

He *was* curious to hear what she'd ask for in return, however. "In trade for what?"

She glanced around, obviously afraid someone might sneak up behind her. "You have to let me and Max stay with you tonight. And you have to take us to Salt Lake as soon as possible. As soon as the van's fixed. I *have* to get out of Nevada."

She was blinking fast, fighting tears. This was no joke. "Please?" she added desperately, as if she expected him to say no.

She'd just offered to sleep with him in exchange for a little human kindness. Scary thing was, she'd done it because she knew he'd probably refuse if she didn't.

God, when had he sunk so low?

With a sigh, he focused on Max's hopeful face.

"I'll be good," Max promised. "Say yes!"

What else could he do? His heart might be three sizes too small, but what was left of it wouldn't let him turn them away. Desperate as Emma was, he feared she might make the same offer to someone who'd take her up on it. Or fall into the hands of the man she feared enough to sacrifice her dignity.

Crossing to the table, Preston thanked heaven he'd hidden the gun in the back of the van and dug under his towel to find his key. Then he handed it to Emma. "Room three forty-one," he said. "I'll be up in a minute."

EMMA STARED at her reflection in the mirror of the motel room's locked bathroom. Wide, frightened eyes gazed back at her, eyes underscored with dark smudges of fatigue and worry. The rest of her face looked pale, almost translucent—and it wasn't any wonder. She'd offered to prostitute herself to the man on the other side of the door, a man she'd known for only two days.

Fleetingly, she thought of her mother and sister in Arizona, and cringed. They wouldn't believe her if she told them what she was about to do. No one would. She could scarcely believe it herself.

"How has my life come to this?" she whispered to her reflection. As a girl, she'd excelled in school and in track. When she went away to college, she'd remained at the top of her class. She'd kept up with her running. She'd volunteered to read aloud twice a week at the neighborhood elementary school. She'd had wonderful, lofty aspirations to make a difference in the lives of the little first-graders she planned to teach one day. Overall, she'd been an exemplary citizen. She hadn't even slept with anyone until Manuel.

Yet here she was, cowering in Preston Holman's bathroom, going through the motions of showering and drying her hair while summoning the nerve to keep the bargain she'd just made.

She hung up the blow dryer and closed her eyes so she wouldn't have to see herself any longer. Sometimes people had to do things they never dreamed they would. It was called real life, *survival,* she told herself. But she knew all the self-talk in the world wouldn't make it any easier. She glanced down at Max, sleeping peacefully on the blankets she'd arranged for him at her feet, beside the tub. Before Preston had returned, Emma had tested her son, fed him a granola bar to raise his blood sugar after swimming, and tucked him in his makeshift bed. She couldn't have him in the room while she kept her promise to Preston.

For the moment, Max was safe. Sheltered. Hidden from the tall dirty man she'd recognized at the Feel Good Motel. Closeted away from Manuel and the threat of abduction to Mexico.

When she looked at her son, no price seemed too high. And at least Preston Holman had an impressive body. His skin was smooth and golden, not apishly hairy. He was young and fit, close to her age. And he smelled good. She'd noticed that earlier, in the van.

Most women would be eager to sleep with a man like Preston Holman. But not her. When Manuel touched her, she felt only revulsion and could no longer imagine feeling anything else. She wanted to retain possession of her own body; she wanted complete independence.

Unfortunately, that probably wasn't going to happen until she reached the midwest and found a job and a home. Until then, she'd have to get by any way she could—and right now, she had no better option than to be where she was.

With a final, bolstering breath, she forced her eyes open. "I can do this," she murmured. "I can do it for Max." Preston had barely spoken to her all day. He'd probably use her quickly and be done with it. And she didn't have to worry about getting pregnant. She'd been on the pill since she'd had Max. She'd known early on not to have another child with Manuel.

The volume of the television dropped, and she quickly scooped the dry clothes Preston had given her off the lid of the toilet seat. Was he getting impatient? She had no idea what to expect. When she'd let him into the motel room thirty minutes ago, he'd asked if she needed to borrow some clothes. She'd said yes, and he'd lent her a T-shirt and a pair of boxers—all he had that might fit her.

After that simple exchange, he'd walked into the bathroom, closed the door while he showered, and returned wearing nothing but a pair of well-worn jeans. Then he'd plopped onto one of the beds and flipped on the television while she took her turn in the bathroom—which included settling Max. Fortunately her son was tired enough not to question his sleeping arrangements....

She was taking much longer than Preston had, which was no doubt becoming quite noticeable.

She held the T-shirt he'd given her to her nose. It was clean; she could smell the fabric softener. But she didn't even have a bra or a pair of panties to put on underneath.

"What are you doing?"

She froze at the sound of his voice. "I'm...um...just finishing up," she responded, but he spoke at almost the same time, and she realized he wasn't even talking to her. He was on the phone.

"Yeah, it's me. I'm fine. I'm always fine, right?"

Slightly embarrassed by her blunder, Emma pressed her ear to the door, curious to learn the reason behind his sarcasm.

"No, I didn't call for that. I've finally found Vince. Christy, did you hear me? I've *found* him."

Emma had no idea who Vince might be, but she could tell by the way Preston spoke that he expected this news to make an impact.

"Because I thought you should know, that's why.... What do you mean? God, have you forgotten Dallas completely?" Anger, accusation and some other emotion, something that sounded a lot like pain, rang through his words. "So we're divorced. Does that mean we can't talk about our son?... Forget it. You're right. I shouldn't have interrupted your comfortable new life with Bob."

So Preston had an ex. And that ex was apparently remarried.

"No, *you* stop. Our son's dead, Christy. Our bright, perfect six-year-old who—" His voice cracked. He couldn't seem to finish his sentence, but he recovered by starting off on a different tack, this time lashing out, obviously trying to hurt. "You might be able to pick up and carry on as if nothing happened, but I can't. At least not until I make it right.... What? Justice!"

He said something else but Emma couldn't quite catch what it was. He must've turned away from the bathroom.

"I was his father," he said when she could hear him again. "He was depending on me.... If it's not my place, then whose is it?... We've gone over this before. That doesn't mean I'll let Vince get away with what he's done.... Fine, call it whatever you want."

Emma winced as certain things became clear to her. Preston had had a son once, too—a son he'd lost.

His strange fascination with her when he saw her carrying Max into their room at Maude's Cozy Comfort Bungalows made sense now. So did everything else. No wonder he couldn't stand the sight of Max. No wonder he was bitter.

She pressed her palms to her eyes as she remembered telling him she'd never met anyone who hated children as much as he did. He'd looked at her as if she'd slapped him. But she hadn't known, could never have guessed, and the thought that she might soon be in a similar situation deepened her resolve. She didn't care if she had to sleep with Preston Holman. She wouldn't be robbed of her son. She'd do whatever she had to.

"I don't care what Bob thinks," he was saying. "What about Billy Duran? And Melanie Deets?" Preston was nearly shouting now. "How many heroes do you know, Christy? When was the last time you read a newspaper article about some doctor in town miraculously saving a child's life?"

What was he talking about?

"It's more than that."

There was a long pause. When Preston spoke again, he sounded deflated. "I have to do what I have to do.... Okay, wait... No, don't cry. Come on, Christy. Please? I'm sorry."

There was another remark Emma missed, then silence. He'd hung up.

Emma waited to see what would happen next, but nothing did. Preston didn't make a sound, and Max kept sleeping. The minutes began to stretch until she felt like a complete coward for hiding out in the bathroom. Preston was suffering, in a way she could imagine all too easily. Yet he'd agreed to help them.

She suspected that had less to do with her offer at the pool than she'd originally assumed. She wasn't even sure Preston remembered she was there. But a deal was a deal. She owed it to him to at least ask what he wanted from her in return.

If he said she had to climb into bed with him tonight, she'd divorce her mind from her body. She'd had plenty of practice doing that. Sleeping with him couldn't be any worse than lying beneath Manuel.

Resigned, she borrowed his toothbrush, then pulled on his clothes.

CHAPTER EIGHT

PRESTON SAT in the dark, next to the small round table in front of the room's only window, trying to block out the echo of his conversation with Christy. He'd been stupid to call her. He wouldn't have done it, except something about Emma made him miss what they'd had—that sense of family, the togetherness. Since Dallas's death, they couldn't speak without arguing. But after two months of silence, he'd called anyway—and he'd upset her. Again.

Fool. She'd been through enough. Regardless of what he'd said, he didn't really begrudge her the happiness she'd managed to find during the past six months with her new husband. He wasn't even sure what he'd hoped to accomplish by telling her about Vince. She'd already dealt with their son's death. He was the one who couldn't get past it.

Vaguely he wondered if the compulsion to call his ex-wife meant he was still in love with her. But it didn't take him long to figure out that everything he'd once felt for her was gone. The events beginning the day Dallas fell ill had swept all positive emotion away.

Twirling his closed pocketknife between his fingers, Preston remembered the panic and worry over Dallas's unexpected illness, the moment their son's weakened body had lost the fight, the friends and family who'd clogged the cemetery the day of his funeral, Christy weeping over his grave. And later, Christy defending Vince and refusing to believe what Preston knew in his gut to be true.

The images parading through his mind made his stomach churn, made him realize that the anger consuming him left no room for love as he used to know it. Maybe he'd always care deeply for Christy, but what he felt, more than anything, was a terrible regret—regret for the loss of their innocence, their marriage and the child they'd both adored.

Light spilled into the room as the bathroom door opened and Emma stepped out. He didn't want her as a witness to the emptiness that surrounded him, didn't want to feel responsible for anyone or anything except the task he'd set for himself. He'd planned to ignore her as much as possible, but he knew immediately that it wasn't going to be that easy. Not now. It was late, and they were alone in a hotel room. He'd let his imagination carry him too damn far in that Jacuzzi.

His eyes fell to the shapely bare legs that extended beneath the boxers he'd lent her, and he couldn't look away. It was two years now since he'd been with Christy. Suddenly those two years seemed like a lifetime.

Maybe a temporary distraction wouldn't be so bad. Maybe a distraction was exactly what he needed to give his mind and body the rest it craved.

Standing there, she hesitated.

"Are you tired?" he asked.

"A little."

He almost told her to go ahead and get some sleep. He knew she probably wasn't feeling the same rush of sexual excitement he was. But another part of his brain—a part run strictly by hormones, if he had his guess—cautioned him not to be too hasty. Maybe he was walking into an emotional

mess, but he was pretty much stuck with Emma and Max anyway, at least until Salt Lake. If he was honest with himself,
he'd have to admit he'd probably wind up taking them to
Iowa. So how could a little positive sensation make things any
worse? She was the one who'd made the offer.

"What are you thinking?" she asked.

"I'm trying to talk myself into letting you sleep."

Her gaze darted to the bed, then returned to his face. "Or…"

"I think you know my other option."

Her eyes widened slightly. She clasped her hands in front
of her, but she didn't step back or shake her head or indicate
in any other way that she'd refuse. "After that phone call with
your ex-wife, I wasn't sure you'd still be interested."

"Maybe that's *why* I'm interested."

"Would you care to explain that?"

It had to do with reaching out to someone. It also had
something to do with interrupting the endless reel of memories playing in his head. But those were his problems. "No."

"I didn't think so." She waited for several seconds before
breaking the silence again, and he wondered if she was scared.

"Does your decision hinge on any one thing?" she finally
asked.

"Definitely."

"What?"

"You."

Her chest lifted as if she'd just taken in a huge gulp of air.
"You don't have to worry about me. We have an agreement.
I won't go back on my word."

"The agreement isn't what's important to me."

"What is?"

He tried to determine what she might be feeling. "Are you
afraid of me, Emma?"

She shook her head, and his heart beat faster. That was good. He could never touch a woman who was afraid of him.

"Then come here."

Emma's teeth sank into her bottom lip, but she moved forward, stopping a few feet in front of him.

He waved her toward him again, and this time she didn't stop until she was standing between his spread knees. He could feel her body's heat, smell the soap she'd just used. He could almost feel the satiny softness of her skin, even though he hadn't touched her yet.

When he stood, the final inches between them shrank to millimeters. He hovered over her for several seconds, searching for any sign of the fear she denied. He could tell she was nervous, jumpy, but he didn't think she was afraid of him. She met his eyes squarely and didn't flinch.

"Relax," he said. "I won't hurt you, okay? I won't do anything you don't want me to."

She didn't answer, but she had to bend her head back to look up at him, and he thought he saw her eyes lower to his lips. She expected him to kiss her. He *wanted* to kiss her. Deeply, hungrily…

Her tongue darted out to wet her lips, and he took advantage of the fact that she left them parted by pressing his mouth very lightly to hers.

She stood, stiff but compliant, as their lips brushed. His blood roared in his ears, but he wouldn't allow himself to put his arms around her for fear she'd feel restricted, overpowered. He simply strung feathery kisses across her cheeks, her forehead, her jaw. By the time he reached her neck, she seemed to understand that he was serious about not taking more than she offered and began to soften. She even leaned toward him a little.

As gently as possible, he let his mouth slide down her slim throat, nipping at her skin, raising goose bumps. "If you don't like something, tell me," he breathed.

She said nothing. She closed her eyes and arched her neck as he moved lower, and he smiled inside. She liked it. Hope began to equal the desire tightening his groin.

Purposefully touching her in ways she'd find nonthreatening, he came up the other side of her neck, traced her ear with the tip of his tongue and used his breath to evoke a shiver. His fingers itched to slip beneath her T-shirt. But this wasn't about getting to the bottom line. This was about discovering that sense of "we" he missed so much. He couldn't achieve it without her full cooperation, without a passionate response. Considering that, her enjoyment was almost more important to him than his own.

Sliding his hand around to the base of her skull, he cradled her head in his palm, being careful to keep his grip loose, so she'd know she could break away if she wanted to. He wasn't worried about pressing her for more. Pressing her would only make him wonder, later on, if he'd gone too far. She'd let him know if she wanted him to make his caresses less innocent. She'd place her arms around his neck, moan when he hit a certain spot or move eagerly against him. A woman could send the signal he was looking for in a thousand different ways, but he had no doubt he'd know it when she did.

Emma didn't send any overt signals, but neither did she withhold. When he kissed her again, as sweetly as before, she gazed up at him for a second, and he thought he read surprise, even curiosity, in her eyes. "You okay?" he murmured.

She nodded, turning her head to catch his lips as they moved softly across her face.

He nuzzled her neck. "You smell good." She felt good, too. Clean. Warm.

He slid the tips of his fingers down her arms, and she slipped them around his neck.

Closing his eyes, he caught his breath at the softness of her breasts against him. She'd chosen to do that all by herself. She was also burying her fingers in his hair and opening her mouth for deeper, wetter kissing.

She was killing him by degrees. The desire to move faster, to feel her naked against him, to see her throw her head back in ecstasy, curled through his veins like smoke. She could wrap him in her innocence and warmth, provide his body with acceptance and release, his mind with a moment's reprieve.

He groaned when she began to respond in earnest. She tasted so good. Testosterone made his heart bang against his chest. As cautious and slow as he wanted to be, he had to bring her closer to him, make her part of him—so he wouldn't have to spend this night as alone as he did all the others.

Slowly he moved his hand to her hip and rubbed his thumb across the bare skin just above the elastic of the boxers. He shook with the desire to cup her breast, to feel her nipple rise against his palm. But he didn't want to *take* anything. He wanted her to guide him.

She didn't lift his hand to her breast, as he wished she would. But she did shift slightly. To make it easier for him? Or had he imagined it? He let his hand glide beneath her shirt but moved instead to her back, where he skimmed her spine, exploring her muscles with his fingers while savoring the softness of her skin.

Then, as her arms loosened from around his neck, his heart

skipped a beat. Was she going to stop him after all? Or worse, offer to perform something that would let him know she wasn't as involved as he thought?

She did neither. Almost curiously, her expression rapt, she brushed her fingers over his bare chest, circled his pectorals, touched one nipple.

His stomach muscles tightened convulsively, and he started thinking about leading her to the bed. But he didn't make his move fast enough. Max must have rolled over inside the bathroom because he suddenly kicked the wall, and Emma froze. Preston could feel her holding her breath, waiting to see if her son would come out of the bathroom.

After several seconds, Max didn't appear. But when Preston tried to kiss Emma again, whatever she'd been feeling before was gone. She was stiff and mechanical.

It was over before it had ever really begun. He'd lost her.

Closing his eyes, he hauled in a deep breath and forced himself to let go. "It's late," he said when he could speak. "Get some sleep."

Then he walked out into the warm night and went to sit by the edge of the glassy pool.

AFTER THE DOOR CLOSED behind Preston, Emma sank onto the bed, too weak and shaky to remain standing. What had just happened? One minute she was in the bathroom, giving herself a pep talk about suffering through Preston's unwanted attentions. The next she was melting beneath his hands.

Blowing out a silent whistle, she lay back and stared up at the ceiling. Her skin still tingled where his palms had moved slowly up her spine, pressing her fully against him. She'd expected him to pull her into bed right away and take what he seemed to want, what his obvious arousal *proved* he wanted.

But surprisingly, he'd held back. He'd been more concerned with what she might be thinking or feeling.

Was this considerate man the same one who'd been so gruff with her and Max today? The man who'd dumped them and hoped to be rid of them?

The two mental images didn't quite match. But that telephone call she'd overheard revealed a lot. What would *she* be like if she lost Max?

Losing Max to Manuel, or even to diabetes, was always a possibility. The worry she carried with her drew closer to the surface, and she went into the bathroom to move her son into bed. Fortunately, he wasn't sweating or showing any other signs of distress.

Once she had Max situated, her mind immediately returned to Preston. Who knew a man could kiss like that? When his lips had brushed hers the first time, so lightly, it was barely a kiss at all. Somehow, he'd made *her* want to seek *his* mouth….

Throwing an arm over her eyes, she remembered the restrained, almost reverent way he'd touched her after that, and marveled at the confidence he must feel to leave so much room for reciprocation. He hadn't pushed her to take more than she was ready to receive. His touch had been an invitation to participate, an invitation to experience something far beyond anything she'd experienced with Manuel.

And she'd almost taken that opportunity. Now that she was feeling more like herself, she was glad she hadn't. She barely knew Preston Holman, and soon she'd never see him again. But for a few seconds, she'd felt as though she needed Preston's hands on her more than her next breath.

So where was he?

Leaving the bed, she went to the window and parted the

drapes but she couldn't see him outside. He wasn't around when she got up to test Max at three, either. She was just starting to worry that he might have gone to another motel and abandoned them, after all, when she heard him come in at nearly four.

Emma feigned sleep as he moved around the room, even though she was fully awake and had been watching the clock since she'd been up with Max. As a single mother with a child to protect and a dangerous ex-lover dogging her every step, she had no business becoming so involved with a stranger. Least of all one caught up in his own past. Still, she couldn't help feeling safer when Preston was around.

From beneath her eyelashes, she watched him cross the room to the bathroom, heard the toilet flush and the sink tap go on. When he returned, he shed the jeans that fit him so perfectly and crawled into the other bed wearing only a pair of boxer briefs.

Emma breathed deeply, trying to determine whether or not he'd been drinking. She hated it when Manuel drank, because it heightened his possessiveness and lengthened the time it took him to achieve an orgasm. But she couldn't smell any alcohol on Preston, only soap and a hint of aftershave.

Her nipples began to tingle as they had when he'd stroked her back, and she wondered what it might've been like to make love with him. Different than with Manuel. Certainly better.

With so much going on in her life, she was crazy to even think about it she decided, and turned over. Slipping her arm around Max's little waist, she pulled her son close to her. Manuel was probably in town by now. He—

Emma didn't want to dwell on that, either. Letting her mind drift back to the man who'd surprised her so much when he'd kissed her tonight, she listened to Preston's breathing grow deeper and steadier until she finally slept herself.

THE FOLLOWING MORNING, Emma began to stir as Preston hung up with the mechanic at Mel's Auto Repair.

"The garage is open," he told her when she leaned up on one elbow.

She yawned. "This early?"

"Yeah." Briefly, their eyes met and last night's intimacy stood between them. Preston had to acknowledge that Emma looked even sexier sleepy and disoriented than she did wide awake and coherent. But he wasn't about to let her affect him the way she had before. Sleep didn't come easy for him as it was. And wanting something he wasn't going to get didn't help.

"If I hurry over there, maybe we'll get out of here today," he said and turned away to pull on a T-shirt. "They have a free continental breakfast downstairs. I'll bring you and Max a plate before I go."

"That'd be great."

He bent over to tie his tennis shoes. "What do you want?"

"What do you think they'll have?"

"Doughnuts, muffins, coffee, juice, cold cereal. Maybe some waffles and eggs."

She shoved a hand through her sleep-tousled hair and seemed to have trouble deciding.

"I want sugar cereal," Max announced, throwing off the covers and joining the conversation.

"No, not sugar cereal," Emma said. "Get him—"

"Then a donut. How 'bout a doughnut? Pul-leeze, Mom?"

"Get Max some eggs, bacon and—" she frowned at her son "—a doughnut, I guess. A small one, if they have it. If they don't have eggs, please get him a waffle and no doughnut. And ask if they have sugar-free syrup."

Sugar-free syrup? Preston had never known a mother more concerned with her son's diet. "What about you?"

"I'll have the same."

He shoved his wallet in his pocket and gathered his keys. "Let me in when I get back. My hands will be full."

"I'll go with you and help you carry everything!" Max cried, and bounded out of bed. But Preston knew better than to take Max. Spending time with him was difficult. And if Manuel was in town, it wouldn't be wise for Max or Emma to leave the room.

"You need to stay here with your mom. I'll be right back."

Max's face fell. "You don't like me, do you."

Preston hesitated at the door. What could he say? He *didn't* like Max. He didn't like him because he was alive and Dallas wasn't. But that made no sense, even to him. "I'll be right back," he said again, and shut the door, hating himself more than anyone.

CHAPTER NINE

AS SOON AS Preston left to take the van to the garage, Emma counted the carbohydrates on Max's plate and administered his morning insulin. His syringes weren't supposed to be reused, but she carefully capped the needle and put it back in Max's tester kit. If worse came to worst and she couldn't buy any supplies this morning, she'd have no choice but to use it again. Insulin couldn't be taken orally. But she only had two more test strips, not even enough to get through the day. She had to do something about his meds as soon as possible.

"Can I have another doughnut?" Max asked, licking the powdered sugar off his fingers with exaggerated satisfaction.

Emma shook her head. He'd already eaten more carbohydrates than he should have for breakfast, which meant she'd had to increase his insulin dosage. Despite her instructions, Preston had brought back doughnuts *and* waffles, with strawberries and whipped cream, and no sugar-free syrup. "Come on, Emma," he'd said softly. "We're on the road. An extra doughnut won't kill him."

Little did he know. She'd almost set him straight. But at that point, Max had grinned broadly at her, as if Preston's generosity signified an acceptance on his part, and she hadn't said a word. She wanted Max to feel normal for a change, knew his illness would only alienate him further from Preston, who was already sensitive about having Max around. She thought she'd better continue to downplay the attention her son required, at least until they could get out of Ely.

"What are you doing?" Max asked.

Emma had picked up the phone, twice, and hung up without dialing. She wanted to call Rosa to see if there'd been any word from Juanita. But she was afraid of what the news might be. She already felt she was balancing on a high wire; it might not be smart to look down, to see how far she had to fall. Especially when she couldn't do anything about the situation back home.

Or could she? Digging the envelope that had come from Juanita out of her purse, Emma stared down at the list of names and numbers on the paper inside it. She wasn't sure it was enough to help her friend, but the possibility gave her hope.

"What's that, Mommy?" Max asked.

"It's nothing, honey." She put her son in the bath, so he'd be occupied while she spoke to Rosa. Then she dialed the number. The call would be charged to the room, but she planned to pay Preston back in cash. Surely he wouldn't mind as long as she reimbursed him.

Rosa answered immediately, as if she'd been sitting by the phone, waiting for it to ring.

"Rosa, it's me," Emma said, listening to Max play happily in the water with his action figures.

"Vanessa? Are you okay?"

"Yes. Why?"

"I managed to reach Manuel last night. He said he's found you, that you'll be home soon."

Emma's blood ran cold. If not for Preston, Manuel would've caught her. He still might.

"Manuel doesn't have me yet," she said. "But I don't know

how much longer I'll be able to avoid him. Where was he when you talked to him?"

"The number on my caller ID started with seven-seven-five."

"That's Nevada."

"I know. I called the operator after we hung up and asked. But she said the whole state, except for Las Vegas, has the same area code, so I can't tell you exactly where he was calling from."

Probably right here, maybe a block or two away. Emma rubbed the goose bumps that rose on her arms.

Max yelled, "Dive! Dive!"

Pulling the phone with her, Emma glanced into the bathroom to see an army guy take a flying leap.

"What about Juanita and Carlos?" she asked, turning away again. "Have you heard from either of them?"

"No, nothing. Manuel says he hasn't seen them. But I know he is lying. I *know* it."

Emma moved back to the nightstand and ironed the wrinkles out of the paper she'd extracted from her purse. Could this information help? She knew threatening a man as vengeful as Manuel was dangerous, but Juanita had risked herself for Emma's sake. Now Emma had to reciprocate. "I'm so sorry, Rosa. This happened because of me. I was so sure he'd never suspect Juanita, or I wouldn't have asked for her help."

Once again, Rosa's voice wobbled. "It's not your fault. It's Manuel. He's the devil."

"Rosa?"

"What?"

Emma heard Max talking in a high voice for one of his "men." He was proclaiming, "Don't worry, I'll save you...."

"I'm in real trouble," she said into the phone. "I have to

buy Max more insulin. If I don't, he could get very sick—or worse." The bathroom had fallen quiet, so she checked on Max again. He was fine.

"What are you going to do?"

"I was hoping you would help me."

Rosa hesitated. "How? Manuel, he...he frightens me."

For good reason, Emma thought. But she couldn't focus on that. A plan was forming in her mind. She knew it wasn't the best plan in the world, but it was the only one she could think of that might throw Manuel off her trail and help Juanita at the same time. "With him and his men swarming the town, I'm afraid to leave my motel room. But..." She twisted the phone cord through her fingers as her mind raced. "What if... What if I called a motel somewhere else, in another town, and rented a room? You could tell him you talked to me, that you know where I am."

"He thinks he already knows where you are."

"But he hasn't found me. You'll tell him he's looking in the wrong place. Offer to trade him my location for information on Juanita."

Rosa was silent as she thought it over. "Do you think it might work?"

"We've got to try something." Emma couldn't risk going any longer without Max's meds. "When you find out where Juanita is, tell him I saw his man go into my motel room last night and hitched a ride to—" Emma searched her mind for a plausible location that wasn't in the direction she and Preston would actually be traveling "—St. George."

"St. George? I don't know this place."

"It's in southern Utah."

There was another long silence. "Why would you need to rent a room there?" Rosa asked.

"Oh, no, it's going off!" Max said, and made explosion sounds.

"As confirmation," Emma said. "Manuel's smart. He may not believe what you tell him. This way, if he calls all the motels in St. George and finds I've rented a room there—"

"It'll convince him."

"If luck is on our side."

"What if he still won't tell me where Juanita is?"

"Then we're not any worse off than we are now, right?"

Rosa didn't take long to decide. "*Sí*. Call me again in fifteen minutes, and I'll let you know what he said."

After she hung up, Emma called information for motels in St. George and booked a room at the Pioneer Lodge in her real name.

Once the room was arranged, she paced until it was time to call Rosa again.

"Mommy, I'm ready to get out," Max shouted.

"In a minute," she said.

Evidently he wasn't completely bored because he went back to playing. She dialed Rosa's number. But she wasn't encouraged by what she heard. Rosa was crying. "What's wrong?" she asked.

"He wouldn't tell me what happened to Juanita. He says he doesn't know."

"Do you believe him?"

"No!" The words turned into a wail.

"Did you tell him I'm on my way to St. George?"

Rosa was crying so hard she didn't answer.

"Rosa? Did you tell him?"

"*Sí*," she said on a sniffle.

Emma was tempted to bite her nails but purposely kept them away from her mouth. "Do you think he believed you?"

More tears.

"Rosa, I'm sorry about Juanita, so sorry, but I have to know if Manuel is going to be here in Ely looking for me."

"I hate him," she said. "I hate that evil man!"

"Rosa, please."

"Mom?" Max called again.

"I'll be with you in a minute, honey!"

This time when Rosa spoke, her voice was so low Emma could hardly hear her. "I think so."

Emma sagged onto the bed. Rosa thought so. They couldn't be sure, of course, but...there was a chance. "Rosa?"

More sniffling.

"Rosa, listen to me. Don't give up hope, okay?" She gazed down at the list. "Juanita gave me something. Something we might be able to use against Manuel."

"What is it?"

"I think it might be proof that he's smuggling drugs into the United States from Mexico."

There was a lengthy pause. Rosa sounded significantly more dry-eyed when she spoke again. "Does he know you have it?"

"Not yet."

"You say it came from Juanita? How?" she asked.

Emma ran a nervous hand through her hair. "Maybe she stumbled on to it. Or knew what she was looking for. Bottom line, it's all we have. And I'm willing to use it."

Rosa started to cry again. "It won't work. Manuel, he fears nothing."

Emma heard Preston outside, asking a maid for extra towels. It hadn't taken him as long to drop off the van as she'd expected.

"I'll have to call you later."

Evidently, Max had decided to get himself out of the bath. He streaked, dripping wet, across the room to meet Preston at the door. "Can we swim now?"

"It's too early," Preston said. Then, seeing Emma hang up the phone, he arched a questioning eyebrow. "Tell me that was your family and they're on their way to get you."

"No." Emma shoved the list of names and numbers back into her purse and tried to ignore his eagerness to be rid of them. "Max, get back in the water. I need to wash your hair."

Preston booted up his computer. "Then who was it?"

"Juanita's sister."

"Who's Juanita?"

"My nanny, silly." Max had hesitated in front of the television, but now he returned to the conversation. "Remember?"

Preston barely acknowledged him. If Emma hadn't been intent on other things, her heart would have gone out to her son. He was trying so hard to win Preston over. But she couldn't do anything to protect Max against such subtle hurts. Not when she was fighting a much bigger battle.

Briefly she considered telling Preston about Juanita's disappearance, and the document she had in her possession. She wanted to talk to someone about the best possible way to approach the situation. If she turned that list over to police, Manuel might go to jail and she wouldn't have to worry about him anymore. Which made doing so very tempting.

But as she took Max into the bathroom to finish his bath, she realized that even if the list meant everything she thought it might—and she had no guarantees—investigations didn't happen overnight. Manuel could be free for months, maybe even years, before spending any real time behind bars. And once she gave up those names and numbers, she'd have nothing to use as leverage to get him to back off, to leave her and Max alone or let Juanita go.

There was also his family to think about. Manuel wasn't involved in the business alone. The people on the list might draw his brothers and uncles, maybe even a few cousins, into the investigation. While Emma wouldn't be sorry to see the whole family in prison, she knew the police would never catch them all. Implicating Manuel would be asking for enough trouble. If her actions brought about the arrest of anyone else in the family, it wouldn't matter *where* she was hiding.

EMMA GLANCED over at Preston, who sat at the table by the window working on his computer, and tried to come up with a good way to ask him to watch Max for an hour or so. She'd waited as long as she could, to give Manuel time to leave town—if he was going to—but she needed a new syringe in about an hour. And just in case Manuel hadn't fallen for her little trick, she was terrified to be seen around Ely, especially with Max in tow.

"What's on your mind?" Preston said without looking up. Obviously he'd felt her interest because she hadn't even said anything yet.

"I—I need to go out for a few minutes."

Finally he turned away from his screen. "Why?"

"Look at us," she said, gesturing at herself.

At her invitation Preston studied her bare legs. But it wasn't the cursory, matter-of-fact assessment she'd been expecting. It revealed the same sexual awareness she'd felt from him when he'd watched her in the Jacuzzi last night.

Heat suffused her cheeks the moment their eyes met and she couldn't help remembering his hands on her bare skin.

"We have no clothes," she said, feeling she should redirect the conversation, although Preston had barely spoken.

"Considering the situation, I think you'd better stay put." He turned back to his work, as though he hadn't noticed the sudden surge of energy between them. "Why not wait until we reach Salt Lake to worry about clothes?"

She suspected he wasn't just concerned about Manuel. He liked seeing her in her swimsuit.

Cursing her elevated heart rate, Emma wondered why this man was having such a strong effect on her. Last night had built her trust. But relief, gratitude, even trust, shouldn't make her mouth go dry whenever she recognized that primitive hunger in his eyes.

She cleared her throat to hide the fact that she wasn't as unaffected by him as she wanted to be. "I'm not comfortable traveling like this. I feel almost naked."

A crooked smile kicked up one corner of his mouth, but she refused to let it distract her. "We have no idea how long it's going to take to fix the van," she went on. "We might reach Salt Lake too late for the stores to be open."

"If you go out, you could walk right into Manuel's arms." The click of his mouse brought up a new screen. "But if you're that uncomfortable, I'll get you and Max some clothes when I finish here."

"Rosa said Manuel thinks I left town. He's searching elsewhere already," she told him, knowing that otherwise he wouldn't see the point of taking this kind of risk. "And I'm just sitting around, doing nothing. Let me shop for what I need, and…and I'll be right back. You wouldn't know what to buy for us, anyway."

The smile disappeared as his eyes went to her again. "Wait a second. You're not thinking of leaving Max here with me."

She curled her fingernails into her palms. "We'd be too obvious if we were out together. And I'm on foot. It'll be easier without him."

Preston shook his head. "No way."

"Why not? I'll be quick."

He scowled. "I don't babysit."

"It won't be like babysitting." She waved at her son. "See? He's so immersed in *SpongeBob SquarePants* he's not even paying attention to us."

"He could start crying the moment he realizes you're gone."

"I won't leave without telling him."

"Where are you going, Mommy?" Max asked, joining in as if on cue.

"I have to run out and pick up some new clothes, okay, baby?"

"What about our old ones?"

"We lost those."

"No, we didn't. They're in the other motel, remember?"

"Someone took them," she said. "Will you be good for Preston if I leave you here with him?"

"No. I want to go with you," he said, but he sounded half-hearted about it, and the cartoon he'd found so fascinating a moment earlier drew him back almost immediately.

"Okay?" she said to Preston. "He's happy. He won't be any trouble at all. You'll be able to—" she motioned toward his computer "—do whatever it is you're doing, and I'll be back before you know it."

She could tell Preston wasn't pleased, but she could also sense him softening. "Come on," she said. "I'll take your cell phone so we can talk if necessary. I'll be an hour at most."

His scowl darkened, but he finally nodded. "Okay. But

wear my ball cap and sunglasses." His eyes flicked over her legs once again. "And unless you want to stop traffic, you'd better put on a pair of my sweats."

Emma couldn't resist feeling somewhat gratified by the compliment, but she chose to concentrate on the practical. "I'll stand out like a sore thumb if I wear sweats in this weather. It's nearly ninety degrees."

"Well, put on one of my T-shirts, at least. It'll hit you lower than what you're wearing now," he said, but he didn't move to get it for her.

"Do you want *me* to take it out of your suitcase?"

"It's open," he said indifferently.

She selected a folded Nike shirt and pulled it over her swimsuit. Then she borrowed his sunglasses, twisted her hair up under his cap and collected his cell phone. "How do I look?"

He stared at her for a moment without speaking. "Keep your head down," he said in place of an answer.

Snatching up her purse, Emma said a silent prayer that she'd be able to find what she needed and get right back. Then she slipped out.

IT WASN'T AS DIFFICULT to locate a pharmacy as Emma had thought it might be. The manager of the Starlight directed her up the street, almost to the other end of town, to Ely Drugs. She and Preston had actually passed this drugstore yesterday. But that was before Emma had needed a pharmacy, so she hadn't really noticed. It had simply blended in with Mr. G's, a boarded-up casino, a series of budget motels, pizza places and other businesses lining the street.

The sun reflected off the glass front of the store, making it impossible to see inside. Her shoulders ached with the anxiety she'd felt as she walked. And now that she was here, her scalp tingled with fear. This was the moment of truth. If Manuel hadn't been fooled by what Rosa told him, he or one of his men could well be waiting for her inside.

She felt so vulnerable. She'd tested Max's blood right before she left to make sure he'd be okay while she was gone. But that meant she only had one test strip now. For his sake, she couldn't run and hide, much as she wanted to. She *had* to do this.

Taking a deep breath, she pulled open the door and stepped inside. Only afterward, when the short jingle she'd set off fell silent, did she breathe a sigh of relief. The store was empty except for a clerk in the gift section, the balding pharmacist in back and an older woman with white hair who was paying for a few items at the cash register.

"Will that be all, Mrs. Williams?" she heard the clerk ask.

Gripping her purse more tightly, Emma moved directly to the pharmacy counter and rang the bell, even though she knew the pharmacist had already seen her coming.

He frowned slightly at her impatience, but didn't let her hurry him.

Come on…come on. Heart pounding, Emma fidgeted with the display of Chap Stick next to a bucket of nail clippers.

The pharmacist finished whatever he was working on, set it aside, and finally came to the counter. "Been swimming already this morning, have you?"

Her cheeks went warm. She was wearing Preston's T-shirt as a cover-up, but she still felt embarrassed parading around town in her swimsuit. "No, not yet."

"Doesn't hurt to be prepared, I guess. What can I do for you?"

She ordered everything she needed, except the emergency glucagon kit. Only the glucagon required a prescription, which she didn't have with her. Reaching Max's endocrinologist through his receptionist and dealing with the necessary red tape would take too long, and if she had to do without something, the kit was the most expendable. It was over a year since Max had been diagnosed with Type 1 Diabetes, and she hadn't needed it yet. Chances were good that he'd be fine without this fail-safe. In a few days, when things settled down, she'd figure out how to come by another one.

Emma's pulse began to slow when no one entered the store behind her or jumped out to grab her. But it was still hard to wait. She needed to make the most of this time. If she could finish here quickly, she could get the clothes she'd told Preston she was going to buy. Then he'd never be the wiser. There'd be no sudden upsets, no surprises and, as soon as the van was ready, he'd have no reason not to take them with him.

"Is that everything?" the pharmacist asked a few minutes later.

She glanced down at the supplies he'd piled on the counter in front of her and nodded. "How much do I owe you?"

"Do you have insurance?"

They had insurance, but she didn't dare use it. She doubted Manuel could trace her through the transaction. By the time he received any type of notice, she'd be long gone. But the authorization would take forever, and because she was out of state she'd probably have to pay for it, anyway. "No."

He whistled. "This stuff's not cheap."

God, didn't she know it. The test strips alone were outrageous, and these supplies would only last a month.

Emma dug into her purse and pulled out three crisp one-hundred-dollar bills while the pharmacist listed all the products she was purchasing. "You from around here?"

"No."

"Just passing through?"

"Yeah."

"Where ya headin'?"

He was being nice, making conversation, but Emma figured the less anyone knew, the better. "California."

"Lots of folks like California."

He said it as though he couldn't understand why, but she didn't respond. She didn't want to encourage him. She had very little time before she had to return to the motel. She had to give Max his lunch; to keep his blood sugar steady, he needed to eat at the same time every day.

She flashed the bills she'd taken out. "How much is it?" she asked again.

When he gave her the total, she paid him, grabbed the bag and walked quickly through the store, pausing only when she saw the clerk dusting a shelf of decorative plates a few feet away. "Can you tell me where I can do a little shopping?"

"For groceries or—"

"For clothes."

"There's a Garnet Mercantile across the street. They took over when the JC Penny went out of business." She pointed kitty-corner from the drug store. "I buy most everything there."

"Thanks," Emma said, setting off the jingle again as she hurried out.

MANUEL DROVE with one hand so he could answer his cell phone. The incoming call had a 775 area code. Nevada.

"Hello?"

"Mr. Rodriguez?"

"Yes?"

"This is Gray Featherstone, the pharmacist over at Ely Drugs."

Manuel's hand tightened on the phone. There were two pharmacies in Ely. He'd visited both and left his card. But when he hadn't received a call from either place, he'd finally decided he was wrong, that Vanessa must have continued on as Rosa had said. He'd started driving to St. George. But he'd only been en route for fifteen minutes.

It was a good thing he'd waited so long. "Is she there?"

"She just left."

Excitement bubbled up inside him as he glanced over at the backpack that held Max's diabetes supplies. He'd gambled on the fact that Vanessa would need to replace what she'd lost before moving on, and he'd won. She might've made it this far, but she wasn't nearly as smart as she thought she was. She never had been. "Can you step outside to see which direction she's going?"

"I don't need to."

"Why not?"

"I know where she's going. She's heading over to Garnet Mercantile."

Manuel smiled. He had her now. "Where's that?"

"On the main drag, a couple blocks west of here."

"*Graçias*, Mr. Featherstone."

"No problem. I hope you get your boy back. I tell ya, I wish someone had listened to me when I went through my divorce. My ex even managed to turn a few family members against me, claiming I abused the kids."

"That must have been terrible."

"It was. Some people really lose it, don't they?"

Manuel made a U-turn and put the gas pedal to the floor. "Yes, indeed."

"CAN WE GO swimming now, pul-leeze?"

Preston gritted his teeth and looked down at Max, who was standing at his knee, wearing the most pathetic expression he'd ever seen. *SpongeBob SquarePants* had been over for nearly an hour, and apparently nothing else on TV could replace it. Emma's son had been bored silly almost from the moment she'd left. "I'm trying to work."

"How are you doing that?"

"Can't you see my computer?"

"Where's your suit?"

Despite himself, Preston chuckled. "My job doesn't require a suit."

"Why not?"

"I'm a day trader. Day traders wear whatever they want."

"What's a day trader?"

"Someone who often loses his shorts," he grumbled.

"Like me and Mom?"

Preston's chuckle turned into a full-blown laugh. "Never mind." He returned to the article he'd been reading on Drawdown Reduction Methods, but by the time he reached the third paragraph, Max was nudging him again.

"What are you doing now?"

"What does it look like I'm doing?"

"Working?"

"Exactly."

"Oh." Max left his side to bounce on the beds, but the noise and activity got on Preston's nerves almost as badly as the boy's constant questions.

"I'm hungry," he announced a few seconds later.

"Stop jumping on the bed," Preston said.

"But I'm hungry."

Preston could tell Max thought those two simple words

would be enough to drag him from his computer, but it wasn't even noon yet, and the boy had eaten plenty for breakfast. "You'll live until lunch."

"I need to eat."

Preston gave up on the article—it was too technical for right now when he had a five-year-old tapping his thigh every minute or so—and clicked back onto the *Wall Street Journal.* He generally had no trouble making money on the Internet, but he'd had a run of bad luck this week—he glanced over at Max—in more ways than one.

"Sorry, pal. It hasn't been that long since breakfast, and we don't have any food in here. We'll grab some lunch later."

"If we can't eat, can we go swimming?"

Preston didn't answer. He wanted Emma to walk through the door, and he wanted her to do it *now.* Enough was enough. He wasn't good with kids, not since his son's death.

Crossing to the room's only phone, Preston called his cell *again,* but it went straight to voice mail.

"I'll give you a million bucks if you'll take me swimming." Max gazed up at him with round, pleading eyes that reminded Preston of a puppy's.

"You don't have a million bucks." Preston hung up and redialed.

"My mom will pay you when she gets back."

Preston thought of the kind of remuneration he'd like to receive from Emma and experienced an immediate physical reaction. "If she felt excited about paying up, I just might do it," he muttered.

"I'll tell her to write you a check."

His call went to voice mail again. Why wasn't she answering?

"Pul-leeze?" Max persisted.

With a frustrated sigh, Preston hung up. There was no help for it. This poor kid was going stir-crazy; he needed to get out. "Okay, I'll tell you what. Let me make one more call, then we'll hit the pool."

"Really?"

"Really," Preston said, and called the front desk.

"Do you know anything about the cell coverage in this town?" he asked when the operator answered.

"Excuse me?"

"I've used my cell a time or two, so I know it works here in Ely, but—"

"Oh, you're talking about cell *phones,*" she said. "I'm afraid the coverage is pretty spotty. From what I hear, some networks do better than others, so whether it works or not depends on your service."

That explained it. "Thanks," he said. For good measure, he tried Emma again but couldn't get through to her. And when Max started running around the room, jumping from bed to bed, chanting, "We're going swimming, we're going swimming," Preston decided to give up. He left Emma a note, in case she missed seeing them out front when she returned. Then he took Max and his laptop to the pool.

CHAPTER TEN

ONCE INSIDE Garnet Mercantile, Emma quickly flipped through several blouses on the clearance rack. She typically wore a size four, but there weren't a lot of smaller sizes.

"Can I help you?"

A heavyset, fiftyish woman smiled when Emma glanced up. Her badge read "Ruby."

"Yes, please. I need a short-sleeved shirt to go with these khaki shorts." Emma held up the shorts she'd already found on sale for fifteen dollars. Fortunately, most of the summer clothes had been discounted to make room for fall merchandise. She'd been able to find Max three pairs of shorts and matching T-shirts for about ten bucks each.

Ruby frowned. "Aren't those shorts you've got made by Bayside?"

Previously, Emma hadn't looked at anything but the size and the price, but she checked now. "Yeah. Bayside."

"Have you tried them on?"

She shook her head and kept digging, her thoughts distilling into a brief mantra: *Shirts and shorts. Pay and go.* She'd been gone more than an hour already. Max had to have lunch soon.

"You might want to do that," Ruby said.

In her worry, Emma had lost the thread of the conversation. "Do what?"

"Try on those shorts. They run small. Generally, I can squeeze into a sixteen. But not in those babies."

Given this information, Emma decided to play it safe. What good would it do her to purchase a pair of shorts that didn't fit? "Then could you help me find a six?"

"There is no six. That's the last pair we've got. Actually, those were a return. Someone bought them without knowing the line runs small. That's why they're marked down."

"I see." Quickly weighing the time she'd need to find another pair against the time it'd take to try on the shorts she already held, Emma opted for the dressing room because it was empty and close by.

"Don't you want to find a shirt before you go in there?" Ruby called after her.

"Grab me something," she called back.

"My, my, aren't we in a hurry," she heard Ruby mutter. Then, louder, "How about something in bright orange? If that doesn't say 'look at me' I don't know what does."

Emma grimaced. Orange was her least favorite color—and she certainly didn't want to draw attention to herself. "I was thinking something understated, maybe in white. Or black, if you have it. Black would match my sandals."

"Conservative. I see how it is."

Ruby said *conservative* as though it meant boring. Emma might have chuckled, except she was growing too frantic to react to anything unrelated to her goal. The minutes were ticking away. Steadily. Inexorably. At this rate, she'd have to jog back to the motel.

Pulling the shorts on over her swimsuit, she quickly zipped and buttoned, then breathed a sigh of relief. She'd lost weight lately. A little too much. But at least they fit.

She was about to take them off when Ruby stuck her head

through the curtain that was supposed to provide a modicum of privacy. "What about this?"

Emma stared at the white, sleeveless sweater tank top Ruby shoved at her, surprised that Ruby had come up with something she liked.

"It isn't marked down," Emma said, checking the price.

"Honey, there's nothing on that sale rack you're gonna like. Conservative stuff don't generally go on sale around here. Neither does western wear, but don't get me going on how badly this town needs a fashion makeover."

The shirt was thirty-five dollars, much more than Emma wanted to spend. But at the moment, she was too frantic to be concerned with price. "I'll take it."

"Well, try it on first," Ruby said as if talking to an errant child.

The salesclerk started to leave, but Emma caught her arm. She was about to say she didn't need to try it on. She wanted to give Ruby her purchases so Ruby could ring them up. But a voice she'd hoped never to hear again reached her ears at the same moment, making the words catch in her throat.

"Excuse me, have you seen this woman?"

It was Manuel. Emma was sure of it. And he wasn't far away.

"I think Ruby was helping her," came the answer.

A wave of dread crashed over Emma. Ruby frowned as though distracted by the same exchange. But when Emma's light grasp on her arm turned into a death grip, the salesclerk looked at her in puzzlement.

"Don't let him know I'm here," she whispered fiercely. "Please."

Standing half in and half out of the dressing cubicle, Ruby blinked, but Emma didn't have the chance to say more. She shrank back as Manuel spoke again, because this time he was right outside the fitting room area.

"Excuse me, Ruby, is it?"

Emma hugged the far wall as Ruby closed the curtain and walked onto the sales floor. "Yes?"

"That lady over there said you might have seen this woman in the past several minutes."

There was a long pause, during which Emma assumed Ruby was busy studying a picture. "I've seen her, all right. She your wife?"

"Yes."

"Was she supposed to meet you here or somethin'?"

"To be honest, she's probably not expecting me. But I need to talk to her. It's very important, maybe even a matter of life or death."

Emma felt her panic rise. Manuel was so handsome, so polished, so *credible.* People generally believed what he said. Life or death... Would Ruby fall for it?

"Whose life are we talkin' 'bout?" Ruby asked.

Manuel's voice dropped, and Emma knew from experience that he was working to create the illusion of intimacy. "Our son's."

"Ya'll have a son?"

"Yes."

"I didn't see no boy with her."

"If I find her, I'll find him."

"I see."

"Can you help me?" he asked.

Of course she could, Emma thought. What woman wouldn't spill all when she'd been told a little boy's life hung in the balance?

Forcing her rubbery legs to move, Emma crept toward the

curtain and peeked through the crack. There was no way she could slip out unnoticed. The slightest movement would draw his eye.

"I'd love to help you, to save your little boy and all," Ruby said, "but I'm afraid your wife walked out just before you got here. If you hurry, maybe you can catch her."

Emma's mouth dropped open.

"Which way did she go?" Manuel asked.

Emma peered out once more to see Ruby shake her head. "Wish I could tell you, but I was too busy mindin' my own business."

Manuel hesitated as though trying to interpret the tone of Ruby's voice. "How long ago did she leave?"

Was that skepticism she heard? Emma prayed it wasn't. *Believe her. Believe her and go.*

"Oh…maybe five minutes."

"Thank you, *señora*."

"That's *señorita*," she corrected.

"*Señorita*, then," he replied. His voice told Emma nothing about what he was thinking or feeling. But he left.

No longer able to remain standing, Emma let go of the breath she'd been holding and sank onto the plastic chair in the corner.

Several minutes later, Rudy slid the curtain aside. "He's gone."

Damp with perspiration, Emma pulled the front of Preston's T-shirt away to keep it from clinging to her body. "Thank God. Thank *you*."

Concern showed in Ruby's dark eyes. "You're white as chalk, girl. You okay?"

"I think so." Emma wiped her upper lip, then managed a smile. "Why'd you help me?"

"Because I've never seen such a desperate expression in all my life as the one on your face when you heard that man's voice." Ruby propped her hands on her wide hips and gave Emma the once-over. "Besides, I didn't like him much. Seemed to think I should do 'bout anything he wanted. Bit too oily for my tastes, if you get my meaning—thinkin' I'm gonna swoon at his feet with all that *señora* stuff. I guess he figured I was some kinda fool."

For once, someone had been able to see through Manuel. It was a good omen, a godsend. Emma felt her lips curve in a weak grin. "I could never thank you enough."

Ruby started to gather up the merchandise Emma had dropped on the floor when Manuel had arrived. "You gonna try on that top now?"

Chuckling, Emma shook her head. "No, I'll take my chances with the fit. I've got to go."

"Go?" Ruby held the garments she'd already recovered to her ample bosom. "Girl, he could be standin' right outside on the street. I didn't lie to that man just to have you go waltzing out of here and straight into his arms."

Ruby was right. Quite likely, Manuel was still close by. But Emma couldn't wait. "I have to get back to my son," she said. "He needs to eat. Right away."

A threatening expression darkened her face. "You didn't leave no child alone…"

"No, of course not. He's with…a friend." She had no idea whether she could really call Preston a friend. He was a handsome, mysterious stranger. But somehow she trusted him.

"Well, you gettin' caught won't see your son eatin' any earlier, will it?"

Ruby didn't understand the urgency of the situation, but explaining wasn't going to change anything.

"No."

"Where's your car?"

"I don't have one."

"How'd you get here?"

"I walked."

Ruby rolled her eyes. "I knew I shouldn't come in to work today. When that alarm went off, I told myself, Ruby, this here's gonna be too fine a day to spend on your feet in a pair of panty hose. But I'm a responsible worker, see. I couldn't cancel out at the las' minute."

Emma searched her purse for Preston's phone. She needed to check on Max. Then maybe she could breathe normally again. "Well, I, for one, am glad you came to work today."

Ruby scowled as she watched Emma punch in numbers. "That cell phone won't do you any good in here," she said. "This building's in a bad spot."

She was right; Emma couldn't get the call to go through. "Is there a back door?"

"A back door? Of course. But it has an alarm. Listen up." Ruby glanced at her watch. "In half an hour, Jackie comes in. As soon as she does, I can go to lunch. You stay in here until then, and I'll give you a ride to wherever your son is."

When Emma didn't immediately respond, she added, "Considerin' you're hidin' out in the fittin' rooms, I don't think you're gonna get a better offer."

The ride Emma appreciated. It was the wait that bothered her. Half an hour...and she couldn't even call Preston to reassure herself about Max.

She shoved the useless phone into her purse. It'd be one o'clock by the time she reached the motel. Two hours after she'd left, not one. But she couldn't walk and get there much faster. And she was probably agonizing over nothing. Stress, anxiety or extra activity could cause Max's glucose levels to fall. But he was sitting in front of the television. That wouldn't raise his stress level or burn many calories.

"Well?" Ruby said. "Should I go ring these up and come for you when I can?"

"Yes. But first, will you please call the Starlight Motel and tell a man named Preston Holman that he needs to feed my son? Tell him you're calling for Emma."

"I can do that." Ruby's panty hose rubbed as she moved away.

Emma remained in the dressing room. Five minutes later, the salesclerk returned, but she wasn't smiling.

"No one answered."

"Are you sure you called the right number?" Emma said.

"Positive. I tried it three times."

Where were Preston and Max? Was something wrong?

Emma didn't know. But she didn't have any options. All she could do now was pray.

"I'LL RACE YOU to the other side," Max said.

Preston flung the wet hair out of his face. He'd planned to continue working while Max swam. But a silent bystander didn't appease Emma's active five-year-old. Max wanted someone to keep him company. Every five seconds, he'd climb out of the pool and pad over to Preston. "Don't you want to swim with me? What about the Jacuzzi? I'll get in the Jacuzzi with you if you want…. My mom likes the Jacuzzi 'cause it's warm…. Watch me dive…. Watch me do a somersault…. Watch me walk on my hands…. Preston? Are you watching? Here I go…."

Finally, Preston had grown so frustrated with the constant stream of interruptions, he'd given up trying to work and dived into the pool. Now he and Max weren't just swimming, they were playing games and staging contests.

Max held up his hand. "On your mark—"

"Whoa," Preston interrupted. "Aren't you tired?"

"No."

"We already raced to the other side."

"So? You beat me."

"That means we do it again?"

"Uh-huh." Max grinned as he nodded.

"Until when?"

"Until I win!"

Preston drained the water from his ear. "I see your tactic."

"What's a tactic?"

"A plan of attack."

"Oh. Well, this time you have to keep one hand behind your back," Max said, as if that was the most difficult challenge ever devised.

Preston arched his eyebrows so he'd look properly challenged. "I already gave you a huge lead."

"Chicken!" Max began to make cackling noises.

Preston hated to admit it, but Emma's son was one heck of a cute kid. He was solid and well-built, expressive, almost always happy. Preston didn't *want* to like him. But there were moments when he couldn't help himself. "All right. If you're so confident you can take me, let's give it a shot."

Hiding a smile, Preston waited for Max to position himself. "On your mark, get set, go!"

Max started off with a splash and swam for all he was worth. Preston waited until he'd reached midway, then kicked off, being careful not to overtake him. When he came up for air at the other end, Max was already there, as orchestrated.

"I told you I could beat you!" he said. He was hanging on to the edge, looking like a drowned rat, but he was wearing a huge grin.

"Good job," Preston said, wiping the water out of his eyes. "Now let's see who can hold their breath the longest."

Max began counting down. When he said, "Go," they both sank under the water, where Preston opened his eyes to watch the concentration on the boy's face. Max was determined, Preston had to give him that.

Max's eyes flew open when he was nearly out of breath. Pretending he couldn't hold out anymore, either, Preston broke the surface at the same time. "Boy, you're good," he said as Max recovered.

"Yeah. I can beat my mom, but not my dad."

Preston was willing to bet Emma lost on purpose, as he'd just done. But he wasn't about to give her away. "How did you get to be such a good swimmer?"

"I don't know."

Preston hooked his arms on the edge of the pool and leaned his head back, soaking up the sun. "Did you have a pool at home?"

"We still do." Max accidentally hit Preston in the chest as he let go of the edge and began treading water. Preston almost drew the boy to him. It was instinctive to help a child who was flailing about in the water. But he knew that wouldn't be a good thing. Holding Max would only remind him of how badly he wanted to hold Dallas.

Max bumped Preston again, but instead of pulling him closer, Preston shoved him over so he could reach the edge. "What was your house like?" he asked.

"Big."

Big didn't tell Preston much. How big was big to a kid? "How many rooms did it have?"

Max screwed up his face while he tried to count. "Twenty billion."

"That's a pretty big house," Preston said with a laugh.

"That includes the pool house."

Preston whistled. Big was probably big even by adult standards if there was a pool house. "What kind of car does your daddy drive?"

"A Hummer. It can go anywhere. Through a jungle and a swamp."

"Does he take it to Mexico?"

"No."

"I didn't know jungles and swamps were a problem in California."

Max didn't catch the sarcasm. He was treading water again, but as he tired, he reached for Preston. "Sometimes he drives Mommy's car."

Once more, Preston guided him back to safety. "What kind of car does she have?"

"Um…a Cougar."

"A Cougar? Are you sure? Do you think your mother could drive…" he searched his mind for an expensive car with a cat name "…a Jaguar?"

"Yeah, that's it," Max said. "A Jaguar."

Preston remembered Emma's concern over the price of a motel room and wondered why she didn't have more money if she and Manuel had been so wealthy. The life she was living right now must come as a shock. Besides what Max had just told him, the size of the diamond studs in her earlobes, the depth of her tan, and the way her toenails were painted with little rhinestones across the top, indicated she probably wasn't used to roughing it.

A flicker of discomfort passed over Max's face. "I'm getting hungry," he said. "Can we eat?"

"We'll have lunch as soon as your mom comes back, okay?"

Max latched onto Preston's shoulder so he could talk without sinking into the water. "But I'm not feeling very good."

"If your mom's not back in fifteen minutes, we'll go to the room and try calling her again." Instead of moving Max back to the edge of the pool as before, Preston tried to tolerate the contact. He managed for a few seconds. But like opening a closet stuffed far too full, he found the memories tumbling out on top of him. Memories of swimming with Dallas in the ocean, of burying him in the sand, of lying down with him at night and reading about dinosaurs and race cars. The memory of Dallas running to him as he walked through the door at the end of a long day filled his mind and weighed heavy on his heart.

Daddy, catch me.... Watch me bat.... Look at that motorcycle.... I'm tired, will you carry me?

Daddy... A lump grew in Preston's throat, nearly choking him, and he jerked away. "Don't touch me, okay?"

Max's eyes widened at the harshness of his tone. "Why not?"

Preston told himself to push those poignant memories back into that closet where they belonged. But the devastation he felt in their wake lingered on.

"Preston?"

The insecurity in Max's voice brought a sharp pang of guilt. "What?" He still sounded angry. He *was* angry. Ever since Dallas had died, a dark rage snaked beneath his skin, like an alligator trolling shallow waters.

"Why can't I touch you?" Max asked.

"I just don't like it."

Max's shoulders slumped. "Okay."

Preston hated the hurt he saw in Max's eyes and cursed himself for not being able to forget Dallas, for not being able to swallow the pain and move on, as Christy had.

Climbing out of the pool, he walked to the fence facing Aultman Street. Where was Emma? She should never have left him with her kid. He couldn't even be kind to the boy.

"Preston?"

"What?" He expected a fresh onslaught of questions or maybe another swimming challenge. But Max didn't respond right away. When Preston turned, he found him resting his head on his arms and looking...blotchy.

"I don't feel good. I—I think I'm going to throw up."

Alarm gripped Preston. The boy's voice sounded reedy-thin. What was wrong? Certainly what he'd said couldn't have caused this bad a reaction, could it?

"But you haven't had anything to eat. You said you were hungry," Preston reminded him.

The boy's eyelids fluttered closed.

Preston couldn't believe it. What the hell was going on? Two minutes ago, Max was acting as normal as could be. They'd been laughing, playing, swimming. And now... "Max?"

No response.

Preston strode to the edge of the pool. "Max! Answer me."

Max lifted his head as though trying to obey, but Preston could see that it required effort and concentration just to move.

"Get out of the pool," he said. "We're going upstairs."

Again, no answer. And no attempt to get out.

"Did you hear me?"

"I can't," he said, sounding breathless. "My legs…and arms won't…work."

Max dropped his head again, then slipped off the edge. Preston watched in stunned surprise as he began to sink without a single squeal or protest.

What the hell? With two launching steps, he dived into the pool. The rush of water felt warm after standing in the open air, but he scarcely noticed. He was too busy forcing his legs and arms to propel him forward as quickly as possible.

By the time he encountered Max's limp body, Preston's heart was pounding. The reverberation of it seemed to echo through his chest as he managed to maneuver Max to the edge of the pool. He rolled him out onto cement that was probably too hot, but Preston was more interested in keeping him from drowning. Hopping out, he quickly scooped him up and laid him on a lounger.

Normal, healthy individuals didn't get sick so fast. And Max had seemed the very picture of health. Was this some sort of ploy to gain attention? Some kids held their breath while throwing a tantrum. Did Max stage a fainting spell when his feelings were hurt? He'd been fine five minutes ago. What had changed?

"Max? Max, if this is a game, I don't like it," Preston said.

"My name's…Dominick."

He could barely talk. "What's wrong with you?" Preston cried. He tried to bridle the terror in his voice, but a memory from that closet in his mind threatened to intrude: Dallas lying on a hospital bed, as pale as the sheets. *Daddy, I don't feel good, will you hold me?*

When Max, or Dominick, didn't answer, Preston gently shook his shoulders. "Stop it, okay? Open your eyes."

Max's eyelids fluttered open and Preston latched on to the

hope that small response offered. "What's wrong with you, Max? Talk to me."

"I—I think I'm going low."

Low? What did that mean? The boy sounded disoriented. Maybe he didn't know what he was talking about. "What's low, Max? What does that mean?"

Max couldn't seem to gather the energy to respond. He continued to lie there, pale and scarcely breathing.

Was he dying? He looked like he was dying....

God, no! A white-hot jagged pain shot through Preston's chest, nearly incapacitating him as the present mingled with the past. *Daddy, I don't feel so good.*

"Don't you dare, Max," he said. But he wasn't commanding, he was pleading. "What can I do to help you, buddy? I'll do anything. What's wrong?" Preston was shaking so badly he wasn't even sure he could support his own weight. He wasn't the right person to deal with this. He felt raw, helpless, completely bewildered.

"Help me!" Preston called to anyone who might be around. He and Max were the only ones in the pool area, but he knew there should be a few maids not far away. They'd been pushing carts from room to room all morning.

He prayed they could hear him. "This child needs a doctor. Get help. Get a doctor!"

"I'm coming," a female voice called. A flash of gray told him a maid from the second story was hurrying toward him, but he feared help wouldn't arrive fast enough. Max was slipping away.

What should he do? He didn't know anything about CPR or first aid, but he felt he needed to help Max breathe.

Flattening the lounge chair, Preston tilted the boy's head back, checked his breathing passage and began mouth-to-mouth. He wasn't sure he was doing it right. He only knew he couldn't let another boy die. Not on his watch.

"Stay with me, buddy, please," he murmured between breaths. "Hang on."

Weakly, Max kept reaching up and pushing at Preston's face, trying to resist. This wasn't working. This wasn't what he needed. But Preston had no idea—

Suddenly he remembered the silver chain Max had pulled off with his T-shirt and thrown on a chair. He hadn't paid much attention to it before. What if…

Leaving Max on the chaise, he ran around the pool to the boy's T-shirt. Sure enough, the chain was tucked inside. The metal tag on the end had a medic alert symbol and a single word engraved beneath it: *diabetic*.

Shit! Max was in insulin shock. His body needed sugar to bring him out of it. Suddenly everything began to make sense. That was what Max had meant by "low." But Preston couldn't believe he'd been with this child for two days and had never guessed there was anything wrong with him.

"Juice!" he cried. "Get me some juice!" He hoped the woman hurrying toward him would hear him and turn back. Max needed food. Fast. *Now.* If he passed out, he wouldn't be able to eat or drink. Then his life would depend on getting him to a hospital, and Preston had no idea if Ely even had a hospital.

Flip-flops slapped the pavement in a rapid staccato. "I'm coming. What's the matter?"

Preston hurried back to Max. "Get some orange juice. Right away!"

She ran off, and he willed Max to hang on a while longer.

The seconds that passed felt like hours. Max's breathing grew shallower. His eyelashes rested on his pale cheeks as his body tried to conserve its sugar to fuel his brain.

Alarm doubled the amount of adrenaline in Preston's body as he lifted the boy into his arms and cradled him against his chest. "It's coming, Max. Don't give up on me, buddy. You're tough, right? You can beat me in a race across the pool. Can you do this, too?"

Max attempted to nod—and it was such a valiant effort that Preston kissed the top of his head. God, this kid was brave. He was deathly ill and yet he was still trying hard to be a good boy and do what he was told. "That's the way." Warm tears rolled down his cheeks. "You're a stud. Don't go to sleep, okay? Fight it a little longer."

The woman finally returned from the front office with a glass of juice. Preston held Max while she lifted his head and helped him drink. More spilled on Preston than went into the boy's mouth, but at least Max still seemed capable of swallowing.

"How much do we give him?" she asked.

Preston had no idea. He'd never been around a diabetic. But he sure as hell wasn't going to risk falling short. "Give him the whole glass and go back for more. Then call a damn doctor."

CHAPTER ELEVEN

EMMA GOT OUT of Ruby's car at the entrance to the Starlight Motel and hurried past the office. *I'm coming, Max. I'm coming.* She'd almost made it to their room when she spotted the little group clustered by the Jacuzzi. Then her heart sank. They were talking low, circling someone on a lounge chair, and she feared she knew who that someone was.

When the maid shifted to one side, Emma could see Preston holding Max, rocking him back and forth, back and forth, and felt her knees go weak.

Dropping her shopping bag, she started running. "Max!" Her hands shook as she fumbled with the latch on the gate. "Max!"

Her son lifted his head from Preston's shoulder and smiled weakly. "Hi, Mom."

As young as he was, Max often tried to ease her worry by assuring her he didn't mind taking shots or testing his blood. She knew that smile was meant to reassure her, but it only made her feel guilty. Somehow she should have thought of another way to get his meds.

He's okay. I'm back now. Max will be fine, she told herself. But Preston's face was bathed with tears. And he looked up at her with such unbridled rage and loathing she knew that even if Max was going to be okay, he was not.

Emma broke eye contact with him. She should've told him about Max's condition. But she'd been too afraid of losing his help. And she'd never dreamed he'd take Max swimming. He hardly spoke to the poor kid.

"Come here, sweetheart," she said to Max. "What happened?"

"I went low."

"At the pool?"

"Uh-huh."

He slipped into her arms, and she buried her face in his hair, absorbing the solid, comforting feel of his stocky little body.

"How bad was it?" she asked Preston.

He didn't answer. Standing up, he stalked off toward their room.

"Lloyd Bannister's on his way," the manager said, filling the awkward silence. "He's a good doctor, been practicing for years. And your boy here seems to be bouncing back already, thank God."

Emma muttered something polite to thank her and the maid for their help, but her attention wasn't really on them. It was on her son, her own relief, and the man who'd left them so abruptly.

Preston reappeared only moments later, wearing a clean T-shirt and another pair of jeans. The sight of him, apparently recovered, gave Emma hope that he'd forgive her for what had happened. But that hope died the moment she saw he was carrying his laptop and his duffel bag.

"I need my cell phone," he said, his voice clipped.

Emma's hands were shaking as she dug his phone out of her purse and handed it to him. She wanted to apologize, but he turned immediately to the manager.

"I'm ready to check out."

Emma watched them both walk away. A few minutes later, Preston stepped outside again. When he squinted against the sun, Emma realized she still had his sunglasses and his hat, and hoped he'd come back a second time. But he didn't bother. He didn't even glance in the direction of the pool. Slinging his duffel bag over his shoulder, he headed down the street.

EMMA SAT on the motel bed in Preston's room, staring at nothing while listening to the water drip in the bathroom. Evidently, he'd been in such a hurry he hadn't even bothered to turn off the faucet properly.

"Mommy?" Max bent down to see beneath the hair that made a curtain around her face. "What's wrong?"

Too discouraged to even cry, Emma shook her head. "Nothing, honey. Don't worry."

"Are you mad?"

She was numb. "No. I'm glad you're okay, that's all."

He climbed into her lap, something he rarely did now that he was getting so big, and let her hold him. She kissed his forehead and hugged him close, taking solace from the fact that they still had each other. His insulin reaction had been the worst he'd suffered so far. She was grateful Preston had had the presence of mind to figure out what he needed.

But not all aspects of the nightmare she was living had ended. Manuel hadn't fallen for her decoy. He was still in town, searching high and low, and the scene down at the pool had caused a stir. She wouldn't be surprised if it made tomorrow's paper: Man at Hotel Saves Diabetic Boy.

She rubbed Max's back as she remembered the fiasco that had erupted once the doctor had arrived. As a family practitioner,

Dr. Bannister had a few diabetic patients, but they were older, Type II patients who weren't insulin-dependent. It had taken her nearly an hour to convince him that it wasn't necessary to take Max to his office for a blood test. An HbA1c would reveal Max's average glucose levels over the past three months, but Emma didn't have the time or money for something that wouldn't, at this point anyway, be of much benefit. They wouldn't even be around when the results came back from the lab. Max's unexpected exercise had brought on a severe insulin reaction, but a little orange juice had fixed the problem quickly enough. Heck, now that he'd eaten the lunch the manager had given him, he was already begging Emma to take him swimming again. *She* was the one who felt she needed to crawl beneath the covers and sleep for a week.

Her son squirmed out of her arms, and she pulled her purse over to count what was left of her money. She'd already spent hundreds, and she'd only been gone three days. At this rate, she'd run out of money long before they reached Iowa or anywhere close to it. But she had to do what she had to do. And that included moving on. Somehow. After the crisis at the pool, she and Max couldn't stay here. They shouldn't have hung around this long, but she'd been hoping Preston might reconsider and come back for them.

Why she'd been stupid enough to let herself hope for that, she had no idea. Obviously it wasn't going to happen.

She'd have to buy the cheapest car she could find. It was her only option.

At least she had Max's supplies and some clothes. She hadn't remembered to buy herself any underwear or even a bra. But she couldn't worry about that. She had to keep looking on the positive side—or she'd be too depressed to do anything at all.

"Let's go," she said.

"Where?" Max asked.

Emma hid her hair under Preston's hat and donned his sunglasses. "We're getting out of here, one way or another."

PRESTON SLUNG his arm over the back of the booth. The restaurant in the Hotel Nevada wasn't busy, but two old cowboys sat against the far wall, beneath an elk head that stared sightlessly down on them, and a few people lingered beyond the restaurant in the open lobby, playing slot machines. The bright lights typical of a casino glittered and flashed, and occasionally the sound of bells, whistles and coins falling rang above the hum of voices and the clatter of dishes in the kitchen across from him. But the midday activity was hardly enough to keep Preston's mind occupied. That incident at the pool had rattled him too badly. He'd left the Starlight nearly two hours ago, yet he felt sick every time he thought of Max's pale face.

Which was why he wasn't going to think about it anymore, he decided.

Pulling a twenty from his wallet, he tossed it into the small plastic tray the waitress had left with his check, then glanced at his watch. Mel, over at the auto repair shop, had told him the van would be ready at four. He had another thirty minutes to wait. Then he'd be on his way with his gun and no one to worry about except himself, sailing down the highway at seventy-five miles per hour.

He smiled. God bless Nevada and its generous speed limits. The added freedom he felt in this lonely state was one of the reasons he liked it. No one tried too hard to legislate the daily details of life. Live and let live seemed to be the motto here. It was Preston's motto, too. And that was exactly why he felt perfectly justified in leaving Emma and Max behind.

He refused to set himself up again; he'd rather play it safe than take the kind of risk that might lead him down the same dark path his life had taken two years ago. The new Preston preferred having nothing to lose.

His cell phone rang. After the trouble he'd had reaching Emma, he was surprised it worked. But who was he to question the gods of cellular service?

Eager to distract himself in any way possible, he grabbed it from the table. Inactivity only invited his conscience to continue pestering him with the same resolve-weakening questions he'd been battling for the past hour. *What's going to happen to Max and Emma now? What if Manuel catches up with them? Could one more day in their company cost me that much?*

"Yes!" he snapped.

"What?" a scratchy voice responded, and Preston realized he'd already punched the Talk button.

"I mean, hello."

"I can see I've caught you in a good mood."

It was Gordon Latham, the private investigator he'd hired to find Vince and probably the only person in the world Preston called a friend these days. Preston could tolerate him because Gordon had no connection to the other stockbrokers from the firm where he'd worked, the guys on the block where he'd lived, the investors he'd wined and dined or the Little League dads with whom he'd coached. Gordon hadn't been part of his former life. Back then, Preston hadn't needed a P.I. Like almost everyone he knew, he'd stupidly believed that nothing truly devastating could ever happen to him.

Until it did.

"No worse than usual," Preston said, and sat up taller. The last time Gordon had called, he'd said that a Dr. Vincent Wendell had opened a medical practice in Cedar Rapids, Iowa. It had taken Preston only a few calls to determine that *this* Dr. Vincent Wendell was indeed the man he'd known as Vince, the neighbor who'd lived down the street from him two years ago. Vince had finally shown up again after disappearing from Fallon over a year ago.

"Where are you?" Gordon asked.

"Nevada."

"What? I thought you'd be on a plane to Iowa the second we hung up two days ago."

Preston couldn't fly, not with a gun. And, considering what he planned to do, it made little sense to go to Iowa without it. "I don't fly," he said, choosing to let Gordon believe he had an aversion to leaving the ground. He used to fly all the time, but that was when he had a home and a family and didn't live out of a van and travel with a loaded weapon.

"So are you on your way there?" Gordon asked.

"I am. It should only take a couple more days."

"Wendell's finally set up his practice again. He's probably not going anywhere real soon."

"Not unless someone tips him off that I'm coming."

"Who would do that?"

"Exactly," Preston said. He figured Vince felt safe now and had decided to put down some roots—which was why he believed it was wiser to go there prepared. As much as he craved getting hold of the man he held responsible for Dallas's death, he didn't want to blow what could be his only chance at a confession.

"By the way, you're one hell of…sly dog…know that?" Gordon said.

Gordon's voice had started cutting in and out, but Preston managed to decipher his words. "How so?"

"…you kidding? I made fifty-thou…stock tip you gave me. Thanks, man."

Preston stretched out his legs and crossed them at the ankles. "I guess I should've taken my own advice."

"You didn't?"

"I bought into something a little more volatile. The gamble didn't pay off."

"How much…you lose?"

Preston did a quick calculation in his head. "Seventy, give or take a few thousand."

"Seventy thousand dollars?"

That came through loud and clear. "Could've been worse. Fortunately, I got conservative at the last minute." The waitress came to collect his money, and he gave her a polite smile.

She smiled back, a little more meaningfully than he'd expected, and he shifted his gaze away so she wouldn't get the wrong idea.

"You don't *care?*" Gordon said, their phone connection improving. "You're not freaking out about losing that much money?"

"As long as I have enough to get by, it's all numbers on a spreadsheet to me."

"With… We're…"

Preston held the phone closer to his ear. "What?"

"I said with a dollar sign attached! We're not playing with fake money here, pal. I'd have a heart attack if I ever lost that much. And if the heart attack didn't kill me, Pamela would."

"Yeah, well, I don't have a wife to worry about anymore, remember?" Preston said.

Gordon fell silent. For a second, Preston was afraid he'd put them both in an awkward position by apologizing for the blunder. But he should've known better. Gordon wasn't that stupid.

"I have something new for you," he said, simply changing the subject.

Preston wiped the condensation from his water glass. "What's that?"

"Wendell and his wife...divorcing."

"You say they're *divorcing?*"

"Right. Your old pal is losing his wife."

It couldn't be. Joanie had always thought Vince walked on water. After Dallas's funeral, when Preston had confronted them with his suspicions, she'd been vehement in her defense of Vince. *How can you say such things? You son of a bitch! I thought you were our friend.*

The two couples *had* been friends. Close friends. At least until Preston had voiced the terrible questions and doubts that had been consuming him, along with his grief. At that point, Vince and Joanie began playing the martyr. *After everything we've been to each other, how can you turn on us?*

Easily. He could do it because no friend meant more to him than his son, and he needed answers.

But they'd only used Preston's accusations to make him look irrational. "It's the grief," they muttered to anyone who'd listen. For a while, Preston wondered if he *was* irrational, if he just wanted someone to blame for his loss. While he was doubting himself and fighting to save his own marriage, the Wendells had sold their house and moved away—with no forwarding address. Gordon had eventually found them in Fallon, but by the time Preston had arrived, they were already gone.

"I'm not sure they'll go through with it, of course," Gordon was saying. "But they filed a month ago."

"How'd you find out?"

"Hey, don't you watch TV? I'm a P.I. I can dig up anything, remember?"

Preston chuckled, but he was so busy trying to work out what Joanie's defection might mean that he didn't see the tall, dark-haired man who'd entered the restaurant until that man was standing in front of him.

"Excuse me, *amigo*. I'm sorry to bother you, but I have a quick question, if you don't mind."

Surprised by the interruption, Preston glanced up, and the man immediately shoved a photograph under his nose.

"Have you, by chance, seen my wife? Or my son?"

Preston stared dumbly at an image of Max grinning for the camera, and a much more sedate-looking Emma. Max's smile appeared to be authentic, but Preston could easily guess that the slight curve of Emma's lips was for the camera alone.

When he lifted his eyes to the clean-shaven man who had to be Manuel, he fought the urge to let his hands curl into fists. Manuel had called her his wife, but according to Emma they'd never married.

"I've got to go," he told Gordon. "Thanks for the info. Call me if you find anything else."

Arranging his expression into one of concern, Preston hung up and accepted the picture Manuel held out to him. It was slightly bent, as though it had been carried in a wallet of some sort, but it certainly wasn't torn and shabby. Like Manuel's blue fitted shirt and black slacks, there wasn't a crease in it.

Preston noted the expensive sunglasses hooked into the opening of Manuel's shirt, the thick gold medallion around his neck and the mammoth diamond ring that glittered on his little finger, and decided he definitely had an uptown flair. Manuel had even splashed on cologne—more than anybody should have the right to wear. Preston could barely stand it.

Evidently, Max's dad took "dressing to impress" to a whole new level.

"She's really beautiful," he said, just to hear Manuel's response.

Manuel's lips thinned. "Have you seen her?"

Preston tilted the picture to the side to get a better look. "Is she in some sort of danger?" *From you, perhaps?*

So far their exchange had lasted mere seconds, but Preston could already feel Manuel's dislike. It came off him in waves and made Preston wonder if his own feelings were equally transparent.

"Possibly."

"I really wish I could help you, but…" Preston shook his head. "I haven't seen them. Do you have a card or something? Maybe I could call you if I do."

Manuel slipped the picture of Emma and Max into his breast pocket and withdrew a card that read "Manuel Rodriguez." Only a cell phone and pager number were listed beneath the name. No profession. No address.

"If you see her, I'd appreciate hearing from you."

"You bet. We can't leave such a pretty lady at risk now, can we?"

When Manuel froze and turned back, Preston knew he hadn't masked the flippant tone of his voice quite as well as he'd intended to.

"Do you live here in Ely, *señor?*" Manuel asked.

They'd gone from *amigo* to *señor.* Not a good sign. Preston saw no reason to single himself out any more than he already had. He'd been foolish to provoke Manuel. It wasn't going to help matters. "Yeah, I grew up here. Why?"

There was that icy smile again. "You don't look like a cowboy."

"Next time I'll remember to wear my spurs."

Straight white teeth flashed as Manuel laughed. "Be careful. A cowboy lives a dangerous life," he said softly. "You wouldn't want to be caught unawares."

Manuel held his head at a haughty angle as he stalked into the dimly lit lobby, where Preston could see him showing everyone the same picture and, no doubt, asking the same question: *Have you seen my wife?*

The tension inside Preston wound tighter as he watched. How many people would Manuel have to approach before someone said, "I think I saw her over by the Starlight Motel." Even if no one gave her away, Emma had a kid and no car. A *diabetic* kid. She didn't stand a chance against the arrogant son of a bitch who was chasing her. If she couldn't get a ride out of town Manuel would probably find her before nightfall.

The memory of Emma arching her neck as he kissed her soft skin flashed through Preston's mind. She'd closed her eyes and held her breath at his touch, as though she'd never felt anything so gentle.

The thought of what she might have endured before caused Preston to crush Manuel's card in his hand.

"Here's your change," the waitress said.

His mind on Emma and Max, Preston waved her off. "Keep it."

She pocketed the money, but paused with a hand on her hip instead of moving away. When he looked up, she grinned. "At least take your receipt."

He accepted the slip of paper. He was about to toss it onto the table when she touched his hand and made a point of turning the receipt over so he could see the telephone number she'd written on the back. "Call me sometime."

As he slid out of the booth, he nearly told her he was just passing through. Even if he'd been planning to stay, he would've offered some excuse. He knew how to deflect interest; he'd become a master at isolation. But Manuel's dogged persistence in the lobby distracted him, grated on his nerves.

Forget Emma. Get out of here. You have enough to worry about. Joanie's divorcing Vince. This could be the break you've been waiting for.

Preston watched Manuel approach an old woman. Smiling broadly, he acted the perfect Latin gentleman. And she was obviously impressed. The old lady beamed as though she'd trade her dentures to be able to help him.

"Shit," Preston muttered. To hell with moving on alone. He'd catch up with Joanie soon, but first he had to get Emma out of Ely, because he wasn't about to let Manuel Rodriguez have what he wanted. Not today.

"Excuse me?" the waitress said.

"Sorry, I was thinking about something else," he said. "I'd love to take you out sometime. But is there any chance you might be willing to do me a small favor first?"

The hesitancy in her eyes said she was leery of promising too much. "Um, sure, I guess. What is it?"

"See that man out there?"

"The one who was talking to you earlier?"

"That's him. Has he approached you yet?"

"No."

"Well, he's looking for my sister and her son. But he's abusive. He's beaten her badly, and I've promised to help her get away from him."

Her eyes went round. "He *beat* her?"

"You should've seen it." Preston let the disgust he felt every time he thought of Emma's burn show on his face.

"That's terrible!"

He nodded. "Do you think you could walk past him? When

he stops you to ask about the woman and the boy in the photograph, tell him you saw them earlier, that they were eating
in here with—" he searched for a lie plausible enough to buy
some time "—a heavyset trucker who mentioned he was on
his way to Vegas."

"A heavyset trucker going to Vegas. Got it." She smiled
freely again now that she knew she didn't have to do anything
too difficult. "So you'll call me?"

"This weekend if I can. But in case I have a conflict, here's
a little something for your trouble."

"You don't have to tip me for such a simple favor."

"You deserve it."

She slipped the twenty he handed her into her apron.
"Okay, but don't let a conflict stand in the way," she said with
a pout.

"I'll do my best," he said, and she headed toward the
hotel's front desk.

Just as Preston had expected, Manuel spotted her immediately. When he crossed to speak with her, Preston slipped
around them and hurried outside.

Parked right out front was a black Hummer. Manuel's car.
It had to be. The license plate read "Rodriquez-1," which confirmed it. The bastard had every advantage.

As much as he wanted to avoid Max and Emma's company, Preston knew he couldn't walk out on them now. He already had more than enough regrets.

CHAPTER TWELVE

EMMA HAD purposely left her cell phone behind in San Diego. If she didn't, she knew Manuel would call her incessantly. She even feared he might be able to trace her if she used it. She'd taken the barest of necessities, exactly what she needed for her plan to work. Only her plan had fallen apart the first day, and now she found herself trying to get by with almost nothing.

Wearing her swimsuit for underwear and holding all of Max's and her possessions in one hand, she stood at a payphone several blocks from the Starlight Motel. Max played nearby. With the highway heading out of town only a few feet away, and nothing but flat land and low shrubs all around, she felt like a target. She could hardly believe Manuel hadn't already pulled up and ordered her and Max to get in the car.

A flash of movement told her Max was too close to the road. "Hey, get back," she called, leaning out of the phone booth to make sure he obeyed. When he started digging in the flower beds again, something she was sure the owner of the gas station wouldn't be too thrilled to see, she put the phone back to her ear. At least digging in the flower beds kept him low to the ground and out of the street.

"I think you must have the wrong number," a voice said on the other end of the line.

The person she'd called had picked up. "I'm sorry. I was talking to my son."

"Oh."

"I'm contacting you about the car you have for sale in the paper."

"I'm afraid that's already been sold. Larry Beecham wanted it for his teenage son."

The woman gave Larry Beecham's name as though she expected Emma to know him. This *was* a small town. Too small. And Emma was growing desperate. If she couldn't get a car, she'd have to spend another night here, or hitchhike.

She wondered if maybe she could buy a couple of sleeping bags and camp out in the wilderness. She knew she'd feel safer beneath the stars in some remote location than she would if she got another motel room in town. But with her luck, it'd rain. Or she'd encounter a rattlesnake.

She focused on her call. "Has Larry picked up the car already?"

"No, I don't think he has. Milt promised to install a better stereo first."

"So it's running."

"Oh, yes."

"I'll pay you an extra hundred if you'll sell it to me instead." Emma felt like a heel trying to buy some kid's car out from under him. But she knew Larry's son couldn't need it as badly as she did.

"I can't do that, young lady. I've already given my word."

"I'd be really grateful," Emma said hopefully, but the woman hung up.

With a heartfelt sigh, she crossed off the two-line ad that read "1979 Camaro, rebuilt engine, new tires, only $1500."

Unfortunately, Ely didn't have a big used-car market. She'd

already called the small Ford dealership across town. They had no cars in her price range, which wasn't really a surprise, and there weren't many automobiles for less than two thousand dollars listed in the newspaper. Two had already been sold. Another three weren't working. *Your husband puts a little elbow grease into this baby and you'll have yourself a fine vehicle.*

What had she expected for the price?

She glanced at the motorcycles for sale and wished she knew how to drive one. At this point, she'd risk just about anything, even taking a bus. But, as she'd guessed, there wasn't any Greyhound service in Ely.

She fingered her diamond earrings. They'd been a birthday gift from Manuel. They held no sentimental value, but she'd worn them when she left San Diego because she could pawn them under desperate circumstances.

Circumstances couldn't get much worse, but there wasn't anything in Ely's narrow phone book under "pawnshop." She'd already checked.

Her eyes flicked over the For Sale ads again, focusing on newer cars, more expensive cars. Could she talk someone into trading a car for a pair of diamond earrings? The earrings had been appraised at ten thousand dollars, but she didn't imagine anyone would take her word on that. Maybe if she could find a jeweler in town to corroborate their value...

She blew a strand of hair out of her eyes and turned to the *J*s. A trade might actually be the smartest way to go. In college, a friend had to pawn his camera and got only ten percent of its value. With a trade, she might net forty, perhaps fifty percent.

Max knocked on the outside of the booth, even though she'd left the door open. "Mommy, I'm hot!"

He couldn't be as hot as she was. At least where he was playing, the slight breeze could cool him. The old-style phone booth cut much of the highway noise, but it acted like a huge magnifying glass in the hot August sun. Beads of sweat rolled between Emma's breasts, and the air was so tight and close, she felt she might spontaneously combust if she didn't get out soon.

She pressed the folding door open another two inches, but it only bounced back. "We'll buy a diet soda in a few minutes. Hang on, okay, pal?"

"But we've been here *forever.*"

"It won't be much longer."

Shoving his hands into his pockets, he kicked dejectedly at a dirt clod that broke apart. "I want to go home."

Emma tucked her sweat-dampened hair behind her ears. "Come on, Max, don't start. I know this hasn't been an easy day for you, but I can't fix it right now."

"Why can't we just go back?"

This wasn't a good time to have the talk Emma knew they needed to have. But her "pick up and move and Max will simply forget" plan suddenly didn't seem fair to him. Young though he was, he deserved an explanation for why his life had been turned upside down. Maybe he even deserved a small say in it.

Holding the door of the phone booth open by putting her back to it, she squatted to face him. "I'm afraid I can't live with your daddy anymore, Max."

His eyebrows gathered over his green eyes. "Why not?"

"He isn't nice to me. I—I can't be happy when I'm with him. Do you understand?"

He scuffed one sandal against the other.

"Max?"

"What?" he said without looking at her.

"You mean more to me than anything in this world. If I thought you'd be better off, I would've stayed with your dad, even though I didn't like being with him myself. But I don't think you'd be better off. Your dad is…changing."

No response. Emma wondered if she was going too far with her little talk, if she was beginning to unburden herself at Max's expense. She didn't want to make the situation any more difficult for him. "At least you and I are together. That's about all I can offer at the moment. You want to be with me, don't you?" she asked.

His chin bumped his chest.

"I know it's hard to think about moving and not seeing Daddy…for a while," she added to soften the blow. "But—" she drew a deep breath "—I hope you can trust me on this."

The sun glinted off his bowed head.

"Can you trust me, Max?"

His nod was barely perceptible.

"Now we need to find a car so we can get out of here, okay? Can you be good just a little longer?"

"What about Preston?"

Emma pictured Preston's face, wet with tears. A man like Preston didn't cry easily, which told her what she'd done to him. "He's left us behind."

"Because he doesn't like me."

"Because I made a bad choice. It had nothing to do with you." She didn't want Max feeling responsible for something he couldn't help. It wasn't his fault Preston had lost a son. It wasn't Max's fault that she'd chosen not to tell Preston about his diabetes. "Do you believe me?"

He shrugged.

"Can you be good a little longer?" she repeated.

"Yeah." Grudgingly, he went back to digging in the dirt.

Once again, she had to depend on Max to handle more than a child his age should have to. Pride nearly brought tears to her eyes when he glanced up and offered her a brief smile. Somehow, he understood that she was doing her best. Even at five years old. Or maybe he only understood how much she loved him. She hoped that would give him enough to cling to until she could get their lives sorted out.

Returning to the phone book, she discovered that Ely had a jeweler who could attest to the value of her earrings. Now if she could just find someone selling a five-thousand-dollar car who might be willing to trade for ten-thousand-dollar studs.

MANUEL PACED the empty men's room of the Hotel Nevada, waiting for his call to go through. He'd already sent Hector to Vegas to chase down the lead he'd received from that stupid waitress. He thought they might be on Vanessa's trail again. But he was angry that he'd come so close—and missed her.

"Guess who?" he said as soon as Rosa answered.

Juanita's sister paused. "What do you want?"

"Funny thing, but Vanessa didn't go to St. George, like you told me."

"You found her?"

"Not yet. But I will."

Silence.

"Rosa?"

"She said she was going to St. George."

Manuel wasn't sure whether to believe her or not. It could be that Vanessa had used her to mislead him, and Rosa had no knowledge of it. Either way, it didn't matter. Now that he knew Juanita had a sister and Vanessa was in contact with her, he could turn it to his advantage. "Has she called again?"

"No. And she probably won't."

"If she's worried about Juanita, she will."

As before, Rosa began to cry. "Where's my sister? What have you done with her?"

"How badly would you like to know?" he asked.

She managed to compose herself. "What do you mean?"

"I mean, if you ever want to see your sister again, you'll find out where Vanessa is and call me."

"I knew you had her." Rosa's voice broke into a wail. "Don't hurt her! Please, don't hurt her."

He slammed his fist into the swinging door of a toilet cubicle. "Shut up! Whether or not she gets hurt is up to you."

"But I don't even *know* if Vanessa will call again," Rosa whined. "And asking too many questions will only make her suspicious."

The door he'd sent swinging still banged open and shut again. "I thought you cared about your sister. I guess I was wrong. She won't be happy to hear it. I'd better go—"

"Wait! I—I'll do my best. I do know something."

The breath caught in Manuel's throat. "What?"

"I heard a voice in the background the last time she called. I—I think she might be traveling with someone."

Someone. Manuel's muscles bunched. Was it the trucker the waitress had mentioned? Or a secret lover? Had Juanita held out on him?

"Is it a man?" he asked, barely able to force the words between his clenched teeth.

"*Sí.* A man."

He pivoted away from the mirror because he didn't like seeing the red in his face and eyes, the vein pulsing at his temple. Look what she'd done to him! "Who?"

"I don't know. As soon as I heard the voice, she told me

she had to go and the line went dead. Now will you set my sister free?"

Manuel heard the pathetic weakness, the supplication in her voice, and felt his gut twist with derision. Juanita had spit in his eye. As much as he'd made her pay for her disrespect, he had to admire her spirit.

Rosa, on the other hand, was nothing. Less than nothing. "When you tell me where she is," he said, and hung up.

TWENTY MINUTES after leaving the Hotel Nevada, Preston stood at the front desk of the Starlight Motel. "How long ago did she leave?" he asked.

The manager who'd helped with the emergency earlier, an older, white-haired woman with the last name of McMurtry, consulted the clock on the wall. "It's been about an hour, I guess."

"Do you have any idea where she might've gone?"

"She asked me if there was a car dealership in town. I told her Elton Lee owned one over on the west side."

So Emma was looking for a car. That told him something. "And did she and the boy head in that direction?"

"No, they went plumb opposite."

Why? In another few blocks, the town gave way to wilderness. What kind of car could Emma have hoped to find going east? "Can you remember anything else she might've said, to you or her son?"

"She asked if you'd been back."

Preston ignored the guilt he felt on hearing this news. Maybe he'd reacted too harshly after what had happened to Max, but he still couldn't think about the boy lying limp in his arms. Not without wanting to throttle Emma. "That's it?"

"Um…let's see." She drummed her fingers on the countertop. "She bought a newspaper at the gas station across the street. I know, because I saw her come out with it."

"Anything else?"

"Sorry."

Preston thanked her and strode across the lobby. The first thing he had to do was pick up the van. It was finally time, and he could cover a lot more ground in a vehicle.

"From what I saw, she needs to take better care of that boy," Mrs. McMurtry said before he could clear the door. "What happened this afternoon was awful."

"She's a good mother," Preston said, then had to ask himself why he'd immediately jumped to Emma's defense. She'd stranded him with a kid who had a debilitating disease without even warning him of the danger.

Preston couldn't forgive her for that; he still felt angry. But not angry enough to leave her to the mercy of a man like Manuel.

"She seemed terribly nervous when she left," Ms. McMurtry added. "Do you know what she's so afraid of?"

Preston thought of Manuel over at the hotel. "There's a man in town looking for her," he said. "There's no telling what he might say to you, but don't believe a word of it. He's dangerous. If he comes by asking about her, tell him she shared a room with some trucker who told you he was on his way to Vegas."

Her light eyes narrowed as she sized him up. "How do I know you're not the bad guy?"

"If I was the bad guy, I would've taken her with me earlier."

She thrummed her fingers on the counter. "Sounds like you should have. Sounds like you regret leaving her."

Preston didn't bother to deny it. "I do. Now I've got to find her before he does."

"Mr. Holman?" she said.

He glanced back a final time to see her smile. "Good luck."

EMMA SAT with Max against the back wall of the mini-mart in the shade of a small bush. Max held a diet soda and seemed to have cooled down, but he still wasn't talking much. Certainly not like normal. Emma wasn't sure if his blood sugar was too high or too low—either extreme could cause moodiness—or if his sudden melancholy resulted from what she'd told him earlier.

"You okay, buddy?" she asked.

The straw in his soda scratched the plastic lid of the cup as he toyed with it. "Yeah."

"Don't you like your drink?"

He shook his head. A cola was the only diet drink most places carried, and diet cola wasn't especially popular with five-year-olds. Max preferred orange soda or root beer.

She ran her hand over the short bristles of his fine hair. "Do we need to test you? Are you going low?"

"No." He wrinkled his nose. "It stinks back here."

Emma didn't appreciate the smell of rotting garbage coming from the trash bin a few feet away, either. But, as much as possible, she'd wanted to stay out of view of the highway.

Craning her neck to look around the corner, she frowned as she studied the road. Going through the rest of the cars-for-sale ads, she'd actually found someone who sounded intrigued by her strange offer. A woman by the name of Amelia Granger was supposed to meet her at the gas station to take a look at the earrings and show Emma the car she had for sale. But Amelia should've been here by now.

Would she like the studs? Would she agree to the trade, let Emma and Max drop her at her house and drive away?

Only time would tell.

The minutes dragged on. While Emma felt safer staying behind the building, she began to fear that she'd somehow missed Amelia. It'd been more than an hour since they'd spoken on the phone.

Deciding to call her again, she stood and brushed off her new khaki shorts.

"Where are we going?" Max asked, hopping up behind her.

"To the phone booth out front."

His shoulders sagged. "Again?"

"This time it'll be quick." She motioned for him to follow her, but as soon as they rounded the building, Emma spotted a black Hummer parked at the gas pumps.

She didn't need to see the personal license plate to know it read Rodriguez-1.

She reached for Max's arm, to pull him out of sight, but he'd already spotted his father's car.

"Daddy's here!" he cried, and started to run.

Emma's heart leaped into her throat. "Max, no," she whispered harshly. She couldn't see anyone inside the Hummer, or near the pumps. Manuel had to be inside the store. But even if he was, he wouldn't be there long.

"Max!" Emma called again.

When he didn't stop, she darted after him. She'd taken off Preston's sunglasses while sitting in the shade, and the sudden brightness hurt her eyes. The hot tar filling the cracks moved beneath her feet with the consistency of Play-Doh; she could feel the heat rising from the blacktop. But all of that barely registered. She had to get her son. Keeping her gaze firmly affixed to the back of his head, she closed the distance between them, but she seemed to be running in slow motion.

At last she felt the cotton of Max's shirt beneath her grasping hand. She grabbed hold and managed to stop him, had nearly scooped him into her arms to head back the other way, when she heard the sound of an engine coming up from behind.

A glance at the mini-mart told her Manuel was on his way out. He stood just inside, his head bent as he did something to whatever he held in his hands. In a split second he could look up and it would all be over....

A brown minivan pulled into the lot, between her and the store. Tires screeched as the driver threw on the brakes and popped the transmission into Park. Then a door flew open and Preston got out. With a cry of surprise, Max was snatched from her and tossed inside.

"It's him," she managed to say.

"I know. Get in," Preston snapped as he jumped behind the wheel.

Emma scrambled into the back after her son, and the next thing she knew, they were careering onto the highway.

CHAPTER THIRTEEN

MANUEL SQUINTED through a pair of Oakley sunglasses at the back of the old van that had just torn out of the lot. What had happened? Had someone crashed into his car? Had he been robbed?

Hurrying over to his Hummer, he checked his license plate to see that his registration sticker was still intact, then looked inside. Nothing had been ransacked. Nothing was missing.

Strange…or maybe not. He'd never understand the stupid rednecks who lived in this godforsaken desert.

With a shrug, he pulled a cigarette from the package he'd just opened and leaned against the car to light up. When he got hold of Vanessa, he'd make her pay for all the trouble she'd caused him. He was tempted to dwell on exactly *how* he'd make her pay, but he needed to concentrate on what to do next.

He sucked the nicotine deep into his lungs, then slowly exhaled. His first impulse was to follow Hector to Vegas because he wanted to recover Vanessa and Dominick himself, or at least be on hand if Hector found them. But there was something about Vegas that didn't feel right. When he'd left the Hotel Nevada, he'd overheard two people talking about a diabetic boy who'd had an insulin reaction at the Starlight. Thinking it might be Dominick, he'd rushed over to the motel. Sure enough, according to everyone around, Vanessa and

Dominick had been there. They were gone when he arrived, but after telling him his son was okay, the manager mentioned the trucker. Only she'd given him a completely different description than the waitress at the hotel had. *Why?*

Putting out his cigarette, he climbed into the Hummer and pulled up to the turnout. He already had someone going to Vegas. He doubted Vanessa would really show up in St. George after using that town as a decoy. So if not Vegas or St. George, where might she be heading? His only other choice, if she was sticking to major highways instead of trying to hide in some backwater town in Nevada, was Utah.

He turned toward Salt Lake City. Hector could always call him if he was wrong.

EMMA GOT her crying son buckled up and moved into the passenger seat, where she immediately realized they were driving in the opposite direction than she'd assumed. "Where are we going?"

Preston checked his rearview mirror but didn't answer.

"Is he following us?" she asked.

"Not that I can see."

"That was close."

"Too close. Now we can't go directly to Salt Lake from here. If Manuel saw us at the gas station, we'd be too easy to spot along the road. We have to do something unexpected."

"Like backtrack?"

"Exactly."

"How far?"

"We'll go the seventy or so miles to Eureka."

"What's in Eureka?" As far as Emma could remember, not much besides a junkyard, a café, a gas station and a couple of quaint churches.

"From there we'll take 278 to Interstate 80. That way if he heads to Vegas, we're fine. If he goes to Utah instead, we should still be fine, because we won't be traveling on the same two-lane highway until Wendover. And we won't be arriving in Salt Lake at the same time. It's only a four-and-a-half hour drive from Ely."

"And the drive we're taking is…"

"I haven't figured it out. Probably eight or nine hours at least. But I think it's worth it to go around, don't you?"

She couldn't believe Preston was changing his precious agenda for their sake. She couldn't believe he'd come back for them at all. "I thought you were in a hurry to reach Iowa."

He scowled at the reminder. Then he glanced over his shoulder at Max, who was still crying for his father, and she figured he probably regretted it already.

Emma nearly shushed her son, then changed her mind and turned to stare out the window. She didn't have the heart to ask one more thing of Max. Of course he was sad. He didn't understand what was happening, only that he'd been ripped away from his father before he could even say hello.

She hated what leaving Manuel meant for her son. But every time she went over the situation, she could see no other way. Even if she could take parting with Max, she couldn't abandon him to Manuel and the future he'd have if she did. And Manuel was not the kind of man to share nicely.

"Max?" Preston said a few moments later. He adjusted the mirror so he could see her son, but Max wouldn't answer him. "I got something for you."

Surprised, Emma twisted in her seat to witness her son's reaction. Max still didn't answer, but his crying turned into an occasional hiccup.

"What is it?" he finally asked.

"Some candy I found at the grocery store when I was looking for the two of you."

"I can't have candy," he said.

He knew he could have candy occasionally, but he was too
busy sulking to acknowledge it.

"This is sugar-free," Preston told him.

Sugar-free didn't mean carbohydrate-free, and it was the
carbs that mattered with diabetes. But Emma wasn't about to
spoil the moment. Max had liked Preston from the start. This
small overture of friendship might just cheer him up.

"What kind of candy is it?" Max asked.

"Gummi Bears."

There was a slight pause. "I like Gummi Bears."

"I figured you might." Preston glanced at her. "Is it something he can have right now?"

It was dinnertime, but that was the least of Emma's worries. She nodded, and Preston took the bag out of a compart-
ment in the console.

Emma read the carbohydrate totals on the package so she
could include them in Max's meal plan, then opened the
Gummi Bears and passed them back without even attempting to ration.

At this windfall, her son's sniffling stopped completely.
Emma tried to smile at how easy to please a child could be.
One bag of candy, and the world was good again. But she
couldn't smile. She was fighting tears. She'd made it through
the close call at Garnet Mercantile, the panic of trying to get
back to the motel, her guilt over Max's insulin shock, the
nerve-wracking hours in that damn phone booth, and the fear
of coming nose-to-nose with Manuel at the Gas-N-Go, all
without a single tear. Yet she was crying now, over a simple
bag of candy.

It wasn't really the candy, though. It was the fact that Preston had thought of Max in that grocery store. It was having a friend when she needed one most.

"Thanks," she muttered, and averted her face so Preston wouldn't notice her watery eyes. She knew she hadn't fooled him when he touched her arm.

"You okay?"

She nodded.

"Emma?" He didn't sound convinced.

"I'm fine," she said. "How did you find us?"

"Amelia Granger."

She turned back, even though she was still trying to blink away the tears she didn't want Preston to see. "How did you come across her?"

"I knew you were searching for a car and that you hadn't gone to the dealership. So I called every ad in the paper. When I got to Amelia, she said she'd spoken to you earlier and was just getting ready to meet you at the Gas-N-Go."

"She never came."

"I told her to hang on so I could swing by and take a look at the car."

"What made you think I might've called about her ad? She was asking forty-eight hundred for her car. You don't think I have that much money, do you?"

"I started with the cheapest cars and worked my way up."

Which was pretty much what she'd done, so it probably hadn't take him long to realize he was on the right track. "I was going to trade her my earrings."

"How much are they worth?"

"Ten thousand dollars."

"It wouldn't have been a good trade."

"Why not? The car's a Mercedes."

He cocked a challenging eyebrow at her. "Do you know how many miles a Mercedes would have to have on it to cost so little?"

She didn't. Manuel had handled all their finances and brought home a new car for her almost every year. "The mileage wasn't mentioned in the ad."

"For good reason. That Mercedes had two hundred and fifty thousand miles on it and looked as though it's spent the past few years doubling as a ranch truck. My guess is it would've stranded you in the desert."

No wonder Amelia had been interested in her earrings. "So you came to get us instead," Emma said.

He didn't respond.

"How did you know Manuel was at the Gas-N-Go?"

"Max told me he drives a Hummer. It's not like you see one of those on every corner, especially out here."

Why *did you come back?* The biggest question of all remained unasked. But Emma didn't want to broach that subject yet. She knew it would lead to why he'd left them in the first place and she wasn't ready to talk about what had happened at the pool. She owed Preston an apology, but she'd only choke up if she tried to say the words right now.

"Have you had anything to eat since breakfast?" he asked.

Emma remembered the lunch the hotel manager had provided for Max. She'd been so concerned about Max getting enough to eat that she hadn't dared take so much as a bite of his sandwich. With Manuel in town, she hadn't dared go out, either.

"I haven't been hungry," she lied.

Preston's eyes swept over her, but the appreciation she'd noticed when he was in the Jacuzzi last night was gone. "You're too thin already."

It bothered Emma that he thought so, but she couldn't think of one good reason it should, so she shrugged off her reaction. "I had a few extra pounds to shed."

"Well, you can't afford to lose any more," he said. "We'll stop in Eureka for dinner."

ONCE HER STOMACH WAS FULL and Max had nodded off, Emma couldn't keep her eyes open. She felt guilty letting Preston do all the driving. Especially now that he was going so far out of his way. But she'd offered to help, and he'd refused.

As she leaned her head against the door, the hum of the motor and the *warp, warp, warp* of the tires worked better than a lullaby. She was afraid that after eating so late, Max's blood sugar might be too high to go through the whole night without more insulin. But she couldn't test him and make any adjustments until the fast-acting insulin she'd administered at dinner had done all it was going to do, which would take about three hours. Then she could get a better indication of whether or not she needed to give him another injection.

"I'll check him when we stop."

"What?" Preston said.

Emma hadn't realized she'd spoken aloud until he questioned her. Obviously, she was half-asleep already. "Nothing. Nudge me if you need a break."

Preston had been quiet at dinner but not resentful, like before. He'd helped with Max, insisted she eat more than she wanted and picked up the tab. Being with him was actually enjoyable—until the waitress told him they were a beautiful family. Then he withdrew.

"I'll be fine," he told her. "We'll get to Salt Lake before too long."

An Important Message from the Editors

Dear Reader,

Because you've chosen to read one of our fine romance novels, we'd like to say "thank you"! And, as a special way to thank you, we're offering you two more of the books you love so well, and a surprise gift to send you — absolutely FREE!

Please enjoy them with our compliments...

Pam Powers

Peel off Seal and Place Inside...

FREE GIFT SEAL

EDITOR'S FREE GIFT SEAL THANK YOU

How to validate your Editor's "Thank You" FREE GIFT

1. Peel off gift seal from front cover. Place it in space provided at right. This automatically entitles you to receive 2 FREE BOOKS and a fabulous mystery gift.

2. Send back this card and you'll get 2 brand-new *Romance* novels. These books have a cover price of $5.99 or more each in the U.S. and $6.99 or more each in Canada, but they are yours to keep absolutely free.

3. There's no catch. You're under no obligation to buy anything. We charge nothing—ZERO—for your first shipment. And you don't have to make any minimum number of purchases—not even one!

4. The fact is, thousands of readers enjoy receiving their books by mail from The Reader Service. They enjoy the convenience of home delivery...they like getting the best new novels at discount prices BEFORE they're available in stores... and they love their Heart to Heart subscriber newsletter featuring author news, special book offers, book reviews and much more!

5. We hope that after receiving your free books you'll want to remain a subscriber. But the choice is yours— to continue or cancel, any time at all! So why not take us up on our invitation, with no risk of any kind. You'll be glad you did!

GET A *Free* MYSTERY GIFT...

SURPRISE MYSTERY GIFT COULD BE YOURS ***FREE*** AS A SPECIAL "THANK YOU" FROM THE EDITORS

THE EDITOR'S "THANK YOU" FREE GIFTS INCLUDE:

▶ Two BRAND-NEW Romance Novels

▶ An exciting surprise gift

YES! I have placed my Editor's "thank you" Free Gifts seal in the space provided at right. Please send me 2 FREE books, and my FREE Mystery Gift. I understand that I am under no obligation to purchase anything further, as explained on the back and opposite page.

PLACE
FREE GIFTS
SEAL
HERE

193 MDL D37U   393 MDL D37V

FIRST NAME	LAST NAME

ADDRESS

APT.#	CITY

STATE/PROV.	ZIP/POSTAL CODE

► DETACH AND MAIL CARD TODAY! ►

(ED1-HQ-05) © 1998 MIRA BOOKS

Thank You!

The Reader Service — Here's How It Works:

Accepting your 2 free books and gift places you under no obligation to buy anything. You may keep the books and gift and return the shipping statement marked "cancel." If you do not cancel, about a month later we'll send you 3 additional books and bill you just $4.99 each in the U.S., or $5.49 each in Canada, plus 25¢ shipping & handling per book and applicable taxes if any.* That's the complete price and — compared to cover prices starting from $5.99 each in the U.S. and $6.99 each in Canada — it's quite a bargain! You may cancel at any time, but if you choose to continue, every month we'll send you 3 more books, which you may either purchase at the discount price or return to us and cancel your subscription.

*Terms and prices subject to change without notice. Sales tax applicable in N.Y. Canadian residents will be charged applicable provincial taxes and GST.

And then what? Emma wanted to ask, but after the day she'd spent, she couldn't face the answer. He'd drop them off at some motel, the way he had last night.

At least Salt Lake was a lot bigger than Ely. She and Max could hide there, take a day or two to rest, buy some underwear and a change of clothes, figure out how to move on.

"Any budget motel will do," she murmured.

"What?"

"When you drop us off." With a brief yawn, she fell into the first dreamless sleep she'd had in a long time.

WHEN YOU DROP US OFF...

Preston frowned at Emma's sleeping form and shook his head. He couldn't drop them off. He'd been trying to ever since they'd met, but something always brought them back together. At this point it'd be better to drive them all the way to Iowa. They might make the trip more difficult, slow him down a bit—this little detour was costing him probably five hours—but he felt the precaution was justified. He could make sure they arrived safely in the Midwest, and then, when they parted, there'd be no guilt, no second thoughts, no doubts.

He just hoped putting several states between them and the man he'd met at the Hotel Nevada would be enough. Manuel seemed pretty determined.

The miles to Carlin and Interstate 80 from Eureka passed quickly. When Preston pulled off at a truck stop on the edge of Elko, Emma woke up. She tested Max's blood and gave him more insulin while Preston filled the gas tank. Then Max and Emma fell back asleep and Preston drove on.

When they reached Wendover, it was midnight, and he was starting to get tired. His eyes burned, and his legs were cramping. But he decided to press on. Manuel could be any number of places, but if he'd headed to Salt Lake from Ely, he would've connected with Interstate 80 at Wendover. Although Preston hoped his roundabout approach had reduced any chance of meeting him, they could be on the same highway now, which made him cautious. Once they reached Salt Lake, he could relax. For one thing, he wasn't sure Manuel was going to Salt Lake or that he'd know they'd be stopping there. And finding someone in a mall was difficult enough; in a big city like Salt Lake, locating Emma and Max without a good lead would be next to impossible.

But they weren't in Salt Lake yet.

Passing through the salt flats seemed to take forever, partly because he was so exhausted and partly because the land deserved its name. It was absolutely flat—and monotonous. The only sign of civilization in well over an hour was the Morton Salt Factory, which sat out in the middle of nowhere, a dark, amorphous shape, half-hidden behind huge piles of salt waiting to be iodized and purified.

As they drew closer to Utah's capital, the Great Salt Lake came up on their left. Its marshy, shallow water reflected the moon's light, stretching as far into the distance as he could see, and he could smell mold. He remembered taking Dallas swimming in the Great Salt Lake, remembered how excited Dallas had been that he could float without a raft because the salt content created such buoyancy.

Tooele, a small community separated from Salt Lake City by a mountain range Preston couldn't recall the name of, appeared next, off to the right. He'd never visited Tooele, but judging by the small cluster of lights, it wasn't very big. He guessed it was like so many other Utah towns—originally settled by Mormon pioneers and organized on a grid, with small brick homes and plenty of well-tended gardens.

A smokestack stood at the point of the mountain like a sentry as they drove into Salt Lake City. He and Christy had occasionally visited the ski resorts in the area, but he hadn't expected to feel such a bittersweet rush of familiarity.

He rolled down his window and waved his hand in the cool night air, wishing he and Christy had moved here that one year they'd briefly considered it. They'd been newly married, just out of college and not quite settled yet. But after growing up in Minnesota, Preston was in no hurry to deal with more snowy winters. While attending UC Berkeley, he'd grown comfortable in the Bay Area. And Christy was originally from San José, so she wanted to be near her family. They'd decided to stay in California, where Preston was hired on at Ebert & Cummings. The year after that, he was named Rookie of the Year and Dallas was born. Three years later he'd made his first million, and he and Christy had moved into a lovely home in Half Moon Bay. They had a good marriage, a child they adored, more success than they'd ever anticipated. Life couldn't have been better.

Six months after that, the Wendells had moved in only three doors down.

Regret bit deeply as Preston rolled up his window. If only he'd insisted on that move to Utah…

Interstate 80 turned into a major freeway, which soon offered Preston several exits. He took 600 South. He and Christy used to stay in Park City, but that was an hour away in the wrong direction. Tonight, he headed into downtown Salt Lake in search of a hotel.

He was immediately presented with several to choose from. Turning left on West Temple, he stopped at the Hilton and left Emma and Max sleeping in the van while he went to the front desk. He didn't see any point in making her pay for a separate room. He was the one who'd chosen a hotel that was, no doubt, out of her price range, and they'd already shared a room once. He supposed another night or two in close company wasn't going to matter.

After checking in, he returned to the van to find that neither Max nor Emma had awakened.

Preston watched her sleep. How had it come to this? Just a few days ago, he was completely on his own without so much as a dog to look after. Now he had a woman and a child traveling with him.

Remembering how she'd staggered beneath her son's weight at Maude's Cozy Comfort Bungalows, he cursed softly. She'd never be able to lift Max right now, not without spending several minutes waking up and gathering her strength.

He swung his duffel bag over one shoulder, released Max's seat belt and lifted the boy into his arms.

As Max settled against his chest, a powerful yearning nearly brought tears to his eyes. The soft, boneless feel of the child's body, even the smell of good old-fashioned dirt in his hair and on his clothes, made Preston curve his other arm around to hold him close. God, he felt good. His weight was just right, nearly the same as Dallas's.

Preston buried his face in Max's neck. *I miss you, Dallas. I miss the messes you used to make, the food you used to waste, the loud cartoons that used to get on my nerves when I was trying to talk on the phone, the baseballs and soccer balls and basketballs all over the house—*

The van door creaked. Mortified to be caught at such a vulnerable moment, Preston jerked his head up. Emma was blinking at him, but she didn't act as though she'd seen him hugging her child. She was too busy struggling to get her bearings. "I—I didn't realize we'd stopped. Are we in Salt Lake?"

"Yes." He held her son farther away in an effort to stem the powerful emotions surging through him.

She stumbled out of the van and squinted at the building looming behind them. "This is…"

"A hotel," he supplied.

"It's the Hilton."

"That's right."

He expected her to say something about the cost of staying here, but she bit her lip instead.

Despite his irritation with the whole unfortunate situation, Preston found himself smiling. He couldn't believe he'd ended up in the middle of such a mess, that he'd walked away once and come back, that he was standing here carrying her kid so she wouldn't have to. But he had to admit she had the kind of face that could make a man do almost anything. And she had an elusive, beguiling innocence about her. No wonder Manuel was chasing her and Max all over Nevada.

She looked momentarily confused by his expression, but gave him a brief smile in return. Then she seemed to recognize that they had no reason to be staring at each other and glanced away.

"Okay, let me get a room," she said. "I'll take him in a minute so you can go."

"I've already paid for the room."

"I see. Well, that was nice of you. I'll pay you back."

"Just grab your purse and my laptop. I've already got my duffel bag."

Her sleepiness seemed to fall away as she riveted her eyes to his. "Your duffel bag? Your laptop?"

"I'm taking you and Max with me to Iowa," he said, and strode off ahead of her.

EMMA FELT GOOD for the first time in a long while. This classy hotel room was more the type of place she was accustomed to staying in. And although he was out of fresh laundry, Preston had lent her the T-shirt he'd worn today, along with the boxers she'd slept in last night, so she was temporarily rid of the pinching elastic of her swimsuit. Max's glucose levels were fine; he was sleeping soundly. Preston was in the opposite bed, only an arm's length away. And much as she didn't want to admit it, she liked being with him. He made her dream of escaping Manuel a stronger possibility. But that wasn't all. When she remembered the way he'd kissed her—or even smelled his scent on the T-shirt that had still been warm from his body when she pulled it on—she felt a riot of butterflies in her stomach. She'd never experienced anything remotely similar. Which meant she had to be careful not to get herself into another bad situation. She already knew Preston wasn't anything like Manuel, but he had his own issues, especially where Max was concerned.

After another ten or fifteen minutes, she realized she couldn't go back to sleep. She forced herself to try a little longer. She had no idea what was in store for them tomorrow. But now that she was awake, she'd started thinking about Juanita. What had Manuel done with her? Had Rosa heard anything?

Preston had rented a suite, with a bedroom on one side and a small kitchen and living area on the other. Slipping out of bed, she moved as silently as possible through the adjoining door and closed it softly behind her. Then she settled herself on the couch and picked up the phone.

CHAPTER FOURTEEN

SOMETHING PULLED Preston from sleep; he wasn't sure what. A restless night wasn't unusual. He always spent long hours thinking about Vince. But for now, he fought to keep the memories, and the emotions those memories evoked, at bay. He'd find the bastard. Soon. No need to rob himself of the few hours of sleep he'd been hoping to get.

Refusing to open his eyes, he rolled over. But the new position made little difference. The snatches of conversation, the signs he should've noticed but didn't, crowded close, bringing with them the anger and the guilt that were his constant companions.

Throwing an arm over his eyes, Preston shifted onto his back as a fresh spring day from three years ago played in his mind.

"Nice shot, buddy," Vince had said, laughing as he slapped Preston on the back. They were at the Presidio, only ten minutes from San Francisco, golfing among century-old eucalyptus and Monterey pine trees. "If I hang out with you long enough, maybe some of your luck will rub off on me."

Preston smiled. For someone who wasn't very good at the game, Vince sure liked to get out on the golf course. "Next time we'll have to bring the girls," he said.

Vince squatted to line up his next drive. "I don't know. They prefer to shop or get their nails done, don't they?"

Christy enjoyed golf. Preston would've invited her, but she'd volunteered to help in Dallas's class that day. "Christy's interested in a lot of things," he said.

After taking a couple of practice swings, Vince sidled up to the ball and adjusted his grip on the iron. "What do you say we go to Carmel next month?"

Vince and Joanie didn't have kids, so Preston knew they'd expect him and Christy to leave Dallas behind. While Christy's parents were generally good about babysitting, he and Christy didn't like leaving their son more than once or twice a year. "Isn't it hard for you to get away as often as you do?" Preston asked.

Vince shrugged. "I'm in a group. We can always go when one of the other doctors is on call, or I can trade with someone." *Thwack.* He hit the ball and they both watched it fly through the air.

"Not bad," Preston said as it dropped onto the green about ten feet short of his own.

Vince leaned on his driver. "See? Your luck's rubbing off on me already."

A cool Pacific breeze ruffled Preston's hair as he hefted his clubs over one shoulder and headed toward the next hole. They could have rented a golf cart, of course, but Preston preferred to walk.

"Are you and Christy still planning to barbecue with us this Saturday?" Vince asked.

Preston hadn't heard anything about it. "Are we supposed to?"

"I think Joanie talked to Christy."

"She hasn't mentioned it to me yet. Can we bring Dallas?"

"Of course."

"Sounds good."

Vince grinned. "We're so glad we moved here. It's like having a new lease on life."

Preston veered around a sand trap, and Vince trailed behind. "Where'd you live before?" he asked, looking back over his shoulder.

"Pennsylvania," Vince said, catching up.

"I don't think you've ever mentioned the town."

"Maybe not. Lockwood's barely more than a dot on the map. Most people've never heard of it."

"What was so bad about Lockwood?" Preston asked.

"It was okay at first—great. But then…" A shadow passed over Vince's face.

"Then…what?"

"One of my patients died. It happens, you know. Being a doctor, it's something I have to deal with. But afterward…" He shook his head. "I don't know. The place just…*haunted* me."

Preston's steps slowed. Generally Vince went on and on about how much he loved his profession. This was the first time Preston had heard him speak of the painful side of being a doctor. "How old was the patient?"

His friend blew out a long sigh. "That's the worst part. He was only seven."

Preston stopped walking altogether. "That *would* be hard. How'd he die?"

Vince's eyes darted to his face. "It was nothing *I* did."

The sudden defensiveness took Preston by surprise. "Of course not. I didn't say it was."

The placating grin that deepened Vince's dimples should've given him away, but somehow Preston had missed it. He'd been too damn gullible, too certain his friend was everything he appeared to be.

"Sorry. You know how it is," Vince had said. "A doctor feels responsible for saving the world and all that. Sometimes it's simply not possible."

Now the truth was so apparent Preston cringed to remember how easily he'd accepted Vince's rationale. "That's a fact of life, buddy," he'd said and started off again. "You can't let it keep eating at you."

"Joanie says the same thing."

"You should listen to her."

Poor Wendell... Tossing on the bed, Preston ground his teeth. How could Vince have painted *himself* as the martyr in what had happened to Billy Duran?

It was almost unbelievable. *Almost.*

He went back to that day....

At the next hole, Preston selected a putter. "You've shown me some of the letters you've received from grateful patients. I know you're a good doctor."

Vince nodded. "Yeah. I saved a little girl in the same town."

"Really?"

"She would've died had she been seeing anyone else."

"That's impressive."

Vince's chest swelled with obvious pride. "They did a big write-up about it in the paper."

"See? There you go." Preston placed his ball on the tee, settled himself beside it and tapped it to within a few inches of the hole.

"Not bad," Vince said.

Preston stood back, out of the way. "So how'd the little boy die?"

No answer.

"Vince?"

"Bacterial infection," he muttered.

Preston waited in silence for him to finish his put. Vince overshot the hole by nearly ten feet, then Preston birdied.

"Can't bacterial infections be treated with antibiotics?" Preston asked as he retrieved his ball from the cup.

He'd only been making conversation, but all hints of the good-natured friend Preston had known for the past months immediately disappeared.

"Don't you think I tried that?" Vince said. "What, are you a doctor now, Preston? It was spinal meningitis. For your information, that's a *very* serious disease."

And then Preston actually tried to placate him. "Calm down, Vince," he said. "I was only expecting you to tell me a little more about what happened. I'm sure you did everything you could."

"Damn right I did!"

Preston almost let the subject go, but even then, Vince's strange response had made him curious. "How'd the boy's parents take the news?"

"I don't want to talk about it anymore," Vince snapped.

A bump in the other room jolted Preston out of the memory. Rolling onto his side, he glanced at the clock on the nightstand. Light peeked through the cracks in the blinds, but he'd only been sleeping for three-and-a-half hours.

Three and a half crummy hours. Where was he, anyway? He traveled so much these days that all hotel rooms were beginning to look alike.

Rubbing his face, he leaned up so he could see the other bed. He wasn't alone, and that brought it all back to him. He was in Salt Lake. With a woman he couldn't seem to lose. And a diabetic boy who'd nearly died in his arms. Both of whom were being chased by an unstable man named Manuel who liked to burn others with his cigarettes.

He groaned and pulled a pillow over his head. And he'd thought his life was bad *before*.

The sound of a television reached his ears, coming from the living room. He scrutinized the opposite bed more carefully. Emma had to be in the living room because Max was still asleep.

Why wasn't she getting what rest she could? Was she okay?

Sliding out of bed, Preston walked toward the adjoining door. Yesterday had been pretty stressful. Maybe she was having a tough time dealing with the residual effects.

He remembered what she'd said to him that first night. *What if the fact that you've considered suicide doesn't scare me? Maybe I understand how you're feeling. Maybe I've been there.*

God, all he needed was for her to crack up.

As he quietly opened and closed the door, Emma sat up on the couch. "You're awake? Already?"

It was a lot brighter out here, bright enough that Preston had to squint against the light streaming through the windows. When he could see, he noticed that Emma's eyes still had purple smudges beneath them. Her hair was mussed, too, as though she'd spent a sleepless night. He could tell she was tired, stressed, but he didn't think she'd been crying.

Maybe life wasn't so bad. Even when she was wiped out, he enjoyed looking at her.

"I'm sorry if the TV woke you," she said. "I had no idea that whoever watched it last had turned it up high enough to shake the building. I turned it down as soon as I could."

"It's fine." Still a little groggy, Preston took in the way the soft cotton of his shirt molded to the naked body beneath, noticed the gentle sway of her breasts when she shifted position—and suddenly felt a great deal more alert.

Her expression told him she'd read his reaction, so he put some space between them by walking over to the kitchen for a drink. He didn't want her to think he expected anything from her. He was helping her for one reason and one reason only: to appease his conscience.

So where was his conscience when his imagination was painting vivid pictures of stripping away that T-shirt?

"Can't sleep?" he asked.

"I shouldn't have napped so long in the van."

He searched for another topic to occupy his mind. He didn't want to start thinking about sex. He'd spent a miserable night after Max had interrupted them in Ely, and he refused to ask for a second helping of the same kind of frustration.

Fortunately, they had plenty to discuss that should go far toward making him want to keep his pants on. "Tell me about Manuel."

Preston hadn't wanted to know anything about Emma's life, hadn't wanted to be drawn into the middle of whatever crises she faced. But that was pretty much a moot point now. He *was* in the middle of it. He figured it might be wise to learn a little more about the man who was causing all this trouble.

Emma turned the volume even lower and set the remote aside. "What do you want to know?"

"You said the two of you never married."

"We didn't."

"Why does he claim otherwise?"

Cocking her head slightly, she studied him for a moment. "You've talked to him?"

"We met, briefly."

She looked as though she didn't know whether to believe him. "Where?"

"In Ely. He was walking around flashing pictures of you and Max, telling everyone you were his wife and kid."

"Oh." She took a few seconds to absorb this information. "So you think I'm lying about being married?"

"No." Preston checked the refrigerator and found it stocked with wine, beer, soda and juice. He selected a bottle of sparkling apple cider. "He just made me curious about the dynamics of your relationship, that's all."

"It's complicated," she said, rubbing her forehead.

"Obsession usually is. A normal man would show more interest in reclaiming his son. Manuel seems completely consumed by you."

She pulled her legs to her chest and wrapped her arms around them. "He doesn't relate to small children. And he isn't pleased that Max is…less than perfect."

His juice made a hissing sound when he twisted off the cap. "How's Max less than perfect?"

She glanced up at him again. "He has diabetes."

"So? Max is—" Preston caught himself. He'd been about to say "great," but that somehow committed him to an opinion he really didn't want to know he held. "A good boy," he finished. "How could anyone be disappointed in a son like him?"

"To Manuel, he's damaged goods. And yet Manuel loves him fiercely, so fiercely that he drives Max to be the best at everything."

"That sounds like an issue of pride—or possession. Far more selfish than love," Preston said.

"You're probably right. Manuel cares a great deal about appearances, about making sure others perceive him as handsome, intelligent, successful…perfect. He wanted me to be perfect, and Max, too."

Preston couldn't see how Manuel could find any fault with

either of them. "Then why didn't he marry you? Make Max legitimate?"

"I told you. His family wouldn't accept me."

"There's got to be more to it than that."

"It was mainly his mother. She's got some serious jealousy issues with her sons, especially Manuel. She's still married to Manuel's father, but she completely runs his life, and she doesn't respect him because of it. Manuel is stronger, more driven, like her. She admires that, sees him as everything she's ever wanted in a man."

Preston raised his eyebrows. "Sounds a little too Freudian for me."

"It is. I knew she hated me the moment I met her. She couldn't stand to see another woman in Manuel's life. I think she feared how much he seemed to care about me. And she rejected Max because she thought that having Manuel's son gave me too strong a hold on Manuel. So she made Manuel feel guilty for falling in love with someone who wasn't of the same background, made him feel he was letting his family down or not taking enough pride in his heritage. And, of course, she found fault with everything Max and I ever did."

"But Max is her grandson."

"To her, he's simply an extension of me. A rival. She treated us as though we weren't good enough for Manuel and tried to convince him of that. What he probably doesn't realize is that she wouldn't approve of anyone."

"So she's as selfish as he is," Preston said, leaning on the counter. "Because, from what I'm hearing, it's all about him."

"It didn't used to be that way. But, with his mother's encouragement and example, the ambition and drive that once attracted me grew out of all proportion, slowly destroying his better qualities," she said. "Until he gets older, Max is just another weapon Manuel can use against me, the most reliable in his arsenal."

"What's the point of forcing you to be with him?" Preston asked. "If you don't want to be there, he doesn't really have anything."

"In his mind, I belong to him, like his clothes, or his car, or his house. He doesn't feel he should have to let me go simply because I want to leave."

"I know this guy isn't normal, but what kind of man—"

"It's possession, like you said. An ego thing, a compulsion to conquer, to own," she interrupted.

So Manuel was your basic nutcase, and Preston might be risking his own safety by getting involved. He waited for that small piece of information to diminish his overactive libido—but it didn't seem to make any appreciable difference. Maybe that was because self-preservation hadn't been a real priority of late. Or else he wanted Emma even more than he'd thought. "You were attracted to this guy because he had ambition?"

"Among other things. He wasn't like this when I first met him." She combed her fingers through her long hair, which fell straight and shiny around her shoulders. "When we first met, he was away from his family. He was younger, more flexible. We were going to school, having fun, falling in love. But once we moved to San Diego, he started…working in the family business. He…changed."

"What's the family business?"

He assumed she'd say they owned a restaurant or a dry cleaner or something, but she didn't. She sighed and said, "You don't want to know."

He finished half the bottle of juice, wondering if he should take her at her word. But he'd always been a glutton for punishment. "Tell me anyway."

"They claim to import marble from Mexico."

Claim seemed to be the operative word. "But..."

"I think they import something besides marble."

"Something like meth or cocaine?"

She nodded. So she was talking about drugs. She thought Manuel's family was involved in drug trafficking.

Preston tried that on for size. Now he was standing between a nutcase who lived and moved in the violent underworld of the Mexican mafia, and a woman and child. Nice. The perfect position, actually—for a man with a death wish. For the past two years Preston hadn't been so crazy about living, but he didn't intend to leave this world without Vince.

He dropped his head in his hand. *Now why did I track them down in Ely?*

Because he couldn't abandon them, or Emma and Max would face the threat of Manuel alone.

"I can tell you're excited to hear this," she said wryly.

He peered up at her. "Ecstatic."

"I won't blame you if you want to go on without us."

Maybe he should've asked some of these questions before. Maybe then he would've been *able* to go on without them.

But he doubted it. And it was too late now. He'd already met Manuel—and he wasn't about to let him or anyone else harm Emma or Max. "What about the police?"

"You'd think they'd be able to help, wouldn't you?"

He straightened. "Theoretically."

"I guess the practical application poses a problem. Manuel has a big family, many of whom aren't even U.S. citizens. And drug smuggling is a tough thing to prove, at least on his level. It's usually only the carriers who are caught."

This kept getting better and better. Yet they were alone in a hotel room with the memory of Ely between them. The sudden image of pressing Emma into the couch as he kissed her made Preston clear his throat before taking a sip of his juice.

Good thing he was a man who knew what was important.

Retrieving another bottle of juice from the refrigerator, he held it out to her. Emma should be eating more nutritiously. She was wearing herself too thin and needed to be healthy if she was eventually going to make it on her own.

"They charge six bucks each for these," she protested.

"Don't worry about it." Opening the bottle, he carried it over to her and sat in the opposite chair. Ever since he'd noticed her burn, he'd been wondering about something, but he was almost afraid to ask. "You said Manuel expects Max to be perfect."

"He does."

"Is he abusive to him?"

"Not abusive. He's hard on him, often demanding that he behave more like a ten-year-old than a five-year-old. He overreacts when Max can't perform, and he's *way* too protective."

"But he's never hurt Max physically?"

"No. At least not yet."

"Was he heading in that direction?"

She leaned her chin on her knees, which she still held to her chest, looking young and vulnerable in her dishevelment. "He was certainly heading in that direction with me."

"Has he done more than burn you?"

"Only in the worst of our fights."

Only. Preston wished he'd decked Manuel when he had the chance. "What did you fight about?"

"Me getting a job. Me pushing for more freedom. Me wanting some access to our money."

"What were you fighting about when he burned you?"

"You can't possibly want to hear the dirty details of—"

Actually, his interest surprised him. "Why not? I might as well know what we're up against."

She seemed to consider his words. "We were fighting about sex."

Okay, so maybe he shouldn't have asked. Not if he wanted to stop fantasizing. But a statement like that absolutely begged a response. "What about it?"

A gleam of defiance entered her eyes. "I wouldn't let him tie me up. I couldn't do it anymore. I *hate* it."

The vehemence in her voice told him how much. It made him go cold and lethal inside to imagine Manuel forcing her. "Did he hurt you when he tied you up?" he asked softly.

She stared at the carpet. "Sometimes he showed…flashes of cruelty."

The knots in his stomach didn't ease at her tempered reply. "By…"

She shook her head, refusing to get specific. He knew he was probably better off not hearing the details—but he did need some kind of reassurance that she was okay despite what Manuel had done.

Moving to the couch, he took her hands. Her fingers felt slim and cool, and he immediately wanted to warm them. "So he liked feeling powerful?"

She looked at his thumb as he made a small circle around the burn on her wrist. "He liked knowing I couldn't say no, that he had free rein to do anything, regardless of how I felt."

"Bastard!"

At his curse, she glanced up. "He is a bastard. And I couldn't stay with him any longer."

It was little wonder. From the sound of it, Manuel was one sick son of a bitch. "Max told me his real name is Dominick."

"It is."

"And yours is…"

"Vanessa."

"Vanessa," he repeated.

"I'm sorry for dragging you into this," she said with a frown. "It's not fair to you. I know that."

He wanted to lean forward and press his lips to hers, to taste her as he'd done before. But after what she'd just told him, he doubted she'd enjoy it. "Manuel's mother must really be something," he said.

"She is. One minute, she's praising him, the next she's belittling him. They have an odd love-hate relationship. Sometimes I wondered if he wasn't striking out at her through me. In any case, his brothers don't treat their wives much better. And—"

Impulsively he brushed his lips across her knuckles. "And?"

She seemed to lose her train of thought for a second as she watched. "Um…I trigger some reaction that frustrates and infuriates him. Because of my refusal to love him the way he wants me to, I guess."

"He could control every other aspect of your life, but he couldn't control that."

"It became almost a game, to withhold the one thing he wanted most."

The more she talked, the more protective he felt. Preston supposed he should quit while he was ahead—but he couldn't. "How long has it been since you considered yourself in love with him?"

"Years. So you can see how that emotional distance might drive someone crazy." She gave him a hesitant smile, her eyes once again watching his lips move over her fingers.

"It sounds to me as though he didn't deserve your love."

She shrugged. "Sometimes I wonder which came first.

Did he feel me pulling away and grow panicked and grasping? Or did he start to smother me first?"

Preston didn't care which it was. If she wanted to break things off with Manuel, she had the right to do so. "Why didn't you leave him years ago?"

"I tried once."

"What happened?"

"He came after me, and—well, let's just say it made him even more paranoid. After that, it was almost impossible to get any freedom or money. And I had Max to think about."

"You mean Dominick?"

"I mean Max," she said. "We've left Vanessa and Dominick behind for good."

"You don't think of yourself as Vanessa anymore?"

"No. I don't want to look back. If I can help it," she added softly.

He forced himself to release her and was somewhat surprised when she let her hand linger on his leg. "How long do you figure you'll have to run?"

Her smile was sad. "Who knows? Manuel's not a man who accepts failure easily."

"But you'll be okay in the midwest, right?" He needed to believe there was an end in sight.

"Sure. As safe as anywhere."

Her answer wasn't too comforting. Stifling a grimace, he got up so he wouldn't be tempted to touch her again. "Don't you have any parents or siblings who can help you?"

"Only my mother and sister are left. They both live in Phoenix, but I can't go to them."

"Why not?"

"That's where I went last time."

"I see." He shoved a hand through his hair. "And I suppose a restraining order wouldn't work."

"There isn't a paper in the world with the power to stop Manuel. All he has to do is take Max and flee to Mexico, and there's nothing the police can do."

"Would he leave you here?"

"There's no telling what he'd do to me. The woman who helped me leave just went missing. I tried to call her last night, but I couldn't get hold of her or her sister. I'm hoping they're still alive."

Still *alive?* Preston blew out a long sigh. He'd heard enough for one morning. "We'll get to Iowa and decide what to do from there, okay?"

"Okay," she said.

"I'm going to see if I can grab some more sleep." He started past her for the bedroom but she caught his wrist. When he looked down, he felt another surge of desire but fought it back.

"I owe you an apology," she said.

"For what?"

"I…I should've told you about Max's diabetes. I would have, but I was afraid you'd leave us. I'm sorry."

"Forget it." He couldn't resist running a finger down the side of her face.

She closed her eyes, as if she welcomed his touch. But he knew better than to take it any further. Their lives were screwed up enough already.

Dropping his hand, he walked away.

EMMA HEARD THE DOOR close and covered her eyes. She'd wanted Preston to hold her, to pull her tired body into his arms, enfold her in his strength. Because she hadn't been able to reach Rosa, she was more worried than ever. But it wasn't just that. She kept imagining what it might be like to kiss him again now that she trusted him a little more.

But she didn't want to get involved with another man. She was going to establish her freedom, live in a little house, teach school and take care of Max—and never have to answer to anyone again.

Her heart raced at the memory of Max dashing across the pavement toward Manuel's Hummer at the Gas-N-Go. If Preston hadn't shown up when he did...

Why *had* he come back for them? She still hadn't asked. And his behavior provided no clues. He hadn't indicated that he expected anything in return for his help. So far, he hadn't even accepted money for food or gas.

Did he still want what she'd offered him at the pool? At times she saw him looking at her and thought so. But he was sending conflicting signals. He'd just had the opportunity to make an advance, yet he'd walked away. Again.

She wondered if he knew that his reluctance to press her made her want him. It was a subtlety she and most other women could easily appreciate—and one Manuel would never understand.

CHAPTER FIFTEEN

LATER THAT MORNING, a small hand tapped Preston's bare arm, making his heart feel light. He was in the bedroom of his home in Half Moon Bay, with Christy sleeping beside him, and Dallas standing by the edge of his bed—everything as it should be.

Blindly, he scooped his son into bed with him, as he had so many times before, and smiled contentedly when Dallas's arms closed around his neck.

"Hi, Preston."

Preston? He dragged his eyes open, and reality intruded with all the finesse of a sledgehammer.

Immediately he let go and slid to the other side of the bed, where he buried his head in the blankets. It wasn't Max's fault that he wasn't Dallas. Max had responded sweetly, innocently, to Preston's brief show of affection. But the disappointment tasted too bitter for Preston to swallow all at once. He wanted to push Max out of his bed, his life. He wanted to forget—

"Preston?" Max said.

Preston gritted his teeth as he wrestled with the emotions that had welled up, seemingly out of nowhere. *Don't move any closer to me.* "What?"

"Where's my mom?"

"Watching TV."

"No, she's not."

Max's response made Preston forget his inner battle long enough to prop himself up on one elbow. He listened but couldn't hear the TV. He couldn't see Emma anywhere in the room, either. Or the bathroom.

His pulse sped up. "Are you sure?"

"Yeah."

Had she left? Had Manuel found her?

Hell! Preston bolted out of bed, but just as he reached the living room, Emma came in, carrying a bag of groceries.

Her eyes went wide when she saw him. Then her gaze slid down his body, and he realized that he was standing there in his boxer briefs.

"You're up." The tinge of pink that stained her cheeks told him she'd noticed his state of undress, but he didn't care if it made her uncomfortable. He would've been more discreet if she hadn't scared the life out of him.

He drew a deep breath. "Where'd you go?"

"There's a little grocery store down the street."

Scratching his bare chest, he scowled. "You frightened Max."

"Max?" she said, arching one eyebrow.

Preston felt his scowl darken at her knowing tone, but he didn't have a chance to say anything before Max came bounding toward her from behind him.

"Mommy!"

Preston took the groceries in time for Emma to catch her son's running leap.

"I expected to get back before either of you woke up," she said. "The store's literally two minutes away."

"It'd be two minutes too long if something went wrong," Preston grumbled, and headed back to the bedroom. The stock market opened at six o'clock. He was running late today, but he stubbornly decided to do what he could.

He booted up his computer but he couldn't concentrate. Emma and Max's voices filtered back to him. They were talking about aardvarks, for whatever reason, and Preston found himself straining to hear. Apparently aardvarks were nocturnal animals that lived in Africa and were good diggers. They burrowed into nests of termites or ants, then shoved their sticky tongues inside to eat the insects.

How long had it been since he'd thought about an aardvark? Or a triceratops? Or any of the other things a child typically loved? The simple curiosities that had nothing to do with anger and revenge and isolation?

He stared at his amber cursor. As much as Max reminded him of the past and the pain, there were moments Preston found his childish voice comforting.

"Preston!" Emma called. "Breakfast is ready."

Preston told himself he should stay away from them and continue working. There was something about Emma and Max that threatened to break through all the layers of bitterness that had insulated him for two years. He found that almost as frightening as it was appealing. But the smell of eggs and bacon and homemade biscuits tipped the scale.

Getting up from the desk, he strode reluctantly into the kitchen, as if Emma's invitation hadn't just given him the very opportunity he'd been looking for.

"Hungry?" she said when she saw him.

He nodded, and she dished him up a plate. He carried it to the table while she recovered a small black bag from her purse.

Preston had seen her use this bag before, but only in a peripheral way while he was going off to the restroom or pumping gas. This was the first time he was actually close enough to examine its contents.

Picking up his fork, he pretended to concentrate on his

breakfast, but couldn't help watching Emma and Max. Especially when she drew insulin out of three different bottles and handed her son a filled syringe.

Max had to inject himself? At five years old?

"Can I do it in my stomach?" Max asked.

Emma frowned. "We decided not to do it there anymore, remember?"

"Why not?"

"You know why."

Preston didn't. He wished she'd explain, but he was too busy faking preoccupation to ask.

"So? It'll be okay," Max said.

"It's not okay. The doctor told us we have to rotate the site, and we decided it was best to listen, right?"

Preston saw some cottage-cheese-like deposits on Max's stomach and thought he could probably guess why it was important to switch sites. Max had already done enough damage there.

"What about your leg?" Emma asked.

Max shook his head.

"I could put it in your bottom," she suggested.

"Mo-om!" He flushed bright red as he glanced at Preston. Preston tried not to smile at his embarrassment.

Emma sighed. "Do you want me to put it in your arm?"

"No, that's only for little shots."

"Little shots?" Preston asked, unable to remain silent.

"The ones at lunch and dinner have less insulin in them," Emma explained. She turned back to Max. "If you won't let me do it in your arm, you're going to have to try your leg."

"Not my leg."

"Max…"

"Okay." The way he puffed out his cheeks and stared at the needle made Preston wish he could take the shot for him. He could tell by the empathy in Emma's voice that she felt the same.

Pulling up the right pant leg of his shorts, Max pinched a roll of flesh on the inside of his thigh. "Here?"

"That looks good," Emma said.

Grim determination claimed his young face. He aimed the syringe at the site—but pulled back before the needle could pierce the skin. "I can't," he said.

The dejection in his voice made Preston burn with guilt for his earlier reaction to the little guy. Max was a good kid who coped with a lot. He didn't deserve Preston's resentment, hadn't done anything to earn it.

"Go ahead and put it in your stomach, then," Emma said, and went back to her cooking as if she couldn't bear to watch. "Just...just try to find a new spot, okay?"

Preston's fork dangled between his mouth and his plate as Max stuck the needle in his stomach and pushed the plunger. The boy counted to three, then pulled the needle out and carried the empty syringe to his mother.

"Good job," she said, giving him a hug. "You're so brave, Max. I've never met a boy so brave."

Preston kept his eyes on his breakfast, but he had to agree. Max might not be Dallas. But he was no ordinary boy.

"WHERE ARE YOU?"

At the sound of Rosa's voice, Manuel sank onto the bed in the motel room he'd rented in Wendover and used the towel he'd draped around his neck to mop up the sweat dripping from his hair. Because he wasn't even sure he was traveling in the right direction, he'd stopped to sleep and work out, hoping Hector would find Vanessa in Vegas. But Hector hadn't seen any sign of her.

Could there be better news already? "Why do you need to know where I am?"

"I think she called again last night."

"Then the question is, where is *she?*"

"I don't know."

"What?"

"I—I missed her call."

"How?" He tossed his towel aside, onto the floor.

"I couldn't bear to talk to her. She hung up without leaving a message, but the number she was calling from came up on my caller ID," Rosa added quickly. "Maybe you can call her, convince her to come back to you."

The area code should tell him something, at least. And maybe he could reach her. Telephone contact was preferable to no contact at all. He'd been dying to speak to her ever since she'd left. What did she think she was doing? Did she really believe this would improve matters between them? Now he'd never be able to trust her again. She'd stolen from him, turned his own hired help against him, lied to him....

Closing his eyes, he took a cleansing breath. "What's the number?"

Rosa gave it to him, and he quickly jotted it down.

"How— How's my sister?" Rosa ventured.

"You'll find out soon enough," he snapped, and ended the call. Once he found Vanessa and the son of a bitch she was with, Rosa wouldn't matter anymore.

The buttons beeped loudly in his ear as he punched in the number he'd written down.

"Good morning. Thank you for calling Hilton Salt Lake City. This is Trina. How may I direct your call?"

The *Hilton?* Rage rose inside Manuel like a great tidal wave. She was staying at a hotel, a *nice* hotel, a high-rise. Which meant that whoever she was with probably wasn't some trucker. Most truckers didn't pull into a fancy hotel. They slept in the cab of their trucks or rented an economy motel.

"Where, exactly, are you located?" he asked.

"We're at twenty-five fifty-five South West Temple."

"Can you give me directions?"

"Let me transfer you to our concierge. I'm sure she can help you."

Elevator music played in the background. Unable to sit still, he began to pace. Where did Vanessa meet her companion? Were they making love right now? Was she laughing at Manuel as she drew another man inside her?

"This is Megan. What can I do for you today?"

"I need you to tell me how to get to the hotel. I'm coming east on I-80."

"No problem, sir."

Manuel scribbled down the directions, which were simple enough, then tossed the pen aside. He shouldn't have stopped last night. If only he hadn't started second-guessing himself. "How long a drive is it?" he asked before the concierge could hang up.

"About two hours."

Two. He felt fairly certain that if he hurried, he could cut that down to one and a half.

PRESTON SCOWLED at his wet toothbrush. There were a lot of things he was willing to share with Max and Emma, but his toothbrush wasn't one of them. Not because he was worried about germs. Well, maybe he was worried about

Max's germs. There was no telling what a boy his age might put in his mouth. But with Emma it was the intimacy of sharing such a personal article that bothered him. They needed to safeguard the barriers between them, not pull them down.

He thought of calling her into the bathroom to tell her so, but when he saw her swimsuit hanging on the towel rack, he didn't have the heart. She'd had to use his toothbrush. She didn't have one of her own. She didn't even have underwear.

Cursing the night he'd stopped at the Cozy Comfort Bungalows, he brushed his own teeth—and tried to pretend he didn't actually like the idea that his toothbrush had been inside Emma's mouth.

"Are you ready to go?" he called into the kitchen as he packed his things.

"I was hoping to give Max a bath before we left. Do you think we have time?" she called back.

He was anxious to get on the road, to get to Vince. But he supposed an hour wasn't going to make much difference. He could do some work, catch up on his e-mail, make a few phone calls while he waited for Max. Or he could leave the room, and pick up the items Max and Emma needed so they wouldn't have to stop later.

Grabbing his wallet from the dresser, he walked into the kitchen, where Emma was examining a sheet of paper.

"What's that?" he asked.

She immediately folded it and stuck it in her purse. "Nothing important. Should I draw the bath or wait until later?"

"Go ahead and bathe the beast. I'm going out for a bit. I'll be back soon."

"What did you call me?" Max asked, tearing his attention away from the picture he was coloring.

Preston smiled. He didn't know why he'd suddenly come up with that nickname. Except, with Max's stocky build and fearless approach to all the shots he put in his stomach, it seemed to fit. "Beast."

Max wrinkled his nose. "That means animal."

"Nicknames aren't literal."

"What does 'literal' mean?"

"You're big and strong and brave like a beast, aren't you?"

"Yeah…"

"So why not call you Beast?"

Max seemed to consider the suggestion. "Okay!" he said, and the way his chest swelled with pride made Preston laugh.

"The male ego in action," Emma murmured. "It starts young." But she was wearing a faint smile and Preston grinned back at her.

"That ought to keep him tough, poor kid," he muttered. "How's he doing?"

She seemed startled by the question. "Fine."

"Have you tested him since breakfast?"

"No. Unless we have some reason to believe he's too high or too low, we only test at mealtimes, before bed and during the night."

After the incident at the pool, Preston couldn't help watching Max with a certain fearful expectation, wondering whether he might have another insulin reaction. "How often does he go low?"

"It can happen anytime, unless we're careful."

Great. Preston shook his head as he scooped his keys off the counter. He had to pick up a woman whose kid could keel over at any moment.

"But it doesn't happen very often," she added.

Thank God. "I'm going shopping. What do you want me to get?"

"I need a toothbrush."

He gave her a meaningful glance. "That much I know."

She blushed. "Sorry. I looked for one at the little grocery store this morning, but they didn't carry them. And I rinsed yours with hot water when I was done," she offered in a conciliatory tone.

His gaze dropped to her full, soft lips. With a bit of encouragement, he'd show her how little the hygiene issue really bothered him. But he knew that wouldn't be good for her. Their futures were too uncertain. "I'll get you each one," he said. "What else?"

"I'm dying for some underwear. I guess I could get that later, but maybe you wouldn't be too embarrassed to pick up a hairbrush, some hair gel, mascara and lip gloss? I feel like I've been camping in the wilderness for a week."

He cocked a wary eyebrow at her. "You want me to buy lip gloss?"

"You're right," she admitted. "It's something I can do without. I just—"

"You look great the way you are."

She straightened as though the compliment took her by surprise. But he didn't know why it would. With her long, silky hair, golden skin and big blue eyes, she didn't need any enhancements.

She did need underwear, though. Knowing she wasn't wearing any was proving more than a little distracting.

He cleared his throat. "What about snacks for the car?"

She seemed as eager as he was to take the conversation in a different direction. "We could always use snacks. Max is supposed to have them mid-morning, mid-afternoon, and between dinnertime and bedtime."

"What should I buy?"

"Fruit. Power bars. Small packages of crackers and cheese. Baby carrots. Anything around twenty-two grams of carbohydrates per serving."

"It has to be that specific?"

"Following a tight meal plan helps control his blood sugar."

He remembered telling her a couple of doughnuts weren't going to kill Max and felt a flicker of resentment that she hadn't been honest with him then. Unfortunately, it wasn't quite enough resentment to make him stop thinking about her lack of underwear.

"I know what happens when he goes low. What happens when he goes too high?"

Max piped up with the answer. "My eyes get all blurry, and I feel like I'm gonna throw up." Doubling his fists, he began to shadowbox. "Sometimes I want to break something!"

Preston looked to Emma for an explanation.

"He never hurts anything," she said. "It's just that blood sugar affects mood. Whenever he gets a dark glower on his face or talks aggressively, I know he needs to be tested."

Diabetes affected every aspect of his life, and Emma's, too, because of the constant care.

"How do you spell your name?" Max asked, his hand poised to write at the top of his picture.

Preston spelled his name slowly and watched as Max did his best to form the letters. The crooked result touched a painful spot deep in Preston's chest. At the same time, it made him smile.

"This is for you," Max announced.

Remembering the pictures Dallas had colored for him, Preston briefly closed his eyes. He'd never expected to get another picture of a red and black Bugs Bunny. But he forced himself to walk over and give Max's gift the attention it deserved. "It's nice," he said, and squeezed his shoulder.

The way Max beamed with pleasure made the effort worthwhile.

"I'll be back soon," he told Emma, starting for the door.

She grabbed her purse and followed him. "Here's twenty bucks. If the total comes to more than that—"

He held up a hand. "I've got it covered." Such minor expenses meant nothing to him. He just wanted to deliver Max and Emma safely to Iowa—and to know they'd remain safe when he drove away. "I'll put out the Do Not Disturb sign. I doubt You-Know-Who is even in Salt Lake, but just in case, don't open the door to anybody."

PRESTON STOOD in the cosmetics aisle of Smith's Grocery and scratched his head. He'd already collected toothbrushes, toothpaste, deodorant, face wash, a pair of flip-flops he thought would be more comfortable for Emma than the stiff leather sandals she was wearing now, a Jazz Basketball T-shirt—also for Emma, because he was out of clean laundry to lend her—and a whole basketful of snacks. But he couldn't figure out what kind of makeup to buy. Picking up a tube of mascara had sounded simple enough. Until he saw that there were at least ten different kinds. Pink with a green lid. Black. White. Brown. Gray. One called Brownish-black, one called Very Black, one called Blue…

Blue? Maybe it was some sort of code word women understood but men didn't, because he didn't think he'd ever seen a woman wearing blue mascara. He wasn't sure he *wanted* to.

He wished he'd brought his cell phone so he could call Emma. But he'd left it charging at the hotel.

With a helpless glance at the cosmetics, he decided to leave. He had to visit a department store to get Emma and Max some underwear. Maybe he'd be able to find a salesgirl who could help him with cosmetics, as well.

CROSSROADS MALL, which was only a few blocks from the hotel, was already packed with back-to-school shoppers.

Preston skirted a group of teenagers with spiky hair, tattoos and black lipstick standing in front of a skater shop, carelessly blocking traffic, to find the directory near the escalators. The smell of fresh-baked cinnamon rolls drifted up from the food court one floor below as he scanned the list of stores.

Nordstrom. Perfect. They'd have underwear.

He headed toward the mall's anchor store. But when he spotted a small, elegant lingerie shop along the way, he hesitated. Racks and racks of bustiers, lacy bras with matching bikini underwear, thongs, transparent nightgowns and silk robes lined the walls and display tables.

"Hi, there. Can I help you?" An attractive young woman hovered at the entrance.

"I don't think so." This place went well beyond basic underwear....

"We have a sale on right now," she said, her voice enticing. "Buy two bras and get a third for free."

How many bras would Emma need? With the sale, he might as well shop here—and get more than one or two.

"Sounds good," he said. "I'll buy four."

"That was easy."

She laughed and waved him into the store. "I'm Felicia. And I'm sure we can find something you'll appreciate."

Something *he* would appreciate? He wasn't here to buy

something *he'd* appreciate. At least in the way this salesgirl meant it. "Just a bunch of basic bras and panties will be fine," he told her.

"You're buying lingerie and you don't want it to be pretty?"

He didn't want knowing what Emma was wearing under her clothes to drive him crazy. On the other hand, it did seem rather wasteful, even rude, to buy her something ugly on purpose. Especially when he saw so many things here that would look beautiful on her.

"Okay," he relented. "Something pretty, but nothing too… bare." Or he'd drive himself crazy *and* come across like a lech when he gave them to her.

Felicia guided him around a rack of robes to a whole section of bras and underwear. "First of all, what colors do you like?"

He studied the mannequins on display. "White." With Emma's tan, white was the obvious choice. "And black," he added, thinking black would be almost as sexy.

"So we'll go with four white bras, and then you can get two black ones free. Okay?"

He nodded.

"Now let's check out the different styles we have available."

She presented him with several kinds. "This one has an underwire to lift and support." She motioned to show how it lifted, and Preston pictured Emma's breasts. The way they filled out her swimming-suit top. The way they curved and swayed ever so gently beneath his T-shirt….

The vision caused a physical reaction he'd rather not have in public. He shoved his hands into his pockets in an attempt to camouflage it.

"This other one snaps in front," Felicia went on, thankfully oblivious. "Then there's the contouring one. It has a little padding, in case your wife or lady friend would like something to make her look a little fuller."

Emma didn't need any padding. Personally, he liked the sheer bra with the underwire. "Let's go with the first one."

"Maybe you should get a few of these and then a few of the one that hooks in front."

Sounded reasonable. "Fine."

"Good. What size?"

He knew he could cup his hand to show her exactly how big Emma was. He'd definitely noticed. But he thought that might be too crude. He tried to translate what he'd seen of Emma to what he remembered from when he was married. Christy had been a "C." Which would make Emma...

"A small 'D'," he said.

The salesgirl laughed. "A 'D' isn't small. Are you sure?"

"She's bigger than a 'C.' But she's not very big around the ribs."

"So you think maybe a thirty-four?"

He hoped that was close enough. "Yeah."

"Now for the underwear."

Preston was already feeling a little warm. And he got a whole lot warmer when she brought over a handful of thongs. One had white lace edges. Another had metal heart cutouts right where the strings attached to the scrap of fabric in front. A sheer black pair especially appealed to him.

Somehow, he hadn't imagined this turning into such an erotic experience.

"Maybe I should go with a more conservative style," he said.

The salesgirl obviously didn't like this response. "Then she'll have underwear lines."

"So? At least she'll have underwear. These are..."

"What everyone's wearing," she finished.

He tried, unsuccessfully, *not* to paint a mental picture of Emma standing before him, wearing the black thong while he kissed her neck, her breasts, her stomach…. "Aren't they uncomfortable?" he asked in an attempt to refocus.

"You get used to it," she said with a shrug.

"Why bother?"

Her lips curved into a suggestive smile and her voice dropped. "Because, deep down, it's every woman's wish that someday she'll have a man just like you looking at her with the stunned, slack-jawed expression you had on your face when I handed you the first pair."

When he was imagining Emma… He couldn't even conceal his interest in her from a stranger.

He tossed the underwear back on the counter. "Give me something my mother would wear."

Her lip came out in a pout. "Really? You only live once."

What she didn't realize was that he hadn't been living at all. Not for two years. If he saw so much as a hint of Emma in any of this thonglike underwear, there wouldn't be a shower cold enough to help him. Besides, he was the one paying for this stuff. That entitled him to get the ones he wanted… er…the ones he *didn't* want, right?

Wait…why was he buying something he didn't want?

"You look confused," the salesgirl said.

He scowled. What was he doing trying to pick out women's panties? He should leave it up to the salesgirl. She obviously regarded herself as quite the expert.

"Fine," he said. "Give me the bras, and several pairs of whatever underwear you think she'd like best, in a size small. And find me a robe."

"What kind of robe?"

He waved her question away. "I don't even want to know."

Her eyes brightened at this newfound trust. "Anything else?"

"Something for her to sleep in, also in a size small. Preferably something that covers her from head to toe."

"What did you say?" she asked when the last of his words faded away.

"I said to get her a nightgown. Nothing too revealing because we've got a kid with us. And throw in one of those bottles of perfume I passed by the entrance."

"Okay," she said, and whipped off to do his bidding. Preston didn't see her again until she took his credit card at the register.

Happily shoving the receipt into the bag, she handed him his purchases. "Thank you and come again."

For nearly six hundred dollars, he'd expected a heavier bag—but he knew better than to look inside. Already, he couldn't get rid of the visions he'd created since walking into this store.

He started to leave, then turned back. "Do you know anything about lip gloss?"

She closed the register and put the pen he'd used to sign the charge slip in a cup. "I go on break in fifteen minutes. If you can wait that long, I'll walk over to Nordstrom with you and we'll get whatever you want." She winked at him. "Maybe even some expensive jewelry."

Because Emma had lost everything, he could justify buying her a small bottle of perfume. Expensive jewelry was another matter.

"No jewelry," he said.

The salesgirl arched her eyebrows. "I'll bet I can get you to buy her a little something."

He slung the bag over his shoulder. "What makes you think so?"

Her smile widened. "Because you already want to."

CHAPTER SIXTEEN

WHERE WAS PRESTON?

Emma reorganized Max's tester kit for probably the tenth time. They'd been ready and waiting for more than an hour. If Preston didn't hurry, she'd have to order room service for lunch. Max needed to eat again soon.

She checked the parking lot through the window. No sign of the van. But she knew Preston was coming back. He'd left his computer, his cell phone and his duffel bag. Thank goodness. She didn't feel like facing the same problem she had yesterday, trying to buy a car on trade. Especially with Max getting antsy and complaining.

He was already bored, and they had space to themselves and a television here.

She should buy him some more toys, she decided. She hadn't thought of that when Preston left this morning. She'd been too busy feeling embarrassed about pirating his toothbrush and too worried about the trouble they were causing him to ask for anything extra. He'd agreed to take them to Iowa, and they were finally on amiable terms. She didn't want to jeopardize that.

"Mommy, when are we leaving?"

She abandoned the window to sit on the couch again. "Soon."

"How soon?"

"I don't know, Max—"

"You're supposed to call me Beast, remember?"

Briefly, Emma thought how much Manuel would hate his son's having such a nickname. It was too informal, too…playful for Manuel, who'd insisted Dominick was the perfect name for their son because it couldn't be shortened into something ending in a "y" sound. Manuel's world was a very serious place. Everything seemed to hold hidden meaning and have far-reaching consequences.

It was those far-reaching consequences that worried her.

Shuddering at the oppressiveness of the house she'd left when she fled San Diego and Manuel's control, she reached over and pulled Juanita's list of names and numbers out of her purse. Since she hadn't been able to reach Rosa, she'd spent the morning wondering if she should call Manuel on his cell. She felt responsible for whatever had happened to Juanita. She needed to do something to help her.

"Mommy?"

"What?" She kept her eyes on the list. *Justin Shepard… Jesus Barraza…Raymond Midon. What do these names mean?*

"Look!"

Emma glanced up to see her son flexing his biceps.

"Do you think I have big muscles?" he asked.

Hiding a smile, she waved him closer. "I don't know. Let me feel."

He retained his pose as he moved toward her.

"Oh, yes," she said, gently squeezing his arm. "You definitely have big muscles, especially for a five-year-old."

"Do you think they'll be as big as Preston's someday?"

"If that's what you want."

"Do you think Preston's are bigger than Daddy's?"

Preston was a little taller, had broader shoulders and a slightly more rugged build. Emma had certainly noticed the physical differences, as well as other things, like Preston's casual acceptance of his looks compared to Manuel's preoccupation with grooming, lifting weights and buying designer suits. But she refused to be drawn into a discussion of Preston's attributes when she was trying so hard to ignore them. "Maybe."

Max dropped his arms. "When are we going to leave?" he asked again.

"Soon," she repeated.

Fortunately, a show came on television that caught his interest. He pretended to be a bunny and hopped away as Emma continued to worry about her mysterious list. She had to stop putting it off and call Manuel. But first she wanted to try Rosa one more time. Maybe Juanita had returned. Maybe she was fine....

She dialed, but the phone rang and rang, like last night. Then the answering machine picked up.

"*Hola.* This is Rosa. Leave your name and number and—"

Emma disconnected. "That's it," she said. "I have to do it."

Max glanced back at her. "Do what, Mommy?"

"Come on."

"We're leaving without Preston?"

"Just for a few minutes."

"Where are we going?"

"Down the street."

"Why?"

"To use the pay phone."

"Can't you use that phone?" he asked, pointing.

"No."

"Why not?"

She didn't want the hotel number or Preston's cell-phone number to come up on Manuel's caller ID. "It's not the best phone to use for what I need to do."

Max was so eager to get out of the room he didn't question her again. "Okay, let's go," he said, and darted off ahead of her.

She jotted Preston a quick note, in case he returned in their absence, and took the extra key to their room. At the last minute she saw Preston's cell phone sitting on the counter charging, and slipped it into her purse. Maybe he wouldn't be pleased about waiting for them should he get back before they did, but he wouldn't want to head to Iowa without his phone. Emma knew it was small insurance. But she felt better having it with her than leaving it behind.

The midday sun was warm but not uncomfortable as she and Max hurried down the street. She could smell the petunias planted in the flower beds, hear the click of heels on the sidewalk all around her. She liked Salt Lake City. It was clean and well maintained, and the mountains rose majestically around her.

Max chased pigeons as they walked, squealing in excitement when he nearly caught one. Emma smiled at his fun, wishing they could have a few days that were free and slow and all their own. Especially when she spotted the phone booth that was her destination. In the next few minutes, she had to confront Manuel. She'd once wanted to marry him. But her fear of him had grown from a few misgivings after Max was born into something large and dark and often suffocating.

Now she could almost feel his hands reaching out from some alley to latch on to her neck, could see the thick-lidded expression that told her it was time to go into the bedroom, where he'd do things he knew she hated just to make her feel powerless.

A cold shiver ran down her spine. She turned, her worried eyes passing over a medley of people.

They were all strangers.

He wasn't here, of course. How could he be?

Still, when Max called out, pointing to another pigeon, Emma couldn't help telling him to lower his voice as they hurried on.

Graffiti covered the phone booth that sat outside the gas station and mini-mart. It had definitely seen better days, but there was a sign that read "This pay phone does not accept incoming calls," which was exactly what she needed.

"Sit right here," she told Max, placing him on the curb near her feet. "If you don't move, I'll buy you a sucker from the mini-mart as part of your lunch, okay?"

"Okay!" He plopped down as though he had every intention of obeying, and Emma breathed a sigh of relief. The next few minutes were going to be difficult enough without worrying about Max running into the street or walking off with a stranger.

Gathering her nerve, she called Manuel's cell. A mechanical voice told her how much to deposit for the long-distance call. She pumped the pay phone full of change, then closed her eyes and listened to her heartbeat while she waited for him to pick up.

"Hello?"

Revulsion made her clench her teeth. She'd grown to hate even the sound of his voice. "Manuel?"

"Vanessa. Thank God."

She sensed his relief, knew it was authentic. As twisted as he was, he honestly believed he loved her—or needed her.

"I'm glad you called, *querida*. Are you okay?"

Querida. My beloved. She grimaced. "I'm fine."

"And my *hijito?*"

"He's fine, too."

"Good." There was a moment of silence. "Is it over, then? Are you ready to come home?"

She thought of Juanita and Rosa. It was far from over. "No."

"Vanessa, make this simple and come back to me. You belong with me. You know that."

"You're wrong."

"You're not thinking. I've been good to you, given you everything. How can you be angry with me?"

"How can I be angry with you? Are you serious, Manuel?"

"Of course."

Emma had meant to avoid personal attacks, but the deep resentments of the past six years rushed to her all at once. "You know how unhappy I've been. You've abused me and manipulated me and—"

"I've bought you a big house and a fancy car. I don't call that abuse. Maybe you should see a doctor for some antidepressants. This is all in your head."

The outrage felt like an alien inside her body, clawing to get out. "You make me sick," she said.

When he paused, she knew the vehemence in her voice had surprised him. But at least he'd stopped pretending he was something he wasn't. "You think I'm going to let you walk away with my son?" he snarled.

"Thankfully, you don't have a choice."

"You filthy whore! When I get my hands on you—"

She closed her eyes. "Shut up! I don't want to hear any more, do you understand me? Not a word! *Just shut up!*"

Silence.

"Mommy?" Max said, looking frightened.

Emma blinked, scarcely able to believe she'd exploded. For a moment, it felt good, liberating. But then Manuel laughed softly.

"*Querida,* your defiance excites me. Hang on to that, will you? When I get you home tonight, we can have some fun with it."

The thought of his kind of fun made Emma feel faint. "Go to hell."

His voice dropped even further, and the amusement in it disappeared. "Feeling brave, are we? Amazing what a little false security will do."

Emma's confidence slipped, as he'd meant it to, but she quickly pulled herself together. He couldn't touch her, couldn't hurt her in front of Max, couldn't take Max away from her. Not now that she was on her own. She'd gotten out of Ely. As far as he was concerned, she could be anywhere. "It's not false security, it's determination," she said.

"I know you're with someone, *querida.*"

"You don't know anything."

"Where did you meet him?"

"Nowhere."

"Don't lie to me."

"What I do is none of your business."

"Have you let him in your pants?"

A picture of Preston flashed before Emma's eyes—Preston, with his long, streaky-blond hair blowing carelessly across his face as they drove with the windows down, his blue eyes watching her, his lips soft and full, surrounded by a perpetual five-o'clock shadow. "Quit being crude."

"I'll kill him, *mi amor.* You know I will."

She remembered the craving she'd felt for Preston's touch

last night, a completely foreign emotion after being with Manuel for so long, and refused to believe he was in any kind of danger.

I'll be with him for only two more days, just until we reach Iowa. Then we'll part and never see each other again. Manuel will never find us. He'll never know who helped me.

She held the phone against her shoulder and wiped her sweaty palms on her khaki shorts. "Stop trying to frighten me, Manuel. I have something to say you're going to want to hear."

"What is it?"

"I have proof."

Silence.

"Mommy?" Max tapped her leg. "When will you be done? I want my sucker."

Emma shook her head and gestured him back to his seat on the curb. The worst was still to come.

"You have *proof?*" Manuel finally repeated. "What are you talking about?"

A lump of fear sat heavy in her stomach. "I have information that can destroy you, your business, maybe even your family."

Another stretch of silence, then, "You're *threatening* me?"

She was shaking now. She felt like she'd just rattled the chain of a very big dog that was certain to come after her—a dog she'd never be able to outrun.

"Tell me what you've done with Juanita," she said.

"I'll tell you what I'm going to do. I'm going to tear your two-timing heart out with my bare hands, you stupid bitch!"

"You'll never touch me again. Ever. Do you hear? I'll send what I've got to the DEA if Juanita isn't home, safe and sound, within twenty-four hours."

"You don't want to start this battle with me," he warned. "You'll be sorry. You won't win."

"This time maybe I will," she said, and hung up.

VANESSA HAD CALLED him from a pay phone that didn't accept incoming calls.

Manuel threw his cell phone across the car seat and heard it bang against the opposite door. "That damn bitch. I'll kill her!"

Why was she doing this? Who did she think she was? And, even more worrisome, what the hell did she have that she could send to the DEA?

He exited the freeway, following the directions he'd received earlier from the Hilton's concierge. As he drove, he considered the possibilities. He'd always been careful about the calls he accepted at home, was cautious enough to lock his office. He would've known if Vanessa had picked the lock and gone snooping. A camera hidden in the bookshelves recorded everything. He'd already had José watch the tape. There was nothing unusual on it.

So where had he gone wrong?

He'd never dreamed this could happen—*that* was how, he realized. He'd thought Vanessa would never really leave him because of Dominick.

You're too damn arrogant, his mother always said. *It makes you reckless.*

His mother was a bitch, too. He hated her *and* Vanessa, and he hated Juanita, as well. Juanita was to blame for everything. She was the one who'd made it possible for Vanessa to slip away. Juanita and Vanessa's new boyfriend.

He'd crush this man, he promised himself. He'd make Vanessa so sorry, she'd beg him to let her have a life half as good as the one she'd known before.

Picturing her naked body writhing on the bed beneath him, crying out in pain and degradation, made him drive even faster. He'd reached Salt Lake in an hour and twenty-eight minutes, but it was already after noon, and she'd called him from somewhere besides the hotel, which meant she might have checked out.

If she hadn't, he'd need a way to get her room number.

After stopping at a flower shop, he whipped into the Hilton's parking lot, grabbed the bouquet he'd bought and jogged into the lobby. Even if Vanessa was already gone, maybe he could glean some clue about where she might be going. He had to find her. The idea that she'd been secretly laughing at him all along, that she'd somehow achieved the upper hand when he thought *he* had control made him livid.

He headed straight to the front desk. A woman with long black hair gave him a smile that brightened when her eyes moved to the flowers. "Hello, sir, how can I help you?"

Manuel set the vase on the counter. "Today is my sister's birthday. I was hoping to surprise her with these."

"She's a guest here?"

"Yes."

She turned to a computer. "What's her name?"

"Vanessa Beacon." It was a long shot, but he had to try it.

"I'm sorry, there's no one registered by that name."

He recalled the name Hector told him Vanessa had used at the motel in Ely. "What about Emma Wright?"

The woman's eyebrows went up, but when he didn't explain, she checked her computer and shook her head. "There's no Emma Wright, either."

"Maybe the room's registered in her husband's name." It galled him to say it, but at this point, he was ready to say anything.

She looked at him expectantly. "And his name is…"

"Let me see…." Manuel snapped his fingers as though struggling to remember. "It's on the tip of my tongue. I just…can't…grasp it. I've never actually met him," he confided, "but they're traveling with my nephew, a blond boy about five years old. Maybe you've seen them?"

"Not that I'm aware of," she said.

Manuel kept his face as pleasant as possible. "Do you know any way I can find her?"

"Not without a name."

"Right. Well…maybe I'll wait here for a bit and hope they come through the lobby."

"That would probably be best," she said. "I'm sorry I can't help you."

So was Manuel. Taking the flowers, he moved into the lobby, searching the face of each person who passed through. But after about ten minutes, he decided he was wasting his time. The lobby was nearly empty. Like most of the Hilton's patrons, Vanessa had probably checked out. Maybe she was leaving Salt Lake right now while he was standing here holding a stupid bouquet of flowers—

The bell of the elevator drew his attention and he turned just in time to see a man waiting there—a man with a face he recognized.

It was the guy he'd met in the restaurant in Ely. The one who'd said Vanessa was attractive. The one he hadn't liked.

Manuel was sure of it. But this man hadn't come in through the front, or Manuel would've spotted him sooner. He must've used a side door, which was even more curious.

The blond-haired stranger glanced over his shoulder, and Manuel quickly stepped behind a pedestal bearing a giant array of exotic flowers.

A second later, the elevator arrived, and the man got on. When the doors swept closed, Manuel left his flowers on a nearby table and hurried across the lobby to watch the lights that signified the floors above.

Eight...nine...ten...eleven. The elevator stopped, then began to descend again.

Hitting the up button, Manuel took the first elevator to arrive. Then, when he reached the eleventh floor, he began knocking on doors. The place was almost deserted this time of day. It shouldn't take him long to find the man who had to be Vanessa's accomplice.

PRESTON HAD LEFT his purchases in the car and dashed through the side entrance of the hotel because it was closest to where he'd parked, worried that Emma and Max were getting anxious. He'd been gone longer than he'd planned. What had started out as a quest to pick up a few basics had become something much more complicated, mostly because Felicia's enthusiasm had become infectious, and he'd bought all kinds of things. Shorts, shirts, a skirt outfit for Emma, several matching shorts outfits for Max, tennis shoes, toys and books for the car, even a minicomputer so Max could learn how to spell while they drove. Preston couldn't understand why buying these gifts made him so happy, but after two years with each new day as bleak and unremarkable as the one before, it suddenly seemed like Christmas.

He whistled as he retrieved the key card for their room. He might have refused the jewelry, but after Felicia had gone back to work, he'd returned to the toy store and bought the bat and ball she'd tried to get him to purchase earlier. He had so many memories of playing baseball with Dallas that it felt like a betrayal to think of playing with Max. But from what

Emma had said, her son liked the game. And Max was probably pretty good for his age if he'd had a private coach. Preston thought it'd be good for him to get some exercise every now and then while they crossed the country.

Today he wouldn't remember what had come before, what he used to have, who he used to be. He'd concentrate exclusively on here and now and the presents he had in the car for a woman and a child who had nothing. Giving made him feel human again. Certainly he could allow himself a brief respite from the grief that had consumed him since he'd lost his son.

Slipping the key into the lock, he entered the room. His things were still there, but the television was off, and he couldn't see Emma or Max.

"Emma?" He walked to the bedroom, then stuck his head into the bathroom before returning to the living room. He was just beginning to worry that maybe Max had had another insulin reaction, that they'd gone to the hospital, when he found her note.

P—We'll be right back.

But where did they go? And why? How long had they been gone?

Someone knocked.

"Thank God." Crossing the room, he swung the door open, expecting to see Max and Emma. Instead he stood face-to-face with Manuel.

The man seemed tightly wound, as though he was ready to fight. "Who are you?" he asked, his eyes narrow and accusing.

Preston wadded the note he still held in one hand into a tight ball and shoved it in his pocket. How had Manuel found them? And so damn fast? "That's none of your business," he said.

"You said you were from Ely."

"I am." He kept his voice careless, unconcerned. "I'm on a business trip."

When Manuel bent his head to look beyond him, Preston shifted to fill the doorway and decided to go on the offensive. "Why the hell are you following me?"

"Following you?" Manuel chuckled humorlessly. "You know what I want. Where's Vanessa? And Dominick?"

"I'm afraid I don't know anyone by those names. But if you're talking about the woman and child who asked me for a lift from Ely, I dropped them off at the airport."

A muscle twitched in Manuel's jaw, and Preston prayed to God Max wouldn't come running down the hall. *We'll be right back.*

"You're lying."

"Believe what you want," he said smoothly. "But after I left the Hotel Nevada, I saw the woman and child in that picture you showed me. They were standing on the street not far from the Starlight Motel. I told the woman that you wanted to talk to her, but she begged me not to call you."

A vein stood out at Manuel's temple. "So you picked her up instead?"

Preston shrugged. "I figured whatever's going on between you two is none of my business and gave her the ride she wanted. I even let her stay here last night."

Manuel hesitated. "But she's gone now."

"I told you, I took her to the airport."

"If that's true, you probably won't mind letting me take a look around."

It was a challenge, a test. Preston wondered if Emma might have left something that would give them away. But she had only the clothes on her back, her purse and Max's diabetes stuff, which Preston already knew she'd taken with her. If she'd left anything behind to indicate she was coming back, it couldn't be much.

Problem was, it wouldn't *take* much.

Pasting a confident smile on his face, he stepped back and waved Manuel into the room. He knew it was a bold move, but he thought it just might work—as long as Max and Emma didn't return in the next few minutes.

"What kind of business are you in?" Manuel asked, moving purposefully through the suite.

"I'm a computer programmer."

"And you're in town for..."

"A convention." Preston's eyes skimmed all the surfaces. He couldn't see anything of Emma's. His bag sat in the living room. His computer waited on the coffee table. His phone...

He glanced back at the counter. His charger was there, but his phone was gone.

"Excuse me, I've got to make a call. When you've seen what you want to see, go ahead and let yourself out."

Manuel marched into the bedroom as Preston sat on the couch and dialed his own number. Which went directly to voice mail.

Come on, Emma, pick up.

He called again—and sagged in relief when she said hello.

"Barbara?"

"Preston?" she replied, obviously recognizing his voice. "It's not—"

"I know. Listen, I'm running a little late. Do you mind if we meet in an hour or so?"

"I don't know what you're talking about."

"Great. Sorry for the inconvenience. Some guy just came to my room, looking for his wife and kid—" He glanced up to see that Manuel had left the bedroom and was watching him. "Hang on," he said, and made a show of covering the mouthpiece. "All done?"

Manuel's gaze raked over him. "Did you touch her?"

The other end of the line fell silent as Preston let his eyebrows shoot up. "Excuse me?"

"Did you have sex with my wife?"

Who the hell did Manuel think he was? Preston wanted to beat him to a pulp, to vent his rage over everything Emma had told him. But he needed to get Manuel out of here. "Listen, pal, I'm on a business call here."

"*Did you touch her?* Answer me and I'll leave."

"You'll leave anyway."

"Preston, be careful," Emma said.

"I've got to go," he told her. "I'll call you right back." He hung up and stood so Manuel would know he was willing to enforce his demands. "I've been more than accommodating. Now get out."

Manuel didn't move. "What airline did she take? Did she say where she was going?"

"Go to hell. I don't owe you a damn thing."

That muscle twitched in Manuel's cheek again, and his eyes nearly glowed red with rage. "You'd better hope we don't meet again."

Preston held the door. "Yeah, next time I might not be so nice."

CHAPTER SEVENTEEN

SITTING IN ONE of the stalls in the restroom located off the main lobby of the Hilton, Emma hugged Max tightly. She'd been about to step onto the elevator when Preston called. If she and Max hadn't spent so much time at the Maverick Mini-store, picking out his sucker...

"Mom—"

She immediately covered her son's mouth. "Shh." Luckily, they were alone in the restroom. The hotel was experiencing the usual midday lull between checkout and check-in.

He pried her hand away. "But I'm hungry," he whispered loudly.

Emma knew it was his way of pressing her for the sucker she had in her purse. He wouldn't leave her alone until she gave it to him.

She stopped worrying about making him eat lunch first and handed him his treat. She didn't want his blood sugar to go low—especially now. And she thought having something in his mouth would keep him quiet.

"Why are we sitting on the toilet if we don't have to go potty?" he asked as he eagerly accepted her offering.

Because sitting on the toilet was better than sitting on the floor, which was their other option.

Preston's cell phone rang, giving Emma a good excuse not

to bother with an explanation. She hurried to silence the noise. "Hello?" she murmured softly.

"He's gone."

"Are you okay?" Her words were barely a whisper because she feared Manuel might be standing outside in the lobby. He always seemed to be a half step behind her. Why? How? It was uncanny how he dogged her every move; it undermined her confidence.

"I'm fine," he said. "And you?"

She released her breath. Preston was safe. After what Manuel had said to her on the phone… "We're okay."

The elevator was just a few feet from the bathroom. She heard the *bing, bing* of the bell and imagined Manuel getting off. Had he left the building or only their room? Was he hovering right outside the door? Hiding behind a potted plant? Lurking outside in the lobby?

"I'm sorry," she said to Preston.

"Don't apologize. Listen, he could still be in the hotel, so stay away."

"Stay away? We're trapped in the lobby bathroom," she murmured, terrified that Manuel might somehow be within earshot.

"Good." There was a pause. "Okay, stay there. Wait fifteen or twenty minutes, then meet me at Temple Square. It's right in the middle of town, within walking distance. If you haven't heard of it, ask someone on the street. Almost anyone can direct you. Got it?"

"Got it."

"I'll be waiting at the entrance on North Temple. I can't remember if there's more than one gate, but if so, go to the one farthest west."

He'd told her to wait fifteen or twenty minutes, but she sat in the bathroom for another half hour, just to be safe. Then she led Max cautiously through the lobby and out a side door, onto the street.

THE SPIRES of the Mormon temple rose up from the block called Temple Square, which served as the very center of the city. Inside the gates, Preston glimpsed beautifully manicured trees, lawns and flower beds, as well as several elegant buildings. But he had eyes only for the two figures huddled outside the square, near the stone fence. Finally, Emma and Max had arrived. Preston had circled the block fifteen times already—until he was crazed with worry that Manuel had caught up with them, after all.

Pulling to the curb, he opened Emma's door. "Get in."

"Hi, Preston!" Max acted as though they hadn't seen each other for days.

"Hi, Beast," he murmured. "Put on your seat belt, okay?"

Emma made sure Max obeyed, then climbed in the front, and Preston merged into traffic.

"You okay?" he asked, glancing over at her pale face.

She nodded. "What did—" She lowered her voice. "What happened?"

Preston checked over his shoulder to see Max staring curiously out the window at people moving along the wide sidewalk surrounding Temple Square. "He came to the room."

"How?"

"That's what I'd like to know."

"What did he say?"

"He wanted to know where you were, of course."

"How did you respond?"

"I told him I gave you a ride from Ely and that you stayed with me last night."

"You *did?*"

"I wasn't sure what he already knew, so I wanted to keep as close to the truth as possible."

"How'd you get rid of him?"

"I told him I dropped you off at the airport. I even let him come in and nose around, hoping to convince him that I didn't have anything to hide."

Relief eased the tautness in her face. "That was smart."

He turned right on State Street. "I'm not sure he bought it completely, but it was plausible enough to get rid of him for the time being."

"How did he know we were in Salt Lake? How did he find the room?"

"I thought maybe you could tell me." He stopped for a light, then turned pointedly to her.

"What?" she said.

"You're not playing games with me, are you?"

Her horrified expression answered that question. "You think I'm leaving bread crumbs? *Wanting* him to follow?"

He sighed. "No." He didn't believe that. Or he wouldn't have gone to such lengths to help her. "I just can't figure out how he's following our every move."

Emma shook her head. "It has to be Rosa. There's no other way."

"Juanita's sister?"

"I've been calling her. You know that. I've never left a message, but I suppose she could've gotten my number off caller ID."

Preston scowled as he opened his window for a little fresh air. "And gave it to him."

She sighed. "Juanita said I could trust her. Anyway, it was a risk I had to take. Juanita helped me escape, and now she's gone missing. I couldn't keep running and not look back! I feel responsible!"

"Sounds like Rosa's not as interested in your well-being as Juanita was."

"I know she wouldn't have done it unless she had to."

They were traveling past block after block of numerically named streets—200 South, 300 South, 400 South. He couldn't remember how to get to Interstate 80 from this part of Salt Lake, but he knew they couldn't be far from an entrance to the freeway. He'd checked MapQuest this morning when he'd opened his trading accounts. Evanston, Wyoming, was only eighty miles away. The route had seemed so clear he hadn't bothered writing down directions.

"What can *you* do to help Juanita?" he asked.

Biting her lip, she retrieved a piece of paper from her purse. "More than you think. Juanita gave me this. I found it in the glove box of my car before the police took it away."

He shot her a meaningful glance. "The same car that was stolen?"

She gave a quick shrug. "Would you have let us ride with you if I'd said the man I used to live with reported me for kidnapping his son?"

"Good point." He took the paper. It was a list of names and numbers, along with a few addresses. At the bottom he found some writing in Spanish. "What does it say?"

"If he finds you."

"Don't tell me this has to do with what you mentioned earlier, about Manuel and his family's 'import' business."

She lifted her chin. "How'd you guess?"

"It wasn't hard," he said. "I just dreamed up the worst-possible scenario, and bam—there you go. Worst-possible scenarios seem to be a given with you."

He thought she might bristle at the sarcasm in his voice, present him with the argument he was looking for, give him some reason not to like her. The concern he felt for her and Max bothered him. He couldn't afford to care about them. He didn't know where he'd be in a few months.

But she gave him no argument. When she spoke, her voice was somber. "You're right. It's not fair to drag you into this. Manuel might decide to hurt you. And I couldn't bear—" Her eyes met his but darted away.

She couldn't bear…what? Part of him wanted her to finish. The other part insisted he was better off not knowing. He couldn't let himself soften where Max and Emma were concerned, or at least no more than he already had. He had to stop Vince.

"We should part company," Emma stated decisively. "Take me and Max to a used-car lot. I'll buy a car and continue on alone."

He doubted she'd get much for her earrings. Considering how he was feeling, he thought she'd do better with what she'd volunteered at the pool in Ely. But he certainly didn't want her to make that offer to anyone else.

"Preston?" she said when he didn't decelerate. "Are you going to stop?"

"No."

She watched him for several seconds. "Why not?"

He knew he should, but he couldn't. Now that they'd come this far, he *had* to keep her and Max safe. Probably because he'd been too blind to protect Dallas. At least he had a clear enemy this time. He *knew* Manuel wasn't his friend. If only he hadn't trusted Vince…

Eventually, it would've happened to someone else's child, he reminded himself. Vince couldn't obtain the hero worship he craved any other way, or he wouldn't have repeated the crime he'd committed in Iowa. Which brought Preston right back to square one. Vince had to be stopped.

"Are you going to answer me?" she asked.

"I said I'd take you to Iowa, and I will."

A road sign pointing to the freeway came up at the next light, and he turned right. He was fairly confident he could catch Interstate 80 if he headed south on I-15.

He handed the paper back to her. "Does Manuel know you have this?"

She busied herself folding it into a neat square and didn't reply.

"Emma?"

He heard her sigh. "He does now."

"How?"

"I called him from a pay phone and told him."

"That's where you went this morning?"

She nodded.

"Talk about stirring up a hornet's nest," he said.

"I had to do it. This is the only leverage I have."

"For what?"

"For Juanita. I told him if she isn't safe at home by tomorrow, I'm sending it to the DEA."

So Emma wasn't just running from Manuel. She had something that could potentially ruin him, and she was threatening him with it. More good news. "I'll bet that went over well."

"It went over about as well as expected."

"What did he say?"

Checking behind her to make sure Max was still staring out the window, preoccupied with whatever he was thinking, she lowered her voice. "Do you really want to know?"

"I wouldn't have asked if I didn't."

"He said that when he gets hold of me, he'll rip my heart out with his bare hands."

Preston gripped the steering wheel so hard he thought he might break it. "That son of a bitch won't touch you."

"Ooh…you swore, Preston. Mommy, Preston swore again."

Max was back with them.

"He didn't mean to say that," Emma said.

"At least he doesn't smoke anymore," Max responded. "That's good, isn't it? I don't want him to get a hole in his throat."

Now that Max mentioned it, Preston realized he hadn't had the desire for a cigarette in nearly two days. "Would you mind not keeping score of everything I do wrong?" he asked wryly.

Max gave him a devilish grin, and Preston would have grinned back. Except that Emma was still very serious.

"I want you to let us out."

"You're crazy."

"You'd be safer."

"Life is a series of risks."

"And this is just another risk for a man who doesn't really care about living?"

He didn't answer her. "Will you go through with what you said and send this to the DEA?"

She cast another concerned glance in Max's direction. "If I knew the police would be able to use it to put him in jail for the rest of his life, yes."

"Who's going to jail, Mommy?" Max asked.

"No one you know, sweetheart."

Preston waited until she focused on him again. "But you don't think that's a possibility?"

"I'm not even sure what this paper means, exactly. And even if—" she smiled at Max, who was now listening intently "—you-know-who went to jail, chances are good he'd get out again in a few years. Then he'd come after me."

Preston thought of Vince. He had enough to do already. Why couldn't he walk away from this? Why did he have to become involved?

Because he was starting to care about them—which was even more reason he should drop Max and Emma off at some car lot and let them make their own way from here on out.

But for the first time in two years, he didn't need to think of a reason to get out of bed.

"How far is it to Iowa?" Emma asked as they crossed the Utah-Wyoming border.

Preston stretched his neck, then settled himself with one arm over the steering wheel. "From here it's about eleven hundred miles."

Eleven hundred miles. She'd never traveled such a great distance by car before. She would've tried to leave Manuel by plane, but she'd wanted the control only a car could provide—to change direction, to stop where she wanted, to move at a moment's notice, to carry their luggage, to sleep in if she and Max got desperate. She'd also been hard-pressed for money and couldn't afford an extra eight-hundred-dollar outlay.

"We go through Wyoming and then…" She rubbed her forehead, trying to decide if Interstate 80 clipped the corner of Colorado.

"Nebraska," Preston said.

She wanted to study his face but kept her eyes on the road ahead. The more she came to know him, the more interesting and attractive she found him—which was surprising, since she'd considered him one of the handsomest men she'd ever seen when they first met. He was still gruff at times, remote with her and Max, hardened by his losses. But there were moments when his unexpected smile nearly stopped her heart.

"It seems I heard somewhere that Interstate 80 goes clear across America," she said, trying to keep her mind on the conversation instead of the shape of his lips. She'd kissed those lips, felt them slide down her neck.

A flood of warmth made her sit up straighter.

"It does, for the most part," he said. "It starts in San Francisco and goes to New Jersey."

"Listen, Mommy." Max pushed one of the buttons on the computerized toy Preston had given him when they stopped for lunch just outside Salt Lake City.

"*B* is for *ball*," the computer said. "Can you spell *ball?*"

Max spelled it correctly, which resulted in a celebratory jingle and a computerized accolade. "Now spell *cat.*"

"See?" Max said proudly.

"Good job, honey. You're learning."

He grinned happily and went back to playing with his new toy.

"Buying that computer for Max was really nice of you," she said to Preston. "It's kept him occupied for over an hour, which means it's a darn good toy."

The side of Preston's mouth kicked up, but he didn't say anything.

Searching for a diversion from her preoccupation with the man sitting next to her, she turned to look out at the brown, treeless landscape, dotted only with scrub brush. "Have you ever been to Wyoming?"

"I've spent a few months here in the past couple of years," he said as they started up a fairly steep grade.

"Doing what?"

"What I do everywhere."

"And that is…"

"Day-trading."

She allowed herself to look at him again—and admired the strong angle of his chin. "Are you very good at it?"

He shrugged, leaving the answer to that question a bit of a mystery. Judging by his car, Emma might guess he wasn't too successful. But she was beginning to believe he drove what he drove out of a lack of concern, not a lack of money.

"So what's this state like?" she asked.

"It's pretty barren in most places. Right now we're going into an area they call the Three Sisters."

"What're the Three Sisters?"

He waved a hand at the landscape. "What you see is what you get. They're hills, basically. But they're famous for bad weather in the winter."

"That's why I've scen so many signs about closing the highway in inclement weather."

"This stretch isn't as bad as Arlington."

"Where's Arlington?"

"You'll see it. It's just before we hit Laramie. Someone once told me they close Interstate 80 down there more often than at any other spot."

She could hear Max spelling *hat* in the back seat. "I'll bet Donner's Summit outside Tahoe could compete for that honor."

"Probably." He turned off the radio because reception had deteriorated to static. "After we climb this, we'll descend to Lazeart Junction, then go uphill again, until we're east of the Leroy Interchange. The view there is spectacular."

She was already enjoying the view—the view she had of *him*—even though she was trying hard not to think about how handsome he was. Developing a crush on the first guy to come along after Manuel was a terrible mistake, but she refused to be too hard on herself. Of course she'd feel something for Preston. He was helping her through a very difficult time. He acted protective, exuded a kind of battle-tried confidence she envied. What she felt was just gratitude—mixed with a great deal of appreciation for his fine physical attributes.

That was where the confusion came in, she decided. But she didn't have anything to worry about. After Manuel, admiration was probably all she'd ever feel for a man. Love was too risky, especially if children were involved.

As if he could feel her watching him, his blue eyes flicked her way, and she quickly averted her gaze. "I take it we'll have one more mountain to climb?" she said, hoping she'd accurately picked up the conversation where they'd left off.

He responded as though she hadn't missed a beat. "That'd be Bigelow Bench. It'll take us into Bridger Valley."

"How far will we travel today?"

"We'll see how Max does. I was hoping to make Cheyenne."

We'll see how Max does? For all his dislike of her son, he sure seemed to be taking Max's needs into account. At lunch, he'd brought out a baseball and bat, and played with Max for nearly forty minutes. Then he'd given him that expensive game.

"How far is Cheyenne?" she asked.

"Another three hundred fifty miles or so."

"I know it's the capital, but is it a big city?"

"As big a city as you're going to find in Wyoming. Cheyenne has about fifty-thousand people, I think, but there are probably less than half a million in the whole state."

"I can see why," she said, staring out at the wilderness surrounding them. "What do people do for a living here?"

"Ranching, mining, oil and natural gas, for the most part. Up ahead there are some trona mines."

"What's trona?"

"It's used to produce baking soda and detergent. From what I've heard, it can only be found in two places in the United States. Here and in Trona, California."

"I've never heard of it."

"Neither had I until I visited here."

"Now spell *far*," Max's computer told him.

"Have you ever been to Yellowstone Park?" she asked Preston.

"No."

"Me, neither, but I'd like to see it someday."

"Manuel wasn't interested in vacationing?"

"He didn't mind going on a cruise or flying to Hawaii, but I could never interest him in anything that might get him dirty."

"Like camping?"

"Exactly. Someday I'm going to Yellowstone Park, where Max and I will camp for as long as we like. And when Max gets to be a teenager, we'll visit the Grand Canyon and backpack down to the Colorado River, and—"

"Sounds as though you plan on being alone with Max for a long time."

She tucked her hair behind her ears. "After what I've been through, staying single is the only way to go."

"Now spell dog."

"It's tough to have any…intimacy," he said, in obvious deference to Max, "when you're not married and you have a kid at home."

She couldn't meet his eyes. Before she left Manuel, she would've sworn she could happily go without sex for the rest of her life. He'd soured her on the whole lovemaking experience.

But then she'd met Preston, and was already wondering if sacrificing that part of a normal existence would be as easy as she'd thought. "I don't care. I'm tired of being dominated."

"I'm not talking about domination."

He wasn't. He was talking about the way *he'd* make love, the give-and-take she'd sampled before, the respect he'd shown for her and her body.

Goose bumps broke out on her arms. "I made one error in judgment. I don't want to make another."

"So that's it? You're never going to make love again?"

"Love and sex aren't always the same thing, right? If I start to miss that…aspect, I'll just have to quit being so conservative and…I don't know, pick someone up, I guess." She knew she'd probably never do it, but taking charge of her sexuality sounded good—as though she wouldn't let herself be deprived simply because she'd screwed up and gotten involved with the wrong man.

If the expression on his face was anything to go by, Preston wasn't happy with her answer. "That's not very safe."

"I'll be careful."

"You're not the type to enjoy casual sex."

"How do you know?"

He gave her a look that said he knew her better than she thought—and he probably did. Although they'd been together a very short time, he'd seen her at her lowest, her most "undone." Her situation hadn't allowed for the usual social masks that made it so difficult to know someone.

"Maybe it's something I can learn," she said.

"How many men have you been with so far?"

She lifted her chin. "What difference does that make?"

His teeth flashed in one of his knee-weakening smiles. "Too many to count?"

"Maybe."

"Or only one?"

She scowled at him. "So what if it's only one? I'm now a stronger, more assertive person."

"Emma, I know you want to believe you can fulfill all your own needs. But I can guarantee that sleeping around will cause more problems than it solves. Besides, it's…empty, meaningless. A woman like you would feel worse instead of better."

"A woman like me? What about a man like you?"

He looked at her frankly. "Actually, I've only slept with three women."

"In the past week?" she said irritably.

"In my life."

This announcement was such a surprise that she dropped her combative demeanor. "Really?"

He nodded. "My wife, a woman I was briefly engaged to before Christy, and a girlfriend I had for over two years in high school."

"Then you don't really know what it's like to sleep around any more than I do."

"I don't have to try it to know I won't like it," he said. "How fulfilling could it be?"

It wouldn't be fulfilling at all. She just didn't want to acknowledge that there seemed to be no good alternative to inviting someone else into her life, giving someone who could be as bad as Manuel the same opportunity to wreck her happiness. How could she trust enough to risk her heart a second time? How could she trust enough to carry another child?

She couldn't. Yet she was only twenty-nine. Was she doomed to devote the rest of her life to Max and Max alone?

"So what do people like me do?" she asked, her mood matching the drab hills around them.

He frowned. "I haven't figured that out yet."

CHAPTER EIGHTEEN

PRESTON MOVED silently through the living room of the suite he'd rented in Cheyenne to the doorway of the bedroom, and leaned a shoulder against the portal. When Emma didn't look up, he knew she hadn't heard him, which didn't come as any surprise. She was too focused on her sleeping son. Worry creased her forehead as she sat on the bed beside him and pulled his hand out from beneath the blankets.

"You've got to test him?"

When he spoke, she glanced up and attempted a smile, but he could tell she was too tired to put much energy behind it. "Five to eight times a day."

The tone of her voice suggested it was a never-ending chore. One she hated—but not because of the trouble it caused *her*.

"Why don't you show me how it's done?" he asked.

She gestured him over, and he sat on the other bed.

"You change the depth of the lancet by adjusting this." She handed him a blue penlike device that turned at the end. "You don't want the needle to go in too deep, or it'll hurt worse and take longer to heal. You want it to go deep enough, though, or you won't get enough blood."

Preston saw that she'd fixed the setting at a depth of two-and-a-half, but he didn't know what two-and-a-half meant, other than that it was greater than one, which was the lowest setting, and less than four, which was the greatest.

Holding the boy's hand to the light, he could immediately spot five or six places on the pad of each finger where Max had been pricked before. "You wait until he's asleep on purpose, don't you?"

"If I can. It's not much, but…" She shrugged. "It's one less poke that he has to know about."

"How badly does it hurt?"

"The finger pricks hurt more than the shots because fingers have so many nerve endings."

Preston resisted the urge to set the lancet aside and begin massaging her back. She seemed so weary, so anxious. He wanted to relieve some of that tension. "Can't you poke him somewhere besides his fingers?"

"I can do some alternative site testing on the forearms, but the reading isn't as accurate, and it's harder to draw blood."

"I haven't heard him complain about the pain."

She smoothed a hand over Max's hair. "He usually doesn't say much about it. He's a brave boy."

Fighting his natural reluctance to do anything that would hurt a child, Preston pricked Max's finger so Emma wouldn't have to. A drop of bright red blood oozed out, which she captured with a test strip she'd inserted into the glucose meter. The meter beeped only a few seconds later.

"How's he doing?" Preston asked.

"He's two-fifty. I'll have to give him a unit of Humalog and get up in three hours to test him again, in case my guess is wrong and the insulin pulls him too low. He also has his background insulin working, which can be pretty unpredictable."

He stared at Max's sleeping form. "Would it hurt him that much to let him stay high, if he's sleeping?"

She pushed a needle into the top of one of Max's insulin bottles and drew out a small amount of clear liquid. "It could, if he went into ketoacidosis."

"Which is…"

"If he doesn't have enough insulin to be able to break down the sugars in his blood, his body will start metabolizing fat to get the energy it needs. When the body breaks down fat stores, it throws off a by-product called ketones, and that's bad for the kidneys. It's bad for the whole body, really."

"So ketoacidosis is what we're trying to avoid?"

"Even if he doesn't go into full-blown ketoacidosis, you have to worry about other things. High blood sugar damages all the body's major organs. Diabetics who don't control their blood sugar end up blind or on dialysis. Some even lose a limb due to severe nerve damage."

"And low blood sugar results in what happened at the pool."

"Exactly." She pinched the back of Max's arm and inserted the needle. He didn't even twitch. "It's all about maintaining the right balance. A healthy pancreas constantly adjusts. There's no way to completely replace that with a handful of shots every day."

Capping the syringe, she dropped it into the paper sack where she'd been keeping all the other used needles.

"If he goes low in the night, what do you do?"

"Wake him up and feed him a small can of peaches."

"What if you're sleeping and you aren't aware that he's low?"

She put Max's diabetes supplies back in the black pouch. "That's the risk I take every time I close my eyes. His brain requires sugar to survive. A body will conserve as long as it can, and shuttle what it has to the brain. But if Max goes too low and there's simply not enough sugar in his blood…"

Her words dwindled off, which was all the answer Preston needed. If Max went too low, he could die. Here today, gone tomorrow. Just like Dallas.

Sorry he'd asked, Preston stood up. He sympathized with the burden Emma was carrying, wanted to help her. But he couldn't help without caring, and he couldn't care because he couldn't withstand losing what he'd lost before.

"I'm going to the Laundromat," he said, and moved abruptly to the door.

"Hurry," she said. "I can't wait to get out of this swimsuit."

Preston thought about the lingerie and other items he hadn't given her yet. He supposed now was the best time to dig them out of the van. She needed them. And he'd be gone when she looked through the sack, so he wouldn't have to hide his reaction when she pulled out those skimpy panties.

Maybe he couldn't offer Emma any *real* emotional support. But he could certainly give her some clothes.

EMMA COULDN'T believe it. Judging from all the tags and the receipts she found carelessly wadded up or tossed into this bag or that, Preston had spent nearly fifteen hundred dollars on her and Max. Yet, when he'd left an hour earlier, he'd handed her the bags without even waiting for her to open them.

Standing in front of the mirror in the bedroom, she admired the elegant cream robe she'd just put on. It was made of silk and fit her as perfectly as everything else he'd provided. Except for a pair of white sandals that pinched her toes.

Astonished that he'd bought her such lovely items, and so many of them, she stared at the stack of clothes she'd tried on several times already: a pair of pajama bottoms with a matching spaghetti-strap tank top, bras and panties every bit as beautiful and expensive as the lingerie Manuel had insisted she wear, another pair of sandals besides the ones that pinched, along with more casual flip-flops, makeup, shorts and shirts. And he'd bought Max almost as much: shorts, shirts, boxers, socks, toys, an expensive pair of athletic shoes, even a pair of cleats!

Why? They were planning to reach Iowa tomorrow. Iowa meant goodbye. And Preston didn't want them along in the first place.

She heard the outside door open and held her breath. He was back. She thought he might poke his head in to see if she liked what he'd given her, to see if it all fit, but he didn't. The door connecting the living room to the bedroom remained shut, and the television went on.

Emma couldn't help feeling disappointed. That was it? He bought her fifteen-hundred-dollars worth of merchandise and didn't think about it again?

Evidently money was as unimportant to Preston as she'd suspected. Which meant the gifts he'd given her were probably meaningless to him, as well. She needed clothes; he'd bought them. Merely a practical, if generous, approach to solving the problem.

She pulled her hair into a ponytail. What had she expected? Too much, evidently. But regardless of how or why he'd done this, he'd been more than kind. She had to thank him.

Tightening the belt of her robe, she slipped into the living room.

He didn't turn at her approach.

"Did you find the Laundromat okay?" she asked.

Over his shoulder, she could see television stations flashing across the screen as he deftly wielded the remote. "Yeah, there was one just a few blocks away."

"That was lucky."

He settled on Conan O'Brien's monologue and started folding the clean clothes piled in front of him.

"Preston?"

"What?"

"Could you look at me for a second?"

A scowl marred his handsome face. "What is it?"

"Thanks for the clothes. I—"

He turned back to the television. "No problem."

Emma wondered if he could be embarrassed by his own kindness. He didn't like to show his softer side, but after everything he'd done for her, she knew he had one. "Okay, well, I'm going to get some sleep."

"Good. You need the rest."

She cleared her throat. "I can tell you don't really want to hear this, but…" He seemed to be ignoring her. "I appreciate all the things you bought us."

"You're welcome," he said. "Good night."

Her excitement over her elegant new clothes dimmed. "Good night," she replied, and left.

PRESTON KNEW he should breathe a big sigh of relief and let Emma go to bed. He didn't want to think about her in that sheer lingerie, didn't want to break down and do something he'd later regret.

But maybe he'd been too gruff. Maybe it wouldn't have killed him to admire a few things, let her feel good about them.

With a curse, he got up. From the glimpse he'd had of her in that silky robe, he knew he was setting himself up for another sleepless night. But he could tell he'd disappointed her.

He knocked softly on the door.

"Yes?"

She was brushing her teeth. Walking into the bedroom, he leaned a shoulder against the wall, so he could watch her. "I've changed my mind."

She wiped her mouth and set her toothbrush aside. "About what?"

His gaze swept over her, taking in the details·of the silk robe. It fell to a low V in front, revealing a generous and very stirring amount of cleavage, and hit her midthigh. Beautiful. Felicia had certainly known what she was doing. "I want to see you in the rest of the stuff I bought," he said.

Her eyebrows shot up. "The clothes?"

Their eyes met, and something powerful arced between them, obliterating the pretense he'd used to let himself come back here. "The underwear," he admitted.

Her eyes widened. "Are you serious?"

He considered her for several seconds. "You wanted my attention, didn't you?"

She nodded.

"You've got it now." He grinned as his pulse sped up. "Is it a little more than you bargained for?"

"I'm not sure." She toyed nervously with the ends of her belt. "I can't think when you smile at me like that."

"Why not?"

"It makes me want to see *you* in *your* underwear."

His breath caught, and he stepped closer. "You've already seen me."

"Which is how I know the sight's worth seeing again."

They were flirting with disaster, and he knew it. They'd be in Iowa tomorrow, faced with saying goodbye. But he couldn't turn away.

The front of her robe brushed against his chest, and he

lowered his voice. "I'll show you mine if you show me yours."

She lifted her chin so she could look into his eyes. "You didn't seem interested a few minutes ago."

"I'm willing to make that up to you." He tugged on her belt, and she grabbed his hand. When he laced his fingers through hers, she stepped back, pulling him into the bathroom with her. The door clicked shut behind him, and it was the most hopeful sound he'd ever heard.

A moment later, her belt slithered to the ground, leaving her standing two feet away with her robe parted.

She was watching him intently, looking just a little unsure. So he was careful not to touch her when he pushed the silky fabric to each side.

No bra. But that was hardly a disappointment. Her breasts were perfectly formed, heavy enough to settle nicely in his hands, pert enough to win any wet-T-shirt contest. The sight of them kicked Preston's stomach into his throat. "You're beautiful."

"Someone has good taste in panties."

He lowered his gaze—and felt his whole body go rigid. She was wearing the black ones. "Those are my favorite."

At the hoarse sound of his voice, she offered him a flirtatious smile. "How do you know? You haven't seen the other ones."

"Oh, yes, I have. About a million times in my mind." He'd told himself he wouldn't touch her, but he'd never expected her to encourage him. A man could only stand so much.

He slid a hand inside her robe to rest on the curve of her waist and waited to see how she'd respond.

Her tongue darted out to wet her lips, and her breathing went shallow. Two very good signs. As he slowly moved his hand upward, she closed her eyes and arched toward him—and suddenly he had both breasts in his hands. He trailed kisses over her soft skin from her collarbone down, thinking she might finally stop him. Part of him prayed she would. But when her hands came up, they didn't push him away. They clenched in his hair and held his head where it was—and she moaned softly as his mouth closed over one nipple.

The sound of her pleasure made him want to feel her, taste her, plunge inside her with eager, powerful strokes. He'd never desired a woman so badly. But he was afraid anything too aggressive would spook her. After Manuel, she couldn't handle too much, too fast.

Raising his head, he kissed the very edge of her mouth, and she turned her head to seek his lips. She slid her tongue lazily against his, as though relishing the sensation it provoked.

That was perfect. He covered her nipples with his thumbs as their kissing grew deeper, more passionate. "You feel so good," he murmured.

She guided his mouth to her other breast. He suckled her until she whispered his name. Then he slipped a hand down her flat stomach, past her belly button and even lower, until he skimmed the top of those lacy panties. She swayed in his arms as he ran his fingers lightly over the fabric, back and forth—and finally delved underneath.

Immediately her legs came together, denying him access.

"Emma…" His voice was raspy, foreign, even to his own ears.

Her eyes locked with his. She looked worried. He told himself to walk away, to put some space between them. Because of Vince, he had no future, no life, no right to be doing this. But he'd never felt so helpless. "Let me touch you, Emma," he whispered.

She bit her lip uncertainly and he kissed her again—long, deep kisses that showed her everything he was feeling. Slowly, her legs parted, and euphoria caused his every nerve to tingle.

"That's it," he murmured. "I won't hurt you. I would never hurt you. You know that, don't you?"

She nodded.

Supporting her back and shoulders with one arm, he watched her face as his fingers searched for—and found— what he wanted.

"Look at me," he whispered, enjoying her expression. "Do you like this?"

Her eyes fluttered open and she smiled faintly. But he didn't need more of an answer. The way her pupils dilated told him enough. And her mouth... It was slightly parted and still wet from their last kiss. She seemed dazed, as swept away as he was.

Nothing seemed to matter beyond the here and now. He claimed her with two fingers, and her eyes opened wide. "Oh!" she said. But he was pretty sure her exclamation conveyed pleasure and surprise, not alarm. She didn't push at him or recoil, but he tried to reassure her anyway.

"You're okay, Emma." He kissed her bare shoulder. "Relax."

He knew she was probably too wound up to relax, too sensitive to his touch, but her arousal fed his own. Burying his face in her neck, he reveled in her musky scent, her silky feel. When she began to rock with his movements, every muscle in his body grew tense. She was moaning softly, clinging to him. Then she suddenly pushed him deeper, and he groaned with her as she shuddered against him.

He was aching to be inside her, but he waited, hoping the passion he'd seen in her eyes a moment earlier wouldn't be gone when she opened them. He wanted to finish what they'd started, but this wasn't about sex. This was about believing in life again.

Finally, she looked up at him. He tried to maintain his composure, to be aloof, indifferent, just in case. But he couldn't manage any emotional distance. The loss of Dallas seemed to bleed like an open wound right in front of her. He couldn't hide his pain or his need.

"Preston?"

He closed his eyes at the sound of his name on her lips. It was tender, knowing. Reaching out, she touched his cheek. Then she began to pull off his shirt.

Her hands felt cool as ice as she ran them over his burning skin. He liked her caresses. Her eagerness carried him to even greater heights. But he stopped her before he lost himself completely. "I want to make love to you, Emma," he said. "But I can't promise you anything after we reach Iowa. There are…things I have to do. You may never see me again."

"I don't want to hear that right now."

"But I can't take any more guilt or regret. If this…if this is going to make your life harder somehow…"

She held his face, made him look at her. "Stopping now would be harder than anything."

"But I don't have any birth control. I haven't been with anyone since Christy."

"I'm on the pill." She gave him a shaky grin. "So help me get your pants off. I can't seem to do it fast enough."

He peeled her panties away first, but left her robe on. He liked touching her while the silk brushed against his arms. It seemed more intimate that way, as if he held the prized, secret key.

When he finally stripped off his boxer briefs, her eyes went round, and he laughed at her quick, shy smile.

"Are you embarrassed?" he murmured, pressing her against the wall and kissing the indentation below her ear.

Her eyebrows arched and her smile widened. "Actually, I'm impressed."

When he laughed again, something cracked inside him, something that allowed a little light to penetrate the darkness of the past two years. He took a deep breath as relief and joy engulfed him. With Emma, he felt healthy and strong, almost like his old self.

"I'll take it slow and easy," he promised, but the moment he felt her tight around him he lost all control. He thought he'd died and gone to heaven.

A few minutes later he was sure of it.

"MOMMY? Are you in there?"

Emma froze, her body still slick with sweat, Preston breathing heavily against her. "Um…" She cleared her throat when her voice squeaked. "I'll be out in a minute, sweetheart."

"Where's Preston?"

She could hear Preston's labored breathing in her ear. "Tell him…I'm in…the Jacuzzi," he said.

But she couldn't manage that many words quite yet. After what had just happened, it was difficult to gather her faculties. She couldn't remember the last time she'd felt like this…if she'd *ever* felt like this. "He…he's gone."

"He's coming back, isn't he?" Max was obviously worried. "He said we'd play baseball tomorrow."

"He'll be back."

"You zapped my strength," Preston whispered to her, laughing softly. "I can hardly move."

She smiled because she was pretty sure that without him

holding her up, she'd crumple to the floor. "Kids have the worst timing."

"It definitely could've been worse."

That much was true.

"I'm scared," Max said. "Will you lie down with me?"

Emma felt Preston kiss her sweaty temple and loved that he didn't seem to mind the messy part of sex. Manuel had always treated her as though she was somehow distasteful to him afterward. "If you'll get back in bed and wait for me there, I'll be out in a minute," she told Max.

There was a pause. "Okay," he said at last.

Silence fell as Max shuffled off, and Preston moved away to run a warm, wet cloth over her body. "You're so lovely," he murmured.

She reveled in the frank admiration in his eyes. She still wanted to be with him, to enjoy the aftermath of what they'd just shared. But her child came first.

She finished washing up and put her robe on while Preston dressed. Then she turned toward him. She didn't know what to say. What had happened seemed too powerful, too profound for words.

Giving her the sexy grin she loved so much, he drew her robe tighter at the top. "What time do you get up to test Max?"

"Three."

"Don't set your alarm. I'll take care of it tonight."

She stared at him. "Are you sure you know how?"

"You showed me earlier, remember?"

"But if you oversleep—"

He cupped her face. "Emma."

Her eyes met his clear blue ones. "What?"

"I won't oversleep. If he's above one-fifty, I'll let you know he needs a shot. If he's under a hundred, I'll feed him."

Preston's offer was *really* nice. But she wasn't used to having help, didn't know if she could accept it. Manuel had never gotten up in the night with Max, not even when he was a baby, and she was terrified Preston might not follow through. "It's okay," she said. "I'll probably wake up anyway."

"Don't. I've got it," he said simply. And when he slipped his hand inside her robe to cup her breast as he gave her a final kiss, she decided to trust him. After all, he hadn't let her down yet.

PRESTON LAY awake on the opposite bed, watching Emma. With her mouth slightly parted and one arm flung over her head, she seemed to be sleeping deeply. The moonlight that drifted lazily through the wooden shutters made the creamy skin revealed by the narrow straps of her tank top glisten like a shiny pearl. He couldn't help remembering the feel of that satiny skin beneath his hands.

He'd thought, after their lovemaking in the bathroom, that he'd be able to forget about touching Emma. At least for a while. But he hadn't gotten nearly enough of her.

With a silent curse, he cut off the memory of her legs wrapping around him. God, he had such a one-track mind. He'd spent two years filled with nothing except a thirst for vengeance and resolution. He still yearned for those things. But now he craved Emma just as much. He tried to blame his rampant hormones on the fact that he'd gone so long without a woman. But he wasn't talking two years anymore. He was talking three *hours*.

Focus on something else.

The numerals on the digital clock on the nightstand flipped from 2:48 a.m. to 2:49 a.m. It was almost time to test Max. He wasn't sure exactly why he'd volunteered for the job. Except that he couldn't imagine how Emma dealt with the constant worry, and wanted to ease the burden if he could.

Climbing out of bed, he retrieved the black pouch and went into the bathroom to get everything ready. While he hoped Max's blood sugar wasn't low, he hoped it wasn't high, either. He wanted Emma to be able to sleep.

When he returned with the meter and lancet, he knelt at the side of the bed and stared down at her son. Max's eyelashes rested against his round cheeks, and his small hand retained the dimples-for-knuckles of a baby's. Dallas's hands had been the same way.

The similarities between the two boys ended there. But Preston still felt guilty, almost disloyal for liking Max. One child wasn't interchangeable with another. And yet he *knew* there was nothing to be gained from resenting Emma's son. Dallas was gone. Nothing could change that.

With a frown, Preston pricked Max's finger, but he couldn't get any blood out. Apparently, he hadn't gone deep enough. He squeezed, but there wasn't sufficient light to see where he'd made the hole. A moment later, an error message on the meter told him he'd have to use a new test strip.

Fortunately, Preston's second attempt met with more success. The test strip soaked up the drop of blood he'd extracted, and the monitor beeped to show it had enough. Preston gave a sigh of relief as a dark line raced around the screen. After a series of beeps, a digital number appeared.

Preston held it closer to the light streaming out of the bathroom. *Forty-six?* How could Max be so low?

Trying not to remember the terrifying incident at the pool, he rushed into the kitchen, where he found a snack can of peaches and a spoon. But when he returned he couldn't get Max to wake up.

"Come on, Beast. I've got something for you," he murmured, dragging Max's limp body up against his chest.

Max's head lolled but didn't rise.

Preston glanced nervously at Emma, who, surprisingly, hadn't stirred. Was her son typically this difficult to rouse? Or had he gone into a coma or something?

"Max?" he whispered harshly.

Max didn't respond or even lift his head. But as soon as Preston put the spoon to his lips, he opened his mouth, chewed and swallowed.

Thank God.

When he'd finished the whole can, Max rolled away without saying a word, as if everything was fine. But Preston still couldn't sleep. He worried that maybe he hadn't fed Max enough. The numbers didn't add up. If Emma gave her son a small can of peaches when he was, say, seventy, she probably had to feed him more when he was only forty-six. That can of peaches had been *so* small.

He hated to wake Emma, but after thirty minutes of worrying about it, Preston decided he'd better check with her.

Kneeling by her side of the bed, he shook her shoulder. "Emma?"

Her eyelashes fluttered open. As soon as she saw him, she jerked further awake. "Oh, no. Max! Did you test him?"

"It's okay," he whispered. "I tested him, but he was only forty-six."

"Did you feed him?" She tried to sit up, but he pressed her down.

"Of course I fed him. I gave him a can of peaches. I just want to be sure one can's enough." He told himself to stop touching her shoulder, but he liked the feel of her bare skin beneath his hand and let it linger. The warmth of her body seemed to spread up his arm like a slow-moving dye, bringing back the memories of a few hours ago.

Slowly the tension he sensed in her dissipated. "It should be enough."

Preston finally let go of her as she pushed the hair out of her face.

"I'll have to test him again in a couple of hours," she said.

"Okay, I'll set the alarm." Their eyes met and he smiled. Preston wanted to kiss her, to carry her out into the living room where they could have some privacy. But tomorrow was their last day together. He knew he should leave her alone. "Go back to sleep for now."

"Preston?"

"What?"

"What's in Iowa?"

He thought of life as he'd once known it, full of love and laughter and family. Emma seemed to offer him everything he used to have. But Vince was in Iowa. And the past wasn't finished yet. "An old…friend," he said bitterly.

"A woman?"

Preston detected a slightly proprietary tone in her voice and felt strangely gratified. Taking her hand, he threaded his fingers through hers one at a time. "No."

She responded by pressing her palm flat to his.

He stared down at their interlocking fingers. He hadn't reached out to another living soul since his son died, and he knew better than to form any attachment to Emma. But they were in such a similar place—cast adrift, living a life they'd never expected to live. That connected them already, like two strangers holed up in the same cave to wait out a thunderstorm.

"Can you tell me what happened to your son?" she asked softly.

He didn't want to talk about Dallas; he *never* wanted to talk about Dallas. That was partly why he'd alienated himself from almost everyone he'd ever known. There was too much self-recrimination mixed in with his son's death, recrimination for allowing someone he knew, someone he loved and supported as a close friend, to hurt Dallas. It wasn't logical. He'd had no idea Vince was the kind of man he'd turned out to be. But that didn't change the fact that, if Preston had only caught on sooner, he could have changed Dallas's fate, Christy's fate, his own fate....

The same thoughts had been whirling through his head for twenty-four months. He was sick of them, sick of the debilitating guilt. Tonight he just wanted to *feel*—feel Emma close to him, joined to him once again, assuaging that ache in his heart.

Preston didn't realize he'd squeezed his eyes shut until she tugged on his hand. When he looked up, she slid into the middle of the bed and pulled him toward her.

He could tell she wasn't offering him anything sexual. But it was crazy for all three of them to be in the same bed. What if he started dreaming and woke up in another cold sweat? Or what if he forgot about Max being there and let his hands wander?

"Preston?"

Her open, honest expression begged him not to say no.

Succumbing to the exhaustion that had settled into his bones several hours ago, he lay down next to her. He'd move to his own bed in a few minutes he told himself, and faced away from her so he wouldn't be tempted to take more than she was offering.

He assumed he'd be too distracted and cramped to sleep. But when her smaller body cradled his, and she wrapped her arm around him, pressing her cheek to his back, he wasn't uncomfortable at all. Soon he grew so relaxed, he was incapable of thinking about anything beyond the soft warmth that enfolded him. She held him fast, kept him from drifting, from dreaming, from tossing and turning. By blocking the memories and the past, by keeping him safe from himself, she gave him refuge.

Finally he slept.

CHAPTER NINETEEN

THE ALARM WAS about to go off. Emma wanted to catch it before the noise could disturb the other two people in her bed. But she was sandwiched between her son and the man she'd made love with in the bathroom last night, and even though she barely had room to breathe, she liked being where she was. Cocooned in their warmth, she felt strangely content—considering the state of her life.

Thinking back to the mornings she'd faced every day in her house in San Diego, with empty hour piled on empty hour, and only Manuel's unwelcome, probing calls to break the tedium, she could scarcely believe she'd managed to flip her life around so completely. No more mansion. No more Jaguar. No more days spent lounging by the pool. But she didn't miss any of it, because there was also no more Manuel. No more isolation. No more helplessness. Manuel had told her so many times that she could never get by without him. Wouldn't he be shocked to see how happy she was!

She didn't need anything. Just her son and—

She turned over to stare at Preston's whiskered jaw. She hated to admit it, since they'd be separating in Iowa, but he was an integral part of the peace she felt at this moment. She could smell the fabric softener in his freshly laundered T-shirt, hear the steady thump of his heart, and was grateful for the opportunity to snuggle closer to him without his knowing. She'd slept deeply for the first time in a long while, and it was because he made her feel safe despite everything.

Max began to stir. "Mommy?"

Emma rolled over to scoop her son into her arms and kiss his forehead. "What, baby?" she whispered.

His eyebrows knit together when he realized they weren't alone in the bed. "Did Preston get scared in the night, too?"

Emma laughed at the thought of Preston needing that kind of security and couldn't believe how carefree it made her feel. How long had it been since she'd found humor in anything? Too long. She'd become old far too soon. But things were going to change.

Her smile lingered as she followed her son's gaze. She, Preston and Max might be a ragtag bunch of misfits, but together they did okay.

"I knew a beast like you could protect me," Preston muttered, letting them know he was awake.

Emma's happiness immediately turned to an acute awareness of the muscular legs entwined with her own, the strength of the male body so close to hers. Waking up with Preston after a night in his arms felt almost as intimate as what had happened between them....

"I'm strong, huh, Preston?" Max said. "I have big muscles. See?"

Preston raised himself on his elbows to watch Max do his flexing. "That's good. Now I can rest easy." He flopped back onto the pillow and closed his eyes. Emma thought he was drifting off again until he nudged her. "Have you tested him yet?"

"I was about to."

"I'll do it." As he got up, Emma's eyes skimmed over his T-shirt and boxer briefs. With his square, unshaven jaw, enigmatic blue eyes and sleep-tousled blond hair, he looked incredibly sexy. And he had the body to go with the face. Even someone as conscientious about lifting weights and eating right as Manuel couldn't make a pair of boxers more appealing.

Emma especially loved how unconcerned Preston seemed to be about his physical assets. Outward appearances, *things,* didn't seem important to him. Otherwise, he wouldn't be driving that van. Or dressing the way he did.

He yawned as he returned, and Emma focused on watching him test her son. Ogling him wouldn't help them get through the day—without winding up back in the bathroom—but she was relieved to know she could actually desire someone. Because Manuel had wanted to make love much more often than she did, he'd occasionally accused her of being cold. Once he'd even called her frigid. But she doubted anyone could call her frigid after last night.

"One thirty," he said.

She frowned at him. "One thirty?"

Preston was obviously surprised by the question. "Max's blood sugar. He's one thirty."

"Oh, right." She smiled to cover her embarrassment. Her mind had been drifting back to the way he'd parted her robe.

He cocked an eyebrow at her. "You're turning red."

She cleared her throat. "One thirty is perfect. I guess we could've slept a little longer."

The look on his face told her he was probably remembering the same thing, and caused a tremor low in her belly.

"Or maybe it's better to get back on the road," she said, knowing she couldn't survive another session like the one last night and still expect to go on as if he was simply some nice man who'd helped her.

"We can cross Nebraska in one day if we get started soon."

"One day? How far is it?"

"I think it's about five hundred miles, but I'm not sure. I've got to do a few things on the computer. I'll double-check while I'm on the Internet."

She stretched, pretending not to notice the way Preston's biceps flexed beneath his smooth skin as he set up his computer. "Should I find a little store and get us some groceries for breakfast?" she asked.

"Order room service," he said. "It'll be faster."

"Okay."

After turning on the television for Max, she carried the sack containing her new clothes into the bathroom and closed the door. A shower would help her wake up, she decided, but as she peeled off the pajamas she'd worn to bed, she couldn't help studying her naked body. Preston had told her she was too thin. But he didn't seem disappointed last night.

She turned to one side and frowned at her reflection. Maybe he liked women with fuller figures.

"Mommy, I'm hungry. What's taking you so long?" Max called.

Feminine insecurity, at a time when she could least afford it. "I'll be out in a few minutes," she called.

She turned on the shower and stepped beneath the hot spray, telling herself she was stupid to become so obsessed with Preston. She'd barely escaped Manuel. But chastising herself didn't do much good. The water sluicing over her body soon became Preston's hands and mouth.

The image of him naked and in the shower with her made Emma feel giddy, breathless. She imagined the slickness of his skin against hers, his lips tracing a drop of water down her body....

Closing her eyes, she arched her back and imagined several different variations of last night. Then she smiled. "Take that, Manuel," she thought. "I'm *not* frigid."

PRESTON FELT more rested than he had in months, which was a definite improvement over most mornings. But being rested didn't alleviate a certain…uneasiness. He suspected Emma had something to do with that uneasiness, but he didn't want to think about it.

Tuning out the sound of the shower and the television, he focused on the list of e-mails filling his computer screen. He'd been so preoccupied with Emma and Max and getting to Iowa, he'd done little on the computer for the past few days. Spam cluttered his in-box, along with several securities newsletters, stock tips from various people he'd met on the Net, and a message from Gordon Latham containing Joanie's new contact information.

Preston was reaching the bottom of his mailbox when he came across an e-mail with the subject header: Maybe you should know. Assuming the attached message would start with "Expand your penis size by three inches," or something similar as most spam messages did these days, he nearly deleted it. But the return address caught his eye.

MellyD8. He recognized that address. It belonged to the Deets family. Their daughter, Melanie, had been a patient of Vince Wendell's when he lived in Lockwood, Pennsylvania. Vince had mentioned the family a couple of times, but Preston had learned most of what he knew by going through the archives of the *Lockwood Gazette*, where he'd stumbled upon an article heralding Dr. Wendell as a local hero. Dated three years prior to the Wendells' move to Half Moon Bay, the article praised Vince for hospitalizing little Melanie when she was showing only flulike symptoms. As it turned out, Melanie didn't have the flu; she had septicemia, the illness that had killed Dallas. But she didn't present the rash that sometimes accompanied the disease, so it was a marvel to most everyone that Dr. Wendell had possessed the foresight to get her the help she needed.

It wasn't a marvel to Preston. He thought Vince *should* know what was wrong with her, since he'd given it to her in the first place.

The article had ended by saying that the city was naming a park after Dr. Wendell. It featured a photograph of a very distinguished looking Vince—a self-satisfied Vince who was obviously at the height of his glory. That picture now served as Preston's screen saver, as a constant reminder that he might stand alone but he would never give up.

When Preston first contacted the Deets to ask about Melanie's illness and recovery, they weren't very forthcoming with the details, even though there was a little boy from the same town, also Vince's patient, who hadn't been as lucky as Melanie. Mere months after Melanie's miraculous recovery, Billy Duran had come down with the same flulike symptoms. His illness turned out to be meningitis, caused by the same bacteria as septicemia. Only Billy went into shock and died of heart failure on his way to the hospital.

Vince's voice played in Preston's head: *One of my patients died. It happens, you know. Being a doctor, it's something I have to deal with. But afterward it just…*haunted *me.*

Preston hoped to hell Billy's death still haunted Vince.

He clicked on the Deetses' message. What did they have to say after so many months? The last flurry of e-mails they'd exchanged had gotten pretty heated. Jim Deets had insisted that Vince would have no reason to harm their child. Why would a doctor, a young man with a beautiful wife, a man who had it all, purposely make one of his patients sick?

That was the million-dollar question, wasn't it? A normal person couldn't understand it. But Preston thought he knew why. He'd seen Vince strutting around their house when Dallas fell ill, telling Christy she'd done the right thing by calling him, assuring them they had nothing to worry about now that *he* was there. Preston had known Vince liked to impress others, that he was trying to impress *them*, but he hadn't realized how far Vince might go in order to accomplish that.

Closing his eyes, Preston shook his head. He should've seen it sooner. Vince lived for praise, fed on attention, craved the limelight. Since Dallas's death, Preston had read about people like him. The disorder appeared more often among arsonists, who started fires to set themselves up as rescuers, but it was their intense need to be perceived as a hero that drove them, and Vince had that same craving.

Preston had told Jim Deets as much, but Jim had refused to believe it. In his last e-mail, over a year ago, Jim had said he'd get a restraining order if Preston ever contacted him again.

So what did old Jim have to say now?

Preston quickly scanned the message.

Dear Mr. Holman:
This is Rachel Deets, Jim's wife. I probably shouldn't be writing you. Jim wouldn't like it. But something odd happened that's got me wondering if maybe you were right about Dr. Wendell. In order to register Melanie for seventh grade, we had to fill out a card listing the dates of her inoculations. When I put down that she hadn't had a shot since she was five years old, Melanie told me that Dr. Wendell gave her one the day she went in for her check-

up, two days before she got sick. She said he did it while I was in the bathroom. But no one mentioned anything to me about an immunization.

Dr. Stone has Melanie's medical records now, but there's no notation of any shot being given. I tried to talk to Jim about it, but he doesn't want to hear. Since her illness, Mel struggles to learn, and Jim's having trouble dealing with it. But she's pretty adamant about what happened. If Dr. Wendell hurt Melanie on purpose... Well, I'd hate to think he's out there, able to do the same thing to someone else's child.

Rachel

PRESTON LET HIS BREATH go in a long sigh. That Vince had given little Melanie a shot sounded all too familiar. When Dallas first fell ill, Christy had immediately called Vince to come over and take a look at him. Since it was late on a Saturday night, it seemed ultra-convenient that their best friend happened to be a doctor. Vince diagnosed Dallas as having a touch of the flu, which was what they'd expected. But then he came over early the next morning with a syringe, claiming a gamma globulin shot would boost Dallas's immune system.

Considering what happened afterward, what Preston had learned since, Preston would bet his life that there was something besides gamma globulin in that syringe.

He sent a quick reply to Rachel Deets, thanking her for writing to him and wishing Melanie the best. Then he printed her message. So far, the police had refused to listen to him. But maybe this would help.

AFTER EMMA HAD showered and dressed, she nudged Max. "Let's draw up your insulin, babe."

He ignored her and continued to stare at the television screen.

"Max?"

"Hmm?"

"Will you put your insulin in a new spot today?" Emma tried to fill her voice with encouragement. Somehow, she had to get Max used to rotating his injection sites. The fatty deposits on his stomach were making it difficult for his body to absorb the insulin when he put it there.

Unfortunately, her light tone had no effect. "No," he said, his expression becoming a dark glower when she handed him the needle.

"Will you at least try?"

Preston glanced over at them from where he was working on his computer. "Come on, Beast. Help your mom out with this, okay?"

Reluctantly, Max turned away from the television and pulled up the pant leg of his shorts. Emma was tempted to stay and watch, but she thought it might be easier for Max if she let him have some privacy to deal with this.

Moving to the nightstand, she perused the room service menu. Max liked having breakfast delivered. At the very least, it'd give him something to look forward to. But she found herself looking over at him every few seconds and biting nervously on her bottom lip. *Come on, baby. You can do it.*

"One, two-o-o…three!" Max's voice held more determination than ever before, which gave her hope. But he still balked at the last second and sat staring glumly at the needle.

"What would you like for breakfast?" she asked Preston.

"An omelette and some coffee."

Max jumped at the opportunity to distract himself. "Can I have sugar cereal?"

"Not today," she replied. "You can have eggs and bacon or oatmeal."

He grimaced.

"Which will it be?" she asked.

His shoulders slumped. "Oatmeal, I guess."

"I could get some strawberries to go with it."

"I like strawberries," he said, somewhat mollified.

She called to place their order, adding some eggs and toast for herself. When she hung up, she turned as Max brought the syringe to eye level. "There's a bubble in it."

"No, there's not, honey," Emma said. "I already checked it."

Hearing the flat tone of his voice, she was about to give up and let him put it in his stomach again, but Preston suddenly crossed the room to sit next to him.

"You think that needle's gonna hurt?" he asked.

Max considered the syringe. "I know it will."

"How bad?"

He shrugged.

"Why don't we find out? Why don't you give me a shot in the arm, then the leg, then the stomach, and I'll tell you which one hurts the worst."

Her son's eyes narrowed. "You're going to take a shot?"

"Why not?"

"Because you can't take insulin, silly."

"Don't you have an empty needle we could practice with?"

"I have a ton of 'em!" he said, and bounced off the bed to get one.

Emma sat across from Preston. "What's going on?"

"Don't worry about it," Preston said. "We've got it under control."

Max returned and handed her the syringe filled with insulin. "Here, hold this so I can give Preston a shot."

Emma watched Max pinch the back of Preston's arm and wondered if Preston was frightened at all. He didn't act like it.

"Are you ready?" Max asked.

Preston nodded and the needle pierced his skin. Max seemed to be taking careful note of his reaction, but Preston merely shrugged. "No big deal, right? You ready to do my stomach?"

Max grinned as Preston lifted his shirt, and Emma felt such an odd mix of admiration for Preston's gorgeous body and appreciation for his support with Max that she knew she was in trouble. She was falling in love with this man. She'd known him a week and already she wanted to spend the rest of her life with him. There had to be something wrong with her. She couldn't even breathe right when she looked at him.

"Where are you going to do it?" he asked.

"Here." Max struggled to pinch an inch of Preston's washboard stomach. Preston didn't have any fat for the needle to go into, but he didn't complain when Max gave him another shot. "Did it hurt?" her son asked curiously.

"Not at all."

Not half as much as it was going to hurt when Preston left her. Emma felt her chest constrict. What had she done? She'd let him steal her heart. And she wasn't even sure when it had happened. Maybe when he'd kissed her that first night but had chosen to walk away when Max stirred.

"Okay. Now your leg," Max said.

Preston moved so that Max could easily reach the inside of his thigh, and Max grinned again. "Here goes."

The needle went in and came out without so much as a grimace on Preston's part.

"How'd it feel?" Max asked.

"No worse than in my stomach," he said.

Skepticism entered Max's eyes. "You're just saying that so I'll do it."

"No, I'm not. It really doesn't hurt. You want to poke me again?"

Max inserted the needle three more times before he was convinced it didn't hurt. Then he took the syringe full of insulin from Emma and injected it into his own leg without even pausing to think about it. "Hey, it *doesn't* hurt," he cried in amazement.

Preston looked at Emma, silently sharing their victory, then ruffled Max's hair. "How could a puny little shot hurt a beast like you?"

"Thanks, Preston!" Max said, and before Emma could stop him, he threw his arms around Preston's neck.

THE IMPULSIVENESS of Max's hug took Preston by surprise. He heard Emma say "Max, no," as if she was afraid he might be rebuffed. But before Preston could decide how to react, his cell phone rang, and Max scrambled off the bed to get it.

"Can I answer?" he asked.

Preston avoided Emma's eyes, even though he could sense her watching him. He didn't want her to know how rattled he was, but the fact that he was off balance probably showed on his face.

Max tapped his shoulder. "Preston?"

It was probably Gordon calling to make sure he'd received Joanie's contact information. Preston couldn't see any harm in letting Max talk to him. But then Preston wasn't sure he could've said no to anything Max wanted at that moment.

"Go ahead," he said, pointing to the Talk button.

Max smiled broadly, acting very important as he pressed the phone to his ear. "Hello?...What?...Beast... That's my nickname.... Preston gave it to me.... Five... My birthday's in—" He looked to Emma.

"June," she supplied.

"June," he repeated. "Yeah, he's here...."

"Who is it?" Preston asked.

Max covered the mouthpiece. "Sarah."

His *mother?* Preston reached out to take the phone, but Max wasn't finished talking yet. "We had a slumber party last night," he told her. "Preston slept in our bed." Max's attention returned to Emma. "She's here.... Yeah, she slept with him, too. She got to be in the middle."

Preston groaned and fell back on the bed.

"Max, hand Preston his phone," Emma said.

Max was having too much fun to pay any attention. "Hey, guess what? I'm wearing the new underwear Preston bought me. They're just like his."

Preston shot upright again. "Max!"

Max blinked innocently at him. "She wants to talk to you," he said.

CHAPTER TWENTY

PRESTON WAS HESITANT to put the phone to his ear. After Max's brief intro, he knew his mother would have more questions than he wanted to deal with.

"Aren't you going to talk to her?" Emma asked.

Reluctantly, Preston dropped back onto the bed. "Hello?"

At the sound of his voice, his mother said, "It *is* you. For a minute there, I thought maybe I'd dialed the wrong number."

Maybe he should've hung up and let her continue to think so.

"What's going on?" she asked.

"Nothing."

"Who was the little boy who answered the phone?"

"No one."

"He said you bought him underwear."

Preston didn't respond.

"He also said his mother's there."

"Mom—"

"Have you met someone? Is this something I should be excited about?"

"No, definitely not."

Emma got up and began pulling Max from the room in an obvious attempt to give him some privacy.

"Who's with you, then?"

"Just someone who's catching a ride. It's nothing." From the corner of his eye he saw Emma pause at the door, and knew she'd heard him. Belatedly, he realized how callous he must've sounded. But he couldn't say anything to soften his response or his mother would jump to the wrong conclusion and start in with how grateful she was that he'd found someone, how happy she'd be to have another grandson, how hard she'd prayed that he'd be able to move on with his life. She was causing enough of a fuss as it was.

"Someone who's catching a ride!" she cried. "A *hitchhiker?* Do you know how dangerous that is?"

And he hadn't even mentioned Manuel....

"It's a woman and a child, Mom. No big deal."

Emma had disappeared into the living room, but his words still mocked him, and not only because of Manuel. No big deal? It had certainly been a big deal a moment ago when Max had hugged him. It had been a big deal when Preston made love to Emma, when he'd held her during the night.

"She could rob you blind and sneak off while you're sleeping!" his mother said.

At this point, Preston was beginning to believe that having Emma and Max sneak out while he was sleeping might be the best scenario for all concerned. Dropping them off and driving away wasn't going to be easy. And if they took a little money when they left—so much the better. Then he wouldn't have to worry about them going hungry.

"I'd probably thank her if she did," he muttered.

"What?"

"Never mind. You wouldn't understand." How could she? Even *he* didn't understand. He spent half his time thinking about Emma and the other half thinking about Vince. If he went after Vince, if he had to take matters into his own hands, chances were he'd go to prison and never see Emma again. But if he couldn't get the police to listen to him…

There was a long pause, then Sarah said, "Christy called me last night."

"What for?"

"She's worried sick about you."

"Why?"

"Because you're still living in the past."

Preston didn't bother to defend himself. "Did she also tell you I've located the bastard?"

"She did. But what good is that going to do? You've tried and tried to get the police to investigate that doctor. They won't do it."

"Because they think I'm just some distraught father who can't get over the death of his son." In the other room, Preston heard Max talking to room service. Their breakfast was here.

"You *are* a distraught father who can't get over the death of his son. When are you going to let go of Dallas, Preston? I loved him, too. Until Michelle's baby, he was my only grandson. But no matter how much you love him, you can't go on like this. You're ruining your life."

"Mom—"

"I'm sorry. I can't bite my tongue any longer. It's killing me to see what you're doing to yourself."

Preston blew out a sigh. "This is something I *have* to do."

"No, it's not. I've tried to leave you to deal with your grief in your own way, told myself to give you time and space, believed you'd come around on your own. But you're not, and enough is enough."

"It'll be enough when Vince pays for what he's done."

"That's it," she snapped. "I want you to seek professional help."

"So now I'm crazy?"

"Christy saw the same things you did, and she's convinced Vince had nothing to do with Dallas's death."

Christy didn't want to face what he'd had to face—that *they* were the ones who'd called Vince. "She's wrong."

"I can't believe that. She's rebuilt her life, while you're traipsing all over the country, living in motels. Usually I can't even get hold of you. When we do speak, you frighten me with your talk of revenge."

"*Someone* has to stop him," he said angrily.

"So what are you going to do when you confront this man?"

Preston had asked himself that question a million times. But he still didn't have an answer. He owed it to Dallas to make things right. He owed it to children everywhere to ensure that Vince couldn't hurt anyone else. But how far would he go?

He thought of the gun he'd been carrying with him for over a year. Would he use it?

"I'll cross that bridge when I come to it," he said. "I'm gathering more information every day. Maybe the FBI will finally look into it."

"That's a long shot, and you know it."

Her words brought back the helplessness he'd experienced since Dallas died. Deep in his heart he knew what had happened, but it was difficult to prove. And because of his grief, Preston had no credibility. His insistence that Vince had caused Dallas's rapid decline merely elicited pity or maybe a sad, patronizing shake of the head. He loathed both reactions. Even Christy hadn't sided with him. Her refusal to support him where Vince was concerned was the deepest cut of all.

"It's been two years," his mother continued. "How long are you going to go on like this?"

He was tired of fighting the battle alone, but he wouldn't give up. He'd made a promise to Dallas. "As long as it takes."

"Preston, please! Dallas might be dead, but you're not."

Preston had been numb and vacant for two years, so he might have argued that point. Except, since he'd met Emma and Max, his life had started to change. Suddenly he was experiencing desire, tenderness, protectiveness, even hope. But these changes brought their own pain, making him wonder if he wasn't better off staying as he was. Especially because he hadn't solved anything. He still had the same obsession that had brought about the end of his marriage; he wouldn't rest until he stopped Vince from practicing medicine and made him accountable for what he'd done.

"I don't want to talk about it anymore," he said. "There's no point. We're not going to agree."

In the other room, Emma told Max to sit still before he spilled his milk. Preston wanted to be with them, eating breakfast. *Why* the day seemed brighter when they were around, he wouldn't consider. He told himself it was simply good to be needed again. Looking out for them gave him a purpose beyond chasing down Vince. "I've got to go. I'll call you when I reach Iowa, okay?"

"Preston?"

"What?"

"Please don't do anything foolish. You may not care about yourself anymore, but I'm still your mother. If anything happened to you—" her voice cracked "—it'd break my heart. It's been hard enough already."

Feeling guilty for his earlier impatience, Preston covered his eyes with his arm. Sarah might not understand what he was doing, but she loved him. She'd been a good mother, and he and his stepsister were all she had since his father's death.

"I'll be careful," he promised.

NEBRASKA WAS as flat as Emma had always heard. Cornfields stretched out on either side of the road, still green although it was late August. Dirt roads dissected the passing countryside and an occasional farmhouse or red barn rose in the distance.

She listened to Max play with his computer speller while imagining what it might be like to live in such a place, with bees humming in the flowers nearby, a small dust cloud following a tractor as it rolled slowly along in the field next door, the wind gently stirring the tops of the corn stalks.

She'd like it, she decided. She wanted to live a simple, clean life, wanted to sit out on her porch with a tall glass of lemonade and let Max play in the yard with a big dog.

"Sleepy?"

She glanced over at Preston, who was driving with both hands for a change, and tried not to remember the conversation she'd overheard between him and his mother. She'd been trying not to think of it all morning, but it kept coming back to her.

Just someone who's catching a ride. It's nothing.

He'd been talking about her. *She* was nothing.

"A little, I guess."

"You've been quiet today."

She didn't have much to say. She felt foolish for the fantasies she'd entertained in the shower, for believing last night had meant anything to him. And she was more than a little surprised to discover how much that realization hurt. A week ago, she'd wanted only to start over, to be independent. But a few days in Preston's company had shown her how starved she was for positive emotion.

She closed her eyes and shook her head. She'd known better than to let herself care.

"Emma?"

"What?"

"Is something wrong?"

"No."

"What are you thinking about?"

"The future."

"What do you see in your future?"

Her eyes open now, she admired the neatly tended rows and patchwork squares of the passing farmland and wished her life could be so orderly. "A small town."

"And?"

"A little yellow house with a white picket fence and flowers in front."

"That's a far cry from a mansion with a pool house. Won't you miss *anything* about living the way you did?"

"Are you kidding? The mansion I lived in was a prison. I don't want anything that reminds me of it. And—" she shrugged "—you can't ask for too much on a teacher's salary. I'm willing to settle for what I can afford."

"Is that what you plan to do for a living? Teach?"

"If I can find a position."

"Where in Iowa would you like to settle down?"

"I don't know yet." She was beginning to wonder if maybe she'd put enough miles between her and Manuel by now. Maybe she should have Preston drop them off at the next town. The sooner they parted, the better. Who was to say Iowa would be any safer than Nebraska?

She unfolded the map he'd shoved onto the dashboard after they'd gassed up this morning. "Maybe somewhere around here would be okay."

He pulled his attention from the road. "Here? Now you're talking about settling in Nebraska?"

"Why not?"

"What happened to Iowa?"

It was another four hours to the border. And he was heading to Cedar Rapids after that, which was an additional five hours. Even though Preston had stopped periodically to play a little ball with Max, her son had spent enough time cooped up in a car. Besides, saying goodbye to Preston might be harder in Cedar Rapids, since he wouldn't be moving on to the next state. She didn't want him close if she was never going to see him again.

"I just want to settle in a farming community where I can live the kind of life I've dreamed about for the past few years. And Nebraska looks like it has plenty of farming communities. It's the Cornhusker State, remember?" She tried a weak smile, but he didn't return it.

"Why are you suddenly in such a hurry to split up?"

She didn't want to address that question, so she kept poring over the map. "Hazard's not too far away. That might be a nice place. Or Rockville or Ashton—"

"Emma."

She heard the serious note in his voice but kept her eyes on the map. "Looks like it might get a little hilly over by the Missouri River, so I think somewhere before that."

"I'm sorry for what I said on the phone this morning, if that's what's bugging you."

"You have nothing to be sorry for." It was her misconception, right? He'd been good to her and Max, done much more for them than she could have hoped. She had no right to complain. "Go ahead and take this exit. I'll start by checking out the job market in Kearney and go from there."

"I didn't mean it."

She finally gave him her full attention. "Of course you

meant it. We're a burden. And now that the pressure is off, there's really no reason for us to trouble you anymore."

Crossing her arms, she waited for him to pull off the freeway. But he sailed right past the exit.

"You didn't stop."

"Now spell *zoo…*"

"What about Manuel?" he asked.

"What about him?"

"He could catch up with you."

"He could catch up with me anywhere. That's a risk I'm going to have to live with. There's another exit coming up."

His eyebrows drew together. "I don't want to drop you off here."

"What's the difference?"

He caught and held her gaze. "Stay with me for one more night, Emma."

He wasn't offering her a night spent with their clothes on. She could tell. And she knew she should refuse. She'd just cursed herself for letting her relationship with Preston become so intimate, for allowing herself to care about him. But there was that hunger in his eyes again, and it so closely mirrored her own she could scarcely breathe.

She thought of how he'd tossed them into the van and screeched out of the Gas-N-Go. She thought of the miles and miles he'd gone out of his way from Ely, his generosity with the clothes he'd bought her, everything he'd done for Max. After Manuel, how could she not fall for a man like that?

"What do you say?" he asked.

The question revealed his vulnerability, his fear that she might refuse. She wished she could. But "no" simply wouldn't come.

"Okay."

As Preston passed a slow-moving pickup, Emma stared down at the cell phone she'd just borrowed from him. "Your number won't come up on his caller ID?" she asked hesitantly.

"Not if you press star six-seven before you dial. That'll block it."

"You're sure?"

He checked his speed. "I'm sure."

Max unbuckled his seat belt and leaned over her shoulder. "Who are you calling, Mommy?"

She didn't want Max to know. Maybe someday in the future he'd be able to speak to his father. But not today. Emma couldn't trust that Manuel wouldn't say something offensive. "Put your seat belt back on, honey. It's not safe to have it off while the car's moving."

"But I have to go to the bathroom."

Emma doubted it. He'd just gone to the bathroom. But he was tired of being restrained. "We'll stop as soon as we can, okay?"

"When?"

"Soon. Get back in your seat belt."

When he finally obeyed, she turned to Preston. "I'll try Rosa first."

"What good will that do? She's feeding information to the other side, remember?"

"Only because she's frightened. Who wouldn't be?"

He didn't answer.

"Besides, I only need to know if Juanita's okay. I think she'll tell me that much."

"I want to talk to Juanita," Max cried. "I miss her."

Emma missed her, too. And hoped to heaven that she was all right. But either way, this call would be difficult to make. If her threat had worked and Juanita was home safe, Emma would know the list meant what she feared it did. Along with that knowledge came responsibilities she didn't want to face. On the other hand, if she learned that something terrible had happened to Juanita, she'd never be able to forgive herself.

After taking a deep breath, she dialed.

Hola. This is Rosa. Leave your name and—

Emma punched the End button. "No one's there."

Preston shifted in his seat. "So what now?"

"It's time to call…our *friend.*"

"Want me to do it?"

She remembered Manuel's threats against him and quickly shook her head. Manuel had already met Preston twice; he'd probably recognize his voice. As much as possible, she wanted to keep Preston from becoming a target.

"Let me," he coaxed.

"No."

He looked unhappy with her answer, but she pressed star 67 and dialed anyway.

When Manuel said hello, the curtness of his voice led her to believe that her disappearance was driving him as crazy as she'd expected.

"Is she home?" Emma asked bluntly.

"It's you."

"Good guess." She twisted around to see if Max was still paying attention and found him staring at her. "Is…our mutual acquaintance home yet?"

"Juanita?"

"Yes."

"How the hell should I know?"

"Don't play stupid with me."

"You think I'm going to let you blackmail me, *querida?*"

"Quit calling me that." Emma shot an uncertain glance at Preston and was surprised when he reached for her hand.

His support made a difference. His warmth seemed to encompass her, lending her the strength she needed.

"I'll call you whatever I want," Manuel said. "You're asking for trouble. You know that."

"Forget it," she said angrily. "I'll go ahead and send what I've got to the DEA. But don't say I didn't warn you." She acted as though she was about to hang up and was secretly grateful when he stopped her.

"Wait!"

"Your memory's improving?"

"Maybe. But my temper isn't. You're going to be sorry—"

"Here we go again. Should I hang up?"

"No."

She hesitated, but he didn't seem in any hurry to say what he wanted to say.

"Are you sleeping with him?" he asked at last.

"That's none of your concern." Preston's hand tightened around hers.

"Like hell!" Manuel shouted. "Tell me the truth! You're still with that guy I saw at the Hilton, aren't you? He was in Ely, too. I should've known. Instead I let him send me on another wild-goose chase. Las Vegas, the airport..."

Emma would not allow Manuel to commandeer the conversation. "What have you done with...our friend?"

"Where did you meet him? Have you two been sneaking around behind my back?"

"I'm going to hang up now—"

"Wow, you're really mad, huh, Mommy?" Max said.

Emma was too wrapped up in the conversation to answer him.

"Juanita's fine," Manuel snapped.

"Prove it."

"Come back to me and I will."

"Never."

At her response, he must've thrown something. Emma heard a loud crash, followed by shattering glass. But it was difficult to determine exactly what had happened with him cursing so loudly. "You can't do this to me! Do you hear? I won't let you!"

The craziness in his voice chilled Emma to the bone, but she refused to succumb to the intimidation he was trying to use against her. She was taking control of her life. She couldn't continue to live in fear.

"You don't have a choice," she said, and hung up. Then she called Rosa again. She started to leave a detailed message on the answering machine, telling her she'd call at a certain time and to please be home, that they needed to talk. But Rosa picked up in the middle of it.

"Vanessa?"

Preston had released her hand when Emma dialed, but she reached for him again. Rosa was wailing and sobbing hysterically. "Yes?" She gulped.

"She's dead. Juanita's dead. The police just found her body."

CHAPTER TWENTY-ONE

MAX WATCHED Preston talking to his mommy over by the bathrooms. They'd taken him potty, tested his blood and promised him a treat if he'd be good and wait in the car for a few minutes. But they were taking so long.

Bored with turning the steering wheel and making car sounds, he opened the console, where he found a pair of sunglasses. He knew he shouldn't touch them, but his mommy had promised him a treat and he *hated* to wait. He needed something to do.

He slipped them on, gazed at himself in the mirror and laughed. He looked silly. He was just putting them away when he saw Preston's cell phone wedged between the seats. He loved to talk on the phone. He liked to pretend he was wearing a suit and working like his daddy. His daddy called people all the time.

Picking up the phone, he pushed the Talk button twice.

Suddenly a voice sounded in his ear, "Vanessa? Is it you? Listen to me—"

Max gasped. *"Daddy?"*

"Dominick?" His father sounded confused.

"Daddy, where are you?"

"Where are *you, hijito?*"

"In the van."

"What van?"

"Preston's brown van."

"Preston who?"

"Holman, silly."

"Preston Holman... Tell me about him."

Max thought his daddy sounded angry, so he searched for something Daddy might like to hear. "Preston plays baseball with me. He says I'm a good hitter."

His daddy made a funny noise.

"Daddy?"

"I'm here, *hijito*."

"He likes me to pitch for him, too."

"Where's your mother?"

Max bent his head to look through the side window. "Outside."

"Doing what?"

"Hugging Preston."

"What do you mean she's hugging Preston?" His daddy's voice boomed loud again, making Max worry that he'd said the wrong thing. He didn't like it when his daddy got mad. It scared him.

"Mommy's crying, and Preston's making her feel better." That was good, wasn't it? Preston was being nice. But his daddy didn't answer right away. So Max hurried to think of something that might make him happier. "Guess what? I can put my insulin in my leg."

"That's fine, *hijito*," he said, but he didn't seem to care much about it until Max added that Preston was the one who'd taught him.

"Stay away from him. Do you hear me?"

"Why?"

"Just do as I say." His daddy covered the phone and spoke

to someone else. Then he talked to Max again. "Look around you, *hijito,* outside the van."

"What for?"

"I want you to tell me what you see."

Was this a new game? His daddy didn't usually like games, but Max *loved* them. "Bathrooms."

"Are there any signs that have words written on them?"

Luckily, Max spotted one right away. "Yeah…"

"Perfect. You're a good reader, aren't you? Can you tell me what it says?"

"Sure." Max thought this seemed like fun. It pleased his daddy when he read. But before he could sound out the first word, the really hard one that started with *N-E-B,* he saw his mommy and Preston move toward the van.

"Uh-oh." He dropped the phone between the seats so he could scramble into the back. He didn't want to get caught touching something he shouldn't. If he got in trouble, he wouldn't be able to have his treat.

"Dominick?" He heard his daddy's voice, tiny now, as if it came from a man the size of an ant.

"Bye, Daddy!" Max called. Then Daddy must've hung up, because as soon as Preston opened Mommy's door, and Mommy asked if they could stop in Omaha for dinner, Daddy said nothing more.

SITTING IN a Salt Lake City restaurant, Manuel waved away the waitress who was approaching to take his and Hector's dinner order. He didn't want the noise. He heard Vanessa's voice; he was sure of it.

Pressing the phone more tightly to his ear, he held his breath and listened carefully. Two car doors slammed, an engine started. Then Vanessa and Preston began to talk.

Preston… Anger made Manuel's scalp tingle. Vanessa's lover had fooled him twice, but it wouldn't happen again. Manuel finally understood what he'd been so reluctant to believe—she had left him for another man. The knowledge stung his pride, yet offered him hope. If not for Preston, she wouldn't have gone. Which meant that once he got rid of Preston, she'd come back. He wouldn't tolerate anyone taking her from him or even helping her leave. Juanita had found that out.

The memory of his housekeeper calling him a disgrace flashed through his mind, but he shoved it away. He wouldn't think of Juanita. Killing her had given him no satisfaction. She made him feel weak. Even in the end, she'd laughed in his face. Sometimes it felt as though she was still laughing at him.

Hector watched him closely, but Manuel knew he wouldn't interrupt. Hector had been around long enough to know better.

"Are you done crying, Mommy?" Manuel heard Dominick ask.

"For now, honey."

"Does that mean I can have my treat?"

"We should probably wait until we stop for dinner," Preston said. "It'll be time to give him his insulin then."

Manuel gripped his water glass so tightly Hector took it away. "You're gonna break the damn thing," he muttered. But Manuel didn't care what he broke. Preston was talking as if *he* was Dominick's father. What gave him the right? A week ago, Vanessa and Dominick had belonged to Manuel. One week ago. A week didn't change anything.

"I'm not sure it's fair to ask him to wait any longer," Vanessa said. "How far is Omaha?"

Preston answered, but his voice was too low to be heard

over Dominick's. "I want my treat *now*. I can't wait any longer. P-l-e-a-s-e?"

Manuel mentally grasped at the words he could barely hear. Omaha? They were in Nebraska?

"Once we reach Omaha, how much farther do we have to go?" It was Vanessa again. What she said confirmed that he'd heard correctly.

"Mom?"

Dominick's voice came through the clearest because of the pitch.

Shut up, Dominick. I need to hear this.

"Another five hours or so."

"I've never been to Iowa, have you?" Vanessa asked.

"No, but I'm pretty sure the Cedar Rapids area has a lot of farmland," Preston said, and Manuel sagged in relief. He had them. He had them, and they didn't even know it.

Manuel wondered how long it might take to fly to Iowa. When he couldn't find any trace of Vanessa at the airport, he'd stayed in Salt Lake and waited for Hector to join him. Now the wait was over.

Static interrupted. Then Manuel heard a crinkling noise and supposed Vanessa was giving Dominick his treat. He knew he'd guessed right when his son remained quiet for more than two seconds.

"Are you ever going to tell me who's waiting for you in Cedar Rapids?" Vanessa asked.

It took Preston so long to respond that Manuel feared, for a moment, the phone had cut out. But finally, the answer came. "Probably not."

His phone lost its signal then, and Manuel cursed. He would've liked to continue listening. But he'd heard enough.

Smiling, he raised his wineglass in a toast. So Vanessa wanted to know who was waiting for Preston in Cedar Rapids?

With any luck, he and Hector would be waiting for them both.

HEADLIGHTS STREAMED toward them, but Max was asleep and Preston was driving, so Emma watched each car pass with half-closed eyes. They'd had dinner in Omaha and moved on, traveling so long she'd lost track of time and place. All she understood was that Juanita was dead and Manuel had killed her.

She'd known there was something wrong with Max's father, but *this*... Poor Juanita. Thinking of what she must have suffered made Emma ill. How could Manuel do such a thing? That question echoed through her mind again and again. She had no answer.

Maybe she should've stayed with him. Then Juanita would still be alive.

Fatigue dragged at her arms as she rubbed her face. She *couldn't* have stayed with him. Living with him was killing her by degrees. She had the right to seek a decent life, didn't she? And what about Max? He, at least, deserved the future she envisioned for him instead of the cold, empty life they'd been living.

"How'd your son die?" Emma asked suddenly. She couldn't stand her own thoughts any longer. She needed to talk. And even though she knew Preston wouldn't appreciate the topic she'd chosen, she was tired of being kept at a distance. He was willing to make love to her, listen to her, comfort her, help her. But he wouldn't let her do anything for him. Most of the time he wouldn't even let her drive.

He glanced over but didn't answer.

"You're not going to tell me, are you?"

"Misery loves company, is that it?"

"You think I'm trying to hurt you?"

He scowled. "There's no point in delving into the past. Forget it."

"Like *you've* forgotten it?"

The veins stood out on his forearms as he tightened his grip on the steering wheel. "You're angry, and you're looking for a target. I'm not going to give you one."

"Of course I'm angry. A wonderful woman was murdered this week—by my child's *father*. I keep wondering how I could have avoided this? Where did I go wrong? I was twenty-two when I made the decision to get involved with Manuel. How was I supposed to know he wasn't what he appeared to be? That he'd change so much? How was I supposed to know that caring about the wrong person could destroy my life?"

"It's a tough lesson to learn, but a lot of people have to learn it," he said.

"People like you?" she asked.

"Stop it, Emma."

"You want to make love to me again," she whispered.

He didn't deny it.

"And you want me to feel something when you do."

He didn't deny that, either.

"Yet you've shut yourself off from me completely."

He wouldn't look at her. "I'm not in a position to give you and Max what you need."

"Bullshit! That's a cop-out," she said. "You *could* care about me, if you'd let yourself. But your grief stands between us. And you won't share it with me, won't allow me to carry some of the load."

"There's more to it than grief, Emma. Let it go."

She didn't want to let it go. Letting *it* go, meant letting *him* go. "Tell me what happened."

No answer.

"Who's Vince?"

A muscle twitched in his jaw. "I'll help you and Max get settled in a weekly motel or a house or someplace like that. Then I'm leaving."

The finality of his declaration took her by surprise—and stung even more than she'd expected. "You're putting me on notice?"

"I've been honest about what to expect all along."

"Expecting more, and wanting more, are two different things," she said softly.

His scowl eased. "What I want has nothing to do with it, Emma."

"So tonight would just be one for the road?"

He sighed and shoved a hand through his hair. "It wouldn't be like that."

She'd been there, knew exactly what it'd be like. She'd give almost anything to make love with Preston again, but she couldn't bear the pain of having him turn his back on her afterward. Trying to rebuild her life after Manuel was bad enough. She couldn't afford to let Preston break her heart when she needed to be strong.

"There are some things I have to do, Emma," he said when she didn't respond. "I don't know what my life will be like after that."

"And you're offering me this great insight into your complexity because…"

"I don't want you to think tonight would be meaningless to me."

"You say this on the heels of 'I'm out of here'?" she said bitterly. "Well, don't bother trying to convince me, because I don't want you to touch me." She was already struggling with her guilt and sadness over Juanita's death and the knowledge that Manuel was now a murderer. She didn't need to add to that any disappointment over the fact that the one man who could claim her, heart and soul, wasn't willing to make the necessary sacrifice. The necessary compromise...

His gaze shifted from the road to linger in all the places she wanted him to put his hands, and for a second he lost the mask of indifference he wore so often. Naked desire showed on his face, riveting, hot. The sheer intensity caused her nipples to strain against her shirt. He made a liar out of her—that easily. She *did* want him to touch her. She just couldn't settle for one last night.

Finally, he met her eyes. "You want to make love to me as badly as I want to make love to you."

She shook her head. She'd already spent six years with Manuel, longing for more than he was capable of. "Not if your body is all you're willing to give me."

He drove in silence for several minutes. "I thought you were going to take up sleeping with any man you wanted," he said at last.

"That doesn't apply to you."

"Why not?"

"Because with you, I couldn't smile and wave when you drove away."

"We've only known each other a week," he said, but there was more incredulity in those words than anything else.

Her chest filled with a bittersweet ache as she looked at the man she knew she'd dream about for years. "But I'm already in love with you."

PRESTON SAT in the Jacuzzi, hoping Emma would be asleep when he returned to the room. He'd managed to find a brand-new motel in Cedar Rapids that had two bedrooms and a small kitchen area, and was available for rent by the week—or would be soon. The motel wasn't officially open for business until next week. They'd happened to catch the owner just as they pulled in, and Preston had talked him into letting them stay. He didn't care about the furniture that still needed to be moved into the lobby, or the doors and trim the owner planned to paint. His only concern was that Emma and Max would have a good roof over their heads, even if they didn't rent a house right away.

He felt confident that he'd found the ideal situation for them. But getting through this last night wasn't going to be easy. Now that they had two bedrooms, he and Emma could have some real privacy—and a bed—if they wanted it. And Preston couldn't go in there without wanting it.

I'm already in love with you.

He rubbed his temples. He wasn't sure how he felt about Emma's declaration. Surprised, excited, torn, even scared. He'd distanced himself from others too long for "I'm in love with you" not to make him nervous. He cared about her, knew she was right when she said he could care a lot more if only he'd let himself. But he couldn't. He was only days away from the moment that would define the rest of his life.

For the first time in a long while, Preston felt like having a cigarette.

Getting out of the water, he searched the pockets of the jeans he'd thrown on a nearby chair and came up with the keys to his van. He'd forget Emma and Max once he spent some time away from them, he promised himself. He'd ignore, forget, deny. He'd gotten damn good at shutting people out, hadn't he?

But when he returned with his cigarettes, he found Emma sitting in the Jacuzzi—and wasn't capable of ignoring her.

She said nothing as he passed through the gate. Because the Jacuzzi suddenly seemed very small, he took a chair near a white plastic table. "I guess you didn't see the sign," he said, striking a match.

"What sign?"

He shook out the match and tossed it in a clean ashtray on the table. "Pool area's closed for the night." He wanted Emma to go back inside. He'd come here to avoid her.

She shrugged. "There's no one around to kick me out."

He inhaled, released his breath. "There's me."

"I'm not afraid of you."

Did it matter if he was afraid of *her?* Of the pain he'd feel when he walked away in the morning?

He tried to concentrate on his cigarette. "Max is in the room?"

"He's out for the night."

"Are you sure it's safe to leave him?"

"What do you care?" she challenged.

He flicked his ashes off to the side. "I can see you're still in a good mood."

She sighed. "Our room's less than ten feet away. I wouldn't be much closer if I was watching TV."

Squinting through the smoke rising from his cigarette, he saw a bead of water roll down her neck and between her breasts....

"You're staring," she said.

He raised his eyebrows. "You *want* me to stare. That's why you came out here, isn't it? To show me what I'm missing?"

She reached for the tie to her swimsuit top. "If I was going to show you what you're missing, I probably wouldn't be wearing this." Pulling the string, she unfastened it.

Preston's mouth went dry as he watched her top fall to reveal the breasts he'd fondled last night. He wished he could act as though the sight didn't knock the breath right out of him, but it wasn't any use pretending. "Turning up the heat a little?" he said.

"Is it working?"

He didn't answer. She had to know it was.

She slid lower in the water, but not low enough that he couldn't see what he so badly wanted to touch. "Actually, I came out to say goodbye. Just in case you weren't planning on being here in the morning."

The water bubbled around her, coaxing him to join her. To free himself from the past. To move on....

But Dallas wouldn't let him.

He leaned over, elbows on his knees, and finished his cigarette.

"That would hurt Max, you know," she said, her tone softening. "He's crazy about you."

Preston closed his eyes and ran two fingers over his eyebrows. *Preston, watch me spell* bear.... *Hey, I can take my shot in my leg now! Doesn't hurt at all, see?... I drew you another picture.... Feel my muscles....*

"You'd never do that to him, would you?" she said. "You'd never leave without saying goodbye."

He didn't open his eyes. "Make sure he keeps up with his baseball. He's got real talent."

It wasn't the promise she wanted, but Preston wasn't sure he *could* say goodbye to Max.

She immediately got out, grabbed her swimsuit top and headed past him, toward the gate. Preston could tell she was upset and told himself to let her go. But his hand shot out at the last second and caught her wrist. "Emma..."

She stopped, but resisted when he tried to pull her closer. "Please?"

She struggled with herself for several seconds—he could see the conflict in her face. But, at long last, she moved between his knees, and he pressed his mouth against the heated skin of her stomach. He knew she wanted him to lower his defenses, tell her about the battles he was fighting, but he couldn't. He couldn't hear her say all the things Christy and his mother had already said. Didn't want her to doubt him— because he couldn't change his course, even for her.

"Preston?" she said uncertainly.

He tried to open up, to trust her. But he could manage only four words: "I need you tonight."

EMMA KNEW she should gently extricate herself and walk away. He hadn't said he'd stay. He hadn't told her what was going on in his life. He hadn't said much of anything. But the four words he *had* said sounded as if they'd been wrenched from him.

Running her fingers through his hair, she tried to offer what solace she could. But she wouldn't tell him she loved him. Not again. She knew it wouldn't make any difference.

"Let's go inside," he whispered, taking her hand. But she didn't want to. Inside, she'd be too conscious of what would happen in the morning. Out here, beneath a pale sliver of moon and a blanket of shiny stars, she could pretend that tonight would last forever.

"I want to make love in the Jacuzzi," she said, and the next thing she knew, their swimsuits were gone, the hot water was rising and falling around them, and all she could think about, all she could feel, was Preston.

CHAPTER TWENTY-TWO

"MOMMY!"

Emma opened her eyes to find Max standing at her bedside.

"Preston's gone."

She already knew that. She'd felt him get up a few minutes earlier. He'd smoothed the hair out of her face and pressed a kiss to her temple. She could have awakened fully, but she hadn't. She didn't want to see him go. She wanted to hold last night close, just a little longer.

But it was gone. It had slipped away with him.

"Did he tell you goodbye?" she asked.

"Yeah."

"He woke you up?"

"No, I was up."

Probably not. But at least Preston hadn't simply disappeared. "Did he say anything else?"

"To be a good beast."

"You *are* a good beast."

Max frowned. "Isn't he coming back, Mommy?"

"I'm not sure."

"What about baseball? He's my coach."

Emma kissed her son's soft cheek. For years she'd longed for a life that was just the two of them. Then why did she feel so incomplete without Preston? She was in Iowa now. She needed to search for a job, find a house, start her new life. Yet she could hardly summon the energy to get out of bed.

"Maybe his plans will change," she said.

"Where did he go?"

Emma couldn't face Max's questions. Not while she felt so bereft. "Want to go swimming?" she asked to distract him.

He perked up immediately. "Yeah!"

"First we'll have doughnuts for breakfast."

His smile widened. "Is this a party?"

Sort of a consolation prize. "If you're going swimming, you'll need the extra energy, right?"

Clapping his hands, he ran for his swimsuit. While he was gone, Emma let her eyes wander around the room. No computer. No duffel bag. No cell phone—

Her gaze shifted back to the dresser. There was *something* there.

Dragging herself out of bed, she moved closer. It was a small bottle of perfume. A gift. And it was sitting on an envelope that contained five-thousand dollars. On the outside, Preston had written "Buy yourself a car." Below that, he'd scribbled his telephone number.

She smiled as she held the perfume to her nose and breathed in the delicate scent. At least he'd given her a way to get hold of him.

She picked up the phone, wanting to hear his voice, even though he'd just left. But there was no dial tone. The motel didn't have telephone service yet, but it would in a few days. Maybe goodbye wasn't goodbye after all.

JOANIE HAD BEEN cool and distant on the phone but she'd agreed to meet Preston for breakfast. He thought he had a chance of getting her to talk. She probably still cared about

Christy. But as he waited for her to join him at the coffee shop she'd suggested, he was thinking more about the recent past. Emma would be up by now giving Max his insulin—

"Preston?"

He glanced up to see a woman standing at his table. It was Joanie, but if she hadn't spoken, he wouldn't have recognized her. She'd gained at least a hundred pounds. Her hands and feet were swollen. Even her face…

"You've changed the color of your hair," he said, to cover his surprise. He started to get up, but she waved him back into his seat.

"You don't have to stand. I know we're not friends anymore."

Grimacing, she maneuvered herself into the opposite seat. "You had to get a booth?"

He hadn't known she'd struggle to fit. "I— Would you rather move to a table?"

"No, we'll make do. And you can't hide your shock so don't even try."

"I'm just…"

"Wondering what the hell happened to me?"

Yes—to say the least. He cleared his throat. "Are you… ill?"

She rolled her eyes. "It's called pregnancy, okay? Weight gain. Water retention. I'm borderline toxemic, which means I swell. Believe it or not, today is one of my better days." She dabbed at a drop of sweat rolling down from her hairline. "God, I'll be glad when it's all over."

He could see why. "Is it Vince's baby?"

She gave him an odd look. "Of course."

"When's the baby due?"

"Six weeks."

And now she was facing a divorce. "I thought you didn't want children," he said.

"*Vince* didn't want children. He didn't want anything to slow us down." She made a noise of irritation. "God forbid we should have to miss a trip to Cancun every once in a while."

Preston motioned toward her stomach. "He changed his mind, I see."

She clasped her swollen hands together on the table. Preston noticed that she was no longer wearing her wedding ring—any rings. With all the swelling, she probably couldn't. "Actually, he didn't. This was my choice. I decided I wasn't willing to give up being a mother just because he didn't want to be a father, so I went off birth control. But—"

The waitress brought Joanie a glass of ice water and handed her a menu.

"You were saying…" Preston prompted as the waitress walked away.

"He nearly had me talked into an abortion. I was willing to do it to save my marriage. Until I caught him in the back room with his new receptionist. Then I decided I was tired of sacrificing my desires for his."

"I take it the interaction between the two of them wasn't exactly business-related."

"You got it."

"So you left him because he was cheating on you?"

"No. Cheating was a pretty common occurrence for Vince."

Wanting a refill on his coffee, Preston pushed his cup to the edge of the table. "As far as I know, he didn't run around on you when we were friends."

She looked at the sheet of daily specials attached to the

front of the menu. "That's because you were there, setting the right example."

Preston leaned forward. "You're giving *me* credit for his fidelity?"

"You were completely committed to Christy. Since he admired you, he followed suit. I should've thanked you." She set the menu aside and rearranged the salt-and-pepper shakers, Sweet'n Low packets and creamers. "But I wasn't too happy with you later on," she added. "How's Christy?"

"Better since she remarried."

"Remarried?"

Preston hooked an arm over the back of the booth. "You didn't know we broke up?"

"Vince and I haven't kept in contact with anyone."

"Why is that?"

"Vince didn't want to look back, didn't want to deal with all the negativity."

"This was when you were living in Nevada?"

"How'd you know where we were living?"

"I've been looking for a long time." He'd nearly caught Vince there, in Fallon, when Gordon said his name had turned up on a credit application. But there'd been no "Dr." attached, and by the time Preston had exhausted all other leads and realized he had the right Vince Wendell, Vince and Joanie had already moved on. Without a trace. "But Vince never set up his practice."

"He was rattled, nervous. He wasn't ready yet."

"You didn't mind that he wasn't working?"

She shrugged. "Not really. I could understand. It'd be hard to have your best friend accuse you of such a thing."

The waitress refreshed his cup, and he slid his coffee back in front of him. "It's even harder to have your best friend do what Vince did," he said levelly, and was astonished when she didn't fly into a defensive rage, as she would have two years ago.

"What happened between you and Christy?" she asked, changing the subject.

"Can't you guess?"

"You let Dallas's death tear you apart, right? I was so angry with you, I *wanted* that to happen. I had everything in Half Moon Bay. My husband had sworn off other women and was treating me right for the first time in our marriage. He seemed to be enjoying his practice. We had a big house, plenty of friends. And then..." She sighed.

"And then Vince ruined it for all of us," Preston finished.

The waitress had put the coffeepot away and returned to take their order, but Preston couldn't eat. He handed back his menu. "Nothing for me."

"Me, neither," Joanie said.

The waitress offered her coffee instead, but she snapped, "Don't you know that caffeine causes birth defects?"

"I—I didn't realize you were—" the waitress began helplessly, but Preston interrupted. "Bring her some orange juice, please."

He watched the waitress scurry off. "God, you're edgy," he told Joanie.

"Yeah, well, I don't have much patience these days with people who can still fit in their shoes." She met his eyes. "And I'm not sure what I'm hoping to accomplish by meeting you."

The conversation had already highlighted the dramatic changes in all their lives. It hardly seemed possible that one man had caused everything. The loss of a child. The loss of friendship. Two divorces. Would it end there? "I think you came because, deep down, you believe me."

"I don't. Or I would've come forward a long time ago."

"Really? What about that big house and those good friends you were talking about? What about the life you didn't want to give up? Are you sure you were looking at the situation objectively?"

She scowled and moved her water around in agitation, smearing the condensation that had rolled down the glass onto the varnished wood. "It doesn't matter how objectively I look at it. It's crazy to think the man I married could be capable of doing…what you said."

"Sometimes the people we love can surprise us."

She didn't respond.

"Don't you at least wonder if I could be right?" he asked.

"No."

It was a lie. She obviously had doubts, or she wouldn't have come today. "I don't believe you."

She turned her hands palms up. "Okay, so there's been a time or two when he's acted…a little odd, and maybe it raised a few questions in my mind. But most people act strange now and then. It doesn't make them murderers."

"That depends."

She pursed her lips, and he knew she was wondering whether to continue this conversation.

"Are you still in love with him, Joanie?"

"No. I'm…well, look at me. I'm hurt, disappointed. Half the time, I don't even know what I'm feeling, and I'm about to have a baby. I can't cope with this, too." She grabbed her purse and started to get up, but he caught her arm.

"How well will you cope if he does it again?"

That got her. Misery entered her eyes, and her shoulders slumped. Finally, she settled back and dropped her purse. "What do you want to know?"

"Why don't you tell me what he did that was odd?"

"He came to me once. Told me he thought there was something wrong with him, that he wasn't normal."

"Did he explain?"

"He said he was tempted to do some strange things."

A shiver of excitement shot down Preston's spine. This sounded hopeful. Maybe, at long last… "Like…"

She rubbed her eyes, and he felt a twinge of sympathy as he realized how tired she was. "I didn't want to hear any more. He was scaring me, and our marriage was already in trouble. I was trying to hold everything together, you know?"

"So what did you say?"

"I told him he was as normal as anyone I'd ever met, and he never approached me with it again."

Preston's heart sank. She'd almost had him. Vince had wanted to talk, and she'd told him she didn't want to hear it. Shit! The frustration and helplessness nearly killed him. "You've never asked him about it since?" he asked.

She eyed him speculatively. "You look good, you know that? You're a little thinner, a little rougher around the edges. But you were always handsome. I used to enjoy going out with you and Christy, just so I could watch you." She chuckled. "Don't get me wrong. I wasn't, you know, *interested.* I loved Vince. But…you're certainly well above average."

Preston didn't give a damn about the way he looked. Especially right now. "Did you ever ask him about it?" he repeated.

"Of course." She moved back so the waitress could deliver her juice. "Toward the end, when we were fighting a lot, I threw it up to him all the time. He *always* denied it."

"That doesn't make him innocent."

"It doesn't make him guilty, either."

Preston stroked his chin. There had to be some way to get to the truth. "Could there be any physical proof?"

"I told you he didn't do it."

"What about Billy?"

"What about him? Every doctor loses a patient occasionally."

Preston had heard the same words before. "And Melanie?"

"She lived, remember?"

"You don't find it uncanny that Vince knew to hospitalize Melanie when almost every other doctor would've diagnosed her as having the flu?"

"He said he knew she had something worse."

"How?"

"I don't know!"

"I was thinking there might be some office records," he said. "Some notes on Dallas's medical chart, or Melanie's or Billy's for that matter, to indicate what might have happened."

"No. Anyway, we got rid of practically everything when we moved from California. The few records Vince kept are stored in his garage. But if he did what you think, I can't imagine he'd keep proof of it."

"Damn it!" Preston dropped his head in his hands. At this point, he didn't care if she got up and left. They had nothing.

But she didn't leave. A few seconds later, he felt her hand on his arm. "Preston?"

"What?"

"I know how much Dallas meant to you."

When he said nothing, she sighed. "Vince came home crying the night Billy died."

Preston studied her, wondering where she was going with this. "He felt bad for Billy's family?"

"No, he was scared."

Preston caught his breath. "What?"

"He was afraid someone would blame him. That's all he talked about. 'What if they think I did it, Joanie? Every doctor loses a patient once in a while, right? Children die of meningitis all the time. They're not going to come knocking on my door, are they?'"

Preston remembered his conversation with Vince on the golf course. *How'd he die?…It was nothing I did.* But Preston hadn't intimated that it was. "If he didn't do anything wrong, why the guilty conscience?"

She raised both shoulders in another shrug. "I don't know. I dismissed it. I guess I was in denial. Maybe that's why I got so angry when you came over that day and accused him of causing Dallas's death. Because I was afraid it was true. I'd seen how Vince had acted with Melanie and Billy, knew the attention he required. And I knew how much he admired you, how much he wanted you to think the world of him."

"I *did* think the world of him," Preston muttered. That was part of what made him so angry. He'd let the wolf in at the door.

She shook her head sadly. "Vince needs constant reinforcement."

The coffee soured in Preston's stomach. One man's vanity had cost him so much. "How did he behave the day Dallas died?"

"Not scared, like before. Disturbed. Anxious. After you accused him, he locked himself in his study and drank for hours. He wouldn't talk about Dallas or you after that. I think he wanted to shove the whole incident behind him, like he'd already done with Billy. Only this time the tragedy involved our best friends and wasn't so easy to forget."

"So you moved."

"Moving was my idea. I thought it might help him recover from what had happened. Leaving Pennsylvania had certainly been a good thing. But our lives haven't been the same since California."

"Why?"

"Vince was always selfish, but he got worse. His ego needed constant support, and not just from me. From everyone."

Preston suddenly understood why his comment that Vince might do it again had struck home with her. She knew he lived for the limelight; suspected—feared—how far he might go to get it.

"Do you have any idea how he might've gone about making these kids sick?" Preston asked. He needed details, something besides doubt and conjecture, something that might make the police finally listen.

"No, but it wouldn't be hard. He's said so himself. Not long after we were married, he came home from being on-call at the hospital and told me he couldn't believe how easy it'd be for a doctor to murder someone."

Joanie's words were chilling. Especially because Vince had made a similar remark to him once. *I could commit murder and get away with it. That's how much trust a doctor holds.*

"Can you find out some specifics?" he asked. "Help me establish a chain of events? Anything?"

"I told you, there're no records left."

"Then you'll have to talk to Vince."

"And say what? He barely speaks to me anymore."

"Tell him you've been thinking about what happened to Dallas, that you're beginning to wonder if I might be right. You could even mention that you're thinking about going to the police, just to get a reaction."

She shook her head. "No way. I'll get a reaction, all right. He'll completely lose it."

"That's why you won't do it in person. We'll do it over the phone."

"We?" she repeated.

Preston stood up and tossed a ten-dollar bill on the table for his coffee and Joanie's juice. "I'll be listening in."

MANUEL WATCHED the stores of downtown Cedar Rapids drift slowly past his window as he drove his rented Town Car down J Avenue North. He was tired and rumpled from the flight into O'Hare, and eager to get a motel room. But at least the drive from Chicago had only taken three hours.

Hector had traveled with him and was riding in the passenger seat. "We're definitely gonna stand out here, man."

"Why's that?" Manuel asked.

"This place is filled with white people."

"You're white."

"Not this white."

"Welcome to the midwest."

"I don't like it here."

"We won't be staying long."

Hector made a disgusting sound as he gathered mucous and spat out the open window. "Are you sure Vanessa's in this Podunk place?"

Manuel wrinkled his nose in distaste. He hated Hector's personal habits, was tempted to roll up the window so he couldn't spit again. But the cool seventy-degree air was beginning to revive him, and men like Hector served a purpose. "I'm sure," he said. "We're only a day behind her. From what I could tell on the phone, Preston has business in this town. I think he and Vanessa are planning to stay a while."

Tapping his fingers on the armrest, Hector rocked in his seat—another habit Manuel found annoying. But at least it was one Hector couldn't help. The twitching came from the drugs. "What kind of business is it?"

Manuel's eyes constantly scanned the street, in case he got a glimpse of Vanessa. "I have no idea. And I don't care because he'll never get the chance to do it."

Hector pulled out the bag of cocaine he carried with him. Setting a hand mirror on the armrest between them, he poured the white powder onto the mirror and used a razor to cut himself a line.

"Watch it," Manuel growled. "We just passed the police station."

"So who's gonna arrest me in this town? Barney Fife?" Hector laughed, then snorted the white powder and leaned back.

Manuel knew he was experiencing that first, thrilling rush. He also knew Hector would snort another line in a minute. Hector lived for dope, had built up a significant resistance. Which made his habit very expensive. Expensive enough that he'd do just about anything for his next fix. In that way, Manuel supposed Hector's dependence was a good thing; it made him very cooperative.

Manuel, on the other hand, wasn't stupid enough to let himself get addicted to the product that was making him rich. He liked a little cocaine occasionally, when he was in Mexico and had a houseful of beautiful women willing to entertain his most sordid fantasies. Other than that, he preferred a clear head.

"We'll start by searching all the motels, like we did in Ely," he said.

Hector blinked at him, his eyes glassy, his pupils fully dilated. "For Preston's name? Or the name Vanessa used in

Ely?" He looked baffled for a moment. "What was the name she used?"

"That stuff's eating your brain," Manuel said. "Emma Wright. We'll check for both. This town isn't that big. It shouldn't take long."

Hector cackled, an overloud sound inspired by the high he was experiencing. "Man, this Preston fellow isn't gonna know what hit him."

"Don't touch Vanessa or Dominick," Manuel said. "I'll take care of them myself."

"But Preston's mine, right? You want me to do him like you did Juanita." He formed his fingers into the shape of a gun and pointed it out the window at some old lady walking down the street. "Bang!" he yelled, and she just about fell off her wobbly high heels.

Hector laughed uproariously, but Manuel didn't even smile. He didn't like being reminded of Juanita. When he wasn't living his "other life" with Vanessa and Dominick, he dealt in a nasty, dark world. But until Juanita, he'd never killed anyone. He saved the dirty work for addicts like Hector.

"Only if I don't get to him first," he said. Maybe killing Juanita hadn't appeased his anger, but it'd be different with Preston. All he had to do was imagine Preston in Vanessa's bed and the blood thirst became so great he could hardly contain it. He wanted to slit his throat in front of her.

"How are you gonna kill him?"

"As slow and painfully as possible."

Hector snorted another line, waited for the rush, then gave him a spacey grin. "You should cut the bastard's dick off."

WHILE SHE DROVE, Emma glanced at the inside of the 1986 Monte Carlo she'd just bought. The seats were torn, the dash was cracked, and the outside wasn't in great shape. Rust had corroded the metal along the bottom. There was a large dent on the left-rear panel. The sun had bleached the maroon paint, especially on the hood. But it had cost only $3100, and it ran. The man who'd sold it to her had originally bought it for his son and daughter-in-law, so they'd have a second car. They'd owned it for nearly twelve years before upgrading and, judging by the service records, had taken excellent care of the engine. She'd gotten a bargain, really. Someday soon, she'd pawn her earrings and the ring Manuel had given her for Christmas and use the money to pay Preston back. But she knew he wasn't in any hurry to be reimbursed or he wouldn't have left the money as carelessly as he did. She should concentrate instead on finding work before worrying about the debt. Work, then a house.

Stopping at a traffic light, she turned her attention to the city around her. At a population of 120,000, Cedar Rapids was a little bigger than the place she'd imagined living. But it had plenty of schools and businesses. She thought she'd be safer here and have a better chance of finding a job. And, despite her earlier feelings on the subject, she didn't want to move anywhere else if Preston was going to be nearby.

"Can we go back to the motel and go swimming again?" Max asked as she pulled into the post office and stopped at the drive-through mail drop.

Emma decided she could watch him while reading the want ads. "In a little while," she said, and struggled to roll down her window. She hadn't seen a car with a hand crank for a number of years, and this one was jammed. Finally, when she couldn't get the window to budge more than two inches, she gave up and simply opened her door.

"What are you doing?" Max asked.

"Mailing something."

"What?"

"A letter." Emma stared down at the address of the Drug Enforcement Agency, which she'd looked up on the Internet at the public library, then gazed from the envelope to Juanita's list of names and numbers. Would the list be enough to put Manuel behind bars? She wasn't sure. She'd put this errand off as long as possible because turning those names and numbers over to the authorities frightened her. To protect herself and Max, she'd made a copy and was sending the list anonymously, with a typed explanation that she'd also prepared at the library. But there were ways of tracking things she didn't understand, which meant there could still be a severe backlash, one that could cost her years and years of running, her life, or even Max.

Still, somebody had to stand up and take the risk. Somebody had to draw a line, or people like Manuel would always win.

She must've sighed because Max leaned over the seat and touched her shoulder. "What's wrong, Mommy?"

Stuffing the list into the envelope she'd already stamped, she licked the seal. "Nothing baby. I'm okay," she said, but she wasn't thinking about her words. She was thinking about Manuel and his family, the clandestine meetings they had, the hushed conversations, the many extended trips to Mexico, the bagfuls of money Manuel sometimes brought home. All of this she'd typed out in perfect detail. The Rodriguez family was breaking the law. She knew she should be turning them in on principle alone. But she wasn't doing this for principle. She was doing it for Juanita.

"Thank you, my friend," she whispered. Then she dropped the envelope in the box, slammed her creaky old door and drove away.

CHAPTER TWENTY-THREE

PRESTON FROWNED at the pack of cigarettes he'd tossed on Joanie's table. He was tempted to smoke. Since he'd left Emma and Max early this morning, he'd nearly lit up at least a thousand different times. But the moment he put that cigarette between his fingers and started to strike a match, he remembered Max and threw it away. He didn't want to do anything he wouldn't want Max to copy, even though Max could no longer see him.

"Are you ready?" Joanie asked.

She sounded nervous. Preston felt sorry for her. The apartment she'd rented was a far cry from the home she'd owned in Half Moon Bay, and it was obvious she hadn't felt well enough, physically or emotionally, to clean it. Dishes cluttered the counters. Clothes covered the floor. The kitchen smelled like rotten eggs.

"Depression," she'd muttered when she let him in.

She'd also said her sister would move in with her soon to help get ready for the baby. Preston thought that was probably a good idea.

"Go ahead," he replied. He turned the tape recorder on, and she dialed Vince at his office.

Once the receptionist answered, she signaled Preston to pick up the extension.

Preston held his microphone to the receiver and listened around it as Joanie asked for Vince.

The receptionist paused. "Is this Joanie?"

"Yes, it is."

"Oh." Another pause. "Hold on a second."

Music came through as Joanie made a face at the woman who'd just put them on hold. *She's the one,* she mouthed to him.

Preston gave her a sympathetic look. Maybe Joanie had her shortcomings, but he didn't think anyone deserved to be married to Vince.

"Is he ever going to answer?" he whispered after another five minutes.

"He's probably lifting her skirt first," she whispered back. "But don't worry. That never takes long."

Preston smiled at her sarcasm, then quickly sobered when Vince picked up. "Joanie?"

"Hi, Vince. I take it you were busy diddling your receptionist."

"I'm busy seeing a *patient.*"

"Well, I hope she isn't married. Her husband might not take his marriage vows as lightly as you did."

"I mean, I'm seeing a patient who's *ill,*" he snapped. "What do you need?"

"Don't you want to know how the baby's doing?"

"If you're calling to—"

"No, this isn't about the baby. I know you don't care about that."

When Vince didn't contradict her, Preston winced at the disappointment and pain she had to be experiencing.

"What is it, then?" he asked.

"I've been doing some thinking."

"Turning over a new leaf?"

Preston was shocked by how antagonistic their relationship had become.

"I guess you could say that," Joanie replied. "Considering I've never gone to the police before."

He fell silent, and she flipped her finger at him even though he couldn't see her.

"What are you talking about?" he asked, his voice suddenly filled with caution.

"I'm talking about Billy and Dallas."

"Why?" He lowered his voice, and Preston guessed the receptionist who'd answered the phone, or someone else, was around. "I've told you before, I didn't have anything to do with what happened."

"Healthy kids don't normally die of the flu, Vince. Left to himself, Dallas would have recovered."

"Dallas didn't have the flu. He had meningococcal septicemia."

"Question is, how'd he get it?"

"You've asked me this before, Joanie."

"I'm asking again."

"One in ten people carry the bacteria that causes meningitis and septicemia. It's passed on by close contact. In a very few people, the bacteria gets into the blood stream and cause meningitis and/or septicemia. Anyone can get it. Anyone can die from it. You can accuse me all you want, but you'll never be able to prove a thing. Now I'm going to hang up—"

"You do, and I'll tell the police how you cried for hours after Billy died, asking me over and over again, 'You don't think they'll blame me, do you?' I don't know about you, but that sounds a little suspicious to me."

"It's been five years since Billy died!"

"And only two years since Dallas did."

"Where are you going with this?"

"I think you'll do it again."

"No, I won't!"

Joanie turned to stare, wide-eyed, at Preston. "Are you admitting you did it before?"

"N-no, I'm n-not," he said. Preston hadn't known Vince to possess any kind of speech impairment until Dallas died. Then he'd stuttered his way through every explanation about what had happened for the next twenty-four hours.

Joanie glanced down at the notes Preston had given her earlier. "I've been doing a little research, Vince," she said. "Less than five percent of people with meningococcal meningitis die of the disease. So far, you've lost sixty-six percent. Two out of three."

"For your information, m-m-morbidity among people who come down with s-s-septicemia, who also show no symptoms of m-meningitis, is around twenty percent, not f-five. I've done my research, too, Joanie. No one's going to pin those boys' d-deaths on me. Septicemia c-can strike within hours."

"Is that why you chose it?" she asked softly.

He paused for a long time. Preston waited, counting his own galloping heartbeat, pressing the microphone closer. *Come on, you son of a bitch. Say something we can use.*

Finally, Vince laughed. "You'll n-never be able to outsmart m-me, Joanie. D-don't even try," he said and hung up.

Preston snapped off the recorder and sank onto the couch.

"He's feeling arrogant," Joanie said. "He thinks he's in love with that stupid little receptionist. Says, 'She makes me feel like a man again.'"

Preston didn't respond. He'd thought having Joanie on his

side would be the break he'd been looking for. But Joanie had done her best and they'd netted nothing except a little flustered stuttering.

A NOISE WOKE Emma late in the night. Someone was moving around. Was it Max?

She listened carefully, waiting.

There it was again. Movement. A rustling sound. But it wasn't coming from Max's room.

Getting up, she hurried to her son's bedside, just in case she was wrong. She lived in constant fear that he'd need her in the night and she wouldn't hear him. But she found him sleeping peacefully.

So what had disturbed her?

She returned to her own bedroom to check the time on the radio alarm. It was after midnight. And she and Max were supposed to be alone in the motel.

Drawing on the robe Preston had bought her, she shoved her tousled hair out of her eyes and tiptoed into the living room. From her kitchen window, she could see the moon reflecting off the pool a few feet away. The water looked like ice.

Chills ran down her spine as she thought she saw someone sitting in the Jacuzzi where she and Preston had made love last night. But it was only the reflection of a lounge chair. The pool area was empty. From her vantage point, she couldn't see anyone lurking around the buildings.

A noise at the front door caused her pulse to jump into overdrive. Leaning closer to the window, she strained to see the stoop—then jumped back when she spotted the shape of a man. There *was* someone outside! Her first thought was to grab the phone, but she didn't have service.

The door handle began to turn. *Click, click... Click, click.*

Pressing a hand to her chest, she moved silently toward it. She tried to peer through the peephole, but it was completely dark. Someone had covered it—probably with a thumb or a finger.

Oh, God...was it Manuel? She'd already mailed the list to the DEA. If he got in, he'd kill her, just like Juanita. And poor Max would probably see it all.

She grabbed Max's bat, which she'd propped against the wall before going to bed. "Hello?" she said, the terror she was feeling evident in the breathless quality of her voice.

"It's me."

Emma's knees nearly gave out on her. It wasn't Manuel; it was Preston.

She put the bat back, removed the chain and opened the door to find him leaning against the side of the building. He had a cigarette in the corner of his mouth, but it wasn't lit.

"You scared me," she breathed. A quick glance at the peephole told her he hadn't covered it at all. The workmen who were putting the finishing touches on the place had taped over it so they could paint the doors.

"I'm sorry. I didn't want to wake you, but my key wouldn't work. I must've demagnetized it somehow, probably by keeping it too close to my cell phone."

She focused on his unlit cigarette. "Looks like you need a match."

He took the cigarette out of his mouth and slipped it inside his shirt pocket. "No. I quit."

The first two buttons of his denim shirt were undone, revealing part of the tanned, muscular chest she admired so much. She remembered the smooth texture of that chest beneath her hands as she'd straddled him in the Jacuzzi, and ached to feel his arms around her again.

But he made no move to come any closer.

"Did you buy a car?" he asked.

She toyed with the belt of her robe. The air around them felt heavy with the things they needed to say. But Preston was the one holding back, and she knew better than to press him. At least he'd come to her tonight. That was a victory of sorts. As of last night, he hadn't been planning on it.

"Didn't you see that beautiful maroon Monte Carlo in the parking lot?" she teased.

His teeth flashed in a grin. "*Now* do you miss your Jaguar?"

"No." She let her eyes caress the face she loved so much. There were lines of fatigue around his mouth, making her worry about what might have happened to him today. What was he going through? And why wouldn't he share it with her? "All I miss is you," she said softly.

He looked torn, but he still didn't move toward her. He pushed away from the wall. "Emma, I can't stay. I only came to check on you."

"Well, I'm fine. Besides buying the car today, I learned about a teaching job. Maybe I'll be lucky enough to find a position."

"Are you going to use your real name?"

"No, I'm Emma Wright now."

"What about housing?" he asked.

"There're a few houses for rent in the paper, but I want to make sure I can get work first."

"A good plan." He frowned at the baseball bat. "How's Max?"

"Lonely without you."

"He's a great kid." He glanced reluctantly behind him. "I guess I'd better go." Bending his head, he gave her a light kiss and started to move away. But Emma had no intention of letting him leave so easily. She wasn't sure what was keeping them apart, but she wasn't going to let it beat her without a fight. Catching his hand, she guided it inside her robe and beneath her T-shirt.

"Are you sure you want to go?" she asked.

"I have to," he said, but he hesitated only briefly before his fingers curved around her breast.

"Will a few hours really make any difference, Preston?"

He opened her robe to take her nipple in his mouth. When he raised his head, his breath was coming quicker, but he was still fighting his instincts. "It'll make a difference," he said. "Every time I make love to you, I—"

"What?"

"Lose a little more of me," he said, his heavy-lidded eyes fastened to where his mouth had been.

She looked at him from beneath her lashes, then leaned in to kiss his neck, to feel his heartbeat at the base of his throat. "Is that so bad?" she whispered, sliding her hands under his shirt to rake her fingernails along his back.

Finally, his desire overcame his restraint. He groaned as his mouth crushed hers in an eager, passionate kiss. "I guess there are worse ways to go," he said, and lifted her in his arms.

LONG AFTER EMMA FELL ASLEEP, Preston lay awake, staring at the ceiling. He'd contacted the police again today, as well as the closest FBI field office. But the effort hadn't done him any good. They'd heard from him before and weren't interested in any new information. When he talked about Melanie and Billy, they talked about coincidence. When he mentioned the mysterious shot Melanie Deets had received, they said Vince might have forgotten to write it down. When he told them what Joanie had to say about Vince's reaction to Billy's death, they interpreted it as sour grapes. Nothing had changed. Dallas was dead. Preston was seen as the grieving father looking for someone to blame. And Vince was still free to hurt another child.

Emma shifted in her sleep and curled closer to him. Preston gave her a soft peck on the lips before carefully extricating himself. He hated to leave her, but all his hopes had been whittled down to one—a direct confrontation. Joanie had given him Vince's home address. If he could get Vince to confess, it would all be over and he could live a normal life again.

But he knew the chances of that were next to nil. Which was why he'd be taking his gun.

"Preston?" she murmured as he pulled on his jeans.

"Hmm?"

"Are you leaving?"

He knelt beside her, his pants still unbuttoned. "I have to."

"Will you be coming back?"

"I don't know," he said. That would depend on whether or not he ended up killing a man.

"HERE HE COMES," Manuel said, and shoved Hector back behind the building.

"We didn't really see his face," Hector whispered. "Are you sure we have the right guy?"

"Positive." Who else could it be? Manuel had known he'd found Vanessa's lover the moment he saw that beat-up brown van passing through town. It was just like the one that had torn out of the parking lot at the Gas-N-Go in Ely, and it fit the description Dominick had given him over the phone, as well. Fortunately, it wasn't difficult to follow. They'd trailed Preston to this motel, one they hadn't checked earlier because a sign posted on the front-office window said the grand opening wasn't for another week.

None of that mattered, though. Manuel had seen Vanessa open the door.

He ground his teeth as he remembered her slipping Preston's hand inside her robe. She'd welcomed his touch, responded to it eagerly. *Slut.*

But he'd take care of Preston. The way Vanessa and Preston had held each other, the way they'd kissed, left little doubt as to what they'd been doing once they went inside. Thinking about it had nearly driven Manuel mad. He'd longed to barge into the room and kill Preston right there, in front of Vanessa, as he'd dreamed of doing. But he didn't want Dominick to see him kill anyone. And he didn't want his son accidentally hurt.

Fortunately, his patience was paying off. For a while there, he thought he'd have to bide his time until morning. But Preston was leaving already, only two hours after he'd arrived. "Follow him," he told Hector as Preston climbed into the van.

Hector pulled a semiautomatic out of his belt and checked the magazine. "You want me to take him out?"

"No, that's my pleasure. Bring him..."

Where? In a few minutes, Manuel would have Emma and Max. And he certainly didn't want to risk letting Preston get away.

"Dead is dead," Hector reminded him. "As long as he's not around, he can't cause any more problems."

They were wasting time. "Fine," Manuel said carelessly. "Do it." It was Vanessa who'd betrayed him; it was Vanessa who'd pay.

"What do you want me to do with the body?"

"Leave it. We'll be in Mexico long before the cops figure out what happened. Maybe they never will."

"But if I take the Town Car, you'll be on foot."

"That Monte Carlo in the lot must belong to Vanessa. I'll use it."

"Where do you want to meet afterward?"

"Nowhere. I'm going to take my wife and kid, and head to Chicago to catch a plane home." He dug in his pocket and handed Hector a wad of cash. "Find your own way to San Diego. I'll wait for you there."

Hector accepted the money and the keys, then hurried around the building.

A moment later, Manuel heard the van start and watched Preston pull out of the lot. Across the street, Hector's headlights came on, and Manuel knew he'd never have to worry about Preston again.

CHAPTER TWENTY-FOUR

SOMEONE WAS at the door. Again. Emma heard the soft knock in her sleep but the sound blended with her dreams, until it grew louder. *Knock, knock, knock.*

She opened her eyes and blinked at the darkness. Was Preston back? It felt as though he'd barely left. She could still smell him on the sheets, feel the strength of the arms that had held her.

Rolling over, she squinted at the clock. It was three-thirty in the morning. He'd been gone only long enough for her to doze off.

She kicked away the covers, then got up and shuffled through the living room. He must have forgotten something.

"I'm coming," she murmured so he wouldn't wake Max. Preston had tested her son's blood before he left. Max was a safe 142, which meant that Emma could catch up on her rest by sleeping late in the morning.

"Preston?"

No answer. Instinctively, she checked the peephole, but that didn't do any good. She'd forgotten to take off the tape.

Retrieving the bat she'd kept close at hand, she unlocked the dead bolt and started to open the door. "Preston? Is something wr—"

A fist smacked the panel so hard it hit her in the head and

knocked her back. She fell as a man's hand slid up the inside of the door, trying to unlatch the security chain. A diamond ring on the fourth finger, barely visible in the dim light drifting in from the outside pole lights, told her who it was even before she heard his voice.

"Open the door, Vanessa. It's all over. You're coming home."

Emma's thoughts scattered in a thousand different directions as she scrambled to her feet. How had Manuel found her? What would he do if he got in? And how could she shield Max from what was coming? He was jostled about in the night so often, with all the testing of his blood and the shots, that he slept deeply. But she had no idea if he'd sleep through *this*.

"Vanessa?" he said, his voice coaxing.

Terror made her heart jackhammer against her chest as she grabbed the bat she'd dropped when she fell. Her hands were already starting to sweat. "What?"

"Let me in." His voice held a threatening note that promised things would get much worse if she didn't. She was so frightened of Manuel, so accustomed to giving him whatever he demanded just to keep the peace, that she almost obeyed.

Almost. Gripping the bat more tightly, she swallowed hard. "No. You'd better leave, Manuel. I've got a bat, and I'll use it if I have to."

"A bat? You think you're going to hit me with a bat?" The chain rattled as Manuel struggled to slide it off.

Emma didn't dare move any closer. She held her stance as sweat gathered on her upper lip and ran down her back.

Suddenly, his voice softened. "I just want to talk to you, *querida*. This is crazy. What you've been doing doesn't make sense. Why would you run from me? I love you."

He didn't love her. He smothered her, wrung the joy from her life.

"I—I want you to leave me alone. Please, Manuel. I don't want to hurt you. Just go. Live your life and let me live mine."

"So you can spread your legs for that bastard who just came out of here?" he cried.

Emma gasped and covered her mouth. Preston! If Manuel had seen him leaving... "Where is he?" she asked. "D-did you hurt him?"

"Not yet, *mi amor.* I won't do anything to loverboy if you'll open the door. Come back to me and everything will be fine."

Fear squeezed her windpipe, made it almost impossible to breathe. *Juanita's dead. The police just found her body.*

Was Preston dead, too? Or was he lying on the ground outside, bleeding?

That thought made her long to throw off the chain and charge outside, wielding her bat. She'd sacrifice anything to reach Preston. Anything except Max. If she let Manuel in, he might disarm her. Then there'd be absolutely nothing she could do.

"Come on, *querida.* If you don't want to be with me anymore, we'll work something out," he said, still groping for the chain. "You should live in San Diego. I want to see my son. I have that right."

Normally a man *did* have the right to see his children. Manuel knew how much she loved her son, knew she'd feel guilty about denying them a relationship. But she couldn't let Manuel see Max. Manuel had killed Juanita, for God's sake. He wasn't sane.

"Not anymore," she said.

"What?"

"You gave up that right when you murdered Juanita."

"Open the damn door!"

Panic stole Emma's breath, but that split second brought clarity. She had only one choice. Letting Manuel in wouldn't help Preston. If Manuel managed to reach her, it would be all over, despite the bat. She'd already sent the list to police. His family wouldn't permit him to forgive her, even if he wanted to. He'd kill her and Preston, too.

The chain was nearly off. In a few more seconds...

Adrenaline had Emma shaking, but she gathered her strength and shoved as hard as she could against the door.

Manuel cried out when the pressure crushed his hand, but she didn't care. She wouldn't let him in, no matter what she had to do. She no longer cared about the noise he was making or the fact that they might wake Max. She prayed the disturbance might rouse someone who could help her.

But she had little hope of that. If Preston was still at the motel, still alive and capable of reacting, he'd be here by now. And there wasn't another soul in the whole complex.

Manuel's screams echoed in Emma's head. She wished she could block them out—along with the revolting feel of his hand in the door. The violence sickened her.

Don't think about it. Just hang on.... Don't let him in.... Don't let him in.... Don't—

Finally Manuel kicked the door, which opened just wide enough so he could retrieve his hand. When it slammed shut, Emma threw the bolt, but she knew Manuel wasn't going to leave. He was cursing loudly, calling her some of the vilest names she'd ever heard.

"You broke my hand, bitch! I'll kill you for that. Do you hear me? You're dead. You're as good as dead! And this time I'll enjoy it."

Emma rushed to the phone. The complex wasn't supposed to receive telephone service until the day before it opened, but she couldn't help hoping….

No dial tone. And Manuel was no longer at the door. He'd moved to the window. She could see his silhouette through the blinds as he tested the lock. At first she thought he was trying to wiggle it open, so the sound of shattering glass surprised her. He was coming in.

Grabbing the bat, she turned to run into Max's room. She had to protect her son at all costs. But the noise had finally awakened him. She nearly tripped over him in the dark as he met her in the hall.

"Mommy?" he said uncertainly.

Emma's eyes darted to the front door. She wanted to scoop her son into her arms and make a run for it, but Max was too heavy to carry far, and Manuel was too close. He'd cut her off before she could clear the portal.

The bathroom! The bathroom had no windows. She'd lock them both inside and hope they could last until the construction workers arrived in the morning. If Manuel got in somehow, she'd use the bat. There wasn't any other way.

"Come on, Max," she cried, and started pulling him into the master bedroom. But Manuel was already in the apartment.

"Hurry!" The bathroom seemed miles away. Emma couldn't breathe, couldn't move fast enough. She felt as if she was running through quicksand, going nowhere….

"What's happening?" Max asked, confused, frightened.

She was too busy dragging him along to answer.

They were only three steps from the bathroom when footsteps pounded behind her. The way Manuel was cursing, the glass made her wonder if he'd been cut. But his injuries didn't seem to hamper his strength when he seized her hair and yanked her back.

VINCE'S HOME WAS two stories high and made of wood and stone. Large and rambling, it sat on a small creek and had one whole wall of glass. A copse of trees off to the side provided a great place to sit and watch what went on inside the house. But late as it was, everything was dark, so there wasn't much to see.

Preston turned off the flashlight he'd been using to weave through the trees and knocked gently on the boards separating the stone pillars of the fence. He heard nothing, but he threw a hamburger into the yard, just in case Vince had bought a Doberman in the past few days. He didn't want to come face-to-face with the fangs of an angry dog. Not that he thought he would. Vince wasn't a pet kind of man. He didn't like anything that required much care. So Preston wasn't surprised when he heard no barking.

Scaling the fence, he dropped silently into the backyard. The grass sloped away from the house toward the creek. It was difficult to tell with the tall trees blocking the moonlight, but Preston was pretty sure he saw a little canoe or rowboat tied up down there. If the creek had been big enough, a river perhaps, Preston felt sure Vince would have owned a yacht. Vince was no slouch when it came to keeping up with the Joneses.

Preston moved toward the French doors on the other side of an elaborate pool and patio area. He passed some fancy brickwork, a built-in grill, lawn furniture. Besides the wind chimes tinkling above him, the creek gurgled nearby and classical music floated from inside. Was Vince not alone?

He probably had his little receptionist with him, Preston decided. Vince didn't like pets, but neither did he like to be alone.

The contrast between Vince's house and Joanie's apartment made Preston shake his head. Somehow Vince always came out ahead.

Good thing that was all going to end tonight. Vince would confess, or his secrets would die with him.

The door was locked. Preston considered the possibility that Vince might have installed an elaborate security system after Joanie moved out, but it wasn't likely. Using the butt of his gun, he broke out a square of glass near the door handle, then waited to see if there'd be any response from inside.

Nothing. Pulling his sweatshirt down to protect his hand, he reached in, turned the lock and opened the door.

The house was clean and spacious and smelled like an Italian restaurant. The music came from a built-in stereo above a big-screen TV in the living room. Evidently, Vince had gone all out when he'd moved to Cedar Rapids. What he'd done to Dallas hadn't set him back a bit.

Preston flipped on his flashlight, then paused to examine the pictures on Vince's shelves. Once there'd been photographs of the four of them going deep-sea fishing in San Francisco Bay, skiing in Park City, shopping in Carmel. Now the only photos Vince displayed were of his parents, who'd been significantly older and had died at least ten years ago.

So where was he?

Preston moved quietly through the house and into the garage. Joanie had said Vince kept a few of his old records out there. He wanted to have a look, just to rule out that possibility.

The file cabinets along the back wall held plenty of folders. But most were empty. Preston couldn't find anything that had to do with Melanie, Billy or Dallas.

Another dead end. Preston's gun pressed into his stomach as he rested his head on the cool metal of the filing cabinets. That was it, then. It was up to Vince to tell the truth. One way or another, the agony of the past two years would soon be over. At least there was relief in that.

Striding purposefully into the house again, Preston climbed a flight of stairs that curved away from a vaulted entry. The carpet was so plush he couldn't hear his own footsteps, and with the music playing, he wasn't worried that Vince might be alerted to his presence.

Several doors opened off one side of a long hallway. On the other side, a banister overlooked the living room. The first three bedrooms were empty. One room was obviously an office. At the end of the hall, Preston found a set of double doors that stood partway open. He'd located the master bedroom. And probably Vince, as well.

Flicking off his flashlight, Preston nudged the door wider. He thought it'd take a moment for his eyes to adjust to the dark, but inside was a huge lighted aquarium filled with dozens of tropical fish. Vaguely, Preston wondered who fed them and cleaned the tank. Probably the same person who did the cooking and housework.

Preston turned his gaze to the lump in the middle of the bed and pulled his gun out of his waistband. To his surprise, Vince was alone. But it didn't appear he'd been that way for long. Preston could smell a woman's perfume.

He strode toward the bed. "What's the matter, Vince, you run out of Viagra?" he said, giving his old neighbor a nudge with the muzzle of his gun.

Vince snorted and rolled over, then raised his head and squinted at him. "Who is it?"

"Have you forgotten me already, old friend?"

"P-Preston?" Suddenly wide awake, Vince sat up. The past two years hadn't been kind to him physically. The blankets fell away to reveal a pudgy, white chest with a sprinkling of dark hair, certainly nothing to impress a cute young receptionist. But then, Preston hadn't seen the receptionist.

"W-what are you d-doing here?" Vince cried.

Preston shrugged. "Thought I'd drop by to say hello. Aren't you glad to see me?"

Vince had caught sight of the gun. He blinked as though he couldn't believe what he saw. Then he inched back against the headboard. "You're n-not the type to d-do this," he said. "You'd n-never shoot anyone!"

Preston tossed the hair out of his eyes. "I'd say that was true of the Preston you knew two years ago. It's a funny thing, though, Vince. You wrong a man badly enough, you never know what he might do."

"B-but you have too much to l-lose."

"Not anymore, buddy. You took what I had away from me when you killed my son. I have no job, no house, no wife, no family."

Briefly, Preston thought of Emma and Max. He did have something to lose. Two people he cared about a great deal. But he couldn't let them stand in his way. He *had* to do this.

The color fled Vince's face, leaving it so pale it nearly glowed. "W-where's Diane?"

"It's past her curfew, evidently."

"D-did you make her leave?"

"I would have asked nicely. But I didn't have to. She was gone when I arrived. So get up. I want to have a conversation with you."

"Can you leave so I can get dressed?" he said, finally overcoming his stutter.

"To be honest, I don't think giving you time alone would be in my best interests, Vince." Preston saw a pair of pants lying on the floor and tossed them over. "Here you go. You won't need a lot."

"What are you going to do?" Vince asked as he got out of bed and pulled on his pants.

"We're going downstairs."

Vince's dark hair stood up on the sides like horns. He nervously smoothed it down as he started into the hallway.

"You don't have to look good for this," Preston told him.

"I know you won't believe me, Preston," he said. "But I didn't do anything to Dallas. Septicemia can strike any child, anytime. I tried to save him. Lord knows I didn't *want* him to die."

"What about Melanie Deets, Vince?"

"She didn't die. I saved her. They—they named a park after me. Ask anyone."

"She used to be a gifted student. Now she struggles to learn."

"Sometimes there are aftereffects," he said. "Why are you blaming me?"

"And Billy Duran?"

"I didn't want him to die, either. I'm—I'm a doctor, but I can't save everyone."

"I'm not asking you to save everyone. I'd be happy if you didn't *kill* them." They'd reached the living room. "Turn on the lights," Preston said.

When Vince did as he asked, a ceiling fan came on at the same time and whipped softly around. "If you won't listen to me, what are you going to do?" he asked fearfully.

"Get out a piece of paper. You're signing a full confession."

"Preston, *please…*"

"Do it."

Vince retrieved a piece of paper and a pen from the built-in desk between the living room and the kitchen. "I—I can't go to jail, Preston. It'd k-kill me. I'd d-die there. I know I would."

Preston grimaced at his whiny tone. "Maybe you should've thought of that before you made my son sick."

"Okay, Preston. You—you're right. I might have…you know…made Dallas a little sicker than he was, but there's something wrong with me." Tears began to roll down his cheeks, but they elicited no sympathy from Preston. Vince was crying for himself, not for what he'd done. "After Billy died, I told myself I'd never take that risk again," he continued. "I was doing well, too. W-we were happy, remember? We had fun together. Then Dallas got the flu, and you c-called me over, and…" He raised a shaky hand to his head. "The temptation. The temptation was terrible. I k-kept picturing how it would feel to do s-something really great for you." He hiccuped as his tears turned to wracking sobs. "It—it got the best of me. I didn't *want* to hurt him—"

Preston banged the butt of the gun on the counter with one whack. "You didn't *want* to hurt him? You killed him, you son of a bitch!" Suddenly, Preston knew he'd have no trouble pulling the trigger. It was almost frightening how easily he could do it, despite Vince's sobs. All he had to think of was Dallas. Vince's total disregard for the lives he'd taken, the suffering he'd caused, enraged Preston. How could a man like Vince expect leniency?

Vince sank onto his knees. "Please, Preston. We were friends once. You—you don't know how much you mean to me. I—I only wanted— I only wanted you to…to l-like me and admire me half as much as I admired you. I only w-wanted—"

Preston aimed the gun at his heart. "Write the confession."

Sweat rolled down Vince's face. His eyes widened, but he didn't move. "It w-won't do you any good. D-don't you understand that? It'll be given under d-duress."

"It'll work if you provide enough details, Vince. I want the information only you would know. How you did it. Why. I want you to lay it all out, step by step. It'll probably take you a couple of hours, so I'll just pull up a chair. But you're going to get it all down. Explain what you did to Melanie Deets, what you did to Billy Duran and—" his voice cracked "—the boy I loved more than life. The boy you took from me."

At Preston's words, Vince managed to climb to his feet. He started writing, but he didn't get past the first paragraph before he stopped. "I'm begging you, Preston," he said, and slipped off the chair and back onto his knees. "I'm not right...in my mind. I—I admit that. I have a problem. I need help. But I c-can't go to prison. They'd *kill* me in p-prison."

Disgust made Preston clench his jaw. "Stand up and take responsibility for what you've done!"

Instead, Vince shielded his head with his arms, and began crying again. "Help me, Preston. I'm your friend, remember?"

Preston's hand began to sweat on the butt of the gun. He wanted to shoot. The desire grew so strong he could imagine the jolt of the gun traveling up his arm.

But before he could make a decision, he heard what sounded like a shot. The window shattered. Then something hit him from behind, knocking him flat on his face.

CHAPTER TWENTY-FIVE

PRESTON'S RIGHT ARM FELT like it was on fire. Rolling over, he pulled himself into a sitting position and used his opposite hand to check the arm. His fingers encountered something wet and sticky. He was bleeding pretty badly. It took him a moment to absorb that and to realize why. He'd been shot. But how? Vince didn't even have a gun.

Dimly, he remembered that the shot had come from outside. He turned to stare at the shattered window behind him. *Who* would be shooting at him?

"You shot me!" Vince was screaming. "I can't believe it. You shot me, and now I'm going to die!"

Preston's jaw dropped. Sure enough, Vince was lying on the ground several feet away, bleeding as badly as he was. Or worse.

"I didn't shoot you," Preston said, trying to convince himself at the same time. He searched for his gun, then realized he'd dropped it when he fell forward. It had slid across the hardwood floor and was lying next to Vince, who was now covering a small hole in his chest and struggling to get up.

"Yes, you did," he said, gasping for breath.

The peaceful strains of the classical music playing in the background seemed to mock the ugly violence. Preston edged closer, wanting to get hold of the gun before Vince could. "No. Someone shot me, too."

Vince seemed to register this information about as slowly as Preston's mind had been working a few seconds earlier. They were both wounded. But Preston had a feeling Vince's injury was worse. Preston's arm hurt like hell, but a person didn't usually die from a gunshot wound to the bicep. Vince had been hit in the chest. Blood streamed down his bare stomach and onto his pants.

"Who?" Vince asked incredulously. "Who else wants me dead? Christy?"

Preston winced at the pain throbbing through the entire right side of his body. "No. Christy doesn't know you the way I do." He was nearly at the gun. He reached for it, but Vince saw what he was doing and grabbed it first.

"Looks like you've lost it, huh?" he said, and tried to chuckle.

Preston frowned at the muzzle pointed toward him. "Whoever's out there might still be—"

A noise, movement, drew their attention back to the broken window. A man loomed outside. Preston was fairly sure he'd never seen him before, but he wasn't positive until the stranger came around the house and entered the living room through the same door he'd used.

"No friend of mine," Preston said when he emerged into the light. "What about you?"

The man was lanky, had tattoos down both arms and wore a bandanna around his long greasy hair. He quickly closed the distance between them. "Get up," he snapped at Preston, but when he saw that Vince held a gun, he grew leery and turned the muzzle of his own gun in Vince's direction. "Drop it."

"If you do, he'll kill us," Preston warned.

"Who...are you?" Vince asked with a groan.

"I have no argument with you. I'm here for him." He waved his weapon toward Preston. "Drop the gun."

Vince shifted to lean against the breakfast bar, and Preston guessed he couldn't sit up any longer without support. "What...what did Preston...do to you?" he wheezed.

"For me, it's just a job. Nothing personal. You can thank Manuel Rodriguez."

Manuel. Preston's heart thumped erratically. "He knows where Emma is?"

"Emma?" The man chuckled. "You mean Vanessa. Of course. He's with her now, probably taking up where you left off, eh?" He winked and the image that went through Preston's mind made him nauseous.

Emma... "How'd he find her?"

"Fate." His black eyes narrowed as he eyed Vince. "I said drop the gun."

Preston itched to feel the cool metal of the trigger beneath his finger. He'd been shot in the right arm and probably couldn't use his most coordinated hand. But at this range, he didn't think it would matter. "Don't do it, Vince," he said. "You can identify him, so he has to kill you, too. Surely you know that."

"I'm dying anyway," Vince said hopelessly, and slumped farther toward the floor. He face grew ashen, his jaw slack.

"Then give me the gun." Preston launched himself toward it and was immediately deafened by gunfire. But he didn't feel any pain. He looked down in surprise, expecting more blood. Then he heard the man with the bandanna gasp, saw him fall.

The smell of gunpowder filled Preston's nostrils as he stared at Vince, whose head had fallen back. He was struggling to catch his breath.

"You got him," Preston said.

Vince's eyelids fluttered open. "Did I?" He smiled weakly.

"Now maybe—" he fought for another breath "—someday you can…forgive me. But—" he swallowed "—I know how much you loved Dallas. I…I shouldn't count on it, right?"

Preston didn't know how to respond. He missed Dallas terribly, would always lament the tragedy of his son's death. But for the first time in two years, he was more worried about the present.

Manuel's man was still moving, but barely. Preston didn't care whether he lived or died. He could only think of Emma.

Fighting the dizziness that threatened to overwhelm him, he rose to his feet, dialed 911, and told the operator to send the police to Vince's house and the motel. The motel first, he said. Then he collected both guns, staggered out of the house and started running for his van.

EMMA'S FINGERNAILS SCRAPED the walls as Manuel dragged her down to the floor. He was nursing his right hand, the hand she'd injured earlier. And his head was bleeding. When Max snapped on the light, she could see a large gash near Manuel's temple, which he must have sustained when he came through the window.

"You stupid bitch. You broke my hand," he said, but it didn't stop him from punching her with the other.

Emma supposed it was a good thing she'd injured his right hand, because his left one was powerful enough. Her teeth clacked together as he connected with her chin and, for a moment, she saw spots.

"Daddy?" Max said uncertainly.

Emma struggled to reach the bat she'd dropped. "Get into the bathroom, Max," she said, tasting blood. "Lock the door. Hurry! Mommy will be okay."

Instead of obeying, Max started to cry. "Don't hurt my mommy," he said. "Please, Daddy. Don't hurt her."

"I'm not gonna hurt her. I'm gonna kill her," he said, and that was when Emma knew rage had carried him beyond all rational thought.

"Go!" Emma cried to Max, but she couldn't get out anything else before she had to use all her energy to swing at Manuel with the bat. It make a sickening thud, but his arm had blocked it from doing any real damage. And he retaliated with a vicious kick to her abdomen. Pain exploded in her ribs, burning so badly she wondered if he'd managed to puncture a lung.

"You think you can threaten me, take my son and fuck any man you want?" he hollered.

Trying to raise the bat again, she stumbled and fell, and he kicked her a second time.

"Mommy!" The terror in Max's voice brought Emma to her feet despite the pain. She lurched toward her son, but she was so dizzy, she couldn't even stand. She collapsed to her knees as Max flung himself at Manuel's leg, hitting and kicking him. "Leave her alone! Don't you hurt my mommy!"

Manuel threw Max off as effortlessly as though he were a rag doll. He slid across the floor and banged against the wall.

My God! Max! He's out of his mind. He's going to kill us both.

"You want to fuck him again?" he cried. "You want to let Preston Holman cost you your life, your child?"

Frantically, she grabbed Max's arm and pulled him toward the bathroom. They were so close. If only she could get inside and shut the door—

But Manuel was on her before she could. Whirling just in time, she hit him with the bat, but there wasn't room for a full swing, and it didn't seem to hurt him too badly. He tore it out of her grasp and slugged her again, and she hit the vanity before landing in the bathtub.

"Stop it!" Max screamed. He must have bitten Manuel because Manuel suddenly bellowed in pain—and lashed out.

Terror seized Emma as Max fell to the floor. "Max!" she cried, but he didn't answer.

Rage flooded through Emma, lending her strength she hadn't known she possessed. She struggled to her feet and shoved Manuel, hard, knocking him back into the door.

She tried to slip past him. She knew she had to get out right away, find help for Max or it would be too late. But he seized her arm and forced her up against the vanity.

Feeling behind her, Emma searched for a weapon. But she didn't wear hairspray, and she didn't have much hope of finding anything else that might be useful among her cosmetics. When her hand closed around one of Max's needles, however, her heart began to thump with hope. The needle was too fine and small to cause much damage. But in the right place…

Manuel's hands circled her neck and he started choking her. She could tell by the look on his face that the effort was costing him. She'd injured his hand, but his anger seemed to compensate. She clawed at him with her free hand as he squeezed tighter and tighter. Soon her lungs began to burn and darkness hovered like a thick, descending fog….

"I…hate…you," she managed to gasp.

When he gritted his teeth and leaned close to respond, she knew her opportunity had come. Whipping her hand around, she stabbed at him with the needle.

He cried out and staggered back, his hands covering his left eye, and she knew she'd gotten him where she needed to. "You bitch!" he shouted.

She dashed out of the bathroom. She had to find a better weapon. Something she knew would stop Manuel for good. Max could be seriously hurt. He needed her.

Manuel came stumbling after her, half-blind and cursing. Emma considered making a break for the door, but even if she could get out, her son might be gone by the time she could bring help.

She swerved into the kitchen instead, and grabbed the only weapon she could that might provide a more effective defense than the bat—a kitchen knife.

Manuel's good eye glittered as he realized her intent. "It's over," he said. "You won't live another five minutes."

She felt the same determination. She'd soon be lying dead on the floor. Or he would.

"Then you'd better make it good," she said, "because I'm not going down without a fight."

The challenge seemed to surprise him. He stopped covering his eye and lunged at her. When she stabbed and missed, he caught her hair and sent her sprawling. As she fell, she hit her head on a corner of the cupboard and blacked out. But she couldn't have been out for more than a second because she woke before he could touch her again.

There was no time to think. She could feel the knife flat against her body, beneath her, could hear him coming for her again. Forcing herself to lie still, she held her breath. He must have seen her lose consciousness. Hopefully, he'd believe she was still out.

Breathing heavily, he leaned over her. He kicked her in the side to see if she'd move, but she absorbed the pain and remained motionless. Then he reached down to turn her over, and she thought of Max lying on the bathroom floor. This would be her last chance to save her son, to save them both!

Opening her eyes, she rolled to the right and plunged the blade deep into Manuel's neck.

THE FRONT WINDOW of the motel room was shattered. Preston swayed on his feet, barely able to hold on to the gun in his hand. Fear numbed the pain in his arm but added to his dizziness. He didn't even remember driving over here. He just knew he'd arrived. Somehow.

Was he too late?

He could hear sirens wailing in the distance, knew the police were on their way.

"Emma?" he called. The front door was still locked, but he could see there was a light on in the kitchen. "Emma!"

No answer.

"Max?"

He climbed clumsily through the window, cutting himself on his neck and arms because he couldn't use his right hand and his left held the gun. But he scarcely felt these new injuries. He knew he'd lost a lot of blood and was on the verge of passing out. He also knew he wouldn't relinquish his hold on consciousness until he discovered what had happened to the woman and the boy he loved. The thought of finding them gone—or worse—tore him up. He'd already lost his wife and son. Emma and Max had filled that hole, made him complete again.

"Emma, it's me."

His words were slurred and difficult to understand, yet he was sure he heard a response. A soft "help us" came from somewhere inside. Where had it come from? Had he imagined it?

"Max?" He trained the gun on the floor as he moved through the suite so he didn't accidentally shoot the wrong person, but nearly fired it blindly when he tripped over something sticking out from behind the breakfast bar.

It was a body. He knew instantly, before he even looked. Nothing else could feel that way. He just didn't know *whose* body, and feared the worst. Had Manuel hurt or killed Emma? Had he taken Max? Had that "help us" been an echo of Preston's own wishful thinking?

Slowly, he lowered his gaze to see…. It was Manuel. Max's father lay in a puddle of blood, a knife in his neck.

Suddenly Preston's senses became more alert. Someone had killed Manuel. Which meant Emma might have survived. Maybe he wasn't too late.

The sirens were growing louder. He staggered into Max's room because the light was on in there, too. The bed was rumpled but empty, so he moved as quickly as he could to the master bedroom. He couldn't see anyone in the semidarkness, but more light crept out from beneath the bathroom door. Using the wall to keep himself upright, he made his way over and tried the handle. Locked. "Emma?"

"Preston?" she cried.

"It's me. Are you okay?"

He held his breath as she fumbled with the lock. What would he see when she opened the door? Anxiety clawed at him while he waited.

When the door swung open, he set the gun aside and sank to his knees. Emma was on the floor, holding Max. Her mouth was cut and bleeding. She had blood all over her clothes and hands, and Max had a big bruise on his temple. But they were alone, and they were both alive.

"Preston!" Max reached for him.

Emma looked up at him in horror. "You've been hurt!"

Preston checked the blood soaking his shirt. "I'll live. I think the bullet went straight through."

"We need to get you to a hospital."

"We'll all go. The police are almost here." The sirens had stopped, which indicated that they'd already parked. He pulled Max to his chest, reveling in the feel of his small body secure in his arms. When he included Emma in his embrace, she winced slightly but buried her face in his neck.

"Are you okay?" he asked her gently.

He could feel the wetness of her tears, but she nodded.

"What about you, Beast?"

"My daddy hit us," Max said, and clung to Preston as though he was afraid to let go. "Mommy says he's gone. That he'll never come back."

"That's true," Preston told him. "But if you want, I'll be your daddy now."

Emma pulled back and gaped at him. "What'd you say?"

Unconsciousness edged closer. Preston shut his eyes, fought it off and leaned against the wall for support. "Marry me, Emma."

He felt her touch his cheeks, his forehead, his mouth. "What about your reason for coming to Iowa? What about the past?"

"It's over." He breathed in the scent of her hair, still trying to reassure himself that she was alive. "So what do you say? I'll buy you that little house you wanted, the one with the white picket fence…here or in Nebraska…. Anywhere you want…. We'll start over."

She smiled through the tears swimming in her eyes. "I'd marry you even if we had to live in the van. I'm in love with you, you know that."

He could hear the cops at the door. "In here," he called as he slid farther down the wall.

"Preston?" Emma's voice was filled with worry. "Hang on, okay? Don't leave us."

"Does that mean we're going to be a family?" Max asked eagerly.

Preston nodded. "You—" he swallowed "—me…and…your mom, Beast."

"What about a dog? We need a dog."

"We'll get…a dog," Preston promised. Then footsteps pounded down the hall and a cop poked his head into the bathroom.

Everything was going to be okay. Knowing that, Preston let himself slip into unconsciousness.

EPILOGUE

One year later...

THE BIRDS CHIRPED loudly in the trees overhead as the first rays of sun filtered through the branches and began to warm the tent. Emma stretched and yawned, then snuggled closer to Preston. She loved camping, enjoyed the solitude, the beauty of the mountains, the wildlife. Fortunately, Preston and Max liked it just as much.

The crack of twigs outside made Emma wonder if maybe a bear had come to visit. She would have known for sure if they'd brought Bob, Max's German shepherd. But they'd decided to leave the dog with Preston's mother rather than bring him into bear country.

Rolling over, she peered through the flap. It was only a squirrel. Their food and garbage was still safely stowed on a pole two hundred feet away.

"You awake?" Preston murmured.

Emma slipped her hand up under his T-shirt to feel the smooth warm skin of his stomach. They'd been married nine months already, but she felt as if they were still newlyweds. "I'm ready to go hiking. What about you?"

"I'm ready for bacon and eggs," he said. "Camping makes me hungry."

Max burrowed out of his sleeping bag, which he'd placed next to Preston. Max worshipped Preston, imitated everything his new daddy did. "Do you think we'll get to see a bear today?" he asked.

Gone were the days when Yellowstone National Park had black bears waiting on the side of the road for handouts from motorists. Now park officials strictly enforced their no-feeding-the-animals rule, which kept the bears farther from humans. But Preston had managed to get them a backcountry campsite. According to the information Emma had pulled off the Internet before their trip, grizzlies were often viewed between Canyon and Fishing Bridge at the northern range of the park. They planned to do some hiking and take along their binoculars.

"Maybe," Preston answered. "Should we test your blood, Beast?"

"In a minute." Max started to get dressed.

Preston faced Emma. "You know what today is, don't you?" he asked, tucking her disheveled hair behind her ear.

She nodded. Today several members of the Rodriguez family were going on trial to face drug-trafficking charges. She hoped they'd join Hector Linz, who was spending the rest of his life in prison for killing Vince Wendell.

He drew her hand to his mouth and kissed the scar Manuel's cigarette had left. "Are you afraid they'll get off?"

"No." She glanced at Max, who was busy pulling on his T-shirt. "I'm pretty sure you-know-who never told anyone I had that list of names and numbers," she said. "If he had, they would've found me by now."

"What do you think stopped him?"

"He probably didn't want the grief he'd get from his mother," she said with a laugh. "And he was probably too confident that he could recover it."

"Sending it anonymously was a good move."

She brushed a kiss across his lips. "Living with Manuel seems like another lifetime. It was worth it because of Max, and chances are I wouldn't have found you if I hadn't been on the run. But I'm glad it's behind me."

He grinned at her. "*How* glad are you that you found me?"

She knew by his expression that he was up to something. "Why do I get the feeling you're baiting a trap?"

"Hey, Max," Preston said.

Max crawled toward him. "What?"

"Should we tell your mom what we want?"

Max looked perplexed for a moment, but smiled broadly when Preston rolled over to whisper in his ear. "Yeah!"

Max agreed so readily that Emma narrowed her eyes. "If this is another plea for a motorcycle, the answer is still no. I'm terrified one of you will get hurt."

"It's not a motorcycle *this time*," Max said.

Emma felt her eyebrows come together. "What, then?"

"We want a baby," Preston said.

"Pul-leeze!" Max added, putting his hands together in a gesture of exaggerated pleading.

Emma's eyes fastened on her husband's. After Max, she hadn't planned on having more children. The way Manuel had used Max against her had been too frightening. But Preston wasn't Manuel....

"What do you think?" Preston asked, hope apparent in his voice. "Can you trust me enough?"

She knew what a good father he'd be from the way he treated Max. He was good to her, too. She'd never been so happy.

A baby... She pictured holding a sweet-smelling newborn—Preston's child—in her arms, and couldn't help returning their smiles. "When?" she asked.

"As soon as you're ready," Preston said.

"Okay." She leaned over to kiss Max's cheek, then Preston's lips. "I guess our family's going to get a little bigger."

"So how do we get a baby?" Max asked.

Emma and Preston laughed. "Your daddy and I will handle that part," she said.

HARLEQUIN *Super* ROMANCE

Big Girls Don't Cry

by
Brenda Novak

Harlequin Superromance #1296
On sale September 2005

Critically acclaimed novelist
Brenda Novak brings you another
memorable and emotionally engaging
story. Come home to Dundee, Idaho—
or come and visit, if you haven't
been there before!

On sale in September
wherever Harlequin books are sold.

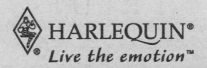

HARLEQUIN®
Live the emotion™